Lion HEART Princess

KAALENA GARCIA

Lion Heart Princess

Copyright © 2026 by Kaalena Garcia

First Printing 2026

979-8-9945209-0-1

Cover design by Kaalena Garcia

Published in the United States of America

To mom, for fostering my imagination so that I may do
what I love

Korzon
Korzon village
Witch Center

Stonehaven hill
The Guard
N
W
E

One

A sound of death—one nobody ever wants to hear.

It slows time. It makes a heart pound. It's a sound of fear.

When the panic sets in, Makeddah wants to run, but why are her feet planted to the ground?

They are being invaded. She has to move, she has to act, but her heart is on the floor and her ears are filled with blood.

Pump, pump, pump. That's all she hears.

Only when her sister grabs her does she notice the screams.

Makeddah's adoptive sister, Rayon, faces her and her sapphire eyes are wide. "Let's go!" It's Rayon who is pulling their little sister Belle as well. "We need to get to safety," Rayon shouts over the alarm as black flashes fly above them. Then another, and another. Soon, all Makeddah can see is black and white flashes of magic.

They start running in the direction of their home. Makeddah thinks of the small and cozy cottage being melted to the ground by the magic. It's going to happen. They are going to die, and her home is going to crumble hard and fast.

They run harder, determined not to be hit. The cottage comes into view, but a man stops in front of them, concealing it again. Makeddah freezes, and her whole world stops again. The second time today, shock paralyzes her.

A man. An actual man. She's never seen a man before.

This man is ugly. He has dark hair and dark eyes, and he's wearing dirty brown clothes. But his skin is white. Even whiter than her sisters. He smiles as if he found a prize, which showcases the nasty yellow and brown set of teeth he's sporting.

Makeddah watches; she seems so far away. It's like she is watching from another room as Rayon uses her magic to fight the man. And she wonders for the moment if maybe this is all fake. If it's a dream and she never woke up this morning.

But she did and she would never have expected her day to turn in this way.

It's a white and black blur of magic, but Rayon only lasts two minutes before he knocks her to the ground. And as he brings his hand up to end her, an arrow flies into his abdomen. He looks up and beyond Makeddah and Belle, then falls backwards to the ground.

Belle looks to Rayon and helps her from the ground as Makeddah whips her head back for the source of the arrow. There is another man running toward them. She can't get a good look at him because of his hood, but as soon as he grabs Makeddah's arm, she thinks he must be just as ugly and rotten as the last one, so she decides she doesn't want to see him. His grip tightens on her, and she tries to pull away, but he is much stronger than her, and he pulls her behind a house for coverage.

Makeddah sees Belle and Rayon following her and the strange man.

Rayons normally perfectly kept cherry red hair is now frizzy, sticking up in places it shouldn't be, and she is sweating hard, but she doesn't look as worried as Belle. Belle's eyes are still wide with fright.

"Get off of me!" Makeddah finally gets away from the man's grip, but she has a feeling she could only do that because he let her.

"Who are you?" Belle asks.

"Shh." He hisses and pushes both Rayon and Belle against the wall. "We need to get to your house. Your great-grandmother and mom will be waiting to make sure you are safe."

Makeddah narrows. "What?"

He doesn't waste time on explaining. He leaves their hideout spot for a few seconds, then comes back and motions for them to follow him. And she's not sure why, but they listen. "Start running, and I will back you up." He says, and the girls nod in agreement. He looks back once more and then tells them to start running.

But as soon as they start running toward the cottage, they see that it's not a good idea.

It's being ransacked by a bunch of the men who are attacking them. Rayon stops, "Let's go this way." She says pulling them to the back alley behind the houses, but there are more and more of those men. "There's a safe house just past that guy." Rayon points out.

The hooded man groans, "Okay, give me five minutes." He starts to walk away, but the girls are following. He put his hand up, "Stay."

They obey and keep their backs as close to the wall as they can.

"What is happening?" Makeddah says.

Rayon sighs, "This must be what mom was talking to High One about yesterday." Both Belle and Makeddah stare. "She was saying that a man was going to take a girl from the Center. When I questioned her about it, well, she basically told me to mind my own business. Now look at the mess we're in."

"Oh, like you could prevent it," Belle says.

Rayon crosses her arms, "Maybe I could have helped."

The girls stand there for what seems like longer than five minutes. The screams have died down, and there is no sign of magic flying around them.

Makeddah takes a breath and remembers only now that she has a sword on her hip. She was so useless. She'd like to think she has some contribution to the Witch Center by being a good swordsman, but she couldn't even pull that off. She feels the soft leather of her sheath.

Rayon lifts off the wall, "I don't think that guy is coming back, and we should really find Mother."

"Okay," Makeddah says, "But we need to stick together." She grabs her sword. "And this time if a man tries to attack us, I'm going to fight."

Rayon smiles, "Good, I can't carry the whole weight of the family. You are the oldest."

But as they start to move, Rayon stops and looks up. Makeddah and Belle glance up at each other, she's getting a witch call.

She stops and looks back at Makeddah and Belle, "It was Mother Lianne."

Makeddah pictures their great-grandmother fighting and being overcome by one of those men, but when Rayon says, "She's okay." Makeddah's body relaxes for a moment.

Rayon continues, "She said to stay put for ten minutes and then meet her at the cottage."

Belle looks around, "But what if they come here?"

Makeddah takes a breath. There is a scream just around the corner that makes her jump.

"Rayon, can you create a shield over us?"

Rayon ponders, "I can but get on the ground because I can't make a big one like Mother does."

They all crouch together as Rayon moves her hands around them and a shimmery globe surrounds them.

The three girls pull their knees tightly to their chest and wait.

"This must be the worst birthday of all time," Rayon says. Belle gives her a look, and she shrugs. "What?"

Makeddah forgot today was her birthday. She knew only an hour ago it was. She opened gifts, ate a good breakfast, and sparred with Belle while Rayon refereed. They went to get lunch, and that's when the alarm started blaring. That must have been when she forgot about her birthday.

Sixteen.

Her first day of being sixteen, and they get invaded by men. This is the worst birthday, and possibly the worst day of her life. She hates sixteen now.

Silence surrounds them, and only the sound of their breathing can be heard.

That gets disrupted by footsteps. Makeddah expects to see the hooded man turn the corner, but it is not him. A man with blond spiky hair walks into the alleyway.

The air seems to have thinned. Belle's hand trembles and covers her lips, her eyebrows creased with worry.

Rayon closes her eyes. She seems to be praying.

Makeddah watches the man as he stops in front of them. He turns his head to the right, staring just above them.

His eyes are as dark as the midnight sky. He's not ugly like the first one she saw, but he does look like he wants to kill anyone in his path.

The shield does not hold as Rayon prays. The bottom is starting to lift. Makeddah tries to warn Rayon by elbowing her. Rayon glares at her but finally sees the problem.

Before she can fix it, the man pulls her foot and drags her out.

The shield vanishes, and the girls are exposed. Rayon kicks and Makeddah draws her sword but there is no need because the hooded man comes back and punches the blond one in the jaw.

"Go!" He shouts as he fights, and Makeddah wastes no time pulling Rayon up to her feet.

Belle grabs Rayon's hand and the girls run out of the alleyway. It seems eerily calm. No men in sight. The alarm is still blaring, but it just seems like a constant buzz in the back of Makeddah's head now.

Their home comes into view, and they see their great-grandmother, Mother Lianne, standing at the door opening looking around for them.

Makeddah opens her mouth to call out, but a black flash comes. It races right between Makeddah and Rayon and goes straight for Mother Lianne. Mother Lianne throws her white magic, but Makeddah doesn't pay attention to where it goes.

"Mother Lianne!" Makeddah and Belle scream at the same time as Rayon screams, "Grandmother!"

This is the hardest Makeddah has ever run in her life, yet she feels like she can go on forever to reach Mother Lianne. They reach the cottage, and Mother Lianne is on the ground, cradling her stomach. "Oh, stars," Makeddah says.

"Oh, stars," is all that she can fathom saying.

When she opens her eyes, Mother Lianne is trying to breathe, and Belle is trying to help her up. "Come on," Belle grunts. Makeddah helps her with Mother Lianne's other side, and they usher her back into the home. When they set her on the sofa safely, Rayon turns and runs out the door.

"What is she doing?" Makeddah shouts, panic rising in her that the same thing is going to happen to Rayon. Belle ignores her and asks for a knife. Makeddah grabs one from the counter, and Belle starts cutting through Mother Lianne's dress. She throws the knife onto the sofa and rips the dress open to see a big black mark on Mother Lianne's abdomen.

Belle stumbles back, "Oh no."

"Grandma." Their mom, Alda, runs into the cottage. Rayon is right behind her and slams the door closed.

"They're early," Mother Lianne whispers.

Makeddah shakes all over. She didn't realize her eyes were filled with tears.

"We have to get to the safety room."

"No, Makeddah…" Mother Lianne tries to stand.

"Stop. Please stop, Grandma." Alda places her hands on her grandmother's shoulders. "I need you, okay? I need you. Don't kill yourself by being stubborn. Please." Alda sucks in a breath and glances up at Makeddah. "Honey, it's okay. We contained them."

Makeddah looks at the door behind them. The magic can burst through it. What if they think they got all of them, but there are more of them coming? Their magic is unlike that of the witches. Their magic is something much uglier. This is dark magic, and if the dark magic hits the door… Makeddah pants, her mind coming to a conclusion.

She moves a rug from its place, and beneath it is a hatch door leading to the safety room. "Go," but Makeddah barely gets her word out before what she feared happens. Everyone turns to the door that just burst from its hinges, and a man is standing in its place. Makeddah reaches for her sword.

He wants to kill them, but she'll go down fighting this time.

Alda blasts the man in the face with white magic. The man tenses up and shouts, and that's when an arrow shoots through his chest and he collapses forward to the ground. With that guy out of the way, Makeddah sees the other man in a hood, saving them for the third time today. He is standing above the dead one—*dead, oh, no, dead.*

"Stars," Makeddah curses. She wipes away her tears and unsheathes her sword. He may have saved them, but she still does not trust him. "Get away from here, or I will kill you." She sounds brave enough, but her hands and body are shaking. Her back is aching. She can feel the earth's vibration strengthen beneath her, climbing through her feet and rising to her chest. "I don't know who you are, but I don't want you here," Makeddah says, slightly shakier.

The man looks from Makeddah to Mother Lianne, who is panting with her hand on her stomach. "Did you get hit?" he asks her.

Mother Lianne swallows and nods slowly. "I will be fine. Rayon and Belle, get in the safety room just in case, and Makeddah…" she swallows, "go with this man, now." She pauses as the room stays still, "Those are not suggestions."

Makeddah has never heard this edge behind Mother Lianne's voice.

Rayon and Belle don't move, and Makeddah feels her body is as frozen as the expression on Rayon's face.

Alda glances at the two. "What are you waiting for? Matt, take her. We will be fine once she's gone. Eliab will be just around the corner. Just take her now."

It sounds harsh, yet fear drips from the words.

Makeddah's sword slips a bit in her hand. "Wait, what? No, I'm not going anywhere."

"Makeddah, go." Alda pleads with a stern look. "Do as we say. We need you to leave."

The hooded man—Matt—takes Makeddah's hand, but she stands firm in her spot. He sighs, then effortlessly picks her up and throws her over his shoulder. And now she understands the meaning of manhandled.

"Wait," she shouts as they walk away from the cottage, seeing it get smaller and smaller. Farther and farther away.

"No, Alda wants this for you. Obey her." Matt looks up and sets Makeddah down.

"What makes you think I won't run?" Makeddah tests him, but he grabs her by the arm and pulls her to the ground.

"Be quiet and stay down," he spits at her.

With a scowl and a glare, she does as he says. Makeddah crouches there as he pulls out an arrow with a rope attached.

She looks back when she hears a shout. Three witches stand together to fight one man. Their white magic pulses against his black magic, but they finally triumph over him and run away, out of Makeddah's view.

She knew they hadn't been contained. Alda lied to her. How many more lies has she told her?

She looks over to Matt as he shoots his arrow over the wall and tells Makeddah to climb. She does so, reluctantly.

When they are over the wall, Matt picks up the arrow.

"Now what?" Makeddah asks, crouching low, thinking the men must be nearby.

"Now, we run."

Two

For years, Makeddah has resented the fact that she was adopted. She always stood out because of it. Being the dark-skinned magicless Parish girl had a toll. Though she herself was not a Parish, she was a Brooke. But Brooke had no meaning to everyone else. She wasn't sure what it meant to herself. But being a Brooke, she knew one thing, that she was the girl whose mother died when she was one.

Parish on the other hand is a well-known name in the Center. Every Parish girl has had a high rank throughout their history. They are also rumored to be descendants of the Stars, the most supreme and original witches.

The Parish girls seemed to be copied and pasted. Beautiful women with long red hair and sapphire blue eyes. Belle's hair was more orange than Rayon and Alda's, and

Mother Lianne's hair is now grey, but they are still clones of each other like most families in the Center.

For these reasons, having Parish as a last name puts her family as a target of gossip.

Many girls have been adopted at the Witch Center due to being orphans, especially after the battle that happened fifteen years ago. A battle that Makeddah is well aware of, but the details seemed impossible due to her ignorance of the world outside of the Center.

Many girls lost their mothers, and the witches come in all different shapes and colors. So being black and being adopted aren't the problem, but they do nothing to help her when her family is neither of those things. And on top of that, she's not a witch.

Makeddah is the only girl who has no inkling of magic.

When you get to a certain age as a witch, you are gifted a blue pendant that flows with magic. It shows that you are a part of the Center and have the magic of a witch in you. When Makeddah turned seven and was ready to be gifted that pendant along with Rayon, her magic pendant was completely drained.

That moment scarred her for life. It might be one of the reasons she has no friends besides her sisters.

Belle, though she struggles, still can spark something, and her pendant holds strong. She has the little lightning between her fingers when she snaps, but Makeddah has none, leaving her as the most gossiped about non-witch *witch* there is.

But still, her family has loved her despite her shortcomings. Her family still says she is a Parish and she belongs in the Witch Center though she may not have magic like them. Her family is still her home.

So, when this stranger man, Matt, says to run, she feels her heart plummet. Run?

Run away from the only family she has ever known and that has loved her? She can't.

"No. I'm not going with you until I know that my family is safe. You can drag me against my will, but I will not go voluntarily. And I will scream, and shout, and kick, and spit at you until you let me see them again." She hates that tears are welling up in her eyes. She almost can't hear her words over her thumping pulse. "I can't leave my family in danger."

Matt lifts his hood to display brown eyes and short mud-brown hair. He has hair on his face, but Makeddah can't remember the name of what it is called. Makeddah remembers her looking at the drawn pictures and calling it a beard, maybe? Rayon loves it when a man has one in her romance books.

Matt's eyes land on hers, and they narrow. Some kind of light ignites in them, but he shakes it off and looks in the direction they were going to go and then back to the wall of the Center. "Okay, fine. But if there is any chance of you dying, I will drag you out of there no matter what. Got it?"

"Got it."

Makeddah starts to stand up, but he tells her to stay down. They wait for what seems like an eternity, but Makeddah knows it is only a few minutes. "I thought we were going to go back inside," Makeddah whispers. "How are we going to protect them from here?"

He holds his finger to his lips.

It is silent in there again, no more sounds of fighting, no more screaming. She notices now that the alarm stopped blaring. Makeddah pushes Matt to shoot his arrow over the wall, but he shakes his head and starts walking around the Center.

"What are you—"

"Shhhh," he snaps like he did earlier. He tells her to crouch down, then he shoots the arrow over the wall. They climb over and land on the blue roses. Makeddah almost forgot the beauty of the Center while this was going on.

The blue roses, though the world was crumbling around them, stood tall. Of all the places they could have landed, it was on a patch of beautiful blue roses. Maybe it is a sign for Makeddah not to be afraid. Her favorite part about the Center is that she gets to see these every day. She gets to walk on them without fear of a thorn pricking her.

They slip behind many homes until they arrive at the window of Makeddah's cottage. When Makeddah peeps inside, she sees Mother Lianne still lying on the sofa, but she is tense. Rayon and Belle are huddled together in the corner. She can't see Alda at first, but once she shifts her stance, she sees Alda standing, mimicking her grandmother's body language.

A man comes into sight. He has two other men behind him, but Makeddah can tell that *he* is the reason Alda is tense. Is that Eliab, the man she mentioned earlier?

"Where is she?"

His voice is muffled by the glass, but Makeddah can make it out.

"Why do you think I have her?" Alda sounds confident. She has no fear dripping in her words; maybe it's because Makeddah is supposed to be far away by now.

"Alda Parish, right? King Haggard told me to come to you to retrieve the girl. He said you were the one who promised him fifteen years ago."

"Well, like I *told* him fifteen years ago, she's not here. I didn't promise him anything. I said we would consent to a search, and that's it. The girl is not here." Alda thinks she is telling the truth. Her shoulders relax. "Eliab, right?"

He narrows, "Where is she, *little witch*?"

Alda stares up and slaps the man across the face, leaving a red mark. Eliab snaps his head back to her but doesn't react with magic. He just glares at her. Alda holds her breath. "Never call me that again." Makeddah can't see Alda's face, but she sees her pointed finger. "Leave. We don't have what you want."

He cracks his neck. Makeddah notices the wiggling of a small earring on the man's left ear. "Okay, but if King Haggard—"

"If King Haggard feels something is wrong here, he can take it up with me himself and not send his *little* sorcerer," she mocks. "I hear he's not as agile as he was, but surely he can still walk without his sorcerers guiding him along by hand?" Alda makes a little skipping motion with her fingers.

Makeddah is surprised by Alda's mocking tone, but she could get used to it. She's wondering now how she is adopted because Makeddah sees herself in Alda right now. Sassy, confident, ready for a fight.

Well, Makeddah thought she was always ready for a fight, but that was when little girls were taunting her little sister. Today proved she is not ready for a real fight whatsoever. But Alda is.

As the man leaves, Matt tells Makeddah to stay and wait. Three minutes later, Alda turns to the front door and uses magic to bind it, then runs to the window. When she opens it, she drags them in.

Makeddah stammers, "How did you—"

"What are you two doing here? You should be long gone. The sorcerers—"

"I couldn't leave knowing you're all in danger." Makeddah hugs Alda so tightly that she forgets her distaste for them. She can't believe she spent sixteen years thinking hugs were weird and uncomfortable. Rayon and Belle rush to Makeddah and Alda, and all of them embrace like she's already been gone for years. They look down at Mother Lianne, who smiles, but is unable to stand.

They shift to her and hold her hands. All of them in the one room, together as a family. Any other way seems wrong so how can she go now?

Just yesterday, she dreamed about leaving the Center, going places—seeing the kingdom and exploring the world—and now the one thing she wants most is to stay.

"I can't leave you." Makeddah says, then turns back to Matt. "I won't."

"You have to," Alda says, moving her hand to Makeddah's cheek.

She feels tightening in her chest. "Those men want me, that's why you want me to go?" When Alda hesitates, Makeddah adds, "Don't lie to me."

Alda closes her eyes, "Yes, they are here for you."

Makeddah steps back. "You've lied to me my whole life about who I am, haven't you? Why else would those men want a girl with no magic?" Alda doesn't answer. "Well, I am not leaving, not without an explanation. A clear one."

"There is no time to explain." Alda takes Makeddah's hand, "Witches are hurt. We have to help them, and you…" Alda opens the window again. "You are right. I lied to you, but I promise I will explain once I know you are safe and far away from here."

Makeddah shakes her head and sits back on the sofa. "I may not be your real daughter, but I am stubborn like you, Mom. I'm not leaving until every witch is accounted for, and the ones who…" she has to breathe before she tells the world the words she's been thinking, "And the ones who died are given up to the Stars. I'm not leaving, not without a proper goodbye." She swivels to Matt again. "And not without explanation. Like, how do you two know each other?"

Alda answers, "Through High One."

High One—no one knows her real name. She is the highest-ranking witch in the Center. Most powerful. So powerful that she has the strength to give witches children through the magic of her hands and mind.

Makeddah remembers the fight between Alda and High One the day Makeddah was supposed to be gifted a pendent. She could never forget the look of anger on Alda's face. She never understood why Alda was upset with High One for her own shortcomings.

Makeddah narrows at Alda. What would High One have to do with this? That day seems murkier in Makeddah's head as she tries to connect the dots.

High One never really cared about or for Makeddah after that day. She wasn't a witch, so she didn't have the attention of the most supreme one. Which makes High One's connection to this even more confusing.

"Then how does Matt know High One?" She asks Alda, though she knows she should be directing her question to Matt. Especially when Alda's left brow goes up and she cocks her head to the side to look at Matt.

Matt rubs his eyes, "We can give the witches up, but we need to be quick if we do this. Alda, is that possible?"

Alda nods. "Yes, of course." She starts walking to the door, "You three, get Mother Lianne to the infirmary. I need to help the other Head Witches."

Rayon steps up, "I can help. They must be all over; I'm sure you guys will need help ghosting them."

Alda nods, "Okay." She takes a breath, "The seal will come off this door as soon as we leave. Please, just be careful. We don't know if there are any more." Finally, after a long look at her grandmother, Alda leaves with Rayon following.

Makeddah feel's uneasy looking around at what stands in the wake of the sorcerers. It's a small cottage, and Makeddah can see all four rooms while standing at the door.

Alda's room door is ripped off the hinges, their washroom door has a big black spot on it, and the table and chairs are all thrown down. The sofa is almost torn apart. Mother Lianne probably isn't very comfortable on it.

They trashed her home just to find her. As she helps Belle take Mother Lianne to the infirmary, Makeddah's brain keeps swirling with one question. *Why am I so important?*

The Witch Center has been a sort of prison for Makeddah. While every other witch would say they got to go to the village at least once or twice a month, Makeddah was stuck there. She felt it might be her punishment for being magicless. Or that it was all a lie. Either option promised no comfort.

That is why until now she'd never seen a man before. Today was the first time she got a glimpse of the world outside. And as much as she wants to embrace it, she senses that something is off. Like she shouldn't be leaving the Center or her family with a man she just met. There must be a reason why she is the only one supposed to be leaving.

She has a gift for seeing when things are out of place, and other than the bunch of men that are lying dead in a pile in front of her, there is more nagging at her.

She watches as they set the men on fire, and her body feels like there are little needles sticking her all over. She reaches around to her back and scratches. It's been bothering her the whole day; the fire is multiplying that.

She grips her sword and backs away from the fire. She needs a moment before she watches more dead people be set aflame. The ceremony will be starting soon, but she first needs to take a breath. She feels suffocated, not the normal being stuck in a prison suffocated either. But she hopes her normal remedy for that will work just the same.

No matter the thing Makeddah is facing she has one way to always clear her head. Lying in the field of blue roses. The way the flowers transition over the year—cobalt blue in the fall, navy in the wintertime, baby blue in the springtime, and sapphire in the summer—it always fills her with a sense of wonder. And she loves the way they sway in the breeze.

The Witch Center is filled with the roses, but they are always protected. As they step, the ground senses it and prepares a pathway above the flowers and under their feet. Makeddah feels the ground transform with every step. She closes her eyes and breathes, trying to calm her racing heart and shaky hands.

"Mak?"

Makeddah opens her eyes at the sound of Rayon's voice. She looks up and sees her sisters walking to her.

"Is it starting?" Makeddah asks.

Belle nods, "Are you okay? Sorry, that's a stupid question. I'm guessing you aren't because we all aren't right now."

Makeddah gives a low chuckle, but it's heavy. "Dead witches, sorcerers, a raid. The worst part is that Mom's been lying to me. And it seems like she didn't just start lying today."

They stay silent for a while.

"Let's go," Makeddah says, and they trudge side by side.

There is always a ceremony for the witches who have died. Whether it be from natural causes, from battle, or any other reason, any witch who has fallen goes up to the Stars. In the ceremony, they lay the witches in the field of blue roses, but these witches actually touch the ground. No barrier lies between them and the earth. All the witches are invited to attend each ceremony, but Makeddah has never been to one herself.

Now, Makeddah stands next to Matt in the back, not wanting to draw too much attention to herself. She doesn't know if any of the other witches know that she caused this, but she doesn't want to find out yet by standing out in the crowd.

Today, eight witches died, along with four sorcerers. Makeddah has never seen anything like this happen before. Matt explains that it would have been worse, but the sorcerers' mission wasn't to kill. "Not this time," he says gravely. The image of the sorcerers being set on fire comes back, and Makeddah squeezes her eyes shut, then looks forward, trying to keep the image from burning in her head.

All of the witches gather around the fallen eight, and High One is to do the ceremony before Makeddah has to leave. The only ones among them sitting are the families of the fallen. They sit and cry, the lives of their loved ones taken so suddenly and unexpectedly. She can see the torment in the eyes of many.

Did I really cause this?

Alda always told the girls stories of a Creator. A God who made the earth and everything in it. And she always referred to this God as a male. Makeddah scoffed at that notion.

Men weren't real. And a God creating the world from nothing. Seems like a fairy tale.

But now seeing a man in real life. It makes her question everything. It makes her wonder if that's true. And if it is, why would this Creator let something like this happen to her family and the people surrounding her?

Makeddah bites her nails and waits for the ceremony to start. Everyone will blame her once they find out. But instead of blaming her at this moment, the witches give dirty glances to Matt and narrow their eyes at her. They must be thinking about why she is with him, so by trying not to draw attention to herself, she did exactly that. But she doesn't know why they stare at Matt. Maybe just because he's a man, but Makeddah wonders if they think he is a sorcerer too, or maybe they just don't like any men.

"Ugh, he stands there like he owns the place," a witch behind them says. "Men."

Yes, they must not like men.

Matt pretends not to have heard it, but she said it loud enough; he heard every word.

Makeddah holds her breath as she watches High One pour water on the fallen witches and put herbs on them. The breeze kicks up a moment later, causing each of the witches to go up in fire. The whole Center seems to hold its breath.

Makeddah sees most of the witches sobbing, some just staring blankly, and others are looking away. She feels her throat tighten and tears start to form in her eyes. She tells herself not to cry in public, that's for when she's alone, but this is her home. It's her family. These are her people.

The realization strikes her. She can't say she has thought of this Center as hers, but today it feels as if it is.

The witches throw flowers into the fire. Makeddah herself throws sunflowers, picked from the garden that Belle has been growing. She watches as it goes up in flames and walks to her family. She needs them right now.

Many of the witches stay for some time to watch the fire, but eventually, the people return to their spots, and the witches fall silent.

She doesn't expect it when a witch starts humming a song—a soft hum with a calm melody line. Maybe it's the sun setting on the horizon, or the heat of the flames, or the strong emotional battle going on within her, but something makes Makeddah sway to the music.

She closes her eyes and grabs both of her sister's hands beside her. Belle lays her head on Makeddah's shoulder, and Rayon grabs Belle's other hand. They are quiet and peaceful listening to the sound of death.

Three

akeddah woke up to smell cinnamon rolls this morning. Her favorite dessert for breakfast. She crawled out of bed and sat with her family at the table.

Alda brought her a box with a nice gold ribbon tied around it.

Makeddah looked up at everyone, "A gift?"

They don't normally give gifts on birthdays. Just good food and dessert and an activity of the birthday girls choosing.

But Alda smiled softly at her and set the present down in front of Makeddah. "Open it."

Makeddah untied the bow and opened the box. She pulled out the dress and saw a beautiful gold shimmer on a knee length dress. It cinched at the waist unlike any of her other dresses. It seemed to be just her size, which is rare.

She normally shares with Rayon, so the dresses are loose enough for both to wear.

She looked up at Alda, "You made this for me?"

Alda nods, "All yours. And there's more."

Makeddah furrowed, setting the dress down and peered inside the box. There was a note from Mother Lianne, one that made her laugh and want to cry. Mother Lianne had never been the sentimental type so Makeddah realized there must be more meaning behind the note but looked past it for the moment.

The last thing she saw inside the box was a black leather sword sheath. It was soft and shiny. It had an emblem of four swords touching at the tips, and in between each handle was an element symbol. At the top was a tree, on the right were waves of an ocean, on the bottom was a flame, and on the left was a symbol of wind.

"What does this mean?"

Mother Lianne and Alda shared a glance before Alda answered, "You'll know in time."

Now looking back to this morning Makeddah wonders if those things were a foreshadow of the events of today.

She touches her sword sheath and thumbs her fingers over the emblems engraved in it.

You'll know in time.

After the ceremony, she watches as everyone disperses, with some still giving Matt dirty looks. High One stares at Makeddah for a good minute and Makeddah stares back into her icy blue eyes. *What does she have to do with this?*

When a witch approaches High One, the staring contest ends and Makeddah follows the others back to the cottage.

For the second time, Makeddah is reminded of the chaos that ensued in her home. She and Rayon fix the dining chairs and table, and Makeddah sits down feeling the aches of her back even more. Matt steps in behind them, sneaking away from the witches. She waits for Alda and

Belle to walk in and close the door before she says anything, but patience has never been her thing.

"Can you tell me why I need to leave with Matt and why we were attacked on my birthday?" Makeddah asks just as Belle steps over the threshold.

Rayon stands by Makeddah's seat and crosses her arms, just as curious. Belle seems to not want to pick sides as she stands at the door.

"We should be leaving," is Matt's answer. Patience might not be his thing either. "I told you explanations come later because we need to leave as soon as possible. So…" He exchanges glances between Alda, Belle, and Rayon. "Say your goodbyes. I'll be waiting out the back." He gives one last look to Alda and escapes through the window.

Makeddah squints at the window where he fled and to the front door, but the thought is distracted by Alda rushing up to her.

She gives Makeddah a long hug, and Makeddah can't help but frown at it. No one is telling her anything and having to leave seems absurd.

But she knows this invasion was all her fault.

She tries to stray away from thinking that and blames everyone else. It is those sorcerers, and Matt. It's them she can blame. Yet, Alda knows what is going on and hasn't said anything to her. Could it have been prevented if she had only told Makeddah?

Rayon is shaking her head. Her arms are still crossed, and her hip is popped out. "No, no." She looks at Alda, then Makeddah again, still shaking. "No, you're not leaving."

"Yes, she is."

"But Mother…" Rayon squeezes her eyes shut, trying to calculate the situation. She turns to Makeddah. "But you're… But…" She pauses, finding her words. "I'm going with you."

"No, you're not," Alda says.

"Yes, Mother, think about it." She stands by Makeddah and takes her hand firmly. "I can help protect her, and we will still have each other, and if that man out there turns out to be evil—"

"He's not evil." Alda shakes her head.

"I'm not so sure," Makeddah and Rayon both say. They look at each other with a small smirk. They are completely different people, but they share a remarkably similar mindset.

Rayon walks to Belle and shakes her shoulders. "Belle can take care of Mother Lianne, and Makeddah has no magic, so I could be of help." Rayon glances up to Makeddah, "I think. But the most important thing is that she has family. And how else will you contact her?"

Alda shuts it down. "I can contact Makeddah if I need."

Rayon sighs, "Okay, what about my other points then?"

Alda looks over at Belle, who is smiling up at her mother with caring eyes. "You know, she's right," Belle says softly. "Like Rayon said, I can take care of Mother Lianne while you are off doing work, and you can take care of her while I'm at school. Makeddah shouldn't go alone."

"We should check on Mother Lianne." Rayon says, starting for the door, but Alda stops her.

"Belle and I will. You two go."

Makeddah and Rayon glance at each other, smiles rising on their faces.

Alda goes to Rayon and hugs her the same as Makeddah. She looks down into her eyes and shakes her head firmly. "You don't get in the way of what Makeddah needs to do. You understand? You contact me every night and tell me you're okay. You both come back as soon as you're allowed." She glances back at Makeddah. "Do you understand?"

They both nod, and Alda swallows. "I promise I will explain everything, Makeddah." Makeddah nods, and Alda says, "I love you both. Now, make me proud."

Alda's eyes glisten at the words.

Make me proud. It rings in Makeddah's head. She doesn't know why Alda tells her this. She doesn't know how she will make Alda proud, but she nods, knowing she'll do anything to obey the command. "I will."

Belle hugs them both and smiles. "I'm the most responsible anyway. I'll take care of Mom and Mother Lianne." Makeddah punches her shoulder, and Rayon shakes her head, but they're both smiling. "Um," Belle points to the window where Matt is pointing at something on his wrist. "I guess you should get going. Contact us when you're there—wherever there is, I guess. I love you both."

"We love you," Rayon says. A few moments later, they walk out together with a sword on Makeddah's hip and a backpack of water containers on Rayon's back.

Matt looks between them both and shakes his head, pointing at Makeddah. "Only her."

"You either get us both or no one. Your choice." Rayon says. She grips Makeddah's hand in hers and grins at her sister, then turns back to Matt and nods.

His jaw fidgets, like he's chewing nonexistent food. Makeddah's never seen a witch do that; it must be a man thing. He sighs and turns away.

"Well, then, let's go."

The girls smile at each other and follow behind the first—or technically second—man that she has ever seen in person. She knew from the moment they said she had to leave that she would go to keep her family safe, but she felt there was something missing.

Maybe the thing missing was her sister by her side.

Now, though leaving feels so wrong, it feels like it might be okay.

Four

It doesn't fully register for Makeddah that she is out in the world. She has actually set foot on the soil outside of the Center. She thought it might feel different. Like she'd finally feel free once she left, but she feels like she is following a man into another prison. Maybe she is, but at least the view is nice.

She looks out at the dark sky through the thick trees, then a small animal crosses her path and moves swiftly, running from them. And all around, she sees the leaves blow from the hot breeze and silently admires the work around her.

She has so many questions that maybe no one can answer. No one but the Creator, who she's not even sure she believes in. Yet she still asks the questions within the confines of her heart, not sure if she's looking for answers. The few fallen trees, what caused them to fall? What makes the green leaves so green? And the large land surrounding them — is this what would be considered woods?

She takes in a breath and smiles; it's finally hitting her. She thinks her mom must be right about this Creator thing because the details she encounters with every step she takes just get more breathtaking.

"So, it seems we have some time now to talk about why you are basically kidnapping me. And why were those…" Makeddah picks her own brain, "Sorcerers there?" She is now walking along on Matt's left side and Rayon is on his right.

He stares ahead when he says, "Someone better qualified will explain."

"Well, why did we have to leave if they weren't coming back?" No answer. "Why aren't you qualified?" Again, no answer. "Then can you tell me where we are going?"

"My stars, Makeddah, give the man a break," Rayon says.

"You're the one who says he is evil," Makeddah says over Matt, stepping over a fallen tree trunk.

"Yes, and I am still convinced he is. But he doesn't want you to keep talking his ear off. I don't half the time." Makeddah glares over at Rayon, and Rayon sticks her tongue out.

Matt stops, which causes Makeddah to stop as well. Rayon walks a few steps, then halts and whips around, "Why are we stopping?"

Makeddah adds, "I thought you wanted to hurry."

"We need to walk faster and stop talking. If they're near, they will find us."

Rayon glances at Makeddah, both shrug—Makeddah with her head, and Rayon with her shoulders. They then follow Matt without one more sound. At least for an hour.

The sun begins to hide from them as they trudge along. And when Matt stops, Makeddah can see the pink hue in the sky through the thick trees.

Makeddah can't tell what he's thinking this time when he glances back at her, so she just stands there looking up at him. He looks over at Rayon. She had been fingering her pendant and staring at the ground until he stopped. Now she's staring at him, too.

He cocks his head, his eyes switching between girls, and points at Makeddah first. "What did you say?"

Makeddah and Rayon have been quiet; there should be no reason to stop. But it seems he thinks differently.

"Nothing," Makeddah's chin juts back. "I swear."

He points at Rayon, and she throws her hands up in the air. "I didn't say anything."

Makeddah swallows as he looks up and glances at their surroundings. She wants to move closer to Rayon, but she's frozen in her place. She needs to break free of this hold that fear has on her. She, at least, is able to slowly pull out her sword and check her surroundings. Maybe her feet will follow her eyes.

There is really no way out if sorcerers encircle them. They're already out in the open, and Makeddah is not used to this circumstance. Maybe her senses are useless outside of the Center. She would run in the direction they have been going, but she's sure she'd soon get lost. As Makeddah looks for escape routes in her head, nothing comes and she gets shaky. She knows nothing about this world.

Rayon shakes her head at Makeddah, then a look falls upon her face that Makeddah can't decipher. That is, until Rayon conjures a glowing orb in her hand. *Then* Makeddah sees it.

Terror.

"Makeddah!" It's all Rayon can get out before a flash of black magic comes flying toward Makeddah.

Makeddah turns in time to hold up her sword against the magic. The sword doesn't fade. "Thank you, Stars, for witch-enchanted swords," Makeddah says after the black bounces off the sword. Her admiration of the witches grows.

Matt's bow is up, an arrow at his fingertips, and he shoots. But he misses as the sorcerer runs straight for Makeddah. Her frozen body finally melts. On instinct, Makeddah stabs her sword toward the sorcerer's midsection, but he catches it. The sword lies flat in his hands, and he laughs at Makeddah, making her feel weak.

She snatches the sword back and swings at his neck. She only nicks him, but it's enough to draw blood. He stops laughing. Makeddah starts shaking. His hand draws up to his neck, and when he pulls his palm away, it's sprinkled with black blood.

The sorcerer takes his gaze off his hand and slaps Makeddah's cheek. The blood from his hand sticks onto her face along with the sting from the blow. Makeddah wants to spit at him but instead brings her sword around with all of her might and goes for his neck again, this time harder.

She feels deep contact, and he crumples to the ground, holding his wound. Makeddah can tell she hit him in the right spot, because he lies there paralyzed for a moment. Another sorcerer comes from the shadows.

The first recovers quickly, and they both snarl at her, walking her way.

Makeddah backs up and bumps into Rayon. They go round, back-to-back, and Makeddah realizes Rayon has two sorcerers on her, and Matt only stands a few feet away, fending off his own. Five against three. And not only does Makeddah have two of them, but it seems like they're determined to take her, more determined than before.

Makeddah and Rayon turn to each other. After losing some of the strongest witches in the Center, they know that it might be over for them as well. Rayon holds Makeddah's hand, and Makeddah knows that Rayon is thinking the same thing. They don't want to go down without a fight.

Rayon grins, and Makeddah nods.

They both turn around toward their sorcerers, who are standing there peering at them. Makeddah has the sword in hand, and Rayon's hands are ready.

Makeddah imagines Rayon being blown away with magic, but she tries to keep her mind from that as she tries to fend off what's coming for her—two ugly and angry sorcerers.

And, with all her force, Makeddah fights. The first sorcerer lunges at her to take her, but she swings her sword, causing him to jump back at every swing. As she swings left and right, the second sorcerer kicks her in the back, making her drop her sword. But she pivots and kicks him and hits him across the face as if it hadn't fazed her. The first sorcerer grabs her arm, and she punches him in the face. Then he's gone like mist.

She cocks her head. This whole time, something had been out of place. How had she not known? Her specialty had failed her when she needed it most. Something so obvious.

Every one of the sorcerers looks alike, she thinks.

"Rayon!" Makeddah screams, but the second sorcerer rises, wiping his jaw off, a red mark where her foot kicked him.

He shoots magic at her, and she's overwhelmed, but more surprised, by the feel of it. It's like something dreadful is growing in her. Like she's dying.

Her breath steadies but slows. Her strength is there, but fleeting. She looks at the sorcerer above her, and he growls at her. "Aren't so bad now, eh?" he says through his gritted, yellow teeth.

"Guess not," she mumbles back.

He takes her by the arm, and she tries to tug away, but he's stronger. Rayon is still dealing with one, but the other is gone. Makeddah looks around for Matt. He's on the ground, clinging to his midsection, but his sorcerer is gone too. Which means Rayon's or this one is the real one.

The earth vibrates beneath Makeddah's feet, and it courses through her body. Her ears pound like her heart, and her body heats up like fire. She feels the heat at her fingertips. She wants to let go of that heat. To push it through her body and into his.

Makeddah grits her teeth and tugs one last time. The tug doesn't work, but she turns and screams at him.

She brings her free hand around and slaps the sorcerer with it, but he doesn't let go, just brings his hand to his face with a hiss. The moment he removes his hand, Makeddah sees a burn mark in the shape of her hand. She swallows hard as he goes for her neck. She does the same, but her hand catches his jaw first.

Her hand burns his skin. Makeddah can see the steam rising from where her hand is connected to his jaw; it unclenches as he cries out against the pain. Makeddah sees a flash of silvery white magic shoot at his back, and he gasps sharply before his eyes go wide and the light leaves them, and he crumbles to the ground.

Rayon is panting and smiling. "Good fight."

Makeddah breathes heavy, holding her neck, where his hands just were. "You too." Her voice comes out rough and scratchy. She looks at the ground where the man is.

"He's not dead," Rayon says. "He'll wake up, so we need to move quickly."

Rayon and Makeddah both look over to Matt, where he lies unconscious. They rush to him. Makeddah puts his bag of arrows around her neck, seeing they have fallen, and Rayon taps him a few times to wake him up. Makeddah picks up his bow as she hears Rayon say, "Come on, Matt. We've got to go. Come on, get up." She groans as she picks him up from the ground. Makeddah helps, and together they get him to his feet.

"It's his side." Makeddah looks through the ripped shirt at the black mark on his side.

Matt was right. The sorcerers weren't there to kill. And they obviously didn't want to injure her because they would have if that was the goal. *Why is she so valuable to them?* Makeddah rubs the sorcerer's dried blood off her face and spits on the ground. *Disgusting* is what comes to mind when she thinks of those men. *Utterly disgusting.*

"We've got to keep moving, or he might wake up," Rayon tells them. "Matt, can you guide us?" Matt nods slightly. "Okay, let's get moving."

Makeddah listens but tells Rayon to wait. She looks around and finds her sword. Bloodied and useful. She picks it up, sheaths it, and they all walk together with Matt's atrocious guidance, Rayon's groaning, and Makeddah's weapons.

They will not die tonight. *No,* Makeddah thinks to herself as she thumbs her sheath. *Not if I can help it.*

Five

Matt points somewhere in the distance. Rayon holds him up a bit more, trying to help him, but it doesn't seem to work. When he coughs and stumbles back into a tree, Makeddah realizes that instead of helping him it just brings him more pain. He slides to the ground and shakes his head.

"Can't you ghost us there?" Makeddah asks.

"I don't know where we're going." Rayon looks at Makeddah, her brows furrowed.

Makeddah almost snaps back at her but when Rayon releases a shaky breath Makeddah see's she is worried. Rayon's eyes are pleading with Makeddah—it's a look she's seen multiple times.

Makeddah is brought back to the day she, Rayon, and Belle were up to no good. Looking for something fun to do that both Makeddah, being magicless, and Belle, being bad at magic, could participate in.

They came across a little abandoned house and found so many treasures. They went every day for a month.

But when High One walked in one day as they were snooping, Rayon had that same look on her face. She didn't want to get in trouble; she is always the most well-behaved Parish.

So Makeddah took the fall while Rayon and Belle snuck out. She still thinks High One knew it was all three of them but didn't rat them all out to Alda.

Now, seeing this look on Rayon's face, it isn't for childish reasons and makes Makeddah's chest feel heavy.

She looks at her surroundings, hoping that any sorcerers haven't followed them, if there are more.

Rayon dips to the ground, and without regard for her white dress, she lets her knees drop next to Matt's leg. "Matt," Rayon says, and his head rolls back. Rayon motions for Makeddah to get water. Rayon pulls Matt's head up. "Matt, can you hear me? Matt, please."

Matt's eyes catch Rayon's. Rayon takes the water and tells him to open his mouth. "We have to keep going. Are we almost there?" He nods. She gives him one more drink of water and hands it back to Makeddah. She tries to help him up, but he refuses her.

Matt slowly forces himself up and stands, leaning against the tree. When Rayon and Makeddah go to hold him up, he pushes them away again.

"Fine." Makeddah crosses her arms. "But we need to go."

"I've heard." He coughs again then pushes off the tree and limps his way forward, holding his side.

Makeddah sighs along with Rayon, and they both follow him. Within ten minutes they are stopped again. This time Matt looks up and back then waves them forward. Makeddah steps forward, feels a strange, warm presence fall over her, and finds herself hidden under dense vegetation. Rayon steps through next, and Matt follows.

Makeddah looks back at the warm air pocket and realizes it has the same shimmer as Rayon's shield but if you aren't looking closely enough you'd miss it.

Matt pulls out a device; it lights up blue. A clear tube-like room seems to appear from nowhere, surrounding them and he grabs Rayon by the waist. "I'll be back," he says to Makeddah. Then he looks down to Rayon and says, "Hold on."

The next second, they are gone along with the tube-like room. Makeddah is alone—scared in the dark woods. It's almost pitch black in this area, just a small bit of moonlight piercing through the trees. She can see the stars in the small gaps between branches, but she still feels uneasy about being alone in the dark woods when sorcerers are chasing her.

And what about Rayon? What if he hurts her? Or what if he's taking her somewhere and Makeddah never sees her again? Now she is panicking, and she is impatient for Matt to come back.

As she goes through all the bad outcomes that can happen in her head, someone does come, but it's not Matt.

The girl appears out of nowhere. Just like Rayon and Matt disappeared to nowhere. Makeddah sees the girl's arms stretch out above her and sweep open. Immediately the trees part to give more moonlight, and Makeddah can see the girl clearly.

She gazes at Makeddah with light brown doe eyes. Makeddah can tell, even in the dark, that this girl's skin is a rich, golden color. She is beautiful and obviously a witch, but Makeddah doesn't see a pendent on her neck so she doesn't understand where her magic comes from.

"You're her?" she asks Makeddah, awe dripping off her voice.

"That depends on who *her* is?"

The girl's eyes sparkle. "The Lion Heart. You're her, right? Wow." Makeddah shakes her head, but the girl ignores it, pulling out a device like Matt's. It lights up blue. "Name's Mira, and you are Makeddah." She tells Makeddah to stand by her and she grabs Makeddah's waist the same way Matt did to Rayon. "You're going to want to hold on." She pauses after Makeddah furrows her brows, "Tight."

So Makeddah squeezes her and the next second, she feels like she is being pulled downward. Her stomach makes weird flips while her head feels like it's going to burst open. She can feel her grip on Mira loosening. Then her feet hit the ground.

Immediately Makeddah falls and coughs.

"I said to hold on tight." Mira bites her lip.

Makeddah looks up at Mira after her last cough. "Well, somewhere in between falling and feeling like dying, I forgot." She stands up straight, wiping herself off. Rayon is standing in front of her, smiling. "What? You didn't do this?"

"No, it just felt like ghosting. Witch,"—she shoots a white ray from her finger—"Remember?" A laugh is hidden in the back of that phrase. Makeddah knows it.

"Yeah." She rolls her eyes. "Right." Makeddah looks at the small room around them, then looks at Matt who is standing against the wall staring out the doorway. He starts limping through it, and they both follow.

The next room is large, and it seems like over a hundred people are standing there staring at them. Makeddah swallows, and Rayon smiles. Makeddah turns to the panting Matt. "One last question, if you don't mind."

"No, of course not. My internal bleeding is no reason to stop your questioning."

Makeddah looks over the room of people. Men and women. Children and the elderly. Brown, white, yellow, black, and red skin. And she twists back to Matt and asks, "Where are we?"

"This place, is just a building." Mira steps up in front of them, and her voice startles Makeddah. "But in these people… in this family," her hand moves over the space everyone takes up, "lies the Guard."

"The Guard?" Rayon asks as her smile grows bigger, and she squeezes Makeddah's arm, whispering into Makeddah's ear. "I like it."

"*I'd* like some help," Matt mutters. Rayon puts her hand on her hip and scowls at him with eyebrow raised. "Please," he adds.

Rayon grins. "Lead the way." She holds him up, and they start walking where he directs them. The people seem too shocked to help them. Mira is the one who decides to go and hold up his other side. Makeddah walks up behind them and makes sure that they don't drop him.

As they walk, Makeddah examines the halls. Everything feels unfamiliar, yes it is just a building like their schoolhouse or like the infirmary at home but nothing seems the same. The walls are not normal walls, she doesn't know what they are, but they're smooth and feel like metal but not as cold. They are a light grey color and curve as they walk through the hall. There are vines and flowers lining the top and bottom as if they are borders for the walls. And the floors are like the fancy ones in the shop at the Center but smooth white, speckled with grey.

It seems like nothing is touched here, it's all so clean. There are no splatters and no splotches, it is all perfectly kept.

There are about a dozen hallways they pass before turning to where Mira is leading them.

They come to a room where a dark-skinned woman is stitching up a young boy. She says something to him Makeddah can't hear, and he runs off with his arm in a cast. The woman looks up and gasps. "Matt, are you okay?" They set him on the table, and she tells them to step back. "Honey, what happened?"

"It's okay, Grace," Matt says to her.

As Matt explains, Makeddah looks around the room. It looks like a witch's room. It has the herbs and shelves of books similar to the ones the witches have back home. Are Mira and Grace witches? They should be in a Center if that's the case.

She drops his bow and arrows, and she feels much lighter with them off of her back.

Makeddah runs her fingers across the books.

"Don't touch that," Grace says calmly as Makeddah comes to a small bowl of liquid. "It could hurt you." She grabs the bowl of clear jelly next to that one and walks to Matt, massaging the jelly onto the blackened area of his abdomen. "You're the Lion Heart, right?" she says to Makeddah.

"I…" Makeddah looks at Rayon who shrugs. "Guess so. That's what Mira said but I don't know, Matt hasn't told me a thing." Makeddah steps up to the table and glares at him. "You probably won't tell me, either." Makeddah pauses, "Not until I force it out of you."

"Oooohh," Mira says from behind her. "I like her."

But Makeddah doesn't mean she will force it out of them violently. She didn't know she could really fight until today—until she had to. Even then she froze up and didn't throw her first punch until maybe an hour ago. Rayon would be the first to actually force it out of them that way out of the two of them. What she means is that she would ask so much that they'd finally fold and be forced to tell her.

By instinct, Makeddah searches for an escape. Ever since she was little, she's always had a feeling that she is trapped in any room she walks in. So, she looks for escapes. She looks for clues, for things that are out of place. It's her way of making sure she is safe. She's never known why she has the instinct to do this, she has never not felt safe with the Parishes and at the Witch Center.

Deep down she feels it's because she lost her mom at such a young age. If her mom could die and leave her suddenly like that then maybe she's never been safe.

Mira is blocking the only doorway she sees. The vent in the floor is too small, and the one on the ceiling can only be accessed through a ladder. Makeddah feels that in this room something is out of place. She looks all around, glances here and there, and then stops searching because she feels it. It's her. She's the one out of place. And the bronze circles on the shelf. "What's this?"

"It's magic binding shackles. Some of the first ever made in Korzon," Mira says. "Have you never seen these before?"

Makeddah shakes her head and takes a deep breath. What else is here that she hasn't seen?

Witches are not fond of worldly items. She didn't know what that meant until she and her sisters found the shed with a bunch of stuff in it that was witch enchanted and deemed to be useless, one being the sword on her hip.

It proved not to be useless to her.

"It's only been in Korzon for about twenty years, so don't feel bad about it." Mira says, "And it was only invented maybe fifty years ago or something."

Makeddah nods, not getting clarification on what magic binding shackles actually are. And Mira must see a puzzled look on her face because she explains, "These are used for anyone with resemblance to magic. It restricts their magic, so they have no way to escape or defend themselves."

Makeddah frowns. She can't fathom how much she is going to learn once these people start answering the questions she really wants to ask.

Instead, she focuses on something she may understand. "You know, if this is an infirmary room it should be much closer to the door. It seems too far away for people who might be injured like Matt."

Grace chuckles, "Well, we try to keep it more central so it can be accessed quickly no matter where you are in the Guard."

"Hm. Is he going to be okay?" Makeddah asks Grace without acknowledging the abundance of questions she now has in her head. "The sorcerers surrounded us." *But it was really only one,* she didn't add, *after me.*

"He'll be fine. At least you… *three* are all right, and they're not able to track you back to us. That would be bad." She leaves Matt's table and goes back to the shelves.

Makeddah watches Rayon leave, yet she doesn't comprehend Rayon is gone. Her head is hurting, and her mind is spinning. She's not sure why. A complete heaviness falls on her chest, but it lifts when Rayon comes back in and says, "Mother knows we're here. She's not sure if Mother Lianne is okay yet."

"Let me show you where you're sleeping," Matt groans as he gets up from his bed. Grace rushes over.

"No, lie down," she tells him. "You need rest." Her hands are on his face, and they are looking each other in the eye. Makeddah looks away because she feels it is one of the intimate moments that she's read in one of Rayon's books. She always cringes at those moments.

"So do they," he replies to her. He gets up from the bed and starts walking to the door.

"Rest. Okay? All of you." Grace sighs and looks at Mira. "Mira, can you help me clean up?"

"Sure," Mira says, and before they leave, she turns to Makeddah. "I think you'll like it here. I *hope* you like it here."

Makeddah doesn't reply. The heaviness on her chest is back and hope is far from her right now.

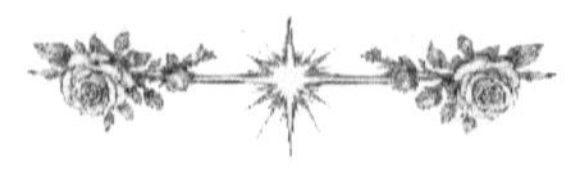

Matt takes them back in the direction they came from and down one of the many hallways. The hallway is short with only 3 doors there and he stops at the one near the end on their left side.

At the end of the hallway, on the back wall, is a small fountain flowing with water which reminds her of the never-ending fountain of water at the Center.

She walks to it and lets the water flow through her fingers. The sounds of the splashing water unclogs her brain. She feels like she's walking straight after having to zig-zag all day.

Everything here reminds her of the Center. Reminding her of how they might still be in danger.

"Mak," Rayon whispers as Matt is checking his pocket for something.

Makeddah walks back to stand next to Rayon. Matt finally finds the key. He takes it out and once he opens it Makeddah is holding her breath waiting for him to say it's a joke. After years of sharing the same room with Rayon and Belle—a small room at that—Makeddah is surprised to see a large room the size of her living room *and* kitchen back at the Center. It only has one bed, but the bed is bigger than any of the ones she's seen at the Center.

Makeddah steps in first. A square room painted blue with white tile floors, a desk, a wardrobe, and a door on the left.

"What's in there?" Rayon points to the door.

Matt steps up to the first door and opens it. "Washroom, which has the second wardrobe." He crosses his arms but uncrosses them and his face goes sour. He must have forgotten about his injuries.

He recovers quickly. "We only expected one of you so there is only one bed and washroom, but does it look okay?" They both nod, without words. "There are some fresh clothes in there. If they don't fit, just tell Grace and she'll get you some new ones in your sizes."

"Thank you." Makeddah looks down at her dress. The dress that was beautiful when she left the Center and is now stained black and dirtied up.

Rayon says, "We would've died if you did, you know? That would've sucked. So, thank you for not dying."

He looks at Rayon and nods with his mouth agape. "I have a feeling that you two would not have died even if I did." He starts backing out of the room. "Sleep well."

Makeddah doubts that she will. All she can think about is black blood, grey faces and yellow teeth. She doubts she will get any sleep at all. But she still nods and says back to him, "You too." He shuts the door, and Makeddah and Rayon look at each other, both speechless at what they've been through in only one day. Makeddah sees flashbacks of the blurry day in her head.

Did she burn that sorcerer's face?

That detail had left her mind until this very moment, and she doesn't snap out of her trance until she hears Rayon's voice. "The clothes should fit you, but I'll need a size or two up, can you tell Grace? I'm running a bath." Rayon says, shutting the washroom door before Makeddah can have a say.

"Why is their blood black?"

"Because they're rotten inside. At least, that's what Mother tells me. Says the Creator distinguishes those who have dirtied their souls to those who can still be redeemed." Rayon says and shifts in the bed. Makeddah can't believe she thought it was all imaginary but there it was happening to her. "Did you burn his face?"

"I think I did." Makeddah yawns.

"Cool."

"What was that trick he did?"

Rayon sighs. "Something witches can't do. He duplicated himself. So, while there appeared to be multiple sorcerers, there was only one. But the duplicates can still take you and beat you up. It was smart." Rayon says after a pause, "It just wasn't smart enough."

Makeddah turns on her back and lays her hands on her face.

She's glad she's not dead, but she's not happy about her circumstance. Trapped again inside a building she's not sure how to escape. But at least her sister is here. At least they can still see Belle and Alda and Mother Lianne soon. And Mother Lianne will be well. She will be perfectly fine when they go home.

She makes this her mantra to keep some sanity.

"How do you know so much about sorcerers?" Makeddah asks.

"Mother and witch history classes."

"Mmm." She sighs, "Men are real,"

"I knew that," Rayon replies.

"But I didn't," Makeddah mutters.

"Welcome to the outside world, Mak. Oh, yeah," Rayon turns to face Makeddah, "And happy birthday."

Six

Makeddah's dreams haunted her all night. Many of them were sorcerers taking over the Center, Mother Lianne dying, and Belle and Alda being taken away. But about three minutes after waking, she realizes she was only dreaming. And two seconds after that, she remembers most of it actually happened.

In other words, it was a sleepless night.

Rayon wakes up this time. She slaps Makeddah's arm and says, "Why do you have to do that?"

"I'm having bad dreams."

"I noticed, but you could be like normal people and just open your eyes instead of popping up in bed *every time.*" Rayon must be looking over, seeing Makeddah shake because she puts her arms around her sister and lays her head on her shoulder, softening her tone. "Are you going to be okay?"

"Why are *you* okay?"

"I'm not, but I can hide it better." Rayon gets out of bed and walks to the washroom, shutting the door behind her.

Makeddah wishes she could see the time; she can always tell when it is morning by the sun, but being underground, that is not possible. She gets out from under the covers and goes to her sword. She wishes Rayon had interests in it. It makes her miss her sparring partner. Belle seemed more excited than Makeddah when they found the swords. She caught on just as quickly as Makeddah did. Those were the times she felt the most free.

 Here, she feels claustrophobic. So anxious to get out of this place. To get all those terrible thoughts out of her head.

And why can't these people tell her what's really going on? They keep saying Lion Heart but that has no meaning to her.

She has to do something about it. She doesn't want to act like she's brave and tough if she isn't, but they don't know that about her yet. So, what if she is? What if she and Rayon play a game on them and lie like they are so intent on doing to her?

It's not so much to ask for answers, is it? Not when it involves you.

Rayon comes out of the washroom and holds up two pieces of clothing, but Makeddah is unsure of their name. Matt was wearing them yesterday, and so was the boy sitting at Grace's table. To think of it, Grace and Mira had them on, too.

"Pants," Rayon says, as if she can read Makeddah's mind. And she probably can. "We can actually wear pants. Not just sports shorts, actual pants. I want to see if they fit." Rayon sits on the bed and examines them.

"Rayon, we need a plan."

"Yeah, yeah."

Makeddah pulls the pants from Rayon and throws them across the room. "We need a plan." She repeats. "I know

Mom trusts these guys, but…" Makeddah trails off, trying to find the right words.

"We don't know them, and it's kind of hard to trust people you don't know."

Makeddah nods. "So, what do we do?"

"We snoop. We can ask Mira about it. She seems trustworthy enough, but we just have to be really careful. We don't want people thinking that we don't like the Guard because they may turn against us for not liking it."

"Dramatic."

Rayon gasps, "I've read that exact storyline before."

"In a *story*."

"A story is just history with made up names." Rayon pouts, "Whatever." She pauses and Makeddah already knows she is going to say something she might not like. "We don't know if we do like this place yet. We might."

Makeddah knows her sister has a point. They don't know if they like the Guard yet. They don't know if it's safe yet, but Makeddah wants to know what it's all about. Find a person or two to tell them more. Mira will definitely be the first target because they know her, or at least met her.

"Get dressed." Rayon throws the pants back at Makeddah. "We have breakfast to attend."

There is a chain of command in the Witch Center.

High One is at the top, being the leader of the witches in the Center. The one that they need to answer to.

Next, there are the Head Witches. There are currently twenty Head Witches, and High One leads them. They are the second most powerful, chosen by the supreme hands of High One and the Stars.

Then there are the older witches, ages thirty and older. The middle-aged witches, from ages nineteen to thirty. The witches in training, ages seven to eighteen. Then the witches who can't train yet, of course, are ages six and lower.

The last person Makeddah sees in the chain of command is herself, a non-magical being.

And as Makeddah and Rayon walk into the lobby to have breakfast, she wonders about the chain of command here.

But that is distracted by every eye being on them. Makeddah finds Rayon smiling again. Of course, Rayon always likes attention. Makeddah, not so much. But she does want to be special and magical, like, and that must come with being stared at.

Somewhere in the crowd, she hears, "The Lion Heart."

"They love you," Rayon says.

"They don't know me."

"They know more than you do," Rayon says matter-of-factly. And she's right.

"Don't worry, they'll get used to you." Makeddah turns to find Mira looking over their shoulders at the people staring at them. Mira moves forward and waves her hands at them. "Keep your eyes on your plates, nothing to see here." The faces turn, and the talking resumes. Mira turns back to them. "Wonderful. Come."

Makeddah and Rayon go to the food bar and get food that looks pleasing—though Makeddah feels she can't eat—and sit together at a table with Mira. All of the walls and floors are so bright, but the tables and benches are all made of dark wood. Some are more prickly than others. The one they sit on is smooth.

There are about ten round tables, all with six chairs, but Makeddah feels that there must be more than sixty people who live here. She hasn't explored it yet, but it seems like a big round circle with lots of hallways and different rooms.

Makeddah stares at Rayon to get her to start speaking because Makeddah doesn't know the first thing to say or what questions to ask about the Guard, but Rayon seems as calm as can be as she looks around the room.

"So," Rayon's eyes focus on Mira, "How long has the Guard been here?" Rayon rips off a piece of toast and asks, biting into it.

"Fourteen years. One year after Haggard took the throne." Mira seems so sure about the answer, like she's been asked a million times. Maybe she has.

"Who exactly is Haggard?" Makeddah asks. She knows Alda was talking about him with the sorcerer, but she can't remember what they were saying.

"The King."

That's right. King Haggard is what they were saying. In books, Makeddah has read that if you call the King by his name, he will behead you. But seeing the confidence in the way Mira talks, that must not be true.

Rayon nods and drinks her water. "I really don't get this place. What is it for? *Who* is it for? How did it get here? Underground, that is." All her questions are more like statements. Rayon's eyes go wide. "A witch must live here, a powerful one."

Makeddah smiles because at those words, Makeddah sees Rayon's real question—*Who is this witch, and how can I be like her?* Makeddah shakes her head and looks to Mira for an answer.

Mira nods. "Well, the Guard started with just a witch and her husband—"

"Witches can't have husbands." Makeddah and Rayon say at the same time.

"It'll be a longer story if I explain everything. So, let's just stick to the basics. The witch and her husband came to Korzon to find her Center, but instead she found devastation. Haggard started to reign in Korzon only a few months before, and her husband died in the midst of his wicked acts.

Men were getting changed into sorcerers, women and children were being killed if the King had no use for them, vendors were being robbed of money, and homeowners' houses were being taken away.

"The skies were dark, and there was a sadness and emptiness over Korzon. So, she found a place and, with the help of some earth full-breds, moved it underground. She began by bringing in the orphans, and giving them homes. Then they began taking in families with elements before Haggard found out. Then everyone realized that they all wanted the same thing. To take that wretched King down."

Makeddah finds her eggs falling from her mouth as she closes it. She spits the eggs into a cloth and looks at Mira, who goes about eating her food. Again, like the story is a normal thing, and she's told it many times.

"He kills women and children?" Makeddah shakes her head. "Why is he on the throne? Can't people remove him? Does he have any magic." But her question seems stupid. Of course he does. How else would he take over an entire kingdom?

She really doesn't know anything about the outside world and is almost frustrated with how wrong all her facts are and how ignorant she is of reality. But that should never be in question when a man does things like that.

"He doesn't have magic," Mira confirms that Makeddah knows less than even she thinks. "He's just a man."

"And they still don't take him down?" Rayon is asking.

"No."

"But *why*?" Makeddah sighs.

"Because he's a man who took down the *real* King and Queen of Korzon and who killed thousands with no remorse. He's the man who took away homes, tore apart families, and created an army for himself." Mira bites her lip, "Though he's just a man…"

"He is not just a man at all," Makeddah nods.

"Yeah, pretty much," Mira says.

But she doesn't understand how one man could do all of that with no power. With no special abilities except for being ruthless, if you can call that special.

Makeddah can't comprehend this idea of a magicless man taking over a kingdom, making sorcerers, and playing King. Why would they bow to him and allow him to still be up there? Is there no one who could take him down? Why haven't the witches done anything about it?

Mira plays around with her food and glances up at Makeddah. "So, are you meeting with Kahlan today?"

Makeddah furrows, "Who?"

"The witch we were talking about, her name is Kahlan. Didn't Matt tell you anything?"

"Not really."

Mira nods slowly. "Well, I'm sure she'll want to mee you. She's cool. Sometimes intense, though. Depends on the situation."

Makeddah and Rayon look at each other. There is wonder behind Rayons eyes and Makeddah can only imagine the worry behind her own.

Seven

It's times like these that Makeddah longs to know her real mother. Was she like Makeddah, always trying to find a way out? Did she ever feel trapped? Did she hate lying?

When Makeddah asked about her real mother, and if she hated lying as much as Makeddah did, Alda would give her a little laugh. "You hate lies because they are wrong. I don't have to tell you where that came from."

Alda, always points things back to the Creator, but it never mattered much to Makeddah because how could she care about something she never believed in.

Now her beliefs are skewed.

She never believed in elemental magic and now look at where she is. A Guard that hides people with those special gifts according to Mira. Still, she doesn't know anything about these elements, full-bred or pure-bred. Those words mean nothing to her.

She craves the knowledge that they are holding back from her.

Reviewing plans on how to gather information from people, Makeddah looks at Rayon, who shares a similar idea. She wonders if their minds work the same because they were raised the same way, or if it's because Makeddah has a trait that comes from her biological family, which Rayon has in common with them.

When they hear a knock on the door, they both jump. Rayon is the one who opens it as Makeddah sits up peering at the door in bed.

It's Matt lingering there, and he doesn't look happy. "I can tell what you're doing. You're trying to find out a way to escape or a reason not to be here. But you can stop now."

"What are you talking about?" Rayon asks. Even Makeddah is convinced Rayon doesn't know anything about what he's insinuating.

"Did you get enough from Mira? No?"

Makeddah and Rayon look at each other, then back at Matt. Rayon crosses her arms. "I don't know why you're so mad, unless you are hiding something." Matt narrows at her. "They were innocent questions. We're just learning about the Guard."

Matt seems to shrink a bit before he stands straighter and says, "Let's go. You have a meeting with Kahlan." He pauses. "She'll answer some of your questions."

"Some?" Makeddah asks, getting out of bed. Matt doesn't respond. She wants every question answered. Is that really so hard?

She can imagine that not very many girls fight off sorcerers and follow the first man they meet to a strange place. But she and Rayon did. And now they give her some answers?

But when she thinks about it, other girls might have fought off sorcerers. Have they? She hates being so uneducated. So ignorant of the world around her. It's like she is sitting down to take a test with material she has yet to study. They expect her to ace it but are frustrated when she asks what class it came from.

Did they keep all this information from her, or was she just too stubborn to believe it?

She knew about sorcerers but didn't really have an interest in learning make-believe stories, so maybe it's her own fault.

They head down in the direction of the lobby but pass through it into a hallway. It's a small hallway, a hard place to escape from. There is a fogged glass door, and outside it are perfectly grown and healthy plants in big white pots.

The moment Matt's hand goes up to knock, the door swings open.

It's a woman dressed in a white robe. Her hair is silky white, and her eyes are an icy blue. Despite her difference in complexion and height, Makeddah is sure she is looking at High One. Or just a High One. But really, this woman is the head of the Guard. Which is technically the same thing, Makeddah thinks.

She's starting to understand the chain of command here. This woman is their High One, and maybe Matt is like a Head Witch.

"Matthew," she says with a small smile, "Thank you for bringing them. Would you like to stay?" Matt stands up straight, and with a small nod, he walks into the room. Kahlan looks at the two girls in front of her and smiles. "Come in."

Once Makeddah steps in, she sees a long table. It has eleven seats, four on each side, two on one end, and one on the other. Makeddah glances at her surroundings. Two swords on the back wall, a cart on the side wall, and books, many books, on the entry wall.

What would be her first escape if they tied them up and tried to keep them captive? First, she'd tell Rayon to cut the ropes with her magic. Next, she'd run on the table, grab one of the swords, and disable the witch the same way she did to the sorcerer. Rayon would disable Matt, and they would make a run for it with Matt's transportation device.

But what if the exit was blocked?

Makeddah is pulled from her thoughts the moment Kahlan says, "Sit, please."

Makeddah and Rayon sit at the end of the table with two chairs. Matt stands in the corner. In that moment, Makeddah wants to read everyone's mind, other than Rayon's, who is probably thinking of how the woman at the other end of the table could have gone against the witch rules and married.

"So, I am sure you have many questions. I will answer what I can."

"Right," Makeddah scoffs. "It seems to me like I should be getting all the answers. My sister and I almost died. Witches did die. We should know why, since our mother refuses to tell us."

"She does, does she?" Kahlan asks, clasping her hands on the table. "Your mother and I haven't spoken personally, but Matthew has told me what she's comfortable with me explaining. And I'm sure she knows that it's best you don't get all the information at once. It's a lot to take in. And it's no small matter. Like the fact that you are a Lion Heart." Kahlan smiles, "I'm sure you've heard."

"Yes, what does that mean?" Rayon asks, her tone not as sharp as Makeddah's. "She can't have a lion's heart inside of her body because she's a human, obviously, so it makes no sense to me."

Kahlan doesn't smile, and she doesn't laugh. She just stares at Rayon, as if she is searching her soul.

"Elements—you two know what those are, I suppose?" They both nod. "Okay. You have fire, water, earth, and, of course, the mixture of air, which we classify as an element. Just as witches and sorcerers are allowed magic, people with elements are allowed elemental powers." She raises a brow as a smirk rises on her face. "They are called Full-breeds—or Pure-breeds if they haven't accessed full power." Kahlan stands. "Follow me. You need to learn a thing or two about yourself."

Within ten minutes, Makeddah, Rayon, Matt, and Kahlan are above ground with four other people. Makeddah didn't know what to call the strange door that transports them above and underground, so she and Rayon decided to call it a ghoster.

Makeddah takes survey of the others there. She only knows Mira.

"Can't the sorcerers see us here?" Rayon whispers.

Kahlan answers, "No, I have preserved this space for the Guard. We are shadowed here."

Rayon and Makeddah both release the tension in their bodies. They'd done so much to stay away from the sorcerers; Makeddah doesn't want to be in their hands again.

"These are all Full-bred elements. Air…" Kahlan motions a man to step forward. "Air has the ability to give breath back to someone who is dying. Air can feel the breeze in a different way, connecting with the flow and life of it. Powerful air Full-breeds can even contain the wind."

The man opens his hand, and an air ball is floating above it. "Or they can make the wind stronger, if they'd like." The ball falls from the man's hand, and he opens his arms wide. A breeze comes, then a wind. Makeddah can hear the wind whistle and see the trees sway around her.

Then the wind stops suddenly, returning the area to the still state it was in before.

"And water." Kahlan narrates as another man steps forward with a water ball an inch above his hand. "Water elements can manipulate any body of water, like the seas, lakes, oceans." The water flows between the man's fingers and swishes around. "They can create rain." His fingers move in a wiggly motion, and raindrops pour out of his hand. "They can hydrate others and themselves. Water is essential for survival."

Makeddah stares at the man, mesmerized by the beauty and clarity of the water. She tries not to look so in awe of this; she shouldn't give away anything she is holding inside. But how can she not be amazed? How did a man just create water from his own fingertips? That seems impossible.

"Fire is the most daunting of the elements." Kahlan brings Makeddah back to her attention. "Fire elements can walk through fire and not get burned." Like the others, a girl creates a fireball, but she throws it to the ground, creating a mighty fire, and walks right through it.

Makeddah is drawn to the flames. She steps up and feels the heat of the fire on her face, but it doesn't burn. Then she remembers burning the sorcerer's face, and she thinks something stupid. *Touch it.* Her thoughts guide her, and when she places her hand in it, there is no burning, just a little stinging. And a fond memory passes through Makeddah's mind of when she was younger.

There had been a fire blazing in their fireplace, and Makeddah had put her hand on the gate covering it, but it didn't burn her. It burned Rayon and Belle, and Rayon had to wait four weeks for her hand to feel better. Belle was a bit quicker to heal, but it still burned her. Makeddah had never given it a second thought; she thought she was just lucky.

Makeddah looks up from her memory and smiles at Rayon, who puts her hand close to the fire but pulls back when she is close. She looks at Makeddah, and her jaw drops. "Whoa," she mouths.

Kahlan continues, "And they can hurt their prey more easily than others." Makeddah almost forgot Kahlan was still there, talking to them. The girl ceases the fire by snapping her fingers. Makeddah steps back at the smell of smoke and looks down to see that the grass and flowers of that area are blackened and burnt.

"Fire, some say, is the best way to make someone feel pain."

Kahlan looks to Mira. "And finally, earth. Earth has the ability to create rock or dirt, manipulate it, and shape the natural world. They feel the vibration of the ground and heal plants." Mira steps up eagerly. She puts one knee to the ground and places her hand an inch or so above the burned area. As she closes her eyes, the patch turns from black to the most vibrant green, and the flowers spring back to life.

"Which is the best of all the elements?" Rayon is always looking for the frontrunner.

"Well, they each have their purpose. Earth is the balance of nature, fire is the sting of it, water is the preservation of it, and air is the life for it. Each element is crucial for us. If we have no Earth, we have no oxygen. No fire, no heat. No air, no life. No water, no life."

"So, what does a Lion Heart have to do with this?" Makeddah is the one who asks now, not to know what's best or to understand it deeper, but to know why she's here.

"Makeddah, the Lion Heart has everything to do with this. The Lion Heart has each element. Do you feel the vibration of the earth? Do you see the clarity of the water? Do you have soundness of mind through the air? Do you not feel the burn of fire?"

Makeddah has always felt the vibration of the earth. The water has always felt like a source of clarification for her, but she thought that was normal. Just like with the air, it makes her feel at peace. She thought this was what everyone felt, that she was like everyone else but with no magic.

Her back tingles now, and she clenches her hands.

Her back is tingling more than it ever has. It feels like it's full of moving bubbles, the way water moves when it's boiling on the hearth. It feels like a war is raging inside of her. She throws her hand to her back and scratches.

The sensation is getting stronger.

"No, Makeddah, it's not you," Kahlan says, moving Makeddah's hand. "It's your birthmark, you've finally found yourself. You've finally discovered your Lion Heart."

"What do you mean?" Rayon walks over to Makeddah and lifts the back of her shirt. Makeddah is about to tell her to put it down, but Rayon gasps and lets it fall herself. "What is that?" Makeddah doesn't understand the horror on Rayon's face. Or is it fascination? For the first time, she doesn't understand Rayon.

"Her birthmark," Kahlan says simply.

"But it's glowing, and I have never seen that before." Rayon lifts the back of Makeddah's shirt again. "She's never had a birthmark on her back."

Makeddah pushes Rayon's hands from her shirt and frowns at her. "I don't want people to see my body, thank you." She sighs and shakes her head. "And why would Alda keep this from me?"

"Come, let's show you what your sister sees on your back."

But Makeddah doesn't move. "What is happening?" Makeddah's chest feels a weight on it again. She wants to be special, to be the Lion Heart they are talking about, but all she can think about is how Alda has kept this from her, how she had sixteen years to tell Makeddah exactly what she is. How she went through all that suffering yesterday. She is the reason those witches are dead. How the women yesterday shouldn't have been scowling at Matt for being a man, but spitting on her for being the reason the witches are dead.

How Alda lied.

Her body starts heating up, and she feels her face burn. Her hands are on fire, but her eyes are set with tears that she wills not to fall. The earth is vibrating even more than before as she grits her teeth and clenches her fists to stop the heat and the tears. Her ears ring, and she can't hear anything besides her loud and dangerous thoughts.

She tries not to show the tears and to hide her face, but her anger doesn't decrease.

But is it just anger?

She has been stuck her whole life, locked up in that Center, thinking she was just an unlucky girl with no magic. Now she has been taken to another place to be locked inside, discovering she might be the luckiest girl. She has wished her whole life to be like the others and cried to Alda about being different and strange, and Alda never said a word.

She has been slapped by a sorcerer, his dirty blood staining her cheek. She fought, actually fought, with her sword, almost killing a man. She has almost given up her innocence, and for what?

"Makeddah, stop!" Rayon's voice cuts through Makeddah's rage. Makeddah's hands relax, and she realizes that fire has risen at her feet. She jumps from it and falls backward onto the ground.

"I believe," Kahlan shakes off the ember that has caught on the sleeve of her robe, "You just found out the reason why you shouldn't know everything right now. Almost everyone starts off this way. They're either delighted or terrified. With this type of news, it's hard to know what to do and how to feel."

Makeddah sits up and dusts herself off. She wants to say something smart back, but she can't even talk.

She looks at the burned ground. Sitting up on her knees, her hands touch the ground, and the dark part turns green without her say.

"I know exactly how to feel." She's surprised at the calmness of her own voice because her body is shaking all over. "How many do you have?"

Kahlan asks, "What?"

"Lion Hearts." Makeddah meets Kahlan's eyes. "How many do you have here?"

"Just you." Kahlan smiles and crouches next to Makeddah.. "That is, if you choose to stay. We can train you and feed you and give you safety from the sorcerers."

"Why are they after me?" Her voice shakes now. The stories she's read never told her how emotionally crippled being sought after makes a person. Did the writers of those stories not know what it was like? How scary it is.

"One thing at a time." Kahlan raises Makeddah to her feet. "Everyone, go back inside."

Mira looks at Makeddah and smiles before being the first to leave and Matt follows. After the others go, Kahlan, Rayon, and Makeddah stand in silence above the ghoster.

"Okay." Makeddah looks at Rayon. Rayon nods—she knows what Makeddah is going to say. "I'm feeling like we don't even have a choice here. Either we can stay and live, or leave and…" she swallows, "Get killed. I honestly don't like the sound of either, so just give us time."

"As you wish." She takes out a device, then gives it to Makeddah. "Here. Your key to the Guard."

Makeddah cocks her head at the small metal thing in her hand. "My key?"

"Yes, because I know you think of us as just another prison, but we aren't. Not for you, not for anyone. However, you do come and go at your own risk. I trust you understand this."

"Yes," Rayon says when Makeddah doesn't answer. She takes the key from Makeddah's hand and pets it with her thumb. "We understand."

"Good. You may think about it as long as you like but while you are here, we'd love to get your training started. I know you've met Grace, she will be your fire teacher. You'll be introduced to the others should you decide to stay." Kahlan turns back to the ghoster and pulls out her own key but stops again. And without turning back, she says, "What did you mean, you know how to feel?"

Makeddah looks at the ground. "I've been lied to - for years I've been lied to."

Kahlan nods but still doesn't turn. "They only ever wanted what's best for you. Soon you'll realize all of this is for you. What we all have done." Kahlan holds her key up and, with a glance back, says, "Rayon Parish and Makeddah Brooke. Welcome to the Guard."

Makeddah stares at the little device—or key, as Kahlan calls it. Rayon holds it up, and they both keep staring at it. At almost the exact same time Makeddah repeats it in her head, Rayon whispers, "Welcome to the Guard."

Eight

"Mak, you have to say something," Rayon says.

Makeddah has been pacing in the room, trying to make her headache go away. With everything that she learned today, she just doesn't have the energy to talk to Alda. So, she looks at Rayon and shakes her head, biting her nail. "No, Ray, because if I speak to her, I'm afraid I'll yell, and I don't want to yell. I don't want to be mad. But I am." Makeddah bites harder. "I'm mad at Mom. Oh, my stars. I don't know what to do."

She's never really been mad at Alda before. She never went through that rebellious stage of saying, "I hate you."

One of the younger witches said that, and she was grounded for a year. All Makeddah ever wanted to do was leave the Center, but that discontent was never pointed toward Alda. It was pointed towards many other things. She's never been mad at her mom; now she knows what it's like.

Rayon stands, walks to her sister, and stops her from pacing. Rayon is good at these things. She doesn't get mad or yell often. She can always look at both sides of things and be a mediator. She can calm Makeddah down during almost any circumstance.

When Rayon squeezes Makeddah's shoulder and smiles, Makeddah feels much lighter.

"You know something? You're special." Makeddah tries not to smile at Rayon's words, but it's hard. "You are outside of the Center like you've wanted your whole life. You've fought and won. And you are the coolest sister in the world. You're *special*." Rayon says it as if Makeddah always has been special. As if nothing has changed about her.

"I'm special," Makeddah says, confident in herself now. Her broad smile surprises her, and she can't control it. "I am. I know that," she breathes, "I know that."

Rayon turns back to the bed. "Go somewhere." She sits. "I'll tell Mother that you're exploring."

"Tell Mother Lianne I say hi, and Belle that I miss her." Makeddah opens the door. "And tell Mom that I'm upset, that way we're not lying."

"Such a goodie, aren't you?" Rayon says. Makeddah frowns at her and she quickly adds, "Got it."

Makeddah nods to her sister in thanks and leaves the room. She steps into the lobby, but doesn't want to be there as soon as she sees eyes on her again. So, she turns and goes down the hall, where she and the others had gone the night before.

She can't help but have these thoughts run through her head over and over. Did her real mom know? Was she actually born in the Center? Did she really die in battle? What else have they lied about? Who else knows?

When Makeddah looks up, she finds herself in front of the room from last night. Grace is at her table writing something in a notebook. Makeddah walks inside without being invited. Thinking that must be rude, she steps back out and knocks on the open door.

Grace looks up. "Makeddah, come in."

Makeddah steps in and watches Grace write for a moment. Then she rotates, looking at the herbs on Grace's well-organized shelf. "Kahlan says you'll be my fire teacher." Makeddah picks up a jar of oregano. *Isn't that for food?* She smells it, then sets it back down.

"Yes, I look forward to it. They say that you were already creating flames today. Very rare for a new student. But I suppose you are neither a Full- nor a Pure-breed."

Word spread that quickly? It's only been two hours. But Makeddah knows in the Witch Center, two hours is like two days, plenty of time to spread gossip.

Grace steps up next to Makeddah. "Need anything?"

"Headache." She looks down at Grace. Though Grace is not short, she is about two inches shorter than Makeddah. Which means she's not tall either.

Grace picks up mint and rosemary first and sets them down on the table, then selects a few other items. As she mashes and mixes the ingredients together, she looks up at Makeddah. "What's wrong? Why the headache?"

"I just feel…" Makeddah doesn't want to tell her. She doesn't want to say everything on her mind. She still doesn't know about how the Guard works and if they are a safe place for her, but as she looks into Grace's brown eyes, she feels that Grace is trustworthy. Why? Makeddah can't explain. "Lied to. And other things, I think." She really doesn't know.

"Your thoughts must be all over the place." Grace mixes the herbs into a liquid that Makeddah hopes doesn't taste like urine, because it resembles urine. She doesn't know what urine tastes like, but that is something she wants to keep a mystery. Grace blends up the ingredients and pours them into a glass cup, and gives it to Makeddah.

Makeddah drinks. No, not urine; it's actually quite good, with a very earthy flavor. "My thoughts are overwhelming. I'm thinking more than I ever have had to."

"About what?"

Makeddah turns and examines the room. "You're a witch?"

Grace laughs. Probably due to the fact that Makeddah doesn't answer her question. "No, I'm a Full-breed fire element, but you knew that." Grace steps next to Makeddah, "I know how to work with ingredients, not like a witch."

Makeddah picks up a drawing that has both grace and Mira smiling on it. "This is amazing."

Grace's eyes light up. "Mira is wonderful at these things. She's my prodigy, and she's like a little sister to me. Plus, she knows her way around some needle and thread."

"For stitches?" Makeddah takes another sip of her drink and finds herself wanting to put it down now. It's not so good anymore. Too much earth.

"No, she makes clothes."

"Oh," She wonders if Mira gets paid. Clothes outside of the Center seem so complex. It must take up most of Mira's time.

Makeddah rubs her head. It does feel better.

Perhaps she *is* overthinking everything. Too much about what she is and what she isn't and who she wants to be. Too much about leaving, like Kahlan says, and having free will to do anything. About what other secrets Alda and the Guard are holding. She just needs to take a break. Maybe being stuck without any place to go is a good thing for her now. She can relax.

But as her mind settles to relax, her body moves, ready to run away. It's another war between the two.

Her mind keeps her body awake at night. Her body tends to walk places her mind knows not to go. And now her mind wants her to relax, but her body wants to react. To push something. To make herself feel less numb about everything. The two things that are supposed to help her are at war, yet again.

"What are you thinking about now?" Grace asks.

"Life."

She looks up at the painting of the sea on Grace's wall above her desk. "That's beautiful."

Grace smiles, "It's where Matt and I got engaged. I had to buy a souvenir."

"It's a good one." Makeddah takes a last gulp of her drink, scrunches her face at the overwhelming flavor at the bottom of the cup, and gives it to Grace. "Thanks."

Grace grabs her hand before she leaves. "Makeddah, you can trust us. And if you don't trust me, trust Matt. If you don't trust Matt, trust Kahlan or Mira. But life is nothing when the only person you trust is yourself." She lets go of Makeddah's hand. After sitting back at the table she was at when Makeddah had first arrived, she adds, "Hope that headache goes away."

Makeddah nods. "Me too.

After her talk with Grace, Makeddah wanders around and stops at the kitchen. There is a large area for the hearthstone, lots of light wood cabinets and countertops, and a single water basin. She watches as a man lights the hearth with his finger, and he doesn't flinch when the hearth lights up, and his finger is still in the flame.

And a woman goes to the water basin, but when she twists the handle, no water sprouts out. She calls out a name, and another woman shoots her finger in that direction, and water starts flowing out of the spout.

"What are you doing?"

Makeddah jumps at the voice when she hears it. She swivels and sees a blond boy smiling down at her. "I'm just trying to see how things work," she says.

"What do you mean?" His blue eyes sparkle at her. It's almost as if he has a literal twinkle in his eyes.

Makeddah sighs, "I mean that I know witches have a hob in their kitchen, but often use magic to make food. And that they plant their own seeds for the fun of growing fruit, but really, they don't have to plant them; they just have to grow the fruit itself. And when they use a spout, the water just automatically turns on as if it has read their mind…" She pauses, "Well, except when Belle uses it. Anyway, did you know that when a witch needs to boil water, they get it from the fountain that is an endless source of water for them? That's where the spout water comes from, too. And High One purifies it." She rambles, "And to close the door, they flick their wrist. How does everything work here? Do other people have birthmarks?"

He doesn't seemed fazed by her rambling. "Yeah, actually. I heard yours is on your back."

That's when Makeddah realizes she hasn't introduced herself yet, but of course, he knows who she is.

He continues, "And that is cool cause we regular elements have it on our left rib." He lifts his shirt, and there it is, a swirl of water moving freely on his rib. And when Makeddah has an urge to reach for it, she instantly blushes. Why? She doesn't really know.

But she clears her throat, and he lets his shirt fall. She asks, "Right, what about food or cooking?"

The boy leans against the wall and looks at the people moving in the kitchen, "Well, some of us hunt to get the meat, others scavenge to get the fruits and vegetables. But the fire breeds normally light the hearth like I'm sure you saw. And we don't have an endless fountain of water, so the water breeds help us there. And the earth-breeds make the wood chairs and tables that we sit on and eat at for all of our meals." He shrugs, "Air breeds can also close the door with a flick of the wrist."

Makeddah shakes her head, "It's crazy how much I don't know."

"Yeah, I think it's crazy that you have to learn the elements for defense and learn to fight instead of learning them for fun."

She glances at him, "How did you learn?"

"When my brother and I found out we had elements, we used them every night in our rooms. My mother told us to keep it a secret." He crosses his arms, "She didn't want us to be a part of the ones who were turned into sorcerers."

"Right, because Haggard is turning people into sorcerers," Makeddah remembers.

"Not people, men." He says, "Any boy or man with an element can be turned into a sorcerer."

"And what about women?"

"There is no living sorceress that we know of, so women cannot be turned." He says plainly, but it confuses Makeddah nonetheless.

"I still don't get it." Sorcerers, sorceresses, witches, elements. It's all too much for Makeddah to comprehend.

"The man who turns a pure- or full-bred into a sorcerer becomes the master. So, there must be a master in order for more sorcerers to be created. Since there are no sorceresses, there cannot be a master and therefore cannot be any women sorcerers."

He must see the gears working in her brain or the confusion on her face because he starts explaining more.

"Also, people can only be turned into a sorcerer if they already have magical ability. And from that point, whenever they use their dark magic, their soul starts to rot. Their blood turns black, and they become more disgusting, and eventually they're just walking zombies."

This part Makeddah understands, which makes her happy. Man must be magical to turn; when turned, if they use dark magic, they rot. Their rotting causes them to have nasty breath and rotten teeth.

"That is why one of the sorcerers smelled like decay, but another sorcerer I saw looked like he was perfectly fine."

"Yep, he must not have been practicing for a long time."

"Did you find out you were an element because of your birthmark? Is there something different about a Lion Heart that would help you recognize it early on? Because everyone knew about me but me, so I know it wasn't because I discovered my abilities. Obviously, I don't know you, and you knew about it too."

The boy scratches his ear, seeming uncomfortable now. "Before Haggard, when a baby was born, a prophet would search their future. They'd find out if the child held magic or not and which kind."

"Why doesn't he do that now?"

"He killed the prophet for not obeying his commands."

"Oh." Makeddah swallows.

"Otherwise, people normally discover their abilities by living life. And one day their birthmark reveals itself when they find their magic."

She glances over at the stranger. She feels like she learned more about the world of magic in the past few minutes than she has her whole life. "Thank you for the history lesson, but now my head hurts even more, so I think I'll just find my sister and relax a bit."

He smiles brightly, "Any time, Sunshine."

Sunshine? She turns to tell him her name, but he's gone.

Nine

Makeddah finds Rayon in the hallway of their room, sitting down by herself, reading a book. Already twenty pages in, and it must've only been five minutes she'd been reading.

"It's been eight minutes," Rayon corrects Makeddah's thought when she sees Makeddah's raised brow.

Makeddah sits next to her and watches a few people pass by. "Mother Lianne?" Rayon doesn't put her book down. That's bad. It either means she's crying, or she's upset, or she's too engrossed in her book. "Is she going to be okay?"

"Maybe." A one-word reply. That's really bad.

"Maybe meaning?" Makeddah tries to make her continue, but Rayon shrugs. "I need to know. She's my great-grandmother, too."

Rayon runs a hand through her hair, and this is when Rayon's red eyes are revealed. "They don't know. High One can't determine what state she is in, and she passed out a few hours after we left, meaning she can't tell them her pain." Rayon buries her face in her book again. Not sure what to do with herself, Makeddah guesses.

"There are so many witches, can't they heal her?"

"No, Makeddah. Witches don't heal." She says gently, "Witches… witch, that's what we do." Rayon sighs and rubs her eyes. "Can we not talk about this right now? I don't want to talk about this right now."

You'll know in time.

That time must be now. She can understand the heartfelt words in Mother Lianne's note were a goodbye.

Makeddah's heart feels heavy as she hopes they weren't her last goodbye.

Makeddah and Rayon fall silent. Rayon reads her book for another eight minutes, and Makeddah doesn't know what to do with herself yet. Not until Rayon sets the book down and studies Makeddah. "I think we should break into the witch's office."

Makeddah swears her mood changes just as her books do. Too quickly.

"What?" Makeddah blinks at her sister—Rayon is serious. "Okay, for a girl who wants to be a Head Witch someday, that's a little un-head-witch-like." Makeddah sighs. "What did Mom say, other than about Mother Lianne?"

"She's sorry." Rayon shrugs as if it means nothing compared to what she's just come up with. In her mind, it probably does mean nothing. "We just need to get in there and get out. I can be the lookout; we can do it. Just make sure she's gone and—" When Mira arrives, Rayon shuts her mouth and smiles as if they weren't just talking about their dying grandmother and breaking into someone's office.

"Hey," Mira says. "Liking the book?"

"Oh, is it you who put it at my door?" Rayon jumps up.

"Yeah. I heard you say something about books yesterday, so…" Mira shrugs and looks at both of them. "I think
lunch is starting soon if you guys want to come with me."

Rayon nods. "Yes." She makes Makeddah stand. "We
would love to."

All Makeddah can think about while fake smiling at her
sister is how weird she is.

They walk down the hallway toward the lobby. Rayon
is talking to Mira about food, which both girls apparently
love. Makeddah is looking at her feet, thinking of what
Rayon had said. Does she really think they could break into
Kahlan's office? Won't that be dangerous?

Makeddah shakes her head at the thought and starts
chewing on her fingernails when she bumps into something
solid, hitting her head in the process. She backs up, rubs her
forehead, and finds the solid thing is a person. Her breath
catches at the sight of two boys. And she finds herself
blushing cause one of the boys is the one who called her
sunshine. The other must be his brother, whom he mentioned.

These boys, like Kahlan, command attention. They look
the same age. And their features are almost identical. Twins?
There are only a few pairs of twins in the Center; High One
hates them for some reason. She once stated that if she ever
had to make another twin, she'd lock herself away until the
Stars agreed to let it go.

The boy Makeddah has run into is stockier; he has wide
shoulders, and it seems like he could break a tree in half just
for fun. The one she was talking to earlier is thinner and just
an inch shorter, but she can tell he is also hiding a muscular
stature under his sleeves.

Makeddah feels embarrassed for noticing so much in
the five seconds she's met them. She can't take her eyes
away.

"Sorry," Rayon says first, and Makeddah shakes out of
it.

The boy from earlier smiles, "No problem, it was as much our fault as yours." The bigger one just stares at Makeddah, and she does the same until she hears the boy from earlier say, "You know, Sunshine, biting your nails isn't a good habit."

Makeddah stares at him and pulls her hand down. He has that twinkle in his eye again. She glances at the bigger one and notices, though their facial features are almost identical, the bigger one doesn't have that same twinkle in his eye.

"You didn't stay long enough to hear my name."

"What?" Rayon asks, snapping her head to look at Makeddah.

"Yes!" Mira claps. "Sisters," she puts her hands on Makeddah and Rayon's shoulders, "Meet brothers. Aaron"—the bigger one—"and Isaac"—the thinner one from earlier.

"Aaron?" Makeddah repeats, "Isaac?"

Mira laughs, "You got it."

Makeddah nods, hoping it hides how weird it feels to say their names. Her unfamiliarity with boys' names makes them they sound foreign on her tongue.

"I know our names are very different from what you've heard, huh? Living in a Witch Center your whole life?" Isaac says as if reading her mind.

Rayon interjects, "She's read books-" then she pauses, "Actually, she mainly just ignores me as I read them."

Makeddah sighs, "It's not my favorite hobby."

"What is then?" Isaac asks.

"Um. My other sister, Belle, and I like swordplay."

Isaac smiles, another darn twinkle. "I like that."

Makeddah doesn't smile back, but she wants to. She just doesn't want to give Rayon any room to say anything later.

Before the silence and stares go on too long, Mira says, "And this is Rayon and—"

"Makeddah," the big one, Aaron, says. "The Lion Heart."

"Why does everyone know about me?" She rolls her eyes.

Aaron replies, short and curt. "Hard not to." And now she feels he is mad at her for some reason.

The two stare at each other. Makeddah doesn't know why *he* is staring. Maybe because she is the Lion Heart, as everyone calls her. But *she* is staring because she's confused. How could someone's arms be so big?

"Okay, let's go back to when you said you two met?" Rayon looks between Makeddah and Isaac.

"Yeah, for a bit."

"Sunshine had some questions."

Makeddah is convinced Isaac is trying to mess with her by calling her sunshine. She can't yet decipher whether she likes it or not.

"Anyway…" Mira says, as the awkward silence becomes too much for her, "We're heading to lunch. Join us?"

"No, we just came back from our mission this morning, we're pretty worn," Isaac says.

"Bring anyone back?" Mira asks, hope filling her eyes.

"No," Aaron says, and Mira falls silent again.

Isaac puts a big smile on his face, "We're not too worn for your graduation, we'll be there."

Mira gasps, "My dress." And she runs away in the opposite direction from where they were headed.

And though Rayon is standing right beside her, Makeddah feels like she is the one the boys are focused on.

Isaac smiles staring at Makeddah with intense concentration, "Will you be at the graduation?"

"Sure." Rayon says, though his eyes don't leave Makeddah's.

When he finally breaks the contact, he glances between the two girls and smiles. "Sisters?"

"Yes. *Brothers?*" Makeddah looks at the two of them. Although they look alike and Makeddah knows he is asking because she and Rayon look *nothing* alike, she still mocks. And she has no idea why. She's not a mocker, that's Belle's thing when she's feeling frisky. But she hasn't felt so many emotions in the span of one day, so now she's just acting out.

To think, yesterday she was just trying on a new gold dress for her birthday. Now, she's staring at a big guy and a smaller guy and wondering how it is that her legs do not know what to do with themselves, or how her arms feel weird and lanky by her sides, or how she is so aware of herself in a bad way. She shouldn't feel this way, yet she does. And now, she wants to get her sword and stab something because her insides are making her feel small and puny, like a little girl.

"Well, nice meeting you." She gives a smile that probably looks as fake as it feels. Makeddah grabs Rayon's arm and rushes forward, whispering in her ear, "I have an idea." Makeddah says.

Rayon smiles. "I'm way ahead of you."

Makeddah smiles, knowing Rayon has already calculated and planned out everything.

"Good."

Ten

Makeddah and Rayon join people as they leave the Guard through the ghoster. The Graduation is outside, which makes it all the better for Rayon and Makeddah's plan.

When they make it outside, they see that people are gathering in front of a stage.

"Whoa, Kahlan must have done that."

"Stop being amazed by her. We don't like her."

Rayon shrugs, "You may not, but I think I'm in love with her power."

Kahlan stands in front of the stage and asks people to move from the area. When they part, she walks down an aisle of her own making, creating rows of seats on either side of her.

People start to find their seats, and when Makeddah catches Isaac's eye, she stills. He smiles, and she wants to bite her nails, but Rayon starts dragging her to a seat.

"Can't we just go now?" Makeddah asks.

"No, we cannot." Rayon says, "We need to make an appearance so no one suspects anything. Also, I really want to see what an elemental graduation is all about."

They wait for a few minutes as everyone finds their seats, and Kahlan stands on the stage.

"Hello everyone and thank you for coming. Many of you have heard my speech before; to those of you who are new here, I always like to welcome the graduates with a few words. We have three brave people graduating today. They came from a world where no one would accept them and their gifts. But they trusted the Guard with that very thing. They have come from the bottom and risen up to their very best self."

People cheer and Makeddah smiles despite being indifferent a few minutes ago.

"When a birthmark is revealed in Korzon, it might be one of the scariest days for a person. But despite that, our graduates are here to fight."

Makeddah feels those words vibrate in her chest. She wasn't ready to fight, but she's here now. Maybe there is a reason why. She is increasingly convinced that she belongs here.

"Now, their birthmarks have revealed to them that they are ready to become Full-Bred Elements. Let's have a round of applause for our graduates. Mikko Waider," a dark-haired man walks down the aisle wearing a black suit, and where his fire birthmark is, there is a cutout so that it is clearly seen. "Warren Esper," a younger man, walks down with light hair and dark eyes, his suit matching Mikko's, his cutout revealing an air birthmark. "And Mira Salt."

Mira walks down the aisle, and Makeddah's breath is taken away by her beauty. She is also wearing a black suit with a cutout where her tree birthmark is, but it has a long black train following her. Her light brown, wavy hair is teased, giving it the look of a lion's mane.

She is beautiful.

Mira enters the stage last, and she walks behind Warren to stand between the two men.

Kahlan steps onto the stage to the left of them and clasps her hands. "Full-bred graduations are symbolic, showing the ones you love what you have achieved." She turns to the three graduates, "I hope you all know that today does not make you any greater than before; you are just merely showing the greatness you already possessed."

Kahlan faces the crowd, "Our graduates will now do a demonstration of their elements." She nods to the graduates and exits the stage.

The two men step forward. All three hold out their palms and wait. Makeddah jumps at the sound of drums playing behind her, and Rayon giggles at her. She looks back and sees the big drums behind her, wondering where they came from.

She moves her attention to the stage again, and the three graduates manifest their birthmarks in their outstretched palms.

Rayon gasps, and Makeddah's jaw drops. Their birthmark actually left their body and is sitting in their palms.

What an amazing sight.

They begin to circle the stage, birthmarks still in hand. And they stop where they first started, but Warren and Mikko stand back as Mira steps forward. She closes her palm, and her birthmark appears on her rib again. She moves her hands freely over the stage, and grass begins to grow with flowers blooming in it, and as she raises her hands to the sky, two large trees form from the ground up.

She holds herself with a serene look on her face, but the drums behind them start clanging something terrible, and Mikko steps up with a dark look on his face. He closes the fire birthmark in his palm and sets fire to all that Mira created.

She stumbles back with fear in her eyes, but the moment she hits her marker next to Warren, she becomes a statue.

Mikko stomps both feet, then rips at his chest, fire welling at his feet and all over the stage. He screams, and Makeddah can feel the whole crowd hold their breath.

But Warren appears beside the huffing Mikko. He closes his palm, and his birthmark disappears as he opens it and places his hand on Mikko's shoulder. Mikko's head drops, and he walks backward to stand next to Mira, and he also becomes a statue.

Warren looks over the fire, a sad look on his face, and he blows at it. Makeddah almost laughs, surely blowing on a huge fire will do nothing, but to her amazement, it does everything.

The air pushes the fire so that embers fly over the whole crowd. He makes a circular motion with his hands, swallowing the fire up in a tornado. And he ceases the tornado with a cross of his arms. He steps back, becoming a statue like the others.

Then they lift their arms to the sky, and between their palms, their birthmarks show up once more.

Beautiful and vibrant.

The drums beating behind Makeddah and the glow in her eyes from the birthmarks leave her speechless.

The three graduates bow, and Mikko speaks, "Use your elements responsibly, kids."

The drums come to a stop as the crowd joins in laughter at the lighthearted joke.

Everyone rises to their feet, cheering for the graduates.

Kahlan enters the stage and displays a bright smile, "Thank you and congratulations to the graduates!" She shouts over the chorus of cheers.

Makeddah is so engrossed in the experience that she barely feels Rayon's tug on her hand. Rayon nods her head to the ghoster, and Makeddah is almost sad that she is leaving, but she sucks it up and follows her sister.

The girls enter through the ghoster. Mostly everyone is at the graduation, but a few stragglers remain.

They enter the hallway to Kahlan's office, and Rayon stops Makeddah in time for them to hear a spout turning off. A girl exits the washroom and holds the door open. Rayon pretends to enter the washroom as the girl walks away, but with one glance to make sure the girl is gone, she smiles.

"Easy peasy." Rayon walks up to Kahlan's office door and checks to see if it is locked. With a twist of the knob, she sees it isn't. Rayon steps inside and tells Makeddah to follow her. "Yay!"

"Shhh." Makeddah hisses.

Makeddah shuts the door carefully and turns around to find files or anything explaining the real reason Makeddah is here.

After two minutes, Rayon says, "I don't see anything under the letter M. What about in that cabinet? Those must be names."

Makeddah looks in the cabinet where Rayon had pointed and looks under M. But they aren't names, just something about witch stuff. So, Makeddah closes that and looks around. They have to do this quickly because if they get caught, Makeddah isn't good at coming up with a lie or an excuse. She should have thought of that before; she should have come up with some excuse for their presence here.

She can fight her way out of things, which she truly found out yesterday, but lying her way out of something is a different story.

Makeddah runs to the other side of the room and searches Kahlan's desk. This is where the names are. But as she pulls out her own file, she feels the ground vibrate. She looks to Rayon to see if she feels the same thing, but Rayon is still searching.

She only takes a moment to feel amazed by her connection to the earth before praying that the feet won't pass the washroom. But they do, and they come close to the door.

Fifteen minutes is all she wants, but she barely gets ten.

"Rayon put it away, *now*," Makeddah hisses. She shuts the desk drawer, goes to sit at the table in the same seat as earlier, and tells Rayon to sit next to her.

Rayon slips into the seat two seconds before the door opens, and they hear an "Oh?" Makeddah and Rayon look back as Kahlan shuts the door. "I wasn't expecting you two tonight, weren't you just at the graduation."

"Yes, well…" Makeddah swallows.

Kahlan stands by the table and looks down at them. In her hands is a jar of rosemary, and she sets it down to talk to them. "What is it you two need?"

"Um." Makeddah breathes, slowly waiting for something to pop into her head. "So—" she looks at Rayon. How is it that the more logical one got them into this situation?

Rayon swallows. "It's okay, Mak, I'll say it since it *is* me who wants to leave the note." Makeddah studies Rayon, who trembles slightly before she opens her mouth and says, "Well, I wasn't really supposed to come here. I was still in training, just for major things, and I have one more year left. Being the only other witch here—you are the only other witch here, right?"

Kahlan nods.

"So, being the only other witch here," Rayon repeats and smiles, "I thought maybe you could teach me. When you aren't busy, of course. I don't require much attention. I just need two studies a week on more technical magic. I wanted to leave you a note to ask you if you would be willing to do that for me."

Kahlan looks at Makeddah first, then her gaze returns to Rayon, and she nods. "I would love to teach you. How about I come up with some good days for training? I'll tell you tomorrow before breakfast."

Rayon nods with a big fake smile that only Makeddah can see through. "Sounds perfect. Thank you, Kahlan." Rayon stands first.

They begin to walk out before Kahlan says, "So I assume this means you're staying?"

Rayon and Makeddah turn back at the same time.

Though Makeddah already had a feeling in her bones during the graduation, she didn't know if Rayon did. If she was the only one wanting to stay, she would deny it if Rayon said did not want to. She'd pretend she didn't ache for the type of control over her elements as the graduates. But if Rayon says yes…

The two girls eye each other, and Makeddah's answer is right there in the glint of Rayon's eyes. They nod once. And in unison with perfect melody, they say, "We're staying."

Eleven

A knock wakes Makeddah. She whimpers, unwilling to leave her warm bed for the cold tile. She wants to keep her eyes closed and fall back asleep.

Her first few hours of sleep were plagued by terrible dreams. Now, as she finally settles into peaceful rest, someone tries to snatch it away. Frustrated at whoever is on the other side, she *really* wants to ignore the door.

But when there are three more knocks, Rayon groans and pushes Makeddah off the bed. Makeddah hears the thump before she feels the pain. She can swear her sister wasn't able to do that two months ago. Where does this sudden strength come from?

Frowning at her sister, Makeddah stands, fixes escaped curls, and walks to the door. She rubs her eyes and opens it a crack. First, she sees a tray of food. Opening wider, her gaze rises to a bright smile.

"Morning, Sunshine."

Makeddah rubs her eyes and grunts, leaning against her door frame. "I have a name, remember?" She yawns, folding her arms.

"I do. But Sunshine suits you." He steps past her into the room and looks at the snoring person on the bed. "Sister, I assume," he whispers. "She seems much more elegant awake." He sets down the tray and a bag and fixes his eyes on Makeddah. "Make your way to the training units in an hour. Water is your first lesson."

Makeddah nods.

"Just don't be late. Your teacher does not take kindly to tardiness." He smiles again, but this time it professional, not playful. He picks up the bag and gives it to her. "Your training suit, and you are in Water Unit number 1."

Makeddah sighs as he leaves the room. She isn't sure how to feel. She is excited but a little intimidated.

Fragments of fear return as she remembers it was on her birthday that men tried to take her and kill her. Now, her thoughts become clouded, especially since the Guard doesn't want to share details about what's happening. Still, after her reaction yesterday, she senses that moving slowly is probably for the best.

She thinks back to a normal Thursday in the Center. She and Belle would wake up and duel, while Rayon watched and made comments or read a book. Alda would bring them breakfast before Belle had to go to her class. Mother Lianne would be the one who made the delicious breakfast.

Then late at night, they would go home and sit by the fire. Rayon would be curled up with a book that she had read a million times before. Belle and Makeddah would be playing Twenty Questions or I Spy. Mother Lianne would be sitting in the chair with her eyes closed, listening to the room around her. Alda would be folding clothes and instructing them to put them away after they'd had enough fun.

Makeddah smiles at the thought. She misses her family—she looks over at the snoring Rayon—her whole family.

Makeddah crawls onto the bed and shakes Rayon. Rayon tries to push her away. But Makeddah holds a biscuit in front of her face, and Rayon is up within a second. Makeddah pushes off the bed and goes to the washroom to bathe.

After she washes up, Makeddah slips into the suit. She realizes instantly that she loves it. It is uncomfortable, but it makes her look strong. It's black, shiny, and slimming—a powerful suit. The back is mesh to make it see-through, but not *too* see-through, she concludes. She forgot she had the Lion Heart birthmark there, it's the first time she is seeing it. It is a big and colorful birthmark.

No, it seems more like a tattoo—one that moves, alive and shifting across the upper part of her back, its vibrant colors almost glowing against her skin. It looks unreal, as if it couldn't possibly be on her body.

It is a sphere and the first thing that catches Makeddah's eyes are the flames flowing at the bottom. The fire is a vibrant red, orange and yellow reminding her of when she created those flames at her feet. The fire burns at the bottom, but above it the earth element shows through branches. But as the air blows, the branches sway and turn into a beautiful oak tree, then transform into a rocky mountain.

She almost is too transfixed by the earth movement that she doesn't see the water flowing at the top. Almost as if it is an upside down waterfall. The water flows upward in the same motion as the fire and the air element is causing all of the others to flow in a beautiful motion.

She touches it and the birthmark flows around her finger imprint then as her skin raises to normal state the birthmark goes on as if it wasn't disturbed.

She giggles at it. It's alive like her. It is her.

She reluctantly leaves the washroom, and when she comes out, half of her biscuit is gone, and Rayon has only left one piece of bacon for her.

"They only gave us four, and you know I like three," Rayon says when she sees Makeddah eyeing the food. Rayon pokes out her bottom lip and sighs at herself. She recovers quickly. "You should eat. You have that lesson, right?"

"Look." Makeddah turns, brushing off Rayon's question, but Rayon doesn't appear to mind as she examines her back. Makeddah feels herself smiling again, confused by how easily happiness mixes with her anger. The strangeness of this place is echoed in how she can feel sad and weak, yet also confident and strong, all at once.

"Whoa." Rayon touches it.

"Can you come to the lesson?" Makeddah begins to eat what's left of the potatoes and bacon. "I want some moral support."

"I wouldn't miss your first lesson." Rayon gawks a few seconds, then goes into the washroom. Two minutes later, she returns, changed and brushing her hair.

"When do *you* start?" Makeddah asks. "With the witch?"

"Tomorrow."

"Fun."

"I think it will be fine." Rayon side eyes Makeddah, "You shouldn't be mad at Kahlan because mom lied to you. She is not the witch in control of keeping your secrets. Anyway, I need to keep up with my magic because when we get back to the Center, I want to be Head Witch." She pauses. "*A* Head Witch."

"You're fifteen," Makeddah says.

"In less than seven months, I won't be. And sixteen is the age that I told myself I wanted to be considered for a Head Witch position. It's not like I can be High One."

"No, but the consideration doesn't happen for another three years. Then, you have to wait another two years to see if the training goes well, and another year to take the test. So, don't hold your breath. You might die." Makeddah feels a pillow hit her in the back. She whips her head around and glares at Rayon, whose tongue is sticking out at her. Makeddah throws the pillow straight at it.

"Ach! Gross." She wipes her mouth. "Tastes like your hair."

It takes fifteen minutes to locate the training units. Ten minutes of them being lost and then another five minutes to reach them after getting direction. Rayon points out three times that her way was the right one.

As the doors open, a slight pressure of air whooshes in their faces. Makeddah looks over at Rayon, and they giggle at the same time. Walking in, the first thing they see is a long, wide hallway. Ultimately, there is a wall and additional sliding doors. Above those doors is a metal sign saying "Air Units."

Makeddah looks around her.

"Earth," Rayon says. To their left, four 12-foot-wide windows reveal Earth Units. The windows reach from floor to ceiling. Next to each is a large metal door with a number: 1, 2, 3, or 4.

To the right are benches, Makeddah guesses for observation of the training. There is also a men's locker room, a women's locker room, and a stand for refreshments.

Makeddah puts her hand to the glass and peers inside; it appears to be less like the dry woods but more wet.

"Is that a rainforest?" Rayon peers inside.

It is beautiful. Maybe if she goes in there, she will feel like she's outside of this cage.

"So, do we just keep going down?" Rayon asks, looking in the direction of the Air Units.

Makeddah backs away from the Earth Unit and swallows. "Yeah, let's do that." They walk through the next sliding doors. It's the Air Units—four, just like the Earth Units. These are plainer. They have bluer skies and sand, with few trees and just one pond each. Next are the Water Units.

Makeddah's mental clock tells her she is a few minutes early. She looks at Rayon before opening the door to Water Unit 1. "Wish me luck."

"You don't need it. You're a Parish."

"I'm a Brooke," Makeddah corrects.

"Brooke by blood, Parish by heart." Rayon taps her book to Makeddah's heart and smiles. "And you always will be. Go get 'em, tiger."

"It's lion."

"Would you stop correcting me?" Rayon raises her hands when Makeddah opens her mouth to speak. "I know, I would do the same thing." She sighs and walks to the bench outside the Water Unit, opening her book.

Makeddah turns and puts her hand on the cold metal door. It is heavier than she anticipates, and when she finally pushes through, she trips.

"Careful, there."

Makeddah looks up and sees Isaac. She wipes herself off and sighs. His first impression: ignorant rambler. Second impression: angry, weird girl. Third impression: clumsy. And she's probably not going to make herself look any better.

She composes herself. "Aren't you a bit young to be a teacher?"

The corner of his mouth lifts into a smirk. "Aren't you a bit young to be questioning your teacher?"

Makeddah walks to what she thinks is the center, where he stands. Inside, the room is an endless sea. From outside, she could see there's no back wall—inside, only two side walls are visible, but the space still stretches forever. She loses herself in the sight of it. What if she just keeps swimming, would there be an end?

Isaac gives a not-so-serious smile. "I like that you're not late. But whenever you can, five minutes early." He pauses. "Not for me, for my brother. Here, it is just fine. For him, on time is five minutes late."

"Noted."

"You look nice, Sunshine. The suit compliments you." He claps his hands. "Okay. So, have you performed any type of water, ever?"

Makeddah shakes her head. "No."

"Okay, then, we'll start with the basics. Hand out." She follows him, putting her hand out. He nods. He's talking faster now, and it makes Makeddah nervous. "I don't know how it'll be for you. If you can connect with only one element, or if you must summon all of them to use one, maybe just try to call up water. No fire, or air, or earth. Just water."

Makeddah looks at her hand and freezes. How is she supposed to do that? Just water. Yesterday, it was like she couldn't control anything. She didn't know that fire was rising at her feet or that wind was blowing. And she hasn't even done water yet. What if she does something wrong?

"Okay, I get it." He steps in front of her and looks her in the eyes. It is then that she realizes his eyes are even more blue than the water. *Is that possible?* "Just breathe. You can connect with your element by practicing slow, deep breathing. By listening to the waves. By closing your eyes. Just find a way that fits you, okay?"

"Okay." She examines her hands. "I'll try and breathe first."

Isaac nods. "Good choice. My brother's favorite." He smiles, "So when you breathe, you must feel it through your body. Starting in the lower abdomen and rising to your chest. Making it rise and fall at your will, because this is also about control, you know?"

Makeddah shakes her head. "No, I don't. I haven't done any of this stuff before."

"Right." He bites the inside of his cheek. "I know what to do. Look at my hand." He sticks it out. "Elements are all about balance…" He creates water in his hand and draws it out into a big circle. "About control. It's just like breathing." The ball in his hand pulses like it's taking deep breaths. "Taking hold of your body and telling it what to do and how to do it."

"My body often denies me the right," Makeddah laughs.

"Mine too. Stubborn flesh." He pinches his skin, shaking his head at it, and when his eyes return to Makeddah, they are crinkled in the corners. She would have found this annoying—an old lady at the Center's eyes did that when she was mocking people—but somehow, his are different. Like they're actually smiling at her.

"Okay, take hold. Close your eyes." Makeddah closes her eyes, and it seems like Isaac's voice is floating around the room as he talks. "Just listen to yourself and listen to your elements. Connect."

Makeddah feels the vibration of his footsteps and his voice as he walks around her calmly. He says, "Good, now you said you're good with a sword. How about you take a fighting stance?" Makeddah does as he tells, pretending she has a sword in her right hand. Isaac moves her hand up and opens her palm out to the world. "Feet closer together. Good. Now, with all that you have, push out flowing water. Imagine it in your mind. Strong, peaceful water flowing from your hands and into the sea."

Eyes still closed, Makeddah imagines it. Her mind blocks out everything else. Even Isaac's voice and the vibration of his steps. And she imagines her elements. Water, flowing from her hands like a spout. And earth, becoming one with her as her feet water basin into the sand. And air, causing wind, just as the man did yesterday. And fire, pushing it away from her body, letting it release like she did yesterday.

Seconds later, she feels a splash of water, and her body comes to life again. When she opens her eyes, she sees that Isaac is gone, and his shirt is just outside the lake, in the sand, on fire. She puts it out with her foot, and the smell of smoke fills her nostrils.

Isaac rises from the sea. He shakes out his long hair. "Good job. Just next time, maybe only think of water."

"Sorry," Makeddah says, but she laughs. "Do you want your shirt?" She dangles it. She isn't sure if it is appropriate for women to see men without their shirts, so she spins away quickly as he rises out of the water. She didn't feel the same way when she lifted Matt's shirt to check the bruise, but that was different.

Now she wonders what Matt is doing. If he still has that bruise, or if Grace has healed it. Then, remembering Grace isn't an actual healer, Makeddah wonders if she made it better for him. If he's still in pain, or if it's washed away, like her headache.

Isaac steps in front of her, and her eyes go down to their feet. He grabs the shirt and pulls it over his head. "Good thing I didn't wear the one piece today." Her eyes shift up. The burn hole is right on his shoulder, big and blackened around the edges.

"I'm really sorry."

"Don't mention it, Sunshine."

She feels small, like a little kid. *Again.* What is it about these boys that makes her feel so weak?

"Let's go again."

And she does. Over and over for an hour, and she finally gets into the focus of the one element of water. Of course, it takes the whole class, and she hates that. But she's doing well, many can't even create a ball on their first day, so Isaac says.

Alda's command comes to mind, and she tells herself not to give up. It's only been one day. It's bound to get better.

Twelve

It doesn't get better. It gets worse.

She doesn't have Rayon here with her as support during training. Makeddah didn't get much sleep last night and isn't even sure she slept at all. When Makeddah arrives five minutes early for her next training, Aaron is already there, waiting. He stands by a table, facing away from her, so she sees him before he sees her. He looks just like Isaac, yet the exact opposite. She doesn't know how that is possible, but it is.

He stands at the table, back to her, turning an object over in his hands. She hesitates by the door, uncertain he's noticed her arrival. Unsure if she should wait or announce herself, she remains still, arms hanging awkwardly at her sides. He shows no sign of awareness that she's there.

Without turning, he says, "Thank you for showing up on time. My name is Aaron. I am your air teacher."

He knows.

"We met already."

He turns, pushing his glasses up his nose, and the first thing Makeddah notices is that he is wearing them. Makeddah cocks her head at the sight. He wasn't wearing them yesterday. "Oh, right." His monotone voice does nothing to soothe her nerves. "Have you ever—"

"No."

Aaron pauses, looking much older than the seventeen years his brother claimed for him yesterday. "Do not interrupt me."

Makeddah's heart pounds. "I just knew what you were going to ask."

"I don't care. I am your teacher now. Your authority. You don't act like I am your friend in our lessons; I'm not here to be your friend." He sighs and pushes up his glasses. He is very much unlike his brother.

"Hey, guys." The door opens, and Mira walks inside. Makeddah is grateful for the attention being drawn from her. Mira walks to Aaron and hands him a cup. "I feel like I haven't talked to you in so long."

"Mira, I'm in a lesson."

She puts her hand on his face, but he backs away. Mira sighs. "Right, well, I'll see you later?"

"Yes."

Mira waves and leaves.

Makeddah furrows, trying to think of what dynamic that was. "You two are—"

"Dating? Yes. But it's none of your business."

"It's just I would have never known if you guys didn't just have that scene in front of me. I barely know now." She crosses her arms, "Matt and Grace are pretty affectionate, so it is odd that you guys weren't. But is that because you're not married and they are? I mean, I know nothing about all this."

"That's right, you know nothing," Aaron says. "So, just make a ball of air. Focus on air... and air only."

Makeddah's cheeks heat up, and she scratches them. Isaac must have told him about the fire incident.

"I want you to focus on keeping it in your hand for long periods of time."

Makeddah walks closer to where he stands and does as he asked. She looks at her hand and envisions air coming from it; nothing happens. She takes two breaths, closes her eyes, and tries again. This time, a small ball of air forms. But it fades almost immediately.

"Well, how do I keep it there?" Makeddah opens her eyes and looks up. Aaron is now standing directly in front of her, blocking her view. She flinches backward before she can stop herself and silently curses her reaction. Aaron calmly strokes his chin, his gaze moving over her, measuring.

Aaron takes her hand. She tries to snatch it back, but he holds it firmly. When he meets her eyes, his brows crease with annoyance. "Just calm down." But his voice comes out in a caring teacher's tone. That's a tone she never thought would come out of him. He takes a stronger grasp of her hand and explores it.

Makeddah glances up at him, then back to her hand, where he is now drawing the lines of her palm. "Do you feel that?" he asks. "Do you feel the way my finger barely touches your hand, and it becomes something of a tickle?"

"Yes." Makeddah holds her breath.

"Focus on that. Focus on the air forming in your hand and giving you that same exact feeling. But when you get the air, you have to focus on *keeping* that sensation." He steps back and crosses his arms. "Go."

Makeddah exhales and holds her hand out, feeling the air skim her skin for two seconds. She repeats this five times. On the sixth try, she extends it to three seconds. But the moment she reaches three, her hand jerks away as if compelled by a force outside her control.

"Don't let go next time, Makeddah. Keep it in your hand. Keep the sensation." He sizes her up. "We need to get you in training."

"I am. Right now, actually."

"No, physical, not elemental. You need to learn to hold things in your strength, in control."

And they work on her time during the entire lesson. She only gets up to five seconds. Her slow progress has more to do with Aaron than her, she tells herself. He looks down on her, she can tell.

And when the hour is up, he walks her to the door and slams it closed before she gets all the way out. She stumbles out of the Unit and sits on the bench across from it.

"He can be tough, sometimes." Makeddah looks up and sees Mira standing there with a smile and crossed arms.

Makeddah groans. "Yeah. I can tell. I think I made him mad."

Mira laughs, "I wouldn't doubt it."

"I just didn't know you guys were dating." Makeddah sighs. "I shouldn't have said anything."

"It's okay. He just doesn't like when I give him a lot of attention." Mira pauses, seeing the look on Makeddah's face, "He doesn't like kissing, hugging, touching or anything in public. He doesn't like the attention." Mira waves it away, "I didn't see the whole lesson. How'd the first part go?" She sits down next to Makeddah.

"Bad."

Mira nods. "Don't worry about Aaron, he's not always mean. He's just passionate about what he does."

"Right. Thanks." A second later, the sliding doors open, and Rayon walks in. She sits on the other side of Makeddah and lays her head on Makeddah's shoulder. "How was Kahlan?" Makeddah asks.

"She told me her life story. I've made a decision; I'm going to leave and marry. I have to." Rayon sits up and shrugs, as if it is her true duty. "If I don't, I will never know."

Makeddah scoffs, "You're a witch, Ray. You can't. And you want to be a Head Witch, remember?"

Rayon scrunches her brows. "Bad lesson?" she asks.

"Worse."

"I think you did great," Mira says. "I think you did just enough to make Aaron *kind of* mad at you."

"What?" Rayon asks. "You got the teacher mad at you already?" She turns to Mira, "Makeddah used to always get the old witch teachers mad in school at the Center. But it was the most entertaining thing. Sometimes I think that I should have been born like Makeddah."

"You don't want to be me." Makeddah takes Rayon's water and sips it. "It comes with baggage." Just then, Aaron walks out. His glasses are off now, and he is holding a bag on his arm.

He stops and looks into the Air Unit, then looks at Makeddah. "Good lesson today," he says.

Makeddah sits up straighter. "Uh thanks."

He licks his lips, looking over the girls, landing on Mira, and she can see a faint smile appear on his lips. Then he nods again and walks away. Makeddah looks at Mira, then Rayon, then stands. "That was-"

"Weird." Rayon ends it with a smile. "And cute."

"Hey, he's mine." Mira laughs, and Rayon and Makeddah giggle.

Makeddah has finished her lessons. Exhausted, she took a nap. Afterward, they ate dinner. Now, at seven o'clock, Makeddah sits on her bed, twirling a pillow, restless. She

97

wants to spar with Belle or watch the sky from the field of roses. Even as she tries to distract herself, she wishes she was home—though she hates to admit it.

Belle is the only witch who understands Makeddah. While she possesses magic, it is not very good at all, so she always felt inferior and different. She and Makeddah are the only ones who love swords. While Rayon would referee, she never participated either.

So Makeddah is stuck, staring at the wall and feeling the weight of missing her family and playing with Belle. Loneliness gnaws at her, sharper than before.

They both were getting pretty good, too. While they didn't know if they were handling it properly, they started to get smoother with their moves, quicker, wittier.

Rayon sits on the bed, reading a book, and Makeddah sits at the desk, playing with her elements. She may suck at it, but maybe she can try. Maybe she could visit the Units and practice some more.

Just as she almost creates a full air ball in her hand, she hears a knock at the door.

Makeddah glances over at Rayon, who is still immersed in her book, and rolls her eyes. "I guess I'll get it."

She walks to the door, and Mira stands there with a smile. "Hi."

Makeddah perks up; Maybe she will give her something to do. "Hi."

Mira hands clothes to Makeddah, "Here are the clothes you wanted taken in."

Makeddah forgot about that. She and Rayon can often fit into the same flowy dresses, but not the same pants. Rayon's dresses have always been a bit tighter because of her thick and curvy frame. Makeddah's have always been loose. They didn't bother to have it tailored at home, but for some reason, Makeddah felt insecure here.

She needed her clothes to fit properly so that she could feel right.

"Thank you." She sets the clothes on the edge of the bed and smiles at Mira. "I'm bored," she complains.

Mira leans against the doorjamb. "What do you guys normally do for fun?"

"Swordplay, watch the sky, sit at tea parties with other witches. Though we often sat at our own table and didn't talk to the other girls. Belle and I also built an obstacle course a few times." Makeddah smiles at the thought. That was fun.

Rayon rolls her eyes, "All I need is a good book, some food, and some magic to have fun."

Makeddah is surprised she actually looked up from her book. She is bored too.

Mira narrows, "Well, we do have this thing we do every Friday. Ever since we had to start training for defense and fights, we started doing a fight night."

Makeddah stands straighter, "Fight night?"

"Yeah, we do it once or twice a week. Fridays and sometimes Mondays too."

"It's Friday, right?" Makeddah asks, excitement growing.

Mira checks the clock. "Starts in an hour. Want to go?"

"Yes!" Makeddah and Rayon say at the same time.

Mira leads them to the training units, which Makeddah thought was strange. Why have a fight night there?

Mira explains on the way, "It is always two of the same elements or two different elements, but in a Unit that does not belong to them." When Makeddah and Rayon don't say anything, Mira looks back. She has a small smile on her face when she continues. "So, fire against fire, but in an Air Training Unit. Or air against water, but in an Earth Unit. Get it?"

"Yeah." Makeddah answers, "Why do they do it that way?"

"We will never be in our natural element outside of the training unless we train outside of our natural element."

As they approach the training units, they see many others flooding in as well. It's like the whole Guard is here.

"We have one match in each different unit," Mira shouts over the noise of others. She leads them to one of the papers on the walls, and Makeddah can see there are eight fights tonight.

The air unit and fire unit fights are at eight and nine. The earth unit and water unit fights are at eight-thirty and nine-thirty. Makeddah knows only one person out of the sixteen people who are fighting.

Isaac.

Aaron is a ref for Isaac's fight at eight-thirty in the earth unit and for a fight at nine in the air unit. Grace and Matt are also refs for a few of the fights.

Mira skims over the lists, and she smiles, "Preston is fighting first in the fire unit." She grabs Rayon and Makeddah's hands and walks them to the fire units. Makeddah has never seen so many people in one confined place.

The witches often held gatherings and parties, but they were mostly held outside in the field of roses. Here, everything is closed off.

They have benches lined up in rows in front of the Fire Unit number 4. Mira snatches the one in front, closest to the wall. Mira sits by the wall, Makeddah by her, and Rayon on Makeddah's left.

Makeddah sees a panel of three people off to her side, one of whom is Kahlan. She leans to Mira, "Why are they here?"

Mira smiles, "Well, Matt will be the ref, but we also need judges to see who won fair and square." She nods towards the three men entering the fire unit. "The dark-skinned one is Preston; the lighter one is George."

"How will we know who wins?" Rayon asks, "They announce it?"

Mira nods, "They normally wave a flag. Green for earth, light blue for air, dark blue for water, and red for fire. If they are the same element, they will announce it by pointing the flag in the winner's direction."

Matt waves the green flag in Preston's direction and the light blue flag in George's direction. Makeddah sits back, and everyone goes still. Then the two men shake hands, and Matt starts the fight.

Instantly, George throws air toward Preston, but Preston dodges it. George tries to run away, but Preston is too quick, yet he's not rushing through his movements.

Makeddah can't tell what it is about him, but Preston has this calm presence. He is moving methodically, not sporadically, like George.

Preston throws up a wall of wood, and George tries to run around it, but Preston nails the floor with big wood spikes, enclosing George.

George seems to panic, and he stirs up a wind, causing Preston to be blinded by dirt. As Preston makes his way to George slowly through the harsh wind, George tries to push the wood spikes out of his way or move through them, but it is not working.

Preston finally reaches George, and the wind ceases. George's shoulders slump, and Matt nods, exiting the room.

Makeddah hears every head turn to Matt as he walks to the judges. They whisper, and Makeddah holds her breath to hear what is coming next.

Matt stands and waves a green flag. And the whole room erupts. Makeddah didn't know she was this excited until she found herself cheering alongside the others. The fight was so brief, and nothing really happened, but it was thrilling nonetheless.

She watches Preston let down his spikes, and he and George shake hands.

Makeddah's blood is rushing now. "When's the next one?"

Mira looks back at the clock. "Fifteen minutes, in the earth unit."

Makeddah is the first to start making her way through the crowd, and they end up in one of the front-row seats in front of Earth Unit 3. She taps her foot on the floor, watching people pass for another ten minutes, then finally, Isaac and Mikko from the graduation walk into the earth unit. Aaron speaks to the three judges before walking in.

When Aaron walks in, he mimics Matt's movements from thirty minutes ago. He waves the dark blue flag in Isaac's direction and the red flag in Mikko' direction. The fight starts.

It does not start off with a bang like the last one, but the men do seem to size each other up. Isaac says something, then Mikko says something, but of course, she can't hear it through the thick glass. She still finds herself leaning forward to read their lips.

Isaac is the first to throw water, but Mikko throws fire back, and both of their elements falter. Isaac pops his neck and pulls from the water in the small lake. He punches three water blasts at Mikko, and Mikko dodges two of them, then gets hit by the third, and he is soaked.

Mikko laughs, but is soon throwing his fireballs at Isaac.

Isaac creates a wall of water, then, in a swift motion, he turns and shoots a stream of water at Mikko. Mikko rolls on the floor and dodges the water stream. He lifts up, crouched close to the ground, and Makeddah holds her breath.

Mikko goes into an archer's position and holds a fire bow, then shoots four fire arrows at Isaac. Isaac catches two of them on his left shoulder, and Makeddah can hear him hiss. The whole crowd gasps, and Makeddah is on her feet.

Mikko lets his bow go down and runs to Isaac as Isaac is stumbling and holding his wound. Mikko flies in the air, then tackles Isaac to the ground, and the crowd erupts before the red flag flies.

Makeddah is not cheering; she is worried. Isaac seems like he got hurt. Do they have someone close by if that is the case? But her worry dissipates as Mikko helps Isaac up and they laugh. Isaac holds onto Mikko' shoulder, like it's no big deal.

Then Makeddah smiles and claps. She can't believe she was bored a couple of hours ago. Now she's the opposite. She's devising a plan.

She wants to be one of the fighters in that ring.

Thirteen

Makeddah trains the next day and the next. This is something she uses to keep her mind straight. She is ready to fight. She wants to be the one in the ring next week, though Mira shot her down and said she would have to train for months to be ready. Also, she'd have to stick to only one element. But Makeddah doesn't see it as a problem.

Training to fight gives Makeddah distractions; it gives her a purpose while they are stuck in this place. And she has gotten so much better. She doesn't want to be the same girl she was a few days ago; helpless and unsure how to fight.

With no more info on Mother Lianne and that stupid lie they told the witch, her mind tries to swerve and go to dark places. She's been tossing and turning at night because of both of those things.

But Kahlan has been lying to her, too, right? Keeping secrets and all. That counts. She is doing the same thing, so it must be okay. Makeddah's just doing what *they're* doing.

Every time Makeddah brings up that she wants to tell Kahlan the truth, Rayon tells her to stop complaining and to just focus on the task at hand.

Which to Rayon is finding out more. To Makeddah it's training to fight.

On Sunday morning, before breakfast, she has her first fire lesson. It is much more tolerable than air and easier than earth. Makeddah had her first earth lesson on Saturday afternoon with Preston, who is now a legend in her eyes—he defeated that man so quickly.

Earth seems increasingly like a disaster the more she thinks back to it. She didn't even get one rock in her hand, which was the only task for the day. She just managed to summon some dirt and a few pebbles. She is considering talking to Aaron about that physical training, but she doesn't want to talk to him more than necessary.

But fire, fire is probably her best. She creates not only a ball of fire but successfully launches it into a shack—a magical shack that rebuilds itself after the fire goes out.

She hates to admit that this place is starting to grow on her.

Grace makes her way to Makeddah, applauding. "You did wonderfully today, Makeddah. Although I hear it isn't too hard for you to let off some steam?"

"Yeah. I guess." She thinks back to burning that sorcerer's face. Fire comes most naturally to her, above the other elements. She never thought of herself as a hothead, but everyone must see her that way with how quickly she can light a fire. "You think I can do better next time?"

"I think that's up to you." Grace looks up as someone enters the room, and Makeddah knows that is her cue to leave. Even as she comes out of a great lesson, she thinks about how weak she is.

Maybe she can be better with a sword if her arms are stronger. She doesn't want to have to talk to Aaron about it, pleading with him for help like a child. He makes her feel like that without her asking for favors from him.

Matt passes by her as she walks through the earth units. He doesn't say hi or acknowledge her at all, which doesn't surprise Makeddah. He hasn't talked to them since they've decided to stay with the Guard. She turns and sees him enter an earth unit and close the door behind him. Makeddah walks back to the unit and comes to a stop.

She's never seen Matt practicing his element, whatever that may be. She peeks in and sits down on the bench across from it.

But he does not practice Earth. He sets up multiple targets on trees and vines. Soon, he is setting up his bow and arrow and shooting at each one with great precision.

Makeddah peels her eyes away from Matt's movements as Mira passes by. She is dripping in sweat, but that does not stop her from sitting right next to Makeddah.

"Hey, wanna get breakfast with me?"

"After you…" Makeddah moves her finger over Mira's body, "Clean up?"

"Yes. Maybe. I don't know, I'm hungry." Mira's gaze follows Makeddah's. "You're watching Matt?"

"Yeah, he's an earth-breed?"

Mira shakes her head, "He's not anything. He has no power. That's why he uses a bow and arrow." She stands. "Come, I won't take long."

Makeddah stands, but she doesn't follow Mira out. "Um… I'll meet you in the lobby."

Mira narrows but moves on.

Makeddah steps up to the earth unit and opens the door. Though earth is her hardest element, it has the most beautiful room. The trees and dirt remind her of her first time being out of the Center, when she first got to see what the world really looks like.

She watches as Matt cleans off one of his bows. He glances back, then his gaze returns to his bows.

"What?"

"You don't have to be rude," Makeddah says, though she is not surprised by his shortness.

She steps up to a tree and pulls an arrow from the target hanging off the large branch. She walks over slowly, hoping he won't snap at her for being there. But she likes him better than Aaron, so that must mean something.

"Thanks." He directs her to a table that he set up himself. "Put it there." She sets it down and watches him clean. "What do you need?" His tone is not harsh, but he picks up a knife, and Makeddah gets nervous, that is, until he starts shaping his metal arrow.

Makeddah focuses on the arrow he's shaping. "Do you train? Like without a bow and arrows. You know, physically."

The arrow slips from his fingers. They both stare at the place on the table where it clatters. He slowly looks up at Makeddah, putting down the knife. She smiles. He tilts his head and asks, "What kind of question is that?"

"You seem… muscular." She must sound so ignorant to him. "I think that's the word. We don't use many masculine words in the Center. Anyway, do you train? With the push-ups and all."

"Exercising?" He nods. "I do that, yes. Don't some witches exercise too?"

"Yeah, but I don't. I forget words that mean nothing to me." He looks her up and down before picking up his arrow again. She sighs, "Could you teach me? I need to be stronger."

He laughs, but there is no humor in it. "First lesson, it can't be taught. You either do it or you don't. I can instruct you, be your personal trainer. But why?"

"I told you I need to be stronger. And I want to fight in one of the fight nights." She smiles, trying to mask the feeling of stupidity.

Again, his gaze is completely focused on her. "No, that is not going to happen." He shakes his head and sets down the arrow.

"But—"

"Why me? I am sure you have plenty of new friends in the Guard now. Especially, some of the—what did you call it? *Muscular* type. They must be all over you by now."

Makeddah does not like what he is trying to say, though she can't exactly figure out what he *is* trying to say. But she doesn't feel right for some reason, like a lapdog. Though she's only seen her neighbors' tiny dog twice, and it seemed to enjoy her lap, Makeddah does not enjoy it.

"No, I don't let anyone be all over me. I have two friends now. Maybe three. One of them is my sister, because I don't care about friends." She says, "I don't have people all over me." He doesn't say anything, so she crosses her arms. "I don't like people to be all over me."

"Oh, really? Then what do you like, Makeddah?" He crosses his arms, too. Mocking her? She cannot tell.

"Well, for one, truth. Which none of you tell me." She feels a pang of guilt for lying to Kahlan but continues. "And two, I like control, but I can't control anything if I'm not stronger. Which leads me to three. I like strength over weakness."

He eyes her. She does the same. Then he sighs, rolling his eyes. "You're not like most girls."

"Because I was raised as a witch without being one. And I was raised by Alda. She is not like most girls."

He glances at her, a hint of a smile tracing his lips. "Fine. I will train you. But you *must* listen to me, okay? Or you'll end up asking one of your two or three friends." His eyebrows raise, waiting for her agreement.

Makeddah smiles. "Pleasure doing business." She starts walking out, but turns back. "You know, you're the one who brought us here. I don't understand why you don't like me and Rayon."

"What do you mean?" He doesn't turn to face her. But even with his back to her, she can tell he is listening avidly.

"You saved me from the Witch Center so I wouldn't be kidnapped by those guys. But now here in the Guard you barely look twice at us. You seem like a happy guy, but you frown every time you see us. Why?"

"I'm not a happy guy; I'm a normal guy who does not need to feel emotions. But maybe I don't like you guys because you're the reason I almost died," he replies. Now he turns, and his eyes land straight on hers. "And for some reason, I knew it before I even met you—you, and your sister, are different, Makeddah. You're—" He looks up, but he must not be able to find another word because again he says, "*different*." He swallows, worry creasing his brows.

"And?"

"Different is always dangerous." And he turns back to his arrows and doesn't say another word.

Fourteen

Makeddah sits across from Mira, who looks much cleaner than when Makeddah left her. Rayon is sitting at the table too, already on her third book from Mira. She only stops reading because Makeddah snatches it from her.

"Hey!"

"Good book?" Makeddah asks, checking the cover, feigning interest. She sets it down on the bench beside her, looking across the table at Rayon.

"Now you've made me lose my place," Rayon pouts and glares at Makeddah. "And yes, it is a good book. Thank you again, Mira."

"The suggestions actually come from my brother," Mira says.

"You have a brother?" Rayon and Makeddah ask at the same time.

"I did. He died along with my mom and dad. But he loved reading; it was his favorite thing." Mira looks up at the ceiling, smiling. "I brought all his books with me so Haggard wouldn't destroy them. He would've been an air teacher by now, graduated to Full-breed for…" she counts in the air, "Two years probably."

"Oh." Makeddah swallows. "Haggard killed them?"

"His sorcerers did. He was a good guy, my brother." Mira looks down at her paper. She had been drawing up garments, but she is frozen now. No sound or movement coming from her.

Makeddah swallows again. Unsure of how to react. Her family are the only people she loves. If they died, she'd be devastated.

So, they sit in silence for a while.

That silence is broken by Makeddah's attention falling on Kahlan. She comes from the ghoster and walks down to her office. Makeddah instantly stands. She doesn't even realize it until she is moving in Kahlan's direction. "I'll be back."

"*Mak.*"

"*Ray.*"

Rayon sighs and stands from the seat. "We'll be back." Rayon stops at Makeddah and turns back to Mira. "And, Mira, I'm really sorry about your brother. About everyone."

Mira's only reply is a smile.

Makeddah and Rayon walk down the hallway that leads to Kahlan's office. Makeddah steps up to the door and stands waiting for her hand to lift and knock on it, ignoring the whispers that Rayon says in her ear. She stops when she hears others in the room, but they're speaking low. Makeddah doesn't remember anyone walking up with Kahlan.

Her hand rests at her side, and she puts her ear closer to the door. There's a laugh and the door's opening. Makeddah stands back, expecting to see Kahlan, but no one stands there.

"Makeddah, Rayon, how may I help you?" It's Kahlan's voice, floating out from inside the room. Makeddah and Rayon glance at each other before stepping in. Makeddah sees Aaron and Isaac first, standing against the side wall, then turns and sees Kahlan in her seat at the head of the table.

"We need to talk." Makeddah glances at Aaron and then back to Kahlan. "Please." Kahlan waves them to the seats, and Makeddah and Rayon sit.

Makeddah waits for Isaac and Aaron to leave, and when they don't, she scratches her cheek.

Kahlan stands and smiles at Rayon. "Why don't you shut the door, Rayon?"

"Really?" Rayon turns back and shuts the door with a flick of her finger. It's basic magic, but Alda never allowed her to do anything as small as that.

"What do you want to talk about?" Kahlan grabs something from the ground and sits back in her chair.

"We lied," she blurts out.

"Lie is a strong word," Rayon says, and one glance at Makeddah makes her finish with, "And very true in this case."

Kahlan sets a crumpled paper on the table and folds her hands in her lap.

Makeddah stares at the paper and continues, "After the graduation, we weren't here to get Rayon lessons with you. We were here to find out why you're not telling me everything. Like, for example, the real meaning for me being here. Because for some reason I don't think the king would want me just because I'm a Lion Heart."

Kahlan nods. "Okay, that may not be the only reason. There are a few, not only one. One of the reasons—"

"I want you to tell me *all* of the reasons." Makeddah shakes her head. "I'm tired of playing this game."

"I don't think that is the best idea. Not with the way you reacted to the first thing we told you." Kahlan shakes her head, "Which was not the most shocking thing to tell you."

Makeddah frowns. "Excuse me, I wasn't reacting to the secret of being a Lion Heart. I was reacting because it had been a secret that could have been revealed to me long ago. And I didn't know that I was doing that, but I can kind of control it now."

"There are more things that your mother has kept from you for your safety. We intend to do the same." Kahlan lifts her folded hands and neatly places them on the table in front of the crumpled paper. As if that's the end of the discussion. As if the paper is the secrets and her hands are holding them from Makeddah.

It's not the end of the discussion, and Makeddah will get those secrets out of Kahlan. Now.

"Then tell me yours. The reason you—The Guard—" Makeddah looks back at Isaac and Aaron when she says this, "Is so invested in me. I have no use if I have no cause."

"That's a valid point," Rayon says, taking the role of commentator. She glances at Makeddah and shrugs. Her gaze turns to Kahlan. "So, are you going to tell her?"

"Yes, of course. We do have a reason to keep you other than the fact that you are in danger of being taken by the sorcerers, but…" Kahlan puts her finger up to stop Makeddah from talking, "It is up to your mother to tell you why they are after you."

"Fine," she sighs, crossing her arms.

Kahlan stands. "But understand this is also a part of the reason Haggard wants you, Makeddah." She walks around the table, her finger tracing its outline. When she gets to Makeddah, she stands with her hands in front of her stomach. "Okay." She exhales. Makeddah didn't know she was holding her breath. "Makeddah, you're here because we need you to do something that no other man or woman has ever had the courage to do."

"That is…?" Rayon says as she leans in when Kahlan doesn't continue.

"That is to stop Haggard. To take him down." She pauses, holding her breath again. "To kill him."

Makeddah stands, shaking her head. "I can't kill sorcerers; how can I kill him? My hands already have blood on them, and you want to add to that? I won't do it, and Alda would never let me come here if she knew this. She wouldn't."

Makeddah is trying to convince herself that it's true, but she swallows hard, knowing it might not be. After all that has happened, she can't tell what is true from what is a lie.

"Makeddah, we hope it won't come to killing him. But we know that you need to take him down."

Her ears ring, and she closes her eyes to collect herself. "I'm sixteen."

When Makeddah said this to Alda two weeks ago, trying to convince her to let her see the outside world, it was for a much different reason. Makeddah tried to explain to Alda. "I should be able to go on the village trips with Ray, Mom, please."

Alda crossed the kitchen and shook her head. "Still fifteen. And no. You will go when it is time." Alda looked at her longingly and Makeddah now knows that time is now.

But she shakes the thought away as she stares at Kahlan and says those exact words again. "I'm sixteen." She takes a breath. "Shouldn't you be asking someone more qualified or older. Like Matt, he's like fifty, right?"

Behind her, she hears Isaac snort; that noise would never come out of Aaron.

"Makeddah, it has to be you."

"Why? Is there like some prophecy or something?" Rayon asks. Kahlan cocks her head to the side, and everyone stares at Rayon. "I read a lot of books. A lot. Many of them have prophecies, and the most unstable-turned-stable people go and fight the big guys and win."

Makeddah mutters, "Which won't happen with me, by the way."

"The stable part or the winning?" Isaac asks. Makeddah turns to see him giving her a broad smile.

She melts a bit before considering his question. "Both," She and Rayon speak at the same time. Makeddah looks down at Rayon, who has already turned to Kahlan again, and asks a simple question.

"Why didn't you tell her this first?"

"Because it's hard to handle many big things at once."

Yes, Makeddah knows this well. She's used to handling too many questions, but when they're mixed with answers...

Makeddah feels the room spin as she thinks of killing a man. Swallowing hard, she finds out she has nothing there to swallow. It's like a dry desert in her mouth, and it tastes like wood. She stumbles out of her chair and shakes her head. "I have to get some air." She staggers out of the room and starts walking to the lobby. When she gets there, she feels like everyone's watching her. She hears whispers in her head like they are talking about her, but it's her own thoughts slandering her. She stumbles to the ghoster and hears someone calling out her name behind her, but she ignores the voice.

Makeddah fumbles for the key, and once she gets it, she immediately presses the button; her head feels like it's being pulled from her body. The sensation of her arms being tugged opposite ways makes her want to throw up, and her whole body goes numb. When she gets above ground, she doubles over, taking a breath of fresh air, and crawls to a tree. She brings her hand to her head to find that she is sweating.

Makeddah coughs and flips around, sliding down the tree until her butt is on the ground. She breathes in the air flowing into her lungs bit by bit. A gentle reminder saying she's still alive and breathing. Still existing. Still innocent.

"Hey, Sunshine." She hears Isaac plop next to her.

Makeddah doesn't look up, doesn't open her eyes. "I can't kill someone, Isaac. I can't."

"I get it." A pause. "I don't want him dead."

Makeddah looks up at him. His eyes hold no lie, and his sad smile makes her believe him. "Maybe that's because he hasn't done anything to you. He hasn't done anything to me."

Isaac nods, picking at the grass and throwing a little pebble he found in it. A chuckle slips through his lips before he says, "He killed my mother and father, and he took over Korzon. But I guess he helped shape me into who I am. If he hadn't become King of Korzon, I wouldn't be where I am now, trying to make people happy. My brother wouldn't be fighting alongside the Guard for justice."

She draws a finger through the grass. It feels so selfish not to kill a man who's killed hundreds, maybe thousands. But that's not up to *her*, that's up to who's in charge.

"Oh, sorry. Then I guess he never did anything to only me."

"But he has. He's sent sorcerers after you, who killed your witches and hurt your grandmother."

She hates to be reminded of that. "But *why*? Why did he do all of that?"

Isaac shrugs one shoulder. "I don't know. She has refrained from telling us that, too. But I trust she knows what's right."

Makeddah brings her finger to her mouth and chews on her nail, then switches hands when she tastes the dirt from the ground. "I don't know what or who I trust."

"You can trust me, Sunshine." Isaac clasps Makeddah's wrist and lowers it. She looks into those steel blue eyes, and they convince her. His smile convinces her. She trusts him. Especially when he looks down at her and says, "You can always trust me."

There it is again. The feeling of weakness. But this time, it almost makes her happy. Which is crazy. She'd never, in her life, be pleased with being weak. Right? You shouldn't be happy about that.

Makeddah stands and bites her nails again. But she finds out her palms are sweaty, so she rubs them on her shirt and scratches her cheek. She feels a hand on her shoulder and turns quickly to find him right there, smiling at her.

"You can't kill him, right?"

"No. I don't think I can." Makeddah shakes her head, her mouth set in a frown.

"Okay." Isaac nods. He folds his arms and looks up to the sky. "Don't kill him, outsmart him, then throw him in jail."

"Me? Outsmart that evil man," Makeddah says, but she is smiling. "How does a sixteen-year-old girl like me go about outsmarting a... I don't know his age."

Isaac just shrugs. "I'm only seventeen and I have done it with Matt once. And he's like fifty remember." They both chuckle, "Only once, but that's all we need for Haggard, just one time. Makeddah, don't let your age define what you can and can't be." Isaac looks into Makeddah's eyes. "You're smart; I'm kind of smart. Your sister and Aaron are undeniably smart. We have Kahlan, Matt, and Grace. We can do it, right?"

"Right." Makeddah nods furiously, then shakes her head. "Right?"

"Yes. And the best part is you will be working right beside me." He steps back and smiles. "That's more for my benefit than yours."

That's when Makeddah feels something she has only felt when she is embarrassed. Heat rises in her cheeks. She's blushing for the hundredth time this week. She quickly turns from Isaac and walks to the ghoster. "Okay, then. Let's start outsmarting."

"So, you'll do it? You'll take down Haggard?"

"No, Isaac." She turns back to him. He drops his shoulders; hope is gone from his eyes. But then she smiles widely. "I can't do this stuff alone. *We* will do it." She takes out her ghoster key, and when she gets to the ghoster, looks at the frozen Isaac and says, "Coming?"

Fifteen

The bench in front of Earth Unit 3 is not comfortable, but Makeddah still leans back trying to find relief from her nerves. Rayon sits crisscrossed next to her. She can't tell why she is so nervous. She shifts in her seat three times before sitting back again, then she scoots one last time and wrings her hands, trying to break the habit of biting her nails. The habit returns just like the temptation to eat sweets while on a diet. Her hand goes up to her mouth, and she chews on her pinky nail, realizing there is nothing left to chew, so she switches to her thumbnail.

"What is wrong with you?" Rayon asks.

"I don't know." She's only going to train with Matt. An hour ago, he told her to meet him in the third Earth Unit in an hour. Makeddah checks the clock behind her. Only six minutes to go. "What if he laughs at me for being weak? You know how much I hate—"

"Being weak. Yes, I know." Rayon looks up to the Earth unit. "Go inside. Let out your nerves by making a rock or something."

Makeddah sighs and stands. Shaking out her arms, she walks to the unit door. When she glances behind her shoulder at Rayon, Rayon is already back to reading her book, not paying attention to her. Makeddah rolls her eyes and pushes into the unit. She instantly feels relief at the smell of moist dirt.

She walks to a tree and places her hand on a large leaf. Her back tingles with excitement. Makeddah loves being a part of the earth, no matter how horrible she is with this element. It connects her to her family in a way she never would have thought possible.

Just like witches are controlled by nature, she is not only controlled by it but is also able *to* control it.

A smile spreads across her lips at the vibration that goes through her body when she sits. She concentrates on her hands, wanting to create something, even though her first attempt with her earth teacher, Preston, was horrible.

She focuses on the vibration, the smell, the feel of the moist ground, and the taste of the humid air. She closes her eyes with her hands laid out in front of her. She feels the pebbles gathering as she closes her palm, then she feels the rock slowly forming.

The door opens, but she doesn't dare look up. She keeps going. And when she feels the fully formed rock, she pops one eye open and gingerly opens her hand. She jumps up and holds her hands out. "I did it!" It's a small stone, but it's something.

Matt walks over and investigates her hand. He narrows his eyes at her, but a smile creeps up on his face. "Good for you." He turns and sets down a bag. "Grace said your first fire lesson went well."

"Hope it did, because fire is my best." She walks over to Matt, stone still in hand, and looks over his shoulder. "What's that?"

He pulls the whole thing from the bag. "Rope." He pulls out a few more things and sets them aside.

"I thought I would be doing the push-ups."

"You will." He walks over to a tree and ties the rope around it. "But that's not the only exercise you will be doing." He dips to the ground and grabs a jump rope. "Jump rope. One minute straight."

"I don't do that anymore." Makeddah shakes her head. "That's a kids' sport in the Center."

He pushes it to her chest. She grabs it on instinct, dropping the stone. "You sound like a princess. Now, jump rope."

Makeddah pouts but does what he says. "I am not a princess," she mutters. She jumps rope as he says, three sets at a minute each with only a twenty-second break between sets. Then she does ladders, something called sit-ups, and some other stuff she forgets the names of.

When she's finished, she's sure she's dead. Her arms feel weak, and her legs are wobbly. Even after doing the stretches, sweat is dripping down her face, and her limbs are shaking.

She collapses to the ground, trying to catch her breath.

"You'll get mud in your hair, princess."

Makeddah glares over at Matt and attempts to stand but falls back to the ground. "Why did you kill me?" she pants.

"If you want to kill Haggard—"

"A little help." She holds her hand out. Matt comes over and easily lifts her up from the ground. She shakes herself off when she stands, then puts a hand on her hip. "And I'm not killing Haggard." She starts to grab the hand towel he left for her but stops. "Wait, how do you know about that?"

He smiles at her. "I know about all your secrets, Makeddah."

"You're evil," she pouts.

"I wondered when you were going to guess it." He turns, tosses her the towel, and puts everything in his bag. "I mean, Rayon did right off the bat. But you took a while." He points to the rope. "Grab that, will you?"

"Sorry, can't walk." She wipes her face to get rid of the sweat. "Legs are too tired." He glares back at her, and she smiles. "I wondered when you were going to guess I was evil too," she jokes. "*Really* evil." She lingers there, but she looks at the rope and doesn't want to leave Matt hanging. So, she grabs it and hands it to him.

"You're not evil. You can't be." He zips up his duffel and swings it over his shoulder. "See you next training where we do 'the push-ups.'"

"Thanks, Matt." He waves with his back still to her and exits the unit. She looks where her stone dropped earlier and picks it up, tucking it close to her chest. She walks out and finds Matt walking down the hall already.

She sits next to Rayon and opens her mouth to talk, but Rayon raises a finger to silence her. She turns the page, gasps, slams the book shut, and shakes her head. She keeps her finger up, then nods violently and turns her gaze to Makeddah. "I hate books."

"You love them."

"Nope." Rayon shakes her head. "I hate them." She finally looks at Makeddah. "Ew, you're all sweaty."

Makeddah lays the towel around her neck. "Thanks." She shows her the stone.

Rayon gasps, "That's amazing! Preston will be impressed."

Rayon may just be saying that to make Makeddah feel good, but she still hangs on to her words.

Makeddah sits next to Rayon on the bed, anxious and excited to see Alda and Belle after not talking to them for so long. She wants to leave all that anger behind. But when Alda's ghost comes up, she finds different words flying from her mouth.

"Why didn't you tell me?"

Alda sighs and nods. "I'm sorry, but it was for your safety. I couldn't have you manifesting your abilities while Haggard was watching."

Makeddah understands, but that anger, she's not even sure if it's anger, it's more like hurt. Her body is empty, like she hasn't had anything to eat for days. Her heart clenches every time she thinks back to feeling lonely. The loneliness that came with being last in the chain of command could have been taken away.

But she's looking at Alda, sure, this hollow feeling will die out in time. Just long from now.

Knowing herself now, Makeddah sees it was the right thing for Alda to do. If Makeddah had gotten too headstrong, she would have left the Center. Snuck out and went to the village to show people what she was made of. Not that she'd leave forever, but long enough for Haggard to see.

Alda snaps Makeddah out of her thoughts. "Makeddah, you know that I love you. If I had lost you, I don't know what I'd do." Alda puts her hand up, holds it out for Makeddah. Makeddah tries to lay her hand on Alda's, but it just goes through her ghost. "I admit that I may have done things a bit backward. I thought I was protecting you."

Makeddah nods. "Yeah." She knows Alda would never want to hurt her, but it still stings.

The silence hangs in the air, thick and dangerous. Rayon's the first to ask about the thing no one wants to mention. "How's Mother Lianne?"

Alda doesn't answer for a while. Holding back tears it seems.

Belle's ghost comes into view, and she sits next to Alda with her head on Alda's shoulder.

"She's not waking up." Alda says finally. "High one says that is never good." Alda's voice is steady, but Makeddah can see the sadness behind her eyes. "We don't have a healer. High One tried to contact a few but…" This is when Alda's voice breaks. It's a slight crack that Makeddah has never heard from her mom before. "I know whatever will happen, happens for a reason."

"Right, the Creator will heal her." Makeddah scoffs.

Alda furrows, "The tone is not necessary, but if he does, then that's amazing. And, if he doesn't…" Her voice cracks yet again.

Makeddah doesn't want to add to the hurt she is feeling so she keeps her opinions to herself.

Rayon grabs Makeddah's hand. "It's okay. She'll be okay," Rayon says. "Right?"

The question hangs in the air as everyone fights off tears.

Rayon starts talking about Kahlan and the tests she's been taking, but it's just a cop out to the silence. They talk longer to get rid of it, to make the air change, to enjoy each other. Is that how it's supposed to be? Do you just ignore the feeling inside and try to change the subject?

Makeddah warms up to talking to Alda again, but it feels different. Is it because she's different? Or maybe it's because Alda is. Or maybe it's because the truth always lets in a certain light that many can't handle, and one of those many is Makeddah. Ironically enough. Blaming all the silence on Mother Lianne would just be her lying to herself.

Alda's and Belle's ghosts disappear, and Makeddah sits silently as Rayon goes to the washroom and takes a shower.

Thinking of Alda just brings more questions. What is the last thing Kahlan is hiding from Makeddah? How are they going to figure out a way to take Haggard down? Why is it that Mother Lianne is not waking up, and when will she? Why does she have to feel so mad or hurt or whatever it is she's feeling?

Rayon emerges from the washroom a short while later, putting a towel on her damp hair.

Makeddah looks up as Rayon leans against the wall. "I wish I were like you."

"Sometimes I wish you were like me, too." Rayon flips her hair, sending a few droplets of water to Makeddah's face. "I'm great."

Sixteen

akeddah throws a fireball at Grace, but Grace comes back with one and at a better pace. Makeddah inhales sharply and rolls into the shack. She tries to think of something clever, but what can she do? Grace is faster and smarter and has been at this much longer. This thinking only makes Makeddah smile. She returns to escape mode; it's her saving grace. If she leaves from the back of the shack, she will not catch Grace off guard. She needs to do something Grace doesn't expect. Like escaping from somewhere else and getting to her from a different vantage point. From behind.

"We can stop if you'd like," Grace says from a distance, victory dripping from her words.

"Nope. I'm doing just fine," Makeddah yells, looking around. "Remember, the first one on the ground loses. I'm not on the ground; therefore, I haven't lost."

Makeddah can hear Grace's laugh. "Yet."

Makeddah takes a breath. She looks at the counter and the vent just above it. She scrambles over there as quietly as possible and removes the cover. It's not a real vent; it's just an opening to get to the roof. Makeddah bites her nail. This place has been burned down too many times. It might fall or collapse on her, but she must take the chance. If she dies, she dies a winner.

Hopefully.

She jumps up on the counter, finding it sturdier than she thought, and reaches out to the roof on her tippy toes. She puts her hands firmly on the roof and prays that the physical training won't fail her now. With all her strength, she pulls herself to the roof, feeling some sweat bead down her forehead. Once on top, she lies flat on her stomach and peeks up to look for Grace. She wipes her hands off from the dust and ash and locates Grace not far away. Grace isn't even looking for her. She's standing there, looking at the back of the shack, as if that is the definite place Makeddah will come from. No one must have tried this on her, it's super risky.

Very slowly, Makeddah stands, pointing her hand at Grace. With an inhale, she shoots fire from her palm. The burning feeling in her hand makes her feel like a winner.

Her thoughts return to the shack, and she takes a breath, hoping it will not cave in on her. She dives and lies flat again on the roof, making sure she's secure.

The flames she made are big and fiery, and Makeddah stands sure that she's won. She shouts for victory, but the moment she stops, a fireball hits her square in the chest, and she falls backward, rolling off the roof, landing on the ground. She feels her back hit the ground hard, and a gasp mixed with a cough escapes her lips as air is sucked out of her lungs.

If the fire were real, Makeddah would be close to death. But right now, she just *feels* close to death.

She composes herself and lies there, staring at the sunset in the artificial sky.

"Sorry, Makeddah, it's just I don't play easily." Grace helps Makeddah up and wipes her off. "But I'm sure if you had stayed low and pushed a little more with your core, you would have gotten me." She hands her a bottle of water. "You got up one minute too soon."

"I was trying to do it the way you said. Without the sting."

"Just because it has no sting, doesn't mean it has no strength." Grace glances back at the clock. "You're all good to leave. Great session today, smart thinking."

She and Makeddah move to the door. "See you tomorrow?" Makeddah asks.

"See you then."

Makeddah walks out of the unit and trails down to the air unit. Her days follow a strict schedule: earth first, then fire, then air. Water comes later—just before or after dinner. And if Matt decides to train that day, it shifts to fit his schedule.

She has improved at everything. Earth still trips her up at times, but the constant training has changed everything.

From where she started to now, she is a like professional. She knows she's not.

But training to be in the fighting ring—and to take down an evil king—has sharpened her in ways nothing else could.

She opens the air unit and sits on the ground, watching Aaron read his clipboard. "You're late again."

"Do I have to tell you again?" Like she has almost every day for two weeks. "I'm on a cramped schedule. I walk over as soon as I'm done with fire." She looks up at the clock. "And I am not so late. Four minutes early."

"Equals one minute late, Makeddah." He puts his glasses down to look over the clipboard.

Makeddah stands. "No, it equals a great student." She walks to him, wiping her face off. He looks down at her, over his glasses. When he turns back to his board, she peeks at it. "Are you writing something about me?"

He snatches the board from her sight and places it face down on the table. "I don't write about you."

"*Okay.*" She puts her hands up in defense.

When she came here on the first day, she expected this lesson to be the most dreaded, but it's become the most pleasant element. She enjoys having the air element. It makes her feel freer than the others do. But Aaron is another story. He does not make her feel free; he makes her feel stupid most of the time. So while she loves this element, she does not particularly like the teacher.

When Aaron does praise her, she feels free again. Like nothing can stop her, but she's not sure if that is the air element or the fact that he does not praise anyone.

"You smell like a campfire," he says with a small smile.

Makeddah smiles back. "Is that a good thing?"

He nods. "It must be nice to be able to be everything at once. I've never met someone like you, and it's amazing." He ponders the thought for a moment, then looks back at the board. He doesn't talk for a while, and Makeddah just stands there waiting for him. "Well, what are you looking at? Practice."

Makeddah rolls her eyes. She thought she was going to have an actual conversation with him. But instead, it's the same thing over and over. Get back to work, get to practice, stop standing around. He's so hot and cold. Praising her one minute and driving her crazy the next. She's been so tired of all of it, she shouldn't expect anything from him. No conversations, just practice. Yet she still tries.

After the long lesson of endless drills sucking the life from her, she asks him, "Have you ever tried this?" She lies on her back, looking up at the sky.

"Looking at the ceiling?"

"It looks like a sky, Aaron." She sighs. "And yes. Don't act like it's the worst thing you can do." Makeddah pats the ground next to her. "Try."

"No."

Makeddah rolls her eyes at him and stands. "Why are you so mean?" He doesn't respond to or acknowledge the question. "Because I'm older than you," Makeddah mocks in her best guy voice. And at her best, it sounds like a dumb girl trying to be a guy, which makes her feel like a dumb girl.

She hears the door open and turns to see Rayon walking in with a book in one hand and a smoothie in the other. "The way she does things is so weird," Rayon says.

Makeddah narrows, "The witch?"

"Can you not say that?" Aaron says as he rips off his glasses and glares at her. "Stop calling her *the witch*. You need to respect her. She has brought you here and let you train. Made you into someone you've wanted to be your whole life."

"Yeah? What's that?" She doesn't shout. She tries hard not to. So peaceful one moment and so angry the next. If she wants to make progress in her anger management, she shouldn't spend too much time around Aaron.

"Special."

"Whatever." Makeddah plops back down to the ground. "She isn't the one who made me special, Aaron. I've been special my whole life, she's just the one who decided to *tell* me that I am." She crosses her arms. "And I can call her the witch because that's what she is, right? People call me the Lion Heart all the time. What's the difference?"

"The *difference* is that they use respect when they say it," he says, pushing his glasses back on his face. Makeddah's surprised they don't break. "You have to stop acting like none of us care for you. You have to stop acting like a spoiled little—"

"Don't you dare say princess, Aaron." She's on her feet again and challenges him to say it. They stand there glaring at each other and Makeddah's heart is racing. "Try me."

"Why shouldn't I, *Makeddah*?" He mocks. "That's exactly what you're acting like."

"I am not a princess." Her voice settles in a threatening tone. She doesn't yell, but she doesn't back down. She hates fighting with a friend, but if it's picked with her, she won't hold back her punches. He's hardly a friend anyway.

He's completely different from his brother. Isaac is nice. She can actually talk to him and not be angry at the same time. They don't have to have an argument every single time they have a lesson. And she hates that word princess. Princesses are not strong; they are always portrayed as little spoiled brats who get whatever they want. She can't believe he actually said that to her. She is so much more than that.

"Can you two stop?" Rayon asks, sipping her smoothie. "You're stressing me out. And with stress comes impurities. And with impurities comes bad magic. Magic that I wish I could do, but my mother would never let me. I don't do well with stress." She flips her hair.

Makeddah glances at her sister and starts walking away. "Whatever." She opens the door and turns back, "You know what, Aaron? Maybe you're the prince, and we're all just prancing around you, making you feel special."

She leaves the room, storming down the hall. She shudders at the thought of being called a princess. That's the second time someone has said that to her. It seems so wrong that she gets given a name like Princess. Matt has called her that enough, and now Aaron? She's not a princess. She's a warrior. She's a Lion Heart. Not a princess.

Seventeen

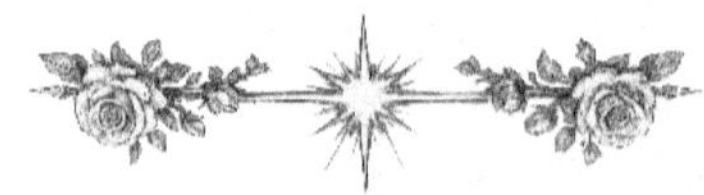

Makeddah avoids Aaron the rest of the day, as usual, since every lesson ends with hurt feelings—for him or for her. She picks at her food at dinner, waiting patiently for the best part of her day: Isaac, who takes her to her water lesson, where they always end up discussing various topics.

She asks about every little detail of the outside world.

"They don't talk like we do in the sophisticated parts of the village, which everyone calls the city," he said last Thursday. "They talk like they always have something up their butts, and they can't use contractions or the words mom and dad. Oh no," he shook his head, "mom and dad are unacceptable."

Makeddah always ends up laughing at how he does things: the way his eyes open wide with childish blue wonder when he tells a story, and how they dilate when he talks about the beauty at the edge of Korzon. She wishes she could go there—she wants to see it all.

When this is all over, she will travel. She will be gone in an instant, with no one knowing where she went. She'll go through mountains and valleys and different kingdoms, trying different traditions. Being who she has always wanted to be…

"Hey, Sunshine."

"Hi." She doesn't expect her voice to sound so dreamy. The second she hears it, she sits up and fixes herself, scratching her cheek. "Hi, Isaac." She giggles. "Sorry."

He gives her a broad smile. "You're mine, right?"

"What?"

"For the lesson? Are you ready?"

Makeddah chuckles, scratches her cheek again, and says, "Yeah…Yup. Mhmm. All yours." She waves goodbye to Rayon and Mira. The training units are always empty at night, and the silence sometimes creeps her out, but that vanishes when she sees her Water Unit and she tingles with excitement.

Pushing into the water unit, Makeddah slips off her shoes by the entrance, letting them clutter by the door. She wiggles her toes in the sand, savoring the sensation as the grains sift around her feet. Throughout the entire lesson, she delights in the constant contact with the sand.

They work hard for the next hour, Isaac teaching her a multitude of new things that she barely grasps by the time the hour is up.

Isaac rummages through his bag for something she can't see. Makeddah steps quietly to the water's edge, watching the ripples.

Their lesson is technically done, but she lingers, reluctant to leave. If it were up to her, she would stay forever. Isaac joins her, standing quietly by her side.

He sits on the edge of the lake, then scoots forward, and his toes dip into the water. "Can you try something for me? I think it's time you manipulate water that's not your own."

Makeddah has done this with fire and manipulates air easily, but earth and water are different. Water is unstable and unpredictable. Still, looking at the clear blue lake and the sea beyond, she feels secure and agrees.

She sits down next to Isaac and carefully rolls up her pants and sleeves, watching his demonstration. Following his guidance, she extends her arms and closes her eyes, focusing on pulling the water toward her palms, just as she did with fire—drawing it, willing it to move.

And nothing.

"Maybe you need a center," Isaac says. "A center helps with control and focus. It's harder for you, I imagine, with multiple elements."

Makeddah blinks at him and a smirk rises on his face.

"Aaron's center is my mom, he thinks of my mom's smile and her laugh, her everything. Mira's center is the thoughts of her family."

Makeddah nods, getting more of an idea of what she can use as her center.

"So, your center is family too or something?" His cheeks go red all of a sudden. Makeddah has never seen that. In her three weeks of knowing men, she has never seen one blush. He looks down at his hands, his smile visible even from the side. "What's your center?" Makeddah asks, curious to know.

"Don't think I'm weird or like a stalker." He stretches his back very slowly as he collects his words. "My center is… you." Makeddah opens her mouth, but he stops her, almost pleading with her with his eyes. "No, listen, okay?"

Makeddah nods and sits patiently, which she doesn't normally do, but she wants to hear this.

"When I first came here, it was crazy. It was like I could no longer breathe, like the earth had shattered on my brother and me. We came as boys in need of a home, because ours had been taken so brutally. *So, so* violently." Isaac stares off into the distance as if watching a memory of his family. "All we wanted was to take him down—Haggard. We wanted him off the throne."

Isaac's voice shakes, then he clears his throat and smiles at Makeddah. "But there was something going around in the Guard. Something of hope. This Lion Heart. 'She will save us,' they all said. And every time I would step into the water unit, I would think of the Lion Heart, the one that would bring sunshine after the rain."

Makeddah laughs. "That's why you call me Sunshine?"

He snaps his fingers. "Secrets out."

Makeddah chuckles. "The Lion Heart is your center."

He licks his lips. "And now I have put a face to her. A very… Sunshiny face." He nods to his hands and stares off into the distance again. "So now, ask yourself. What is your center? What is your hope? What is your peace? What is the thing that makes you want to smile?"

Makeddah looks down at the lake. "If I travel the world, would you travel with me?"

Makeddah's heart pumps and she feels the same panic she did the day they got invaded.

Why would you ask him that? she thinks.

When she doesn't get an answer, her heart pumps faster. "I want to bring my sisters, Belle and Rayon. Rayon won't come unless it means finding a way for her to have a husband. Maybe I could convince her. Belle would definitely go. I want to ask Mira too; she'd be good at helping us if we were injured, sewing clothes and stuff."

Makeddah nods, trying to get out all she wants to say. "And you, because you seem to know a lot about the outside world. And Matt, because he can still train me. And Grace, because she's his wife and awesome. We could bring Aaron, too." She looks up at him. "I just… I really want to travel, but I don't want to be alone."

Isaac smiles. "Why not? What is it that makes you so independent, yet you can't be alone, huh?"

Makeddah's smile turns into a frown. "I… I don't…"

"I was kidding." His smile falters.

Makeddah looks at him and tries to laugh, but it sounds more like a choke. She stands. "I have to go. Thank you for the lesson."

"But wait," she hears him say, but she rushes out. She hears him call her name, but doesn't turn back. She hugs herself and starts jogging out of the air units.

Why was she so stupid to ask him about traveling with her? That isn't realistic. Who besides Rayon and Belle would want to travel with her? What would possess anyone to invite someone to travel alongside them? Do men ever do that with women? Her face burned with embarrassment when he didn't say yes. How could she claim independence and yet dread being alone? The urge to disappear, to collapse inward, is overwhelming.

He said she was his center, and now he must think he made the wrong choice. Maybe he thinks she's just a silly girl and will change his whole outlook on her.

Ugh, so ridiculous of her. When she exits the units, she finds that the halls are empty. She realizes it's almost ten o'clock—everyone is probably in their rooms.

Entering the lobby, she grabs an apple. She plans to tell Rayon what an idiot she was and hopes for some solidarity.

But then she hears something. She stands still. The ghoster. She watches the doorway, waiting to see who will come in this late but her mind starts to go fuzzy. Her vision blurs.

She loses balance all of a sudden and reaches for the nearest thing. When she feels the cold metal from the refreshment bar, she steadies herself, blinking the blurriness away.

She sees a flash of white, followed by a flash of red. "Hey, can you help me get to Grace? I don't know what's happening, but something's wrong with me."

She hears no response, but her heart pounds faster as footsteps approach. Even though she can't see, a chill creeps over her skin—something is wrong. The apple slips from Makeddah's trembling hand, and it seems like forever before it hits the ground with a hollow thud, making Makeddah flinch. "Um, Hello?"

The person laughs, and it makes Makeddah shiver. What is going on?

"Okay, I'll just go to Grace myself," she says and tries to balance herself, but the person grabs her.

"Don't move, it's okay," It is a woman who speaks.

Makeddah's heart leaps. She knows the voice, but her mind swims as she searches for a name. It's distant and haunting, yet close enough to send a tremor along her skin. The words float above her in a whisper, but the sound is clear and sharp, cutting through the haze.

Makeddah wants to throw up now.

She tries to lean closer to see better, but the woman moves her hands from Makeddah, and she feels wet. Makeddah examines her arm closely but pulls away quickly at the sight of the blood.

"Oh, Stars, are you okay?" Makeddah asks.

"Oh, Makeddah, it's not my blood," the woman says.

"What? Whose blood is it?" Makeddah asks, shaking now. How is she supposed to respond? Is she supposed to scream?

She decides, yes, but as she tries, her voice fails her. Not because her mind is warring with her body again, but because she feels completely stuck, like she's in the wind, withering away and drowning in water at the same time.

She can't see, she can't hear right, and she can't move. She's stuck.

Makeddah heaves as the woman backs away. Ice creeps up her spine, and Makeddah feels the goosebumps rise as she notices the chilled air.

"Oh, Makeddah. You shouldn't have seen this," the woman pouts. Makeddah cries out in her head, but it doesn't come out, like her lips are sealed shut. "Well, I guess you can't see much anyway." She laughs, "And everything happens for a reason, right?" The voice is still fading in and out, but Makeddah can sense the low and devilish tone. "Knock her out gently, please, she's still valuable." The woman walks away into the hallway that leads to Kahlan's office.

Makeddah looks around to see who she is talking to, but she can't see anything. She tries to run, but her feet are planted, frozen to the ground. Unmoving like her lips.

Then she sees them. Grey eyes fixed on her. Almost like a shadow. A shadow of a person, but she's sure there is no one there.

She feels the temperature turn hot and cold at the same time. Then ice-cold fingers touch her head, and she starts sinking to the ground, unable to find the strength to stay standing. Unable to cry out, unable to run.

The one time her brain and body work together, and she's not able to use it.

The cold fingers press harder at her forehead and stretch to the crown of her head. It almost feels like something is being pulled from her brain. Then she falls onto her back, looking up at the white ceiling, which seems to be moving, but she is unsure where she is or what has happened to her.

Her mind goes blank as her eyes shut.

Eighteen

akeddah, wake up."

She hears the voice. "Makeddah, wake up." But she can't obey the command. That is, until water is poured onto her face. Then she's awake in a second with a coughing fit to follow.

She looks up and sees Isaac. "You really had to do that?" Aaron asks. Then she sees Rayon—the voice that tried to wake her up.

Rayon stands with a gasp. "I should get Grace."

Makeddah intends to ask why, but instead she shakes, holding her arms close to her chest. Cold fingers touch her every nerve, but on the outside, she feels like she's burning up. Her teeth chatter, and sweat drips from her face. When she looks up, she sees that whatever is going on with her isn't affecting the others.

This sudden fear hits her, but why? She's forgetting something. What is it?

The last thing she remembers is asking Isaac to travel with her, which was stupid, but that's not why she's scared.

Then Makeddah remembers the grey eyes, but that's it, nothing else. Why is she in the lobby? And why is she on the floor? No one has grey eyes here.

She racks her brain trying to remember what happened. She knows that something is amiss. Her superpower fails her and does not reveal that thing.

Makeddah sits up, wiping the sweat from her neck and trying to control her chattering teeth. "Don't get Grace."

"Too late." Grace comes in through the ghoster with Matt behind her. "I go out one night with my husband, and I come back to this?" Grace looks nice. Her dark skin is complemented by a blush pink dress and pearls around her neck and in her ears. She drops her handbag and rushes up to Makeddah. "What happened?"

"I fell, I think."

"You fainted," she says more like a statement than a question. "Why? Are you being overworked?"

"No, no, that's not it." Makeddah looks past Grace and at Matt, who's not paying attention to her like everyone else. He's paying attention to the room around them. He shivers and his jaw works. Then his gaze goes to Makeddah. *He feels it too.* The iciness, the chill up her spine. He has the same chill. Makeddah keeps her eyes fixed on Matt as she says, "I didn't eat enough today. That's probably it."

"Come with me," Grace says.

"You two look nice. Special occasion?"

Grace helps Makeddah up and pulls her along. "Makeddah, come with me." They walk down to Grace's workroom. When Grace unlocks the door, she turns and tells everyone else to leave them.

"But I'm her sister," Rayon says.

"Please." Grace sounds sincere enough, but Makeddah knows that she's not taking no for an answer.

Rayon looks at Makeddah, and Makeddah shakes her head. Isaac and Aaron leave, and Rayon glares for another second before going also. Matt kisses Grace's cheek, and with a glance at Makeddah, he's gone.

They enter Grace's workroom. "Now what's really going on?" Grace has that look that Alda gets sometimes— tell me or I'll find out another way.

Makeddah sits down at the table. "I don't know."

Grace stares at Makeddah. "Are you sure? You can tell me anything." Grace waits for the answer, but none comes. "Okay." She gets busy working stuff up to test Makeddah. "It *was* a special occasion tonight, by the way. I told Matt some big news."

"What?"

She grabs a thermometer and sticks it under Makeddah's tongue, then puts her hand to Makeddah's damp forehead. "I say you're too hot, but the thermometer says you're too cold. Hmmm." She mixes some stuff up and looks back at Makeddah. "I'm pregnant."

"You're what?"

"Pregnant. He's going to be a father, and I'm going to be a mother." She looks at Makeddah's blank stare. "What?"

"I didn't know you guys wanted to have children… and… never mind." She doesn't know the mechanics but doesn't want to ask. Did Kahlan give her the baby, or is there another High One?

Makeddah never truly understood how High Ones gives babies to the witches. And anytime Alda brought up the Creator stories, Makeddah would say, "Sure a man created us, but High One, a female, is the one who gives babies to witches."

Alda's answer was always simple. "How do you think High One got that power?"

So now, sitting in front of Grace, she wonders silently how the babies truly have come to be. Who was the first baby? But she doesn't take the thought too far, her head hurts enough already.

Grace hops up on the table next to Makeddah, taking her from her thoughts. "I really want a boy. Someone like Matt. A little Matty," she says as if Makeddah never said a word.

Makeddah puts her hand on Grace's. "You'll be a good mother." Makeddah nods and attempts to get off the table, but she stops and shakes her head. "I did something awful."

"Awful?"

"Worse than lying to Kahlan." No one thought that was that bad except for Makeddah. "I asked Isaac to go traveling with me. What kind of person does that? What possessed me to ask him that crazy question? Why am I telling you this? There must be something wrong with me. Am I sick? I'm sure I'm sick."

Grace giggles and grabs Makeddah's hand in both of hers. "You asked Isaac to travel with you?"

"Well, it wouldn't be just him but yes." Makeddah hops off the table, but Grace keeps her grip. Makeddah looks at the smile on Grace's face and somehow feels worse. "I'm going to go to sleep. That's what I need. It's just my insomnia that made me pass out. I just need sleep."

"Wait." Grace finally lets go of Makeddah's hand and grabs something from the small fridge she has. "Drink this tonight, and you should feel brand new in the morning. If you don't, come back to me." She pauses, "And you like Isaac."

Makeddah takes the drink. "What, no. Wait." Makeddah is sure she doesn't mean like in friendship, she means as in romance. "I don't. I wouldn't know how to anyway."

"It just happens, Makeddah, there's no right or wrong answer to it. No manual teaching you." Grace smiles.

"Isaac's a good kid, and I know he adores you. You should definitely try it out."

Makeddah blushes and starts to walk out, but turns and says, "Congratulations."

"Thank you, Makeddah. I think you'll have good luck with your traveling." Grace's big smile makes Makeddah embarrassed and happy at the same time. How does she do that? "Tell Isaac, he'll want that."

Makeddah nods. She may never tell him, but Grace makes her feel like it's okay to.

Nineteen

*T*here is so much beauty in the calmness of the morning. The sun gives the perfect amount of warmth, the fresh air is the most wonderful scent, and the grass is the comfiest bed. Everything is at its best right now.

But her head.

It hurts from thinking so much about what she's missing from last night. The drink Grace gave Makeddah did make her feel better, and she slept soundly. And though it is Friday, the day she's been looking forward to all week, she doesn't know if she wants to go to fight night tonight.

If the headache persists, she may not. This morning, she wants to relax and escape the noise and chaos.

Which is why she and Mira are sitting outside, within the veil Kahlan produced to keep sorcerers away. Rayon was pouting when they decided to get some fresh air—she has a lesson with Kahlan that she wouldn't miss for the world—but she said she'll join them when she is done.

Mira takes off her shoes and steps onto the ground. Her toes scrunch up in the grass, and it turns much greener than it was. Makeddah watches as the sunlight hits Mira's face perfectly, and her wavy hair seems blonder now in the natural light.

When Mira looks at Makeddah, her hazel eyes give off a glint of something beautiful, and Makeddah wonders if she ever looks that way. Maybe her eyes can give off something, too. Maybe she can be beautiful.

She almost laughs out loud at the thought. No one in the Center cares about beauty, not even Rayon. They care about order and cleanliness. Even though the Parish women are the most beautiful that Makeddah has ever seen.

Makeddah always thought she was above caring too. Isn't she? But lately, everything feels unsettled. When Isaac is around, her certainty buckles; it's different with him. He makes her question who she thought she was.

"Try it," Mira says.

Makeddah slides out of her shoes and tiptoes along the grass. She watches it turn greener at her touch and smiles. *I don't deserve this*, she thinks. *The earth is always kind, even when I can't return the favor. The vibration settles her, coaxing out the small part of her that's still healing.*

Makeddah hears rustling in the bushes a few feet away, outside of the veil. She sees the most stunning creature jump from it—a beautiful deer.

"That's amazing." Mira whispers in awe. "And *that* is why I'm a vegetarian,"

Makeddah raises an eyebrow. "Wait, you're what?"

Mira sits on the ground and watches the deer as it jumps away. "Vegetarian. It means I don't eat meat."

"I know what it means," Makeddah says as she sits beside her, scanning Mira's face. "Three weeks, and I never knew that about you. Why don't you eat meat?"

Mira doesn't glance at Makeddah. "Long story."

Makeddah leans back on her elbows. "I have time."

Mira sighs, chewing on her words before explaining. "Haggard once robbed my family. I was seven, maybe. I had a pet pig. The first thing my parents bought my brother and I in years. My brother didn't care, but I *cherished* it. Then Haggard came."

"He took your pig?"

"No, he took our money." She swallows. "My father came home and said we had no food. Just the pig. I *begged* him not to take it away. I was *so* desperate. It was the first happy thing in a long while." Mira chews on her cheek. "I was clinging to it when he took it away. I heard it squeal as... I was only seven," She shakes her head, tears welling in her eyes, "I loved him. I couldn't eat meat after that. I starved that night. I swore I would not kill another living thing."

Makeddah feels her instincts push back—was Mira really so changed by a pig? But when Mira draws a finger through the grass and confesses, "It was my family. Haggard made my father murder my family,"

Makeddah's skepticism dissolves. No matter if it is animal or human, blood or not, they can still be family. And they ripped that away from her.

Loss can shape everything, she realizes. "I'm sorry."

Mira wipes her cheek. "Guess it wasn't a long story, just a sad one." She chuckles.

Their attention is drawn to the ghoster, where they see Aaron exit. He avoids eye contact with Makeddah but grabs Mira's hand to help her stand.

"Thought I'd find you here. Grace was looking for you." He squints. "Were you crying?"

"Just telling Makeddah a story." She grabs his hand. Makeddah sees him shrink a little, but he doesn't pull away. "I'm going to see what Grace needs."

Makeddah nods. She reaches over to where she was walking in the grass and grabs Mira's shoes, handing them to her. "See you guys later,"

"See you later," Mira says, she and Aaron walking away and disappearing through the ghoster.

Makeddah takes out her key and hangs back, waiting a few minutes to go through it. She doesn't want to run into them and have to say goodbye again.

When she decides it's been long enough, she presses the button on her key and ghosts. Inside, she runs into the one person she'd wanted to talk to last night.

"Matt," Makeddah whispers, but it's not a very good one. Almost everyone in the lobby turns their heads to look at her. She probably should have waited to announce herself until she blended into the crowd.

Matt's back is to her, but he stops and slightly turns his head. "Can I talk to you?" This whisper is quieter.

He turns around and grimaces at her. "Congratulating me?"

Makeddah blinks. "About what?" Realization dawns, and she shakes her head. "I've only ever congratulated women. Do you want one too?"

"Please don't."

Makeddah nods, scans the crowd, and grabs Matt's wrist. She whispers, "We have to talk somewhere private." He shakes his head, but she grabs him by the wrist and drags him to the training units, entering Earth Unit 1, shutting the door.

Matt turns his wrist a few times. "You've got a danger-ous grip."

"I'm a swordsman. Also, personal training—thanks for that." Makeddah sits and pats the ground for Matt. He sits, hesitantly. She exhales. "You felt it too—the chill up your spine last night?"

His face becomes blank, then he cocks his head. His lip twitches. "The chill?"

"Yeah, I saw you shiver. What was it?"

"You felt that?"

"Yes, Matt, and no one else did. Why just us? *What was it?*" she asks. He stands, but she grabs his wrist. "What do you know? I don't understand what happened last night. Excuses don't help."

"I don't know, Makeddah," he says sternly, but one look at her and his face changes. He shakes his head and sighs. "It scares me too. But I—"

"Know what it is, you just don't want to tell me?" She finishes his thought and lets go of his wrist.

"I'm not sure."

Makeddah groans, frustration leaking through. "Matt, come on. Enough with the secrets." She hates that he's lying to her right now.

"Makeddah, please. I know it's hard not to know everything, but the fact is that you shouldn't. I will tell you when I find out." He shrugs, which he never does.

"Or you won't, and that's okay." She's surprised to find she means it. Maybe she's tired of fighting for every answer. She's not angry at him—she's angry at herself for not knowing what happened. "I just want to know, am I in danger?"

Matt shakes his head. He hesitates before saying, "I would never let anyone hurt you."

Makeddah looks at the ground, kicks it lightly, then leaves. He follows. "You would tell me if something was killing me, right?" she asks over her shoulder.

"Yes, Makeddah. If it were life or death, I would tell you."

"Good." They walk in silence, going down to her room. Makeddah slows until Matt is shoulder to shoulder with her—though his shoulders are about four inches taller than hers. "You'll be a good father. I just know it."

He stops and turns. She stands in front of her door, putting her hand on the doorknob. His face is apologetic, as if he has done something wrong and now wants to make amends. He hesitates then he smiles. "You think so?" He smiles a little brighter. "I hope. I never envisioned having a kid but might be fun."

"Oh, hey." Makeddah turns to see Rayon. She takes out her key and opens the door. "Oh, congrats, Matt." She doesn't wait for a reply; she steps inside the room.

His face returns to a frown. "Should have never put that poster up," he mumbles.

Makeddah chuckles, but her smile vanishes as she hears Rayon squeal and bump into the wall. Makeddah looks inside, sees Rayon whimper and point at the wall. She enters her room and looks to where Rayon is pointing and nearly collapses.

Matt rushes in and holds her up. "What is wrong?" He searches her face, then looks around, and finally his eyes land on the same thing they see.

Sunset on Monday.

It's written on the wall in red. Blood, Makeddah realizes. But what scares her most is staring into a witch's eyes.

A witch's head.

Torn from its body.

Hanging from the wall next to the threat.

Twenty

B ut we must be able to do something about it," Isaac says, pacing in Kahlan's office. Aaron and Matt are standing in the back corner, both have their arms crossed, and only one looks like he is really paying attention—Aaron.

Makeddah is trembling next to Rayon, and Rayon is holding her hand. Makeddah squeezes it every time Rayon is about to whimper. They just saw the most terrible thing anyone could see. A witch woke up this morning to die and be mutilated.

Grace keeps glancing their way and finally pulls a chair on Rayon's other side and rubs her shoulder.

Makeddah brings her free hand to her mouth and chews her pinky nail.

"We can do something," Makeddah says, and wipes her mouth. "We can fight them."

She says it confidently, but her gaze stays focused on the glass of water in front of Kahlan. If she looks her in the eye, she might just break.

"Oh, no." Kahlan shakes a finger. "You are *not* ready."

Makeddah stands up and slams her palm on the table. The force knocks the glass of water off the edge; it crashes to the floor and shatters.

"They killed one of mine, again! From *my* Center!" She shouts, her voice breaking, louder than she expected to come out. Her eyes flash with rage and grief. "They attacked us and killed eight witches before I came here. Now, they double down and—" She almost can't say the words but she has to. Kahlan must feel the weight of this. "They tore her head from her body and hung it in my room. They wrote in her blood, Kahlan. I will not stand for that." Her fists shake with fury.

Kahlan sits, her demeanor changing. "Makeddah, they aren't ready to see you—"

Before Kahlan can finish, Makeddah's hands are in the air, and she's saying, "Who cares what they are and aren't ready for. They call a battle, and we battle. I don't care if they aren't ready to see me. I don't care!"

"There's a traitor." Aaron mumbles.

The whole room turns to look at Aaron.

"What?" Kahlan rubs her temple. "Can you speak up?" Makeddah can tell her patience is running thin, but Makeddah's is too.

"There is a traitor," Aaron says aloud. So loud it rings in Makeddah's ears for a minute, and her blood begins to boil. "How else would the sorcerers get into the Guard? How else?"

Matt now is paying attention. This realization seems to make Aaron as angry as Makeddah. And when he glances to her, a silent union is formed.

Kahlan blinks at him. She seems to be coming up with the right words. "Yes, I believe you are correct."

Makeddah scoffs. "And you're not going to stand for that, right?"

"Makeddah, please—"

"No. I will not take your plea. When I left the Center, it was to protect the witches." She's not shouting anymore; she doesn't have the energy to. "But now they are put in harm's way again, and you can't say that it isn't my fault. You just can't, unless you want to lie straight to my face."

Kahlan folds her hands on the table. Again, choosing her words before they reach the air. "Okay. We battle, but you're not strong enough alone. Stay with someone. Better yet, support from the shadows, don't lead." Kahlan rubs her eyes. "We need to make sure the witches know. Get them hidden, keep them safe…"

Makeddah listens as Kahlan lists a plan of action.

"We only have three days," she finishes.

"I will prepare everything," Grace says.

"You're *not* going," Matt and Makeddah say together.

At the same time, Kahlan says, "No, no, no."

"But—" Grace tries to protest.

"You're pregnant," Matt says.

"I need to be there if someone from the Guard gets injured. The witches can guard me and I'll be fine," Grace says. She puts her hands on her hips. "You are not keeping a hungry, tenacious, pregnant woman from what she wants. You understand?" The room falls quiet. "Do you understand?"

Everyone mutters yes, even Kahlan.

"Good," Grace says and leaves the room.

The silence in her absence is heavy. Everyone must be thinking the same thing.

This is a disaster.

Kahlan is the first to disrupt the silence. "Aaron, Matt, come up with a battle plan. Isaac, I need your help in determining who entered and exited the Guard, as well as the exact times of entry and exit. Makeddah and Rayon, I need to know everything you two did today." Kahlan sounds worried. She is more troubled than she wants to admit.

When Rayon doesn't respond, Makeddah nods and goes back to holding her sister's hand. Rayon looks up at her, as if she had forgotten that there is still a world living and breathing around them, that they were still in the room, talking to Kahlan.

Makeddah knows why she's so shaken up.

It was Rayon's favorite teacher. Rayon's favorite teacher's head was hanging in their room, and she was the first to witness it.

Makeddah gives her sister a sad smile, and Rayon stands.

"We'll do that," Rayon says.

"Okay, then let's get to work."

Makeddah grabs an apple but drops it. The apple rolls across the ground. A chill runs up her spine. She looks up and meets Kahlan's terrified gaze. Kahlan's eyes are fixed on Makeddah's hand. Makeddah follows that gaze and sees that the apple has left a smear of red liquid on the floor.

It looks like blood.

Makeddah reaches out to pick it up and notices blood smeared across her own fingers. Her mind flashes to the witch's head, recalling her hands scrawling a message on the wall in blood. She snaps back to the present as Kahlan screams at her.

"What have you done, Makeddah? What have you done?"

Makeddah stares at her trembling hands, knuckles white and slick with blood. She scrubs frantically, but crimson stains reappear. Her scream is jagged, desperate. Her eyes jerk and dart. "What did I do?" The cold pricks at her spine, fighting the suffocating heat pressing in. "What did I do?" Sweat pools along her brow, streaming down as she lifts her gaze—and meets those piercing grey eyes. "Wha—?"

"Go to sleep. Makeddah, go to sleep."

Makeddah gasps. "What?"

"Wake up, Makeddah, wake up."

Makeddah coughs in bed as she brings herself back to reality. Rayon jumps up. "Whoa."

"Sorry." Makeddah brings a shaky hand to her mouth.

"Bad dream again?" Rayon asks, staring down at her.

"Yeah."

"Me too. The wall, it just—"

"Yeah, I know." Makeddah reaches out for her sister's hand, and they both sit in silence, staring at the wall that had blood and a witch's head on it just Friday morning. The wall that haunted her dreams all last night and again tonight.

Now, she wants to haunt the sorcerers' dreams.

What she doesn't understand is why her dreams feel like memories. Why is she always the one killing the witch?

The grey eyes appear in her dreams too, and she still wonders why she knows them but does not remember anything surrounding them.

A terrifying thought crosses her mind that she is the one who committed the crime. In that blackout moment after the grey eyes, she hung that head. Drew the words with her hands.

But the thought is impossible. Makeddah would never be capable of such a thing.

Right?

"You don't have to come back, Ray." Makeddah would hate to be alone, but she knows how bad that messed with Rayon's head. It's messing with her head, too, and it wasn't her favorite teacher. "After we fight them, you don't have to come back. I wouldn't judge you if you wanted to stay with the witches who didn't want to fight either."

Rayon doesn't answer for a while, and Makeddah almost thinks she's fallen back asleep. But she's not snoring, so she knows she has not fallen asleep yet.

Finally, Rayon says, "I'll think about it."

Then they roll over, and Makeddah has another nightmare.

Makeddah puts on her best training suit, one that's not beaten up and burned through. She sheaths her sword and raises her curly hair into a ponytail, fingers fumbling with the hair tie. When she stares at herself in the mirror, she can see the anger in her face. Her mouth is set in a hard line, eyes blazing.

What good is being with her family again if she is angry? She groans.

At least she gets one day with them before the fight tomorrow at sunset.

She looks down at her sheath. She's abandoned it for the past few weeks, so focused on her elements and now she looks at it and misses the passion she had for it.

Rayon steps in beside her. "I've made a decision. I'm coming back with you when this is all done." She runs her hand through her hair a few times to comb it out. "I've realized something."

When Rayon doesn't go on, Makeddah says, "What?"

"You're my best friend. And it's so sad that people like Mira, who have lost their family, can only lean on friends when it comes to stuff like this. I still have you, Mom, and Belle. And you can still have me here. I'm staying." Rayon looks in the mirror. "I don't ever want to leave your side."

"Thank you." Makeddah wants to hug Rayon, but instead she jumps at the knock on their door. She runs into her room and gathers the bags from her bed, giving Rayon hers. When Makeddah opens the door, she sees Matt. "We're ready," she says before he has the chance to ask.

Rayon throws her backpack over her shoulder, and they both walk out to the lobby with Matt.

Mira, Isaac, and Aaron are already out there with Grace and Kahlan. They all wait around while Kahlan, Grace, and Matt talk to each other.

Kahlan finally turns to them with two small cups in her hand. Matt has two, and Grace has one.

"Drink this." Kahlan hands her cups to Makeddah and Rayon, Matt gives his to Aaron and Isaac, and Grace gives hers to Mira.

Rayon cocks her head at it but drinks quickly. Mira smells it, pulls away, and hesitates to drink. Isaac looks at it and grimaces, then gulps it. Aaron drinks it without any hesitation or grimacing.

Makeddah eyes it. "What is it?"

"It's a potion. It will shield you on your journey. It lasts four hours. If you get to the Center and you are still invisible, just wash it away with water."

"It's that easy to make it go away?" Isaac asks after gagging from the drink.

Kahlan sighs, "Magic has its limits."

Makeddah looks at the cup and nods, then drinks.

"It has a special ingredient to allow you all to see each other, and it will activate soon." Kahlan sets two packs down. "Isaac and Mira, you take these. Rayon, contact me when you are there. Aaron and Makeddah, you two will ensure everything is in order upon your arrival. Prepare the witches for safety, and those who wish to fight may do so. Don't deny them their chance to fight for their home." Kahlan looks over every one of them and nods. "Get there safely."

Kahlan is no longer looking Makeddah in the eye, or anyone for that matter. The invisibility potion must have kicked in.

"Matt and Grace will be behind you by a few hours, and we will gradually send everyone to the Center. You all understand?"

"Yes," the five say in unison.

"Good. I will see you all soon." Kahlan turns.

Makeddah watches as Kahlan walks away, then points to the ghoster. "Let's go."

Twenty-One

It takes them a few minutes to get on track. Aaron is a know-it-all, Isaac wants to be the man, Mira tries to explain the way, and Rayon and Makeddah barely remember anything from when they came with Matt. But as soon as the boys listen to Mira, they are off.

"It's just like going to the village." Mira saunters in front of everyone.

"It'd be easier to use my ghosting," Rayon says to everyone. "But, no, Mother doesn't want me ghosting so many people out."

"Why?" Makeddah snaps, even though she already knows the rules. Witches who haven't graduated can't use magic unsupervised; their magic isn't stable enough. But she asks anyway—she can't stand walking right now.

"It's like she doesn't realize I am very good at my magic and can control it better than most girls my age." Rayon shrugs. "So, we have to walk for two hours."

"It's not that bad," Mira says, and then she repeats, "It's just like going to the village, but when we get to the—"

"We get it now," Aaron says, going up to lead.

Makeddah doesn't hear Mira's muttered comment about Aaron as she hurries up to walk beside him. She glances back at the others before leaning in so no one can hear.

"Do you know a lot of things about the magical world?" Makeddah asks him.

Aaron shrugs. "Depends."

"Do you know about something with grey eyes that gives you a chill yet makes you hot to the point of sweating?"

Aaron glances down, then shakes his head. "No. What are you talking about?" he asks.

"Never mind." She hikes her pack higher on her shoulder. Figures he wouldn't get it. Only Matt knows.

Makeddah remembers the fear on his face and her stomach twists. What if it's something really bad? Is that why she ended up on the floor? Maybe she passed out from fear. She remembers the thing that scared her—nothing else. When she brought it up to Rayon yesterday, she brushed her off with every excuse: it was a dream, her vision was blurry, it wasn't grey eyes, just screws in the wall.

Whatever it was, it had to mean something. That weird heat and chill—it wasn't a normal scare. She can't stop shaking, even just thinking about it.

Her dream. Blood on her hands, Kahlan afraid. It felt like a memory, except it was just a nightmare—her worst kind, the ones that come when she finally sleeps. Nights of witches dying, heads rolling, and battles. She hates being an insomniac because when she finally sleeps, dreams always bring horror. And she has to keep reminding herself it was only a nightmare.

Like this battle.

Sometimes she wonders if she is still dreaming and if she'll ever wake up from the nightmare. This gnaws at her—she's trapped, nothing but a shadow, condemned to stay quiet and obey. The frustration simmers until it explodes. Maybe that's why she snapped yesterday. Not just the witch—not just fear. It's the silence, the reality of swallowing her voice, until she finally lets it out. It wasn't Kahlan's fault. But Makeddah needed a target.

And yet again, Kahlan gets the brunt of her frustrations. She never wants to admit that to Aaron so before she says anything along those lines, she asks him another question.

"Have you ever had a dream that felt like a memory?"

Aaron glances over, "Doesn't everyone?"

"I don't know. That's why I'm asking." She snaps, voice brisk. Sensing him closing up, she quickly softens. "Sorry. I mean bad dreams where you've done something wrong."

"I don't know Makeddah." *He closed up.* "Bad as in?" *Or maybe not.*

"Hypothetically, you have blood all over your hands," she says.

"Hypothetically?" He shakes his head. "Sometimes people have repressed memories. Like they had something so traumatic happen to them that they forgot what it was. Or they did something so traumatic that their brain locks it away from them. So maybe the dream *is* a memory."

That does not comfort her.

"Hypothetically," Aaron speaks. "This person with blood on their hands, did they feel guilty, scared, or was it their own blood?"

"It's hypothetical how should I know?"

He narrows over at her, "Is the blood on their hands symbolizing sacrifice or murder?" She doesn't answer. "You can't know what's happening in your dream until you know what's happening in your dream."

She frowns. He's trying to be helpful, but she doesn't know if she will understand any of it by the information he's given.

She thinks it comes back to those grey eyes.

She needs to figure out who would know about that, cause maybe something is repressed in her. "Do you know anyone else who'd actually know about the grey eyes?"

Aaron nods. "No one I know, but I've heard of a guy that would know."

"Really, who?"

"His name is David Bower, he's only sixteen, and he is currently in the castle's jail, so it's probably not best to go to him," Aaron scoffs. "But he knows about our world, just about everything that goes on in it, so I've heard."

She glances up at Aaron. "Oh, okay." She scratches her cheek. "I'm sorry for being so difficult." Makeddah has learned that the only route to feeling like an equal around these boys is to get on the same level as them. She doesn't think she can accomplish that with Aaron, but she wants to at least try.

They take two steps forward and three backward whenever they talk.

"I'm difficult, too." He raises his brow. "At least Isaac says so. What are you talking about anyway?"

Maybe this is the right time to bring up Kahlan.

"About Kahlan," Makeddah remembers the scared face in her dream. "For calling her 'the witch' instead of her name. You were right, I was disrespecting her." He doesn't respond. Makeddah feels her heart hurt a little more. "The thing is, I know my mom was lying to me. And Kahlan has been holding things back, so my anger was pointed toward her. I was raised by a witch, taught by witches, and lived with witches. They have been my whole life. I feel horrible for disregarding her in that way." He looks down at her, and she tilts her head enough to see him out of the corner of her eye. "Everything happened so fast. I didn't want this to be fake, but I didn't want it to be real. I feel like I have to pretend to not feel weak."

"Pretend?"

"Yeah. I was doing the one thing that I hate—lying—and I was doing it to myself. Being here made me feel things I never have and that meant I was trying to act tough though I wasn't. Made me a difficult person." She tilts her head. "But I don't understand why you were so angry about it."

Aaron glances back, then pushes aside some overgrown bush from their path for Makeddah and continues to walk. "You don't understand how much respect you owe her."

Makeddah sets her jaw. "Okay, but why am I supposed to owe Kahlan anything? What did she ever do for me?"

"She sacrificed herself. She stopped looking for her Witch Center. She fought and stood up against Haggard. She lost everything, for us."

"For us?" Makeddah asks.

"Yes. Why else would one woman stay?"

Makeddah still isn't convinced. "I think that's the problem Aaron. You don't know how to separate things. Stop acting like she did this for me."

"Makeddah, she was there for everyone in their time of need with no promise of power. It's not as if she can be the Queen when all is said and done. She has no benefit for herself; she did this for us. For the people of Korzon, who may not even be her people. She could belong to Zaridon, or Kinghone, or Garideem, any of the other kingdoms in our sect, but she came here and did this for Korzon."

Makeddah scowls. "Okay, I get it. Maybe not those kingdoms or names you mentioned, but I get the respect part."

"I'm not sure you do. I'm not sure any of us do or ever will, because we're not her."

Makeddah steps over a fallen branch, hiking her pack up on her shoulder again. Aaron only speaks when he has something to say; he always has a point. That's why he's odd. He's usually right, but he stays silent if he knows someone else is right.

He was so passionate about this. Maybe that means she should listen.

Makeddah sometimes wishes to be like that.

After about an hour, the steady march comes to a halt as Mira asks to stop and get a drink of water. Makeddah unzips her backpack and hands out a bottle to everyone. She sits by Mira on a rock, gazing out at the sun, and wonders how it shines so brightly on a day like this—one where she has to tell the witches she's put them in danger yet again, where everything feels so dark.

When Aaron calls them to start moving again, Makeddah lingers behind with Rayon and Isaac as Aaron and Mira take the lead. It's rare to see them in front of people, holding hands—Mira trying to intertwine their fingers, Aaron whispering something that makes her laugh.

"Can I talk to you?" Isaac asks, looking her in the eyes, but she doesn't catch his gaze, just stares ahead at Mira and Aaron. "Alone." Rayon glances over, and she walks up to Aaron and Mira, giggling. Makeddah can see she is whispering to Mira about it because they both start giggling.

Isaac takes a deep breath. "So, you've been avoiding me."

"No, I haven't." Makeddah scratches her cheek. "I mean, I avoid Aaron, and since you're always with him, I naturally avoid you, too, I guess." She is talking too fast. She slows her pace, hoping it will also slow her heartbeat, but that doesn't work.

"Okay, well…" Isaac catches up. "Are you mad at me?"

"I told you I'm not avoiding you." It's true. She's not. She hated what she said to him, but everything had been so messed up that she'd forgotten about it. Until now.

"Well, if you had been avoiding Aaron, you wouldn't have talked to him back there. And if you weren't avoiding me, you would still be engaging in conversation with me. *And* standing at least within three feet *and* looking me in the eye." Isaac looks at Makeddah again. "So, what was that you were saying about you not avoiding me?"

"I'm not. I haven't even had time to avoid you. I promise, I'm not. I'm a little embarrassed but—"

"You didn't even let me respond, you know."

She scratches her cheek. "Yes, you did. You said something about independence."

"I was kidding, Sunshine." Isaac laughs.

"But you weren't going to answer. You just sat there when I asked, and I just," she pauses, "I don't know, felt so… I don't know, okay?" Makeddah crosses her arms. Grace and Rayon have their own ideas about why Makeddah ran away from the conversation, but she just tries to cut both of their voices from her mind.

"I would," he says.

Makeddah tries not to glance over but fails and gives him a half glance before turning back and cursing herself. "You would what?" She swallows.

He smiles. "Travel with you and whoever it is you want to bring."

Makeddah looks up at him. "So, you don't think I should travel alone?"

"I would never suggest anyone travel alone. There's something about the company of people while taking an adventure that just warms you." He says, staring off into the distance.

"And you would know?"

He nods. "I would know. So, even if I didn't go, you should definitely take your sisters. It will make it better."

"Thanks." Makeddah smiles at him. Should she even be smiling? This time tomorrow, she will be preparing to fight off sorcerers.

She should not be feeling happiness, yet, talking to Isaac eases her.

"Grace told me something about liking someone." She is an open person and talks about most things, but discussing this is unusual for her. She just met him three weeks ago, and she's having romantic feelings for him. That seems too fast and unfamiliar.

He tries to hide a big smile. "And?"

"And have you liked someone?"

Isaac nods. "You mean before you?" Makeddah instantly blushes and pushes him. "Ow, you're strong now, Sunshine." He rubs his arms and smiles at her again. "I've thought girls were pretty, but I've never liked someone like I like you."

Makeddah instantly wants to change the subject because it makes her feel all warm and twisty inside, and she hates it. "Do you get scared of killing someone? Like in this sort of thing, with the battle."

Isaac's face is blank. "Wow, big change of subject, thanks for the warning." But he clears his throat and says, as if ashamed, "No, I don't. The sorcerers are bad, Makeddah."

"But what if they have families? The ones who were older when Haggard turned them. What if you're killing someone's brother, father, uncle, husband, or guardian? What if you're killing someone who could have mattered or made a difference for you and others? Doesn't the thought scare you?"

His mouth tightens and turns into a scowl. "It does now. But what if they weren't any good for those siblings or loved ones? What if they weren't any good for their friends and the people they used to wave to at the shops and vendors? What if what I did was good?"

"Murder is never good," Makeddah says.

"Yeah, I guess so. But sometimes called for."

Makeddah thinks of a conversation she and Aaron once had. If someone murdered another in the past, they would be hanged for their crimes. However, it appears that Haggard is opposed to that law, and it is no longer in effect. If there were a murderer, maybe Makeddah's death would be beneficial; it would be the law. But just the sound of agreeing with murder in her head makes her mouth taste like bitter fruit. She can't find a genuine way to justify taking one's life. She just can't, and maybe that's bad, maybe it's wrong. Perhaps she *should* consider that it's sometimes called for.

"Well." A few feet ahead, Aaron clears his throat.

"What's wrong, Aaron?" Makeddah rolls her eyes.

He rubs his nose and joins the conversation. "We're in a battle. You wouldn't save the man's life who is killing your people. You take your weapon, and you aim. It's not murder if it's your duty."

"Then what is murder?" Rayon asks beside him.

Aaron replies, "When you take your weapon and aim at them for anything other than defense or duty. When you go outside the law and kill. But this is a battle. When you kill here, it shouldn't be for you; it should be a duty to your Kingdom, to your Witch Center, to Korzon."

"What if that is someone's motive? To just kill for themselves." She asks him.

He shrugs as if the answer is obvious. "Then they shouldn't be here."

"Sunshine," Isaac says lower. "Don't change."

Makeddah looks up at him, confused.

"You're innocent. Not just by hand but by heart and mind, there's not enough of that nowadays. Even I could find a way to say that bad things are okay. Don't find a way."

Makeddah nods. "I like you too." She doesn't stop the words from coming out because she wants him to hear them. That conversation is long gone, but she wants some more light.

He smirks, "Okay, now tell me all the things you like about me."

Twenty-two

As time passes and the sun starts to set, Aaron tells them that they are close. Mira follows by saying, "He only knew because I told him."

Makeddah watches as they emerge from the last of the trees and find themselves in an open field of grass, and just ahead is the Witch Center.

She looks over to Rayon, who is already smiling at her. The two run, though they know they should probably stay back with the others. Makeddah can't help but smile at the sight of their home; She wants to throw herself into Alda's arms. Most nights, she and Alda have talked, but their conversations never feel the same as being together.

They run for five minutes. Makeddah is surprised at how fast and long Rayon runs. While Makeddah herself has been training with Matt for weeks, Rayon seems just as fit.

Is it determination, a longing to see her family as much as Makeddah does, that drives her?

Makeddah stops at the big stone wall. Rayon ghosts them inside the Center. They run to the cottage and up to the window. Makeddah and Rayon both press their faces against the glass, peering inside.

Inside, Alda sits at the table knitting, her scarf trailing over her knees. Belle, wearing an apron, stands by the hearth, cooking and gently swaying. Makeddah hears birds chirping outside, their song saying, "Welcome home".

She smiles at Rayon, but Rayon keeps her gaze fixed on Belle and Alda as Makeddah taps the window.

Belle turns to look at the window, confusion flickering across her face as Alda's head snaps up, eyes wide. They share a silent glance that screams, "You heard that too?" Makeddah frantically washes away the invisibility potion, water splashing everywhere, and Rayon stands grinning, uncaring about the mess. When recognition strikes, Belle's breath catches—her words rush out, voice trembling with relief: "They're home."

Rayon went back out after the reunion to ghost in the other three, and Isaac still hasn't recovered. "Water." Isaac pants. He's doubled over, catching his breath, as Mira and Aaron stand outside the cottage with curiosity. He moves his hand over his face. "Still invisible."

"Oh, right," Makeddah says. She sprays them down with water, and they are revealed to Alda and Belle.

Belle squeezes Makeddah from the side, not caring that she's still dripping water. She has been clinging to Makeddah since they arrived. Makeddah and Aaron air-dry everyone with their elements. Then they all walk into the cottage, feeling its warmth and smelling the rolls in the oven.

She is finally home.

"I wish you were here under better circumstances, but I'm glad to see my girls," Alda says after she shuts the front door.

Makeddah says, "I don't want to talk about why we're here right now. I just want to be happy." She glances over as the window shuts. Belle returns to the kitchen, where she was making what Makeddah guesses is some kind of soup.

Aaron stands awkwardly in the small space, Isaac looks around smiling, and Mira is already talking to Belle as if they've known each other their whole lives.

"Belle and Mom. This is Mira, Aaron, and Isaac." Makeddah points as she says their names.

"Hi." Isaac waves at the same time Mira says, "Hey."

Rayon mutters something and walks off to their room.

"I know you know, Matt," Mira says. "He wanted me to give you good news and tell you Grace is pregnant." Mira shakes her head. "Matt's wife, Grace."

"Yes, I know, Grace. She's a good woman, met her after the High One introduced me to Matt." Alda walks to the sofa and props up the pillows. "Sit, please. You all must be tired." Alda walks back to her chair and resumes knitting. "Grace is pregnant? That's great. Are they here?"

"No." Makeddah shakes her head and takes a seat next to Alda at the table. "A few hours behind us."

"Oh." Alda smiles up at Makeddah with glassy eyes and puts her hand to her mouth. "I didn't realize how much I've missed you until now." She starts to cry.

Belle dips to Makeddah. "She's been emotional lately. I think it's because of Mother Lianne." Makeddah nods. Belle stands straight. "Why are you here? Are you done? Can you come back?"

"No." Rayon shakes her head. Makeddah didn't notice her come back into the room. Rayon glances at Alda, who shakes her head.

That's when Makeddah realizes, Belle doesn't know why they are there. Rayon should not be the one to relay that information, yet Makeddah is frozen, her lips sealed.

Mira sits next to Isaac on one of the sofas, facing Belle.

It is Isaac who talks. "We're here to tell the witches about the threat against them. A battle, tomorrow,"

Alda nods, wiping the tears that barely fell. "Belle, we found Ms. Nadine yesterday. She was murdered. You should probably go because the details are gruesome. I don't want to—"tired?

"No." Belle stops her. "I can take it. What happened?"

Alda sighs, accepting that her daughter won't leave. "The sorcerers hung Nadine's body on a tree just outside the Center. Her head detached, a note in its place warning us about the battle."

Rayon can't hold back her tears.

Belle puts her hand on Rayon's back. She frowns and looks at the others, "How did you all know about it?"

Glances go around the room. "They hung her head in our room." Rayon's voice is low as she adds, "We have a traitor. Kahlan is staying back, figuring out who it is."

Alda shakes her head. "What is she going to do?"

"We don't have a plan yet," Aaron says.

Isaac folds his hands and leans forward, resting his chin on them. "As soon as this battle is over, we'll work something out. First, we must find out who it is. Kahlan and I went over who entered and exited today. We only checked a few people so far and haven't found anything suspicious yet."

"Couldn't someone just have forgotten a key somewhere and the sorcerers found it?" Belle asks, going back to stirring the pot on the hearth.

"Yeah, but no one is that careless around the Guard," Mira says. "We only let the most responsible people out in the field. Everyone else has to stay inside the veil."

"Or in my case, if you're endangered—for a reason no one has told me yet, might I add." Makeddah raises a brow to Alda, who ignores her.

"Do the witches already have a plan of hiding?" Rayon asks.

Alda nods, and Mira perks up, "Why do they have to hide?" She looks at Rayon, then Alda, "Aren't witches just as powerful as sorcerers?"

"Well," Alda seems to think of her words before saying them. "Sorcerer magic is a magic of death. Witch magic is a magic of life. We are just as powerful as they are, but in a different way. Sorcerers can cause more damage since witches' magic is not necessarily for defense or to harm."

"Oh," Mira says, sitting back.

"Is High One fighting?" Aaron asks now.

Alda shakes her head, "No, we don't want our only magic source on the battlefield."

Mira cocks her head, but Makeddah puts a hand on her shoulder. "Long story for another time." And Mira shrugs.

Makeddah sits back in her chair and realizes how abnormal her family is. One is gathering books to send to the Guard, another is swaying at the hearth, and their mother is knitting a scarf. There is a battle tomorrow, and they are aware of it, but they aren't worried.

Then she finds she isn't either. She knows something bad might happen, but she has only really been worried about one thing.

"Do all the witches hate me? For putting them in danger?" Makeddah asks, her eyes closed, bracing for the answer. "Do they hate me?"

Someone's hand is gentle on her back—Belle's touch, steady and reassuring. Alda clasps Makeddah's hand with trembling fingers. Then Rayon silently appears, nestling beside Makeddah's chair and resting her head on Makeddah's leg. The warmth flooding Makeddah feels different: it seeps right into her bones, wrapping her in real, unspoken love. For the first time in weeks, she feels truly safe and seen.

Alda rubs the back of Makeddah's hand. "They don't hate you."

Makeddah sighs, "But High One—"

Alda shakes her head. "No one hates you."

"I think it's too hard, Sunshine."

"Yeah," Mira nods. "The first time I saw you, I already loved you." Then Mira glances at Aaron and kicks him.

"Ow." He walks over to the wall, out of reach of Mira, and looks at Makeddah. "I don't know why we have to give you a bigger ego." He glares at Mira. "You are hate-able despite what they say. But most people tend to go the other way when it comes to you, so I don't think you have to worry."

Belle crouches to Makeddah's ear again, this time with a smile. "I like him."

Makeddah giggles. She looks right at Aaron as she grins and gives a small shrug. "Eh."

Rayon smiles, her gaze right on his eyes, too. "He's okay."

Makeddah tries very hard not to laugh out loud at the rising color in Aaron's cheeks. No wonder he doesn't like attention; he shows his emotions all too well. And for once, she is the one making him feel uncomfortable. Then she looks at Isaac, the guy she likes and the one who likes her.

She's not worried at all.

Twenty-three

Makeddah throws on a dress, feeling good to be home, even if just for a day. Once, dresses were all she wore; now, she only wears pants. Three weeks ago, she was certain she'd never put on another dress. Now, she's glad she gets the chance for normalcy.

Mira stayed with them last night. Isaac and Aaron slept in an empty cottage with Grace and Matt.

When she hears ramblings in the kitchen just outside her door, a warm feeling spreads through her—her home is full in a way it never has been before.

As soon as she steps out into the main room, Makeddah sees Alda talking to Aaron and Isaac near the doorway. Rayon is at the hearth, cooking something. Grace and Matt sit at the table, talking with Mira, while Belle sweeps the floors. Music plays softly nearby. Makeddah looks for the source, finds it hidden in the bookshelf, and walks over to turn it off.

"Hey!" It's three people who say it.

"You always had to spoil the music." Rayon flips her spoon in the air, sending a potato chunk flying across the room.

"Mom likes it," Belle says, leaning against the broom.

"It's soothing." This comes from Aaron. Makeddah stares at him. "Oh, come on, don't tell me you don't like music. Even the sorcerers like music."

"I don't like music." Makeddah grabs her sword from the corner of the room. "Let's go out before breakfast is ready," she says to Belle, excited to reunite with her sword alongside her sister.

"I can't. I have to clean and train for my last spring test." Belle sticks out her lip and shrugs. "Maybe later?"

"Later, I have to shoo away some sorcerers." Makeddah scratches her head. *As if anyone could forget.* Belle still doesn't say yes. Makeddah knows she wants to, but she also wants not to fail. Makeddah sighs and sits on the sofa next to her mom.

"I'll do it," Isaac says, rising as she sits.

"You're a swordsman?" Makeddah asks him, trying to hide her smile, but failing miserably.

"Yeah, we both are." Isaac picks up the second sword that must've been there since her birthday. "I would say that I am a worthy opponent." He throws the strap around his shoulder. "Yeah?"

"Okay." Makeddah stands with him.

Mira stands. "I'll judge."

Aaron clears his throat. "You don't know how to judge." Mira frowns at him but agrees. "I'll judge, you watch."

Without hesitation, Makeddah leaves the room, with Aaron, Isaac, and Mira following behind her.

She wants some time close to Isaac before the battle tonight, but with his brother and their friend there, it doesn't seem right, so she stays quiet. Their conversation has been on her mind. Though she's not sure what it all means, they like each other. It makes her feel fuzzy inside.

So even with the audience, she still sneaks a few glances and smiles at him as they all make their way outside.

Moments later, they arrive at Makeddah and Belle's favorite spot, the only area where the High One allows their swordplay on the blue roses. Mira stands back with Aaron while Makeddah and Isaac move into position, shaking out their arms to get ready.

They face each other and smirk as Aaron calls for them to start.

Isaac lunges first. Makeddah blocks, but he's quick, feinting for her leg. "These need guards," he says, pulling back.

"Guards are for boys. We girls like the real thing."

"She's not wrong," Mira says with a laugh and a nudge at Aaron.

Makeddah steps back, readying herself. And they go again and again. Isaac gets two hits, and she gets none by the third time they move in on each other. He almost comes into contact on his second swing, but pulls away quickly like the first time.

"You guys should try fencing. Much less dangerous."

Makeddah rolls her eyes. "Come on, Isaac. You of all people should know that danger is half the fun."

She turns at full speed, his sword clinks with hers. She comes around and goes for the neck. One hit. She goes for the leg, but he blocks. She comes up for the head, and he's there too, pushing her back.

"Wow, you're stronger than I thought," Isaac grunts, pushing harder.

Thank you, Matt, Makeddah thinks. "And more in control," she says, pushing harder. He swings around to hit her side, but she slides to the right. Isaac finds himself off balance, and Makeddah kicks him down, poking her sword at his chest. "Now, we're even."

"And the woman is left standing." Mira claps. "Meaning she wins."

"You don't make up the rules," Aaron says.

Mira scoffs. "Those are always the rules. You're just upset your brother lost." She sticks out her tongue.

Aaron furrows, "Very mature."

Makeddah looks back as Mira quickly gives him a kiss on the cheek, then turns away from him and stands.

"Fun's over. Time for battle prep," Mira says, pushing back her wavy hair. Everyone moans. "Grace put me in charge."

"Funny, Matt put me in charge," Makeddah replies, sheathing her sword.

"Oh. You handle those here, I'll brief the newcomers?" Mira asks.

"Sure," Makeddah shrugs.

"See, boys? That's how you work out a conflict." Mira slings an arm around Makeddah. "Good work out there. The sorcerers should be scared of you."

"Yeah, I wish I could train more before I have to leave again. I never knew if I was actually doing well with a sword, but it seems like I am a pro."

The fun moment comes to an end when she spots the infirmary. She doesn't want to be distracted going into battle, but her heart is tugging at her.

"You know what, I'll meet you back at the cottage." She tells Mira, "I have to go see someone first."

Makeddah doesn't wait for Mira to answer. She takes a deep breath and heads toward the infirmary. She walks through the gardens, then reaches the infirmary door and pauses. Wishing she'd showered first, she wipes her face, feeling grimy, but reassures herself that Mother Lianne won't notice.

With a swallow, she pushes herself inside. Only one witch is working right now. She doesn't bother to greet Makeddah or look up. But when Makeddah steps up to the counter and dings the bell, she glances up with a faint smile. "Hi, Lola." Makeddah smiles back.

"Hi, Makeddah. Good to see you back." Lola finally meets her gaze. "She's in room five."

"Thank you." Makeddah taps the counter, then walks to the hallway opening and turns right. Room five—the third door on the left. Makeddah sees it open, which isn't normal for witches in a coma.

She walks inside and sees Rayon sitting at the side of the bed. The slight shake of her body and tremble in her sniffing tell Makeddah she's crying. Makeddah looks up at Mother Lianne. Her great-grandmother is still, color gone from her face. She looks calm and peaceful, but the sight makes Makeddah want to scream.

Makeddah walks up and reaches for Mother Lianne's hand.

"No." Rayon's voice cracks. "High One says no touching." She stands, wiping her face.

Makeddah's voice is low as a tear runs down her cheek, and she says, "What kind of nonsense is that?" She wipes the tear away. "If I want to hold my grandmother's hand, I'm going to."

"Makeddah…" Rayon wipes her face and walks to the other side of the bed next to Makeddah. "We should just listen to her. We don't want to make it worse."

"How would that make it worse?" Makeddah means to only say it in her head, but she mumbles it out loud. "She must be so cold." Makeddah doesn't only mean on the outside; a blanket covers her, and it's warm in the room. She means on the inside. Just a touch from her family has given Makeddah warmth beyond what fire can give. She wants to do that for her grandmother.

She doesn't hold Mother Lianne's hand. To fight the instinct, she grabs Rayon's hand and squeezes so hard that Rayon fidgets but doesn't pull away.

They sit in silence but for the sound of Rayon's sniffles and the people walking outside the door, then Rayon coughs. "We should go. You need to eat and tell everyone the plan, like Matt said."

"Okay."

Rayon turns to go but stands still. She turns back to the bed and kisses her hand, then blows it to Mother Lianne. "Love you, Grandmother. Get well, please. Please."

Makeddah has a bad feeling that it will not happen.

Makeddah asks to be alone for a while as she mentally prepares for the battle. She takes a shortcut through the gardens to get to the field of roses. She wants to get her jitters out. Sit down and relax before getting back to the crowd.

Though she remembers the breakfast Rayon made, it is probably cold and she can't think about eating right now. She contemplates doing some jumping jacks or going for a run. Maybe that will keep her mind off her dying great-grandmother. Or off of Isaac and his cuteness. Or the imminent fight happening in thirty-two hours.

As she walks through the garden, she hears voices, and they don't sound happy. Her first instinct is to hide. Why? She doesn't know. She hasn't done anything wrong by walking here, but she still hides.

It only takes a moment to recognize the voices.

"But we've done so much better," Mira says. "I was happy that you held my hand the whole journey here."

"I'm sure you were." Aaron is talking now. "But I wasn't."

"What is so wrong with me that you can't hold my freaking hand, Aaron?"

Makeddah can't see Mira's face, but she hears the anger in Mira's voice, mingled with sadness—right now, anger wins.

"You said you understood. When I started this, I told you that it made me uncomfortable. I can't help that."

"I thought—"

"You thought." Aaron raises his voice, but he's not yelling. "You thought you could change me. That if I liked you enough, then I would change, but that's not how it works. I'm a private—"

"Oh, don't get me started." Mira sounds annoyed. "You and your privacy. Tell me again where you and Isaac go when you take your little mission trips? Oh, right, you won't tell me."

"They are mission trips in the village."

"Partly bogus, Aaron, and I knew that from the beginning. You don't take two weeks for a mission trip. You're in and out so that you're not caught. That's how it's supposed to be." She pauses. "Frankly, I'm done with your privacy and I'm fed up with it."

"Well, you're not going to change me. I am who I am. I like you, Mira, and I would love for you to accept my quirks, but it seems like you can't."

"I can't accept that you won't hold my hand without me feeling like I'm forcing it down your throat, no."

"Then you shouldn't be with me."

Makeddah is shocked at the even temper Aaron holds in his tone. He raised it a bit, but he has not once shouted or shown anger in his voice.

"Maybe I shouldn't," Mira says, anger still dripping. Finally, she speaks again, and Makeddah hears tears in her voice, "Maybe we should break up."

"There is no maybe, Mira. Tell me you will live with my privacy, tell me you will accept that it will take me time to get there, or tell me it's done."

"Don't put it on me, Aaron."

Aaron sighs, "You made your choice then."

"Wha—"

"You should have known the answer, but the fact that you're weighing your options lets me know. I am just an option, I'm not a choice to you. I deserve to be someone's choice."

"Aaron—"

"We're breaking up." He says, finally.

Silence hangs in the air like a storm cloud.

"Fine." Mira is quieter now, but she's still angry.

Makeddah is frozen in her place. She hears the footsteps coming toward her, but her heart is racing. She just listened to the most intimate conversation, and now she knows way more than she should.

Aaron finally comes in sight, and he turns the corner to see Makeddah. Her mouth is agape, and he is still. There are tears in his eyes, but they haven't fallen.

He's like Makeddah in that way; they hate letting the tears fall.

She closes her mouth and swallows. *Should I say something? Is he going to madder if I do or I don't?*

But before she can make reality of her thoughts, Aaron takes a breath and moves on, brushing past her.

She just ruined her chances of relaxing and Aaron's wish for privacy.

Twenty-four

The plan seems solid, but as she shares it with the eight already there, anxiety insists that something will go wrong. She worries Kahlan might learn they defied her wish for Makeddah to stay hidden. Without Makeddah, how will they scare off the sorcerers? She hopes her choice keeps more people safe.

Still, her hands sweat and her heart races, fearing something will go amiss. Matt even warns her to expect it.

Worry twists her gut. She's terrified Mira and Aaron won't work together.

Mira has been angry and moody since this morning. Aaron is his usual quiet self. They haven't told anyone. Makeddah waited all day for Mira to speak to Rayon. When

Grace met them for lunch, she waited then too. But Mira remains silent.

So, as she watches Aaron and Mira pout, she repeats for everyone to be ready. But she knows she's not. All the witches hid; only five agreed to fight, including Alda and Rayon. Makeddah hoped few would join—she can't bear more sorrow. They've had enough already.

Rayon's motive for fighting is *because* they've had enough sorrow. She claims she wants to bring justice, so here she is.

The sorcerers will be here soon. All Makeddah can think of is how Rayon shouldn't be here. Makeddah herself doesn't belong here. None of the witches should face this. Still, it's reality, all because of Makeddah. Yet, believing it's her fault isn't so easy. What makes her so important to them? Why is it so dangerous for her to know? Makeddah screams inside. She's relieved nothing escapes her lips to give them another excuse to keep her out—unstableness.

She knows she's unstable, and the weight of it exhausts her. Just sixteen, her emotions swing wildly. How can the others not see the storm she fights daily? Sometimes it shows in her actions—inside, it feels worse. Turning sixteen only amplifies the turmoil, and she fears it will get harder.

Makeddah shudders.

She feels a warm hand on her shoulder—Matt. She bolts upright, shaking her head. "Kahlan was right. I'm not ready."

Matt looks disappointed. "You're ready, Makeddah. I'd know." She looks down, but his hands squeeze her shoulders. "You're ready."

Makeddah gives him a fake smile. "Well, look who likes me now."

"I've never *not* liked you," Makeddah gives him a look, and he nods, "Okay, but that was before I knew you. And sometimes I wish that I still didn't like you... or even knew you."

Makeddah peers through the crowd. "Grace?"

"Invisible and staying inside the walls."

"You?"

"Ready," Matt says, propping up his bows and arrows. "It's time."

Makeddah turns to the door, her heart hammering. "It's time."

Makeddah stands in front, Mira on her left, Matt on her right.

The sun begins to set. Makeddah tastes the rain in the air, sensing the shift in the weather from warm to cool. Adrenaline surges from the earth, heat rising within her. Her heart thunders loudly. She hopes the sorcerers can't hear it.

And when she sees them, she stops breathing. They all walk up slowly. Makeddah expects there to be more. She was worried they wouldn't have enough people from the Guard. But they do. There are only around fifteen sorcerers. And when they stop, one man walks forward.

Sixteen, Makeddah tells herself.

"What is this?" The sorcerer asks. "Only three? Let me guess, you want us to feel threatened by putting the big bad people out to play. Hi, Matt. How's that family you tried to rescue? Oh, right, dead." Matt stiffens beside Makeddah. The man squints at Mira. "I remember you. My brother enjoyed killing your father. Rest in peace, I guess." The man grins.

Makeddah recoils—she registers the rotten teeth and the grotesque, nauseating stench rolling off the man. The gray pallor is nothing compared to the rot clawing at her senses. She swallows against the urge to gag. He's so close she can feel it crawling on her skin.

They are all hard on the eyes, appearing to decay whilst alive. Only a few in the back look normal.

"And who are you?" He asks Makeddah. "Since you're the only one I don't know."

Makeddah studies the sorcerer, weighing possible threats. She quickly looks back at Matt to seek his support. Matt, without turning, gives her a reassuring nod, signaling her to proceed.

Makeddah glares at the man, scowling as she turns. She feels the breeze pass through the mesh fabric on her back, revealing her glowing birthmark to the sorcerers. The men gasp, surprised either by the birthmark or her status as a Lion Heart. As she faces them again, the front sorcerer's face breaks into a grin.

"That must mean you are the…" He glances back at one of the sorcerers who is a bit younger and not hard to look at.

"The what?" Both Matt and Mira ask in unison. They share a glance with each other before looking back at the sorcerer.

"Oh, never mind that."

Outrage simmers in Makeddah's chest. The earth quivers beneath her feet, echoing her fury. The sun drops lower as her hands flush red with heat, flames pulsing at her fingertips, barely contained. "Who are you?" She demands, masking her rage behind tight control. She's relieved that her voice doesn't betray the anger boiling inside.

"My sorcerers and I were sent here by our master, Eliab. *Eliab*." He repeats it slowly as if she were a little child. Emphasizing Eli and making her hear the very specific "-eb" sound at the end. Like she should know the name if it's brought to her ears that way.

"I'm not interested in *Eliab*." Makeddah mocks, crossing her arms. "I'm interested in you."

"Funny that. I'm pretty interested in you, as well. Tell me, what is your name?" He rubs his shoulder, and his brown eyes follow Makeddah's every twitch. When she moves her fingers, he's watching. When she shakes her knee, he sees. And when she puts a hand on her hip, a very Rayon-like move, he smiles again.

"I'm tired of you already." She says, even though adrenaline still hammers in her veins. "Don't you think we should get this over with?"

He shrugs, "I don't care. You'll die either way."

Makeddah rolls her eyes, remembering Belle's advice that provoking them could make them reckless. She says, "Sure, I will," forcing as much attitude as she can. Even though the smirk she puts on is difficult to hold, she manages, challenging, "Your move."

The sorcerer chuckles. "I kind of like you, and I kind of hate that I do."

Makeddah glances back at Matt with a smile. "That's what they all say." She focuses on the sorcerer again. "I wasn't kidding. Your move." A raindrop falls on Makeddah. Then another.

"If you say so."

Makeddah sees a flash of black and, on instinct, throws up a firewall. The moment she lets it down, she hears them shouting and sees the sorcerers running toward her. The other four jump into action, coming from the walls of the Center and the trees behind them.

Alda and a few other Head Witches follow after them, flying from the walls and shooting white beams of magic.

None of the sorcerers approach Makeddah; instead, one targets Matt, grabbing his bow from his hands. Makeddah starts to help, but Matt shouts, "Help Mira!"

Makeddah turns, and a slight drizzle of rain comes from the sky, making the grass sleek. She tries to step up to help Mira. Mira looks over to her, and her eyes are wide. "Behind you, Makeddah," Mira says.

Makeddah turns, knowing this would be a good time to whip out her sword, but she's shaking. She finds the lead sorcerer face-to-face with her. "Guess your friends are all tied up." His breath is even worse than his body odor.

Like in a fight with a little kid, he shoves her, causing her to slip on the wet grass. He runs off. "Oh, no." She looks back at Matt and Mira—they're busy. She glances at Rayon, who battles with Alda against two sorcerers. Makeddah pursues her opponent, reassuring herself she'll manage alone.

She ducks as a beam of white magic passes overhead. She looks back to see Alda in a fighter stance, creating small needles of white magic. When the sorcerer charges her, she shoots them at him, and he cries out in pain. Each little needle pierces somewhere in his body.

Makeddah focuses on her sorcerer and runs into the trees, stopping abruptly. Chest heaving, she scans the shadows. No sign of him—he wanted her isolated. She wasn't supposed to let that happen. She went anyway, thinking she was strong enough. What if she was wrong?

She turns to run back, but she ducks as black magic flies over her head, just missing her. She looks back. "Hi." It's a different sorcerer. One of the ones that is less hard to look at.

"Where'd the other one go?"

"I told him I had you." His fingers twitch, and he takes a breath. She tries to leave again. "Wait, Makeddah."

She turns slowly and stares at him, knowing her face is full of surprise. "How do you know my name?" She heaves.

"I don't want to fight. If I can just take you—"

Makeddah laughs, and it sounds like a maniac's laugh. Who is this man to think that she'll let him take her anyway? "Too bad, I want to fight." She pushes fire from her hands, but he dives out of the way.

"Fine, I guess we'll do it the hard way," he screams, pushing black magic at her head. Makeddah throws up a shield of air covering her, then throws fire straight at him.

She sees the tree above him, hoping to make it fall, but that doesn't happen. She's not practiced enough.

She punches him in the face and kicks him. He blocks both and goes for her stomach. She grunts as his fist makes contact, feeling a second later like she might throw up the fruit she had two hours ago. He stands above her as she falls to the ground. A thought comes to mind. She's important. They want her, and they don't want to kill her. Not now, anyway.

"Will you let me take you, now?"

Makeddah gives a short laugh. "No." She kicks him in the knee, and he falls back. It's hard for her to get up, but it is for him too. They stand at the same time, he is holding his knee and she is wringing her hands. He runs to her and tackles her to the ground, trying to put one hand around her neck, but she goes for his hand and burns it. He screams out.

The moment he falls back again, Makeddah stands. She goes for her sword, but he throws magic at her abdomen. Her breath is gone. That feeling of the last sorcerer she fought a few weeks ago comes back. Darkness. Emptiness. And, she realizes, rot. But it isn't as strong as the magic of the first sorcerer she fought.

She tries to cough, but when she inhales, her breath doesn't come.

Her head is empty, her heart is slowing, and she realizes she was wrong. It is okay to kill her. It must be because she can feel her breath leaving her. She's about to die. As soon as she falls back onto the ground, tears fill her eyes. She tries to bring a hand to her mouth, but her arms are too weak.

She rolls her head to the side, the wet grass grazing her cheek. Rain is pouring now, but she can't feel much under the thick canopy of trees. But she can hear it. She can hear the rain and everything else. Hear the battle going on. Hear people fighting.

And she feels herself giving up.

But something rises in her. Like a certain kind of strength she's never felt before. When she feels it, she knows it's her adrenaline pumping. She is now able to move, getting up on all fours. The sorcerer is standing now, panting against a tree.

"Tired?" she asks, getting her breath back.

He glares at her but doesn't say a word. She sees the thick branch he is holding with his unburned hand. Walking over to her, he says. "Let me take you, or I'll hit you with this because you give me no choice."

"Well, then, I give you no choice, because I'm not *letting* you."

"I have to do this, Makeddah, you don't understand." Makeddah is not sure if it's sweat, tears, or rain running down this man's face, "He makes me."

"Stop saying my name like you know me," she says through her teeth. She would never associate with a man like him.

"I do know you; *everyone* knows of you. But yourself it seems." He pauses. "I guess we're all better off, anyway," the sorcerer says. He starts to raise the branch above his head.

The adrenaline surges through Makeddah's whole body, strengthening her muscles, and suddenly she's standing. The sorcerer's bottom lip twitches, and he staggers back. She conjures a ball of elements in each hand. One of air and one of water. She still feels the pain, but it's withering away, power and strength taking its place.

"W-what? That's not..." The sorcerer shakes but doesn't miss a beat, throwing the branch at her head. She ducks, and it misses her by an inch. Something tells her to push air at him, and she does, blindly. Her force seems to have the strength of a hurricane, because it makes the sorcerer fly backward a few feet. He skids on the ground before a tree stops him.

Makeddah marches over. "Why does everyone know me?" Black overcomes her vision, and the pain is coursing back through her. Her burning hands reach down for both of his wrists when he doesn't answer right away.

"What do you mean?" he asks with a yelp.

Her grip tightens on his wrists, letting the burn sink into his veins, and crouches to be eye to eye with him. "That sorcerer said that being a Lion Heart meant I must be something. He looked back at you, didn't he? And you said everyone knows me but myself. So tell me, who am I?"

The sorcerer laughs, sweat dripping from his brow. "You. Y-you don't even… don't even know." He coughs, and dark blood drips from his bottom lip. "Y-you're the P-P… the Princess."

Twenty-five

Makeddah stumbles back in horror. "What? What did you just say?" Pain floods her vision, and she clutches her stomach, hitting the ground and rubbing her head. Looking up, she sees the sorcerer, free but unmoving. Instinctively, she throws puny vine chains on his wrists. The burns make his skin appear as if it's boiling.

He doesn't resist; it seems he doesn't want to leave. "Did I do that?" she asks, pointing at the burn marks on his wrists. She truly doesn't remember.

The sorcerer laughs. She crawls to him, holding her stomach, and lies against the tree. She notes that the sorcerer doesn't look angry, but he looks ready. "Yes, you did this. And yes," he says, his words faltering, "I am serious."

He catches his breath. "Y-you are the Princess of Korzon. I n-need you to listen."

She nods, not able to form words.

"I'm sorry," he says, shaking his head. "I didn't want to take you. He made me do it. Thought I could convince you, not the other guy. I'm sorry. I-I didn't mean to hurt you."

"I understand." Her lip trembles. "Actually, I don't, but I don't know if I want to." He nods in silence. "I need to get you back to the field; they'll know what to do."

He shakes his head. "It's okay, I'm a bad guy when I'm alive. I don't want to be a bad guy anymore." He exhales. "You can kill me."

Makeddah wrings her hands, dread twisting inside her. How could he ask for something so terrible? The fear that's haunted her every step—taking lives, losing those she loves—churns in her chest. "No. I don't want to do that. I can't kill you."

"You'd be putting me out of my misery." Makeddah looks over at him, but he stares ahead, not meeting her gaze. "But it's fine, you can just sit here with me like I'm not your enemy."

She does. She sits with him like nothing's wrong. "I thought you hated me. You should, you're supposed to."

He shrugs. "Right now, I'm loose from the chains of sorcery, and I feel as free as a bird. That is, u-until these chains are off me and I'm free to do as M-Master calls."

"Oh."

"If you don't kill me, Makeddah, let someone else do it," he sighs. "I want to be dead; I want to be rid of it. I want to meet my Creator."

That's when she notices his blood is red. She thought sorcerers were irredeemable and that their blood was black to show that.

Maybe Alda and Rayon are wrong.

She stares at his red blood, silent. She cannot answer him. His words feel like a cold, heavy stone. A drizzle of rain sneaks through the thick trees, matching the ache in her stomach. She wipes her brow, shuddering. "Is the pain supposed to be like this?"

"It's not like I was going to kill you. I have never killed anyway."

"I thought that's what you wanted to do—kill me."

He licks his lips, "Not me, the King."

She hears people calling her name, but she doesn't look up until she hears their gasps. She sees Isaac and Rayon, both staring at the sorcerer bound by vines.

"Here you are," Isaac says, running to her and helping her up. "With him."

"Vines?" Rayon chuckles. "Mak, I thought you were dead." She sweeps her sister into a hug, making Makeddah even wetter. She quickly pulls back. "Are you hurt? Do you need to get to Grace? Come on, let's go."

"No, I'm fine. I'm not hurt." Makeddah swallows, looking at the sorcerer. "Ask him," she says, pointing to Isaac. "He'll do as you wish." She pulls the sword from its cover and hands it to Isaac. "You may need this."

They start moving, Rayon supporting Makeddah step by step. Once they are out of sight of the others, Makeddah halts, startled by a faint cry of pain from behind. She realizes, trembling, that Isaac must have just killed the sorcerer. When Isaac rejoins them, he gives a silent nod, and they continue as if nothing happened.

Even the sword is free from any sign of what occurred.

Outside the tree line, the rain pours, and the battle continues. Only a few sorcerers remain. Isaac says something to Rayon and runs off. Makeddah doesn't know or care what he said. They hobble forward, nearly among the others.

The last four sorcerers are fighting hard. The Guard members and witches are fighting back fiercely, and despite her pain and the questions swirling in her head, Makeddah needs to join them. Alda and one of the other witches are in a full-on light magic and dark magic battle. Pushing and pulling against each other.

Matt aims at the sorcerer fighting Aaron. Aaron's air tightens around the sorcerer's throat as Matt shoots an arrow into his back.

Makeddah watches a sorcerer about to fall. He shoots magic at something she can't see in the moonlight. Mira runs at the dark spell and dives in front, but it misses her and continues on.

Makeddah stops holding on to Rayon. She takes a defensive stance.

The sound of thunder booms in the sky, followed by the shriek of a girl. Makeddah stops and covers her ears. The shriek is so high and so unsettling that Makeddah almost falls to the ground.

Matt shoots an arrow at that sorcerer. He goes down, sounding like a falling leaf where Makeddah stands. And then the rain lets up. The downpour stops. Not a single drop remains in the sky. As if by magic.

She hears the shriek again, louder this time, and sees Mira collapse to her knees. As Mira's knees strike the ground, the earth shudders, lightning flashes through the trees behind Makeddah, and thunder rolls. Fissures crack open behind Mira, stretching far into the distance as Makeddah watches.

All the sorcerers—dead, living, wounded—fall into the earth. The ground seals itself, as if its job had been done.

People are standing there, looking at the sobbing Mira and the person in her arms.

"No," Makeddah chokes out as the figure becomes clear. "No!" She bolts, desperation making her limbs heavy and wild, nearly collapsing as she arrives beside Mira and Matt. Her heart screams for mercy as she slides down next to them.

"Grace?" he says. "But the baby, but the baby. No, Grace, please."

Makeddah lays trembling hands on Grace's neck. The sight of the vacant eyes, the open mouth—the terror lodges in her throat and she breaks down. "Grace, please. Be alive. I can't have this, no, *please,*" Her voice shudders.

Grace wheezes awake with wide eyes. Matt gasps, Makeddah smiles, Mira laughs.

"Don't trust them," Grace says, looking right into Makeddah's eyes. "It's them." Then her eyes close, and her head falls. And Makeddah whimpers.

Mira's laugh turns into a silent and heavy cry. Matt just stands, running his hand through his hair.

"What happened?" Alda rushes up. Makeddah notices everyone around them.

"The rain. It washed her off," Aaron grumbles. His voice seems so low that Makeddah can barely make out his words. Alda shakes her head and grabs Rayon, hugging her close.

Isaac drops his sword. "But…"

"She's dead!" Mira snaps. "She's dead!" Mira cries into Grace's hair, and Makeddah only thinks of one thing.

It's all her fault.

Twenty-six

*T*ravelling back, the witches ghosted them to the Guard. They brought Matt and Grace last, to give him some time to grieve with her alone.

All Makeddah can do is blame herself. She keeps replaying the events, convinced that Grace died because of her actions. Why didn't she consider the risk of the rainwater washing Grace off? It's so obvious now. She remembers smelling the rain before the sorcerers arrived. She felt it coming yet did nothing. The weight of her regret is suffocating.

Makeddah can't understand the silence around her. She wonders if everyone else is lost in their own regrets, as she is. Is everyone replaying 'what ifs'? What if they'd told Grace to stay back, or stopped the sorcerer sooner? The questions echo in her head, making the quiet almost unbearable.

There she was sitting and talking with one of them, feeling bad for him. Should she have questioned his wickedness? Of course she should have. Sorcerers did this to Grace, they all deserve to be brought to justice.

Matt and Mira grieve the worst of all. That is Matt's wife. He was the one who allowed her to come. And that is Mira's best friend, someone she calls a sister. Although they are not related by blood, Mira must feel she has lost another family member just hours ago.

Makeddah tries to imagine losing those she loves: Belle, Alda, Mother Lianne, and then Rayon, too. The thought makes her feel as if her heart would rot from sadness, freezing her in a world of regret, guilt, and loneliness. She can hardly breathe under the weight of it.

Grace is dead, Makeddah tells herself for the thirteenth time. *And it's my fault.*

Makeddah stands outside the Guard, under the invisibility veil, hoping to get fresh air. She waits for all of them to go through, wanting to not to have to face anyone.

Matt grabs Makeddah's shoulder and squeezes. She didn't know he was here already. Makeddah looks up at him. Her vision is blurry—not from the sprinkling rain that started up again a half hour ago.

She can't look him in the eye for long. He must be thinking it is her fault. Everyone must be thinking that.

"It's not your fault." Matt answers her thoughts.

"How did you…" Makeddah holds tight to her arm. "But I'm the reason they went out there. It *must* be my fault, Matt."

"If it were your fault, I wouldn't be beside you right now." Matt makes her turn to him. His eyes are red, filled with tears, and his mouth is set with a sad smile. "Listen to me." He shakes her shoulders. "It's *not* your fault."

She inhales a shaky breath. "Okay."

He stares at her for what seems like forever. She pulls from his grip and nods. Somehow, she knows he is telling the truth. Yet, she does not feel that way.

They both walk to the ghoster, and Makeddah goes inside after Matt. She finds many people surrounding Grace, Kahlan calling out orders.

Makeddah waits for Kahlan to finish and says, "Can I talk to you? I didn't have time to talk to my mom, so I need to talk to you."

Rayon looks at her from behind Kahlan. Makeddah keeps her gaze on Kahlan. She hears someone come up behind her. "What's going on?" When he whispers to Makeddah, she knows it's Matt. No one else seems to hear.

"Yes, my office," Kahlan says. This is the first time Makeddah has seen Kahlan look tired. They all follow behind as Kahlan leads the way. Makeddah walks first, Rayon and Matt behind her. When she steps inside the office, she sees Isaac in there, waiting for Kahlan. "Boys," Kahlan says to both Matt and Isaac, "give us a minute, please."

"It's okay, this will be quick," Makeddah says. She doesn't care who hears; she just wants to know the truth.

Rayon sits, but Makeddah paces the room, biting her nails. "Sit, please." Kahlan motions to the chair as she sits.

"Can't." Makeddah crosses her arms and faces Kahlan. "This must be the worst time in the world for me to say something. It must be. All I can think of is how Grace is dead, how she was pregnant. But something is warring with that thought in my head." Makeddah stands behind Rayon's chair, gripping the back of it. Her knuckles turn white. "The reason Haggard wants to kill me himself."

Kahlan's mouth opens. "What…?"

"A sorcerer told me." As if she needs to be reminded, she says, "Before I let Isaac kill him." Makeddah is surprised by her steady voice because she is trembling inside. "Is it true?"

"I don't know what you're saying," Kahlan sighs. "Please be clearer, Makeddah."

Makeddah laughs.

Clearer? How can she be clearer when she herself doesn't understand what this means.

But she puts her words together quickly, "You do know what I'm saying, because you know the reason Haggard wants to kill me. He probably thinks I'll try to take his position, right? What I don't get is why his traitor inside the Guard hasn't just snatched me already. But you know, the pieces start to come together after you think about it for a while." Makeddah tries to get back on track, but her mind is going all over the place.

"I remember the stories, the ones I didn't believe. Of a Queen and King living a good life, having a child, and one year later being killed, and their kingdom being taken away." She pauses. "The princess survived. Someone, *somehow*, saved her."

The stories rush back to her. Even Mira's words when they first arrived at the Guard seem much clearer.

"Mak, what are you talking about?" Rayon asks in a shaky voice. It sounds like she hasn't talked for a long time.

"I'm talking about the fact that *I* am that Princess. The one who survived. I didn't believe my own story." She bites her lip and sighs. "Haggard didn't kill me, but he meant to, right?" Makeddah crosses her arms and shakes her head. Her tears come, but she doesn't back down. Her voice stays steady. "That means my mother didn't abandon me. It means I had a mother *and* a father. Doesn't it?" Now her voice shakes. "And they were killed."

"Makeddah—"

"Just tell me, Kahlan, if I'm right? Is that why Haggard wants to take me? Were my parents the King and Queen of Korzon? Am I the Princess?" She pauses, lowering her voice, "Are my parents dead?"

Kahlan stands and nods. "Yes." She pauses. "To all of the questions, yes."

Makeddah stumbles backward. Isaac catches her, but she throws off his hands. "Thank you for the information. I will be in my room if you need me. Mourning the death of the five people I've lost today."

"Five?" Rayon asks.

Makeddah stares ahead. "My mother, my father, Grace, Matt's child."

"Who's the fifth?" Isaac asks.

Makeddah looks at the door. "Myself." She leaves and walks numbly to her room. Sitting on her bed, she realizes no tears come. It feels like a part of her died when the sorcerer called her the Princess. Now, she doesn't know who she is. She can't be Makeddah anymore, but she can't become the Princess either. She only knows she's not the same girl.

She tries to summon anger, but nothing comes. She searches for sadness, then happiness, for how long Grace lived, but feels nothing but numbness. Even if numbness is still a feeling, at least it's something she recognizes—empty, but certain.

Makeddah wonders why she can't cry or feel anything intense—no anger, no grief. She knows she should be reacting, but instead she just sits on her bed, thinking of all she didn't know, all that was kept from her, and how Grace's child will never get a chance to live.

Makeddah thinks of Grace's smile. Of the way she could handle fire. The way she loved Matt so much. How she would kiss Matt's head when he was grumpy. She would often joke about other elements. The way she talked about family—about Mira.

Then Makeddah's mind goes to Mira. How she screamed.

She was barely breathing when Grace's life slipped
away. How she laughed so hard when Grace's eyes opened,
but then she said her dying words.

It's them.

What did Grace mean by that? Makeddah sits back in
her bed and hears the door creak open.

"I would like to be alone."

"And I like to be alone, but you never let me. *And* you
never like to be alone."

Rayon lies on the bed holding Makeddah's arm. Makeddah hates being alone; she depends on Rayon so much.
Is it because her mother was like that? No. She can't imagine
the Queen as that type of person. But what kind of person
was she? Would Makeddah suffer in that castle? A castle she
hasn't even seen yet? That place was supposed to be her
home, not the home of the man trying to murder her.

"Who would I be today if I had lived with them?"

"Well, you wouldn't be my sister," Rayon says. "You
would probably be boring and hate witches, because you'd
be a bigshot Princess about to be married."

Makeddah scoffs, "I'm sixteen."

"It's Korzonian law. You can be crowned and married
as early as sixteen. Of course, the Queen was eighteen because she wasn't betrothed to the King. And her father
didn't want to give her away until then anyway. But the lat-
est for Royalty to be married is twenty, so you'd still have to
be married in the next four years anyway."

"How do you know that?" Makeddah jumps up.

"Because I used to read about the King and Queen and
royalty. A lot actually." Rayon looks up thoughtfully.

"So, you knew?" Makeddah asks.

"No." Rayon looks offended at the thought, "when
they announced you as their baby, all the papers would call
you the Princess. One said that you weren't named, another
said they hadn't announced your name yet, and a bunch of
other stuff. You're not supposed to give the name of a royal

baby to the public for a year in Korzon. They were setting a date, but never got to it," she quibbles. "That's so weird. Saying the Princess is you, but she is. You are."

Makeddah shrugs. She feels that she and the princess are two different girls.

Rayon hits her. "Come on, Mak. You are something legendary. I wish I were legendary."

"You are, or can be. I'll make you my secondary Princess."

"Doesn't work that way."

"Well, you'll be a witch in the Head Witch group by eighteen."

"Not possible," Rayon sighs.

"Make it possible, Rayon. You're a Parish."

Rayon smiles at Makeddah. She sounds like her.

"And so are you. But you're also a Brooke. Can't believe I didn't put two and two together." She shakes her head. "You're the Lion Heart Princess. Now if that doesn't make you jealous, I don't know what would."

Makeddah says, "It doesn't, because I'm her."

Rayon grins. "Exactly."

Makeddah leans back against the headboard and holds Rayon's hand. "I did die. When I said it back in the office, I meant it."

"Makeddah—"

"Nothing is going to be the same, Ray. I have a different purpose in life now. But it's not only that." She rubs her eyes, her mind focusing on a totally different thing now. "I let Isaac kill that sorcerer."

"He wasn't innocent."

"But he was." Makeddah stands. "It's not his fault; Haggard made him that way. He said he hated being the bad guy, Ray."

Rayon isn't convinced. "That's all talk Mak."

"No. His blood was red." Makeddah whispers as if telling the world a secret. She shakes her head. "What if mom has been wrong the whole time?"

Rayon doesn't get the chance to answer as they hear the door click open. They fall completely silent as Mira crawls into bed next to Rayon.

She lays her head on Rayon's shoulder. Makeddah instantly moves to the other side of the bed to sit next to Mira and lays her head on her shoulder. There is barely any room left on the edge of the bed, but Makeddah doesn't care.

She inches a little closer to Mira. This is a time of comfort, not space. It's a time of silence.

Soon, Mira falls asleep, silently crying on Rayon. And by the sound of Rayon's snore, Rayon is asleep as well. Makeddah looks up at the door. She raises her hand to close it with air, but Isaac pops up through the door. He looks in and sees Makeddah.

She sticks her head up.

"You okay, Sunshine?" He mouths. Makeddah nods. "We'll talk tomorrow?" Makeddah nods again. The door opens wider, and Aaron and Matt are both standing in the background. Isaac and Aaron both leave with a wave, but Matt stands there looking in.

"Are you okay?" Makeddah mouths to him.

He peeks further inside. He comes in, grabs a blanket from the closet, and stands by the bedside. He swings it over Mira and Makeddah since Mira fell asleep on top of the covers, and Rayon is the only one under them. He looks down at Makeddah and whispers. "I don't think I'll ever be okay. But thank you."

Makeddah sighs. "I'm so, *so* sorry."

"Me too." He steps back. "Get some sleep."

And a moment later, the light goes out and the door closes. And Makeddah feels all alone.

Twenty-seven

So many thoughts course through Makeddah's mind in the dark room. Something Makeddah doesn't understand is how she can feel so sad when she is so special. She always thought once she became somebody worth something, everything would fall into place, and she'd be fine, no matter what, she'd be okay.

Throughout her life, she has always wanted to be special, and *now* she is. And *now* she feels like crap. But that doesn't really matter, right? She *has* been special her whole life. Just hadn't known about it. She's been the lost Princess this whole time; she's been a Lion Heart this whole time. So, why doesn't she feel special or good about life when she has so many promises to look forward to?

Alda's Creator must be laughing at her right now. He must hate her to have dealt her these cards. She feels numb to all the things she's been exposed to.

It seems like the only thing she's feeling is alone.

It's probably because her titles don't matter—Lion Heart and Princess—because that's all they are after all. Titles.

And those titles have only brought her destruction.

So, what can she do to feel better in a time like this? She's not only lost a friend, but herself.

Her parents are gone, too.

It's crazy to think how she had no emotion about the King and Queen's death before, but now it's tearing her apart inside. She already knew her mom was gone, but now she has two parents, and both of them are.

As she stares blankly at the pitch-black room, she comes to the conclusion that she will do what Rayon did— look up the King and Queen. She glances down at Mira, sound asleep under the blanket. Rayon is definitely sleeping. Her snoring isn't too loud, but loud enough for Makeddah to hear.

Makeddah glances at the clock on her side table, but she has to light it up with fire to tell the time—two in the morning.

Makeddah slides out of bed, grabbing the slippers Rayon placed neatly under the bed the previous morning. She reaches for the shawl on the side table and tiptoes to the door. With one last glance back, she escapes through the door into the eerily quiet hallway. She pulls the shawl tighter around herself and ganders at the lobby. There is nobody in sight.

Strangely enough, she is fine with being alone. The loneliness that felt suffocating moments ago now feels freeing. Where before it felt like her end, now solitude offers a kind of beginning. She relishes being in the open, unobserved, able to move where she pleases without anyone knowing. The change surprises her, but she follows the feeling, heading down the hallway to the lobby. She vaguely remembers Rayon mentioning the library's location, though she hadn't planned to visit before. Hesitantly, she guesses which way to go, and is pleased when she's right.

Instead of regular walls, the library features glass walls that surround it. She peeks through the glass wall, but the shelves of books on it barely let her see in. All she gets glimpses of are more books and one table.

The lights are still on, so she assumes it's unlocked. She opens the heavy glass door and walks inside, the smell of old books overcoming her. She doesn't even know where to begin. How does this library even work? The one back at the Witch Center had rows of books; this one only has four walls—two of them not glass—and books filling them up. Does she look under letters or…? Makeddah stares at all the books on the wall in front of her and swallows. This is not her area of expertise.

"Looking for something?"

Makeddah twitches at the voice. She turns and sees Aaron on the ground, leaning against the bookshelf to the left of the door, glasses on top of his head, book propped in his hands. So much for no one knowing.

"Yeah. A book or paper or anything about my mother and father."

"Oh, right."

"What?" Makeddah looks at him, her brows furrowing. "Do you think I'm stupid for trying to do this? Am I? I can't decide." She hates the note of desperation in her voice.

"You're not." Aaron stands with a grunt. He rubs the back of his neck. "I would want to know, too." Setting down his own book, he looks through books on the opposite side of Makeddah. Makeddah walks over and stands next to him as he takes out a few books. He pauses as he puts his hand on the newspaper that lies on top of the stack, "I didn't know—we didn't—about you being the Princess."

"Why would it matter to you?"

Aaron just shrugs. He puts his glasses over his eyes and scans the newspaper. "Here." He hands her the three books and the two newspapers. "I'm not sure if everything in those is true, but this one was actually written by your mother's maidservant."

"Really?" She looks at the book entitled *Nzuri*. "Is that my mother's name? Was."

"Yeah. Queen Nzuri and King Stellan," he says. "Those were their names."

Makeddah smiles at the book. She looks up to Aaron. She almost hugs him. She wants to tell him how she feels right now. To open up to someone, somehow. To tell him and Isaac, Rayon, Matt, and Mira how hard life is right now. But what would they all think of her, crying about her life when Grace has just lost hers? They would think she's crazy, or that she needs to suck it up, or that she's thinking too much.

So, she fights the urge and smiles up at Aaron, nodding. "Thank you."

"Have you seen Mira?"

Makeddah gives a small nod, "Yes. She was sleeping with us. I'm sure she's still there."

"Can you tell her I'd like to see her?"

"I will when I see her." Makeddah pauses, "I'm so sorry about hearing that the other day."

Aaron shrugs, "I don't even want to know how much you heard. Let's just pretend I never saw you."

Makeddah scratches her cheek, "Okay." And with that she leaves, trying not to overstay her welcome.

Makeddah walks out to the lobby but then looks around and realizes people will be out here in a few hours, so she moves along and walks to the units. She looks at the schedule, then walks to the fourth earth unit. It is so peaceful in here, and she could read here until noon before someone needs it.

She looks at the newspaper first. She's never had a newspaper with actual pictures in it. The witches would publish newspapers every week with updates, but they were all text, no pictures.

There are several drawings of her mother and father, however, they are of poor quality. But she finds one stunning drawing. Makeddah traces the black and white with her finger. Her mother and father when they were first courting.

She notices her mother has a kind smile, but her father doesn't. Was it drawn while they stood there? Or copied from other pictures? She reads the headline in big, bold, black letters.

Prince-Turned-King Stellan Has Found a Maiden
Below is a description of her mother.

Nzuri, princess to the northern kingdom of Zaridon, the largest kingdom in the On Kingdoms.

The article goes on to say her trip to the southern kingdom went better than expected. It states that Nzuri's father and Stellan's father govern their kingdoms in a similar manner. Their people are in constant good health, free from drought, well-fed, and safe. They both unite the four elements, and they are both against sorcery.

Then Makeddah sees the emblem. The four swords touching at the tips with the elements in the empty spaces between the handles.

She gasps.

Her sheath, did it belong to her mother? Father? Is it a sheath that people within the kingdom use?

She looks for more clues as she searches for more information on her parents.

The next newspaper clipping features a picture of her father. Makeddah looks like them both. Her mother's skin is a deeper brown; her father's is lighter. Makeddah must get her color from him. She gets those rounded almond eyes and small, plump lips from her mother. This makes her wish she could see them both up close. She still doesn't know whose hair she has, or whose ears. Her mother's hair is pulled back—her ears are drawn very poorly. Her father's hair is cut short. In the next drawing her father is standing next to her mother as she sits on a big plush throne.

Makeddah smiles when she sees the sheath on his hip. It was his.

A tear is brought to her eye, but she keeps it from falling.

Alda was already drawing the connection from Makeddah to her parents. She just didn't know it yet.

You'll know soon enough. The words echo in Makeddah's head.

As she stares at the pictures of her parents she thinks of how beautiful they both were. Makeddah can tell, even just looking at the photos, that they were in love. The only time he smiled was when he looked at her. Makeddah then opens the book that Aaron said the handmaid had written.

It was published twenty-one years ago. Only five years before Makeddah was born.

She opens the book and sits back against the window, starting to read about her mother's life.

"Makeddah. Makeddah. Mak!"

Makeddah jumps up, rudely awaked from her sleep. She sees Rayon, Mira, and Matt standing over her. She rubs the sleep from her eyes and stands, yawning, the book falling to the ground. Makeddah dips down to pick it up, but Rayon snatches it up instead.

"Oh, I read this."

Matt steps up and wipes the side of her mouth. "You drool." He wipes it on his pants and picks up the newspapers, but discards them just as quickly. This is when Mira steps up and fixes Makeddah's hair and straightens her clothes.

"Thanks." Makeddah wipes her mouth with her sleeve. "What time is it?"

"Nine," Mira says. "I need this unit to vent my emotions." She points a thumb at Matt. "And he wants to punch something."

"Me too." Makeddah wipes her back of dirt. She stops Mira before they join Rayon and Matt. "Hey, I saw Aaron. He said he'd like to see you."

Mira's face changes, but Makeddah can't decipher it. "I don't want to see him." She turns. "Actually, everyone should know that I broke up with Aaron. We are no longer a thing, and I think it's better that way, cause he would not be able to support me like I need right now."

"What?" Matt sounds groggy.

"What!" Rayon sounds like the world is falling. She walks over with a frowning face. "You two seemed so great."

"Not everything is as it seems. I can't deal with him, especially today." Mira trudges off.

"The, um," Rayon leans to Makeddah and whispers, "Letting go ceremony is tonight. Kahlan just announced it."

Makeddah looks at Matt, who is sitting against a tree with folded arms and a hood pulled over his eyes. Makeddah can tell by the way he is so silent that he is either thinking too much or crying. She only thinks this because she would be doing one of those things.

She starts to walk over to him. Maybe there is some way she can comfort him. But suddenly the room gets hot. She looks up and around to find those grey eyes because she knows this feeling. It feels as if an ice cube is sliding down her back while heat rises around her body.

It's back. The thought stops dead in her tracks.

She looks at Matt. His eyes are wide, searching the unit, meaning he can feel it too. So, she starts to walk to him again, but as she does, she trips. It feels like she hangs in the air for a split second, and something burns her hand as she does. She cries out in pain when she hits the ground.

She holds her hand tight to her and sees the steam rising from it. Whimpering, Makeddah looks and sees what she thinks is blood before her hand is snatched from her.

"Ow," she hisses, both from Rayon pulling her arm and the sting on her hand when it's forced open.

Mira searches the ground. "There's nothing here. Did you burn yourself?" She glances at Makeddah's hand, and her eyes widen.

"Matt, come here," Rayon says, still looking at Makeddah's hand. Makeddah tries to yank it back, but Rayon gives her the death stare. Makeddah lets Rayon keep her hand until Matt examines it. "What could do that? Did you burn yourself?"

Makeddah pulls it back with success this time. "No, I didn't. I promise." She looks at her hand. It seems like a burn, but Makeddah's not supposed to be able to feel pain like that from fire.

She glances at the ground, and her hand starts throbbing. She realizes the burn is in the shape of a star. She looks up at Rayon, then Matt.

A dread passes Rayon's face, and her features darken. Matt's eyes go wide. "I don't get it," he ponders more to himself than anyone else. He leaves almost instantly after whispering this. But Makeddah walks out after him.

"Matt." She says before he walks out of the training units. "What is going on?" She stops in front of him. "Does this have to do with the traitor?"

"I… I don't know. I told you I don't get it. Why is this happening?"

But Makeddah can see something is out of place, the way he is fidgeting. Ready for her to stop talking so he can leave.

"Matt, you aren't telling me something. Why?"

"Makeddah, I want to find this person just as much as you. Stop asking questions. You haven't stopped asking questions since the moment I met you."

Her shoulders drop, "Can you blame me?"

Matt shakes his head, "No, I can't. I'm going to talk to Kahlan."

"Okay, but—" she stops short. She doesn't fully trust Kahlan, but she won't voice that to him. If he doesn't tell her his secrets. She won't tell him hers. "Nothing."

She lets him go and drags herself back to the Earth Unit, where Rayon and Mira are. Rayon just said something, but Makeddah only hears Mira's response.

"I know him best," she says, "but I have no idea what that was about. Did you find out?" She turns to Makeddah.

"No," Makeddah says, and Mira sighs, then runs out.

Makeddah holds her hand to her chest. "I felt it again."

"Felt what?"

Makeddah had told Rayon about the first time she felt it, but Rayon was half asleep at that time, and she didn't really believe Makeddah then. "The chill and the heat. I felt it. Like the night I passed out."

"Oh. You think that's what it is?" Rayon asks, no sign of doubt in her voice this time.

Makeddah gazes up at her sister. "I know that's what it is." Rayon sits by Makeddah as Makeddah continues. "We need to figure out what *it* is."

Rayon nods. "Yeah, okay. After today. Let's just get through today." Rayon lays her head on Makeddah's shoulder. Rayon's right. They just need to get through today. But after that, Makeddah's doing everything in her power to figure this thing out.

Twenty-eight

lack is worn throughout the Guard. It seems like all of them are here now. It took twenty minutes for everyone to get above ground, and the silence was worse than the wait. But now that everyone is above ground, they are moving.

Matt wanted the ceremony similar to that of the witches. He said he thinks that would honor Grace and the baby best.

Aaron stands in front, his air bed holding Grace up. Matt and Mira are right behind him. Makeddah is on Mira's side holding fire up, and Rayon is on Matt's side holding up a glowing orb of white magic. It's sunset, but under the thick trees it seems like it is nightfall.

Makeddah watches Aaron set Grace down at a tree, where little slivers of sunset flow through the leaves. He steps aside, and Matt steps up setting a white rose on her chest. He gives her a kiss on her forehead and one on her stomach. When Matt takes a knee, Makeddah can see his body shaking. And while no sound escapes him, she knows he's crying as he places his head on her stomach.

Starting with Aaron, then Makeddah, Rayon, and Mira, everyone takes a knee. Three minutes of silence. Three very tear-jerking minutes. Three minutes to think about every little thing they could have done to save her life but didn't.

Three minutes to be completely immersed by her death, then give it up. Understand their guilt and shame, then let it go.

Kahlan steps up as everyone lifts their head. She throws herbs on Grace's body, like the witches at the Center did. Then others start putting flowers on her. Makeddah puts a large sunflower on her chest and a small one on her stomach. She steps back to let others say goodbye, then Kahlan signals her to do the rest.

Now, Makeddah comes up, and the body is covered in roses and daisies and tulips and sunflowers. Makeddah heats up her hands, fire courses at the tips of her fingers, she presses her fingers to Grace's body, and it starts flaming. The fire reaches the flowers, and Makeddah sees the most beautiful thing.

The fire turns into her body, like she *is* the fire. It shapes into the flowers, floating up to the sky, feet first and flowing up until it reaches to her head. The fire flowers go all the way to the top of the trees, and when Makeddah looks down again, Grace's body is no longer there, and it's time to let go.

"There is something I have to tell you all," Kahlan says.

The ceremony just ended, people are still crying, but Kahlan calls everyone to take a seat in the lobby.

Makeddah sits next to Rayon and Mira in the lobby as others find seats around them.

"I know this is a sorrowful time, losing one of our own. She was a wonderfully talented woman, who was pregnant with her first child. Great in the infirmary, and an even better teacher. She will be missed by many. But I do have good news to share." She nods at Makeddah and Makeddah goes still.

Now is not the time, Kahlan, she thinks as Kahlan goes on.

"I have been keeping a secret, a big one, and I'm sorry." She looks over the crowd, her eyes landing on no one person. "Haggard being gone will not leave the throne of Korzon empty. Right here in our midst we have the solution."

Mira wipes her face and looks up at Kahlan with puffy eyes. "What are you saying?" she asks. Makeddah didn't tell her, and now she'll hear from Kahlan.

"The Princess is here. Our new Queen." She looks at Makeddah. "Our very own Lion Heart Princess."

The room stills.

Makeddah closes her eyes against the silence, starting to shake. What are people thinking? Do they hate her for getting attention right now? Do they feel she doesn't deserve it? Do they care?

Rayon stands. Every eye goes to her, and though she's not showing it, Makeddah can tell she is taking it all in and loving it. "To the Lion Heart Princess."

Isaac is the next to stand. Then Matt. Then Mira. And Makeddah smiles when she sees Aaron, her earth teacher Preston, and a few people she doesn't really know stand.

She doesn't even know how others can praise her right now. She's done nothing to earn it. As soon as the smile comes, it leaves, and she finds herself standing and running off to her room. She tries to shut the door, but Rayon is right behind her. "I can't," she tells Rayon. "Let me be normal for a few more days. Please. Let me be sad and depressed, let me dwell on my thoughts. Let me not be the one to rule Korzon, because I can't."

She turns and finds she's facing Mira too, but Makeddah still looks at Rayon. "This is not going to be easy for me. You understand that?"

"Yeah, Mak, I do."

"I want to focus on the traitor and on my parents and on Grace. Not my multiple titles. *Please*." She looks down at her hand, where the nasty star-shaped scar lies. It is a reminder of her pain. Of her simplicity washing away. A reminder of mourning. She doesn't know how, but she knows it's there for that reason.

"I'm with you." Rayon grabs Makeddah's hand. "I promise." Rayon squeezes Makeddah's hand with a grin on her face. "I'm with you all the way."

Makeddah looks up into her sister's eyes again. No matter what happened in her past or what blood pumps through her veins, she will always be a Parish. She's lucky she can still say she has a family. She squeezes Rayon's hand back.

This is only the beginning.

Twenty-nine

Makeddah forces herself into a different thought process by focusing on her birthmark. She tries to concentrate, her head pounding, mingling the ache with her memories of Grace, who once cured her pain at the Guard. Her concentration slips. She can almost sense the air around her wavering as her thoughts scatter. Aaron catches her lapse, and tension fills the air.

"Why can't you just make a windstorm? You did the fire tunnel. I saw."

"Because Grace was a better teacher." But truthfully, she would be nowhere without air and him teaching her. Grace died, and that was because of Aaron. She shudders. "Are you sure you know nothing about the grey-eyed thing?"

"Makeddah, focus on the lesson."

"I can't." She slouches. "How can *you*? There is so much more going on."

"I can because I want you to take down Haggard," Aaron says, narrowing his eyes through his wire-rimmed glasses.

"Yeah. That's one thing you have to worry about. I have that, *and* the traitor, *and* being the Princess—and don't forget the Lion Heart thing. My adoptive great-grandmother is not waking up, my real mother is dead, and I found out I have a father who is *also* dead. The person whom I went to for headaches is dead."

She kicks the ground, then throws her hands in the air. "May I remind you that the King of Korzon is out to kill me for being the Princess who survived. I don't even know how that happened. It's not even my fault! Did he even *try* to kill me?"

"Probably."

"Well, there you have it. Maybe that's why everyone around me seems to be dying, because I was supposed to a long time ago. Now, they have to endure the pain while I live like nothing happened." She falls to the ground and sighs.

"I just need you to focus for a few minutes, okay? My way of mourning is to vent with my air. Maybe you should try it too." It sounds odd. He was sincere despite her having just yelled at him. Aaron glances at his watch. "Never mind, I have to go."

"Where?" Makeddah asks, suddenly disappointed. "I'd like to yell at you some more, please."

"I'd love to stay, believe it or not." He frowns at her. "But Isaac and I have a mission trip. We won't be back until Sunday. It will be easier to do with the ball going on." He starts packing up his papers from the wooden table she had set up for him after breakfast.

Makeddah is reminded of what Mira said about their mission trips. She wonders what Mira meant by their trips not truly being for missions. What does she think they do?

"Can I go?" Makeddah pleads. Maybe she could find out. "I need to work it out by being out."

"Funny." He slings his backpack over his shoulder. "You shouldn't be out in the village. Remember? Evil King out to kill you."

"Why will you guys be out there so long anyway?" Makeddah asks as he opens the door to the Unit. She runs up to the door. "It's only twelve hours there and back, right? Two days is plenty, but four whole days?" He continues to walk away, leaving her hanging out of the air unit door. "Fine, don't tell me. See you later!" she calls.

A single hand goes up in the air, him waving goodbye.

Makeddah watches the sliding doors open for Aaron as he leaves. Moments later, Mira enters through the same doors and quickly scolds him. After the scolding, she saunters straight to Makeddah.

Even with knowing all that personal stuff with Aaron and Mira, she's glad she can act like herself with them both. She is a bit more on Aaron's side, but she can't show that.

They both just had their heart ripped out, so she reminds herself to stay neutral.

Makeddah hops out of the Unit and shuts the door. "Hey, sorry to bother," Mira says.

"No, it's fine," Makeddah replies. Mira holds out a sheet of paper. Makeddah looks at the drawing of the most beautiful dress she's ever seen.

"How's this?"

"Beautiful," Makeddah says, observing its every detail. "You did this?"

"Yeah, it's one of my earlier designs. All it needs is an adjustment for you," Mira says. "I'll need your measurements; I already have Rayon's."

"What?" Makeddah looks up into Mira's eyes. "Wait, this is for me? Why? What is it for?" She looks at the dress. Too fancy to just walk around in.

"The ball," Mira says. "The one that Kahlan told us about yesterday before sending Grace." Makeddah stares blankly. "The one in the King's castle—or your castle, depending on how we're looking at it, right?"

It hadn't even clicked when Aaron mentioned the ball. Kahlan was talking about that yesterday, but Makeddah had been zoning out, her thoughts sinking back into memories of Grace. Thinking of her poor parents. Thinking of being the Princess.

She blinks, returning to the present. Studying Mira's busy hands, she asks, "Don't you think you should take a break from being so busy? You should slow down, Mira."

"No. The last thing I need is to slow down. I've decided that right now is my stage of denial, then in a week or so, I will have a complete breakdown and be depressed for twelve days, then try to start fresh, then break down again for three days. I need to mourn a whole year before I really get on my feet and do what Grace would want me to. I haven't decided what I want to do about the rest of the year just yet."

Makeddah nods, slightly lost.

"With my parents and brother, I went through a serious rebellious phase. Of course, then I found Grace... I'm not going to think about it now. Denial phase. I need that. So, come by my place later?"

"I don't know where it is," Makeddah realizes. She has known Mira for over three weeks, and she doesn't recall ever seeing her room.

"Rayon knows," Mira says.

"Okay, then yes." She takes another look at the dress design. "Aaron just said I shouldn't be in the village. Should I even be going?"

"Kahlan snatched four invitations, and it is your kingdom, so you should be one of the couples. Plus, Aaron doesn't know what he's talking about." Mira rolls her eyes. "Kahlan is going to use her magic and change your whole look, remember?"

Kahlan's name brings something to Makeddah's mind. "Oh, I almost forgot. I have to go." She starts walking off, then stops and looks back at Mira. "See you tonight."

Makeddah leaves Mira and makes her way from the Units down to the lobby. She told Kahlan last night that she wants to start searching through the files. She wants to help as much as she can while the traitor is still here. She still doesn't understand why they don't just take her; they've had plenty of opportunities. Why won't they get it over with? She wishes she could have all the answers now; she's strong enough for them.

Heading upstairs to Kahlan's office, Makeddah knocks on the door and discovers Isaac and Aaron inside. She notices they must be going through some files as well. She thought they were leaving already, but she didn't ask why they hadn't yet.

"I'm here for the records," Makeddah says after another glance at Aaron. "I think I should go through a few of them today."

"No." Isaac gives an unamusing laugh behind her. "It's no use. This person has done nothing but rat us out and kill. I don't know about you, but I don't want to be the next victim."

Makeddah almost can't believe it's coming out of his mouth.

"Then what do you say we do?" Makeddah crosses her arms. "Sit around? Do nothing?" Makeddah's gaze falls solely on Isaac. "Haggard is bringing so much pain to families. Killing mothers, changing fathers, taking money. He needs to be set straight. If they kill me, they will kill all of you."

This is the first time she's felt anger toward Isaac. It is stirring in her, and she wants to slap some sense into him.

His voice softens, "If they wanted to, why haven't they already?" He says what she was just thinking. And she can't help but agree, yet something still stirs in her when he says it. Something towards him.

He runs a hand through his hair. "They've lived here among us for who knows how long. They have trained with us and made friends with us. They have been keeping lies from us—"

"And what exactly have you been doing?" Makeddah asks, trying not to raise her voice. *It's Isaac,* she has to remind herself. And even now, his anger isn't toward her, but she takes it personally. She hates to show him just how vulnerable she is to the pain inside of her. "Last time I checked, the Guard was lying to me. *You* didn't tell me I was the Princess. *You* neglected to tell me I was a Lion Heart for fifteen years. Who knows what else you're keeping from us all?" Makeddah says.

"Okay, Makeddah, that is enough." Kahlan stands. "I understand you're upset—"

"Yes, I'm upset." Makeddah frowns. Her voice is low now, but deadly. "My parents are dead, and I didn't even know them. Haggard killed them, and you," Makeddah points to Isaac, "you just want me to sit around? Let him kill me, let him kill *you?* Like he did to my parents. No, I won't. I wish you people knew me by now."

Isaac looks hurt, but she doesn't care. Makeddah steps up to his chair. "Done with these? I'm sure I'd do a better job, anyway. You should just go on your trip." Makeddah gathers the files and drops them in the box. "The sooner you leave," she says as she picks up the box, "the better for the rest of us."

Makeddah walks out the door, fire working in her body. Why would Kahlan allow someone who doesn't even care to work on the files? *It's only Isaac, Mak.* What if Kahlan had let the traitor work on the files? *It's Isaac; he's not the traitor, Mak. Calm down.*

Calming down is hard when you're fuming. She paces her room, clenching her fists, trying to shake off her anger. She scolds herself silently. For every step she takes, frustration lingers. She knows she doesn't have what it takes to do this—to take Haggard down *and* be the Princess, *then* become Queen, all while pretending she doesn't feel lost. Still, she moves, hoping action will quiet her doubt.

She rubs her head as she slams the door to her room and stares at the palm of her right hand. So much going on in her head, and barely any time to think about it. She hears the knock on her door.

"Sunshine?"

With a deep breath, she opens the door and says, "I didn't mean it."

He looks behind him and puts a finger up, then slides into the room and shuts the door. "Be mad at me, be mad at me all you want. I killed the sorcerer, and I know you hated it." He grabs her chin and makes her look up to him. "Makeddah, I really like you, and if you need your anger to be pointed toward me, I get it, but please know that I would never do anything to hurt you."

She looks into his twinkly blue eyes, and she knows he's not lying; he is sincere. "I am mad," is all she says before he pulls her into a hug. She lets go of the anger and hugs him tight.

He pulls away and kisses her on the cheek, and she blushes. Her whole body is crawling with goosebumps and bubbles. "I'll see you soon, Sunshine." He escapes through the door, and all that's left is her, the files, and her thoughts.

Thirty

Having all the files in hand, Makeddah and Rayon head down to Mira's room, which Makeddah soon finds out is not a room but a small house. Rayon calls it an apartment. "It's like a cottage but a part of a building." Rayon knocks.

The door opens. Mira smiles—Yep, she's in full denial. "Welcome to my place. Come in." Makeddah walks in first, amazed by how accurate Rayon is. It has a kitchen with a hearth, cooler, and water basin. The counters are a white slab, and the cabinets are a deep mahogany.

It's surprisingly very clean, but for a few papers and three sets of keys on the counter.

"You can set that down there." Mira points to the raised bar counter.

Makeddah sets the files down and glances around. The floors are the same white tile as Makeddah's room. However, she has a small living room with a sofa and a few mannequins. There are four doors. Four bedrooms.

"Nope, only three," Rayon says as if reading Makeddah's mind. Makeddah peers at her and Rayon grins. "I could just tell you were thinking it."

"Whose are these?" Makeddah asks, picking up the extra keys.

"Matt's and Grace's," Mira says, sitting on a stool at the counter. "That's their room." She points to the door on the west wall. Makeddah stares at the door. That's when Makeddah notices the two hooks next to the door, one with a bow and one with a bag of arrows hanging on it.

This whole time, she has known all three of them; she never knew they lived together.

Mira hops down from her stool. "Come here, I need to measure you."

Makeddah walks over, pointing at the door. "How long have you lived with them?" She stands motionless, still staring.

Mira pushes Makeddah's arms for her to lift them. Makeddah complies, and Mira starts at her bust. "Well, I first lived with Grace while she dated Matt for two years. Then she and Matt were married, and I lived with them for three years. Now I just live with Matt." Mira looks over her shoulder and shouts. "Who needs to clean the dishes!"

She holds a pencil in her mouth and measures Makeddah's bust again. "Thirty-one," she says as she writes on the paper. Next, she goes for her waist.

The door to Matt's room swings open, and Matt leans on its frame, evidently having heard Mira comment about the dishes. "If you could leave me alone for just one day,"

"No," Mira says through the pencil. "Twenty-eight." She talks again as she writes on the paper.

"I don't care if you are going through a denial phase. I'm not. I'm actually confronting my ghosts." Matt says and Makeddah glances up and sees he is in a regular nightshirt and plaid night pants. Inside his room, it is dark.

Makeddah's not sure if it's just because of the circumstances or not, but she feels as if his beard has grown, and it has barely been two days.

"Well, at least I came up with a plan of grief and don't deny the things that I still need to do." Mira folds her arms at him, but her voice softens. "Gracie wouldn't want you like this."

"Gracie would at least give me a week!" Matt yells, but it's not out of rage. He's yelling a fact. "You know what?" He rubs his temple. "I can't deal with you right now, Mira. Not you and not your insanity." He slams his door.

"Very mature, Matthew."

"Shut up," he shouts on the other side of the door.

Makeddah almost laughs at how much they seem like siblings. Many girls were like that at the Center, and probably still are. But Mira has never referred to Matt as a brother, only Grace as a sister. She wonders if Grace had to deal with this all the time.

Mira narrows her eyes at the slammed door, then turns around and puts the measuring tape around Makeddah's hips. "Feet out slightly." Makeddah spreads. "Thirty-four," she writes down on the paper. "Perfect." She scribbles something out. "Okay, let me just see the arms, and then we can work on the traitor files. Oh, actually, Rayon, I lost your waist and hip measurement."

Rayon smiles, "Thirty-seven and forty, respectively."

Mira mumbles something and writes it down on another paper.

"How is the whole grief process working for you, by the way?" Rayon asks. "The denial stage?"

"It's wonderful. Still have six more blissful days of hard work." Mira writes down a few things after measuring Makeddah's arms. "And happiness."

Mira hops on the stool. Makeddah is impressed by how well she is playing the part. Denial is not an easy thing when something is weighing heavily on your heart. But it can also be the easiest thing in the world, if you just let it be. And maybe that's what she's doing—letting it be.

Makeddah can't imagine it. Maybe denial is not an option for her, but it's the only thing Mira has. Makeddah wishes that she could just smile right now and save her grief for some future, preplanned-out time. But most of the time, planning ahead doesn't work; things just happen. Mainly because her body does what it wants.

"I wish I could go with you guys. A ball sounds like so much fun," Mira says. "Matt and Preston will be attending with you both. The sorcerer who knew Matt is gone, so he's safe to go into the village. We think he'll have the best shot at investigating the castle grounds."

Preston, Makeddah's earth teacher, and the legend that won the first fight night. He is very different from the other men she's met. He's almost like Aaron in the way that he is a man of few words, but he speaks when he wants to. He's like Matt in the way that he's humble about his talent. He's like Isaac in the way that he's sweet and funny. But he's a different kind of funny, more like a quiet funny.

"Oooohh, like they'll be on our arm?" Rayon says. "How exciting."

"Yeah, Kahlan wanted Isaac and Aaron to do it, but they took a last-minute mission trip, and Matt volunteered. Good thing, cause Aaron would have been insufferable."

Rayon sighs, "Oh, come on, you liked him so much. There were good things about him."

"Maybe," she says.

"So are you just going to hate on him from here on out?" Rayon crosses her arms.

"Yes," Mira says with her nose up. "Cause he deserves that."

"He doesn't talk about you like that," Makeddah says, and now she feels like she should have shut up. "But to each their own."

Mira grabs a banana from the fruit basket. She peels it open and eats it. "Yeah, he should have bad things to say about me. His fault for not voicing them." She says with a full mouth. "I'll take a third of the files."

She finishes her banana and then retrieves her files, plops onto the fluffy white rug on the floor. Makeddah takes some files and goes to the sofa. Rayon goes through the cooler and grabs a bowl of leftover chili. "Thought you were a vegetarian."

"Matt's," Mira calls without looking up. "Bread is in the pantry."

And so, Rayon warms the chili and bread, and she sits at the bar and looks over her files.

Makeddah gets the A's. Mira gets the B's, and Rayon grabs the C's.

Makeddah sees the first A as Aaron. She holds up a printed copy he made of hers and Rayon's actions of the day and looks at the trips he took out of the ghoster, but Makeddah knows he isn't the traitor. Not only does she not believe he could do something like that, but his ghoster trips were two the day they found Nadine, and that doesn't match with the traitor's activities.

She immediately moves on. The next few files show no evidence of scheming. She came across only one that seemed suspicious, but it was discounted because it was a group of people who had gone out to spend a birthday together outside.

Curious after seeing Aaron's, she grabs the I bin and looks through those. In big letters it says, *Isaac.* He also didn't do it. He hadn't even left the ghoster except for with Aaron the night before. But did they go after Makeddah

passed out or before? The timestamps indicate 6:30 and
7:00, during dinner. Makeddah remembers. They left and
came back with some fresh raw meat for the kitchen, which
many people had grimaced at, and Mira looked away, saying
"la, la, la" the whole time.

It is obviously not them.

Makeddah feels more files fall onto her lap. Rayon
smiles down. "You've got J's." She hadn't noticed Rayon
left and come back with two more file boxes.

Makeddah groans. "Did you find anything yet?"

"No but still worth a try looking through more." Mira
says.

"And aren't you the one who wanted to do this in the
first place?" Rayon says, somehow popping more food in
her mouth. "We're only doing this for you, Mak."

"I know." Makeddah pulls some more files open. She
feels like a hypocrite getting frustrated after yelling at Isaac.
"I know."

Makeddah sits down in Kahlan's office. Mira has her dress
all ready for the ball tomorrow. They've found nothing
about the traitor, which only upsets Makeddah. She's been
working so hard. She's been trying to get all her elements in
order, making sure that she's working twice as hard as she
was before. That's going well enough.

She's been training physically by herself. That's not as
good. She misses Matt. He's been holding up in his room
the past two days. She wants to talk to him about the chill
and the scar on her hand, but she also wants to give him
time to process.

He's here now, but it's still not the right time. He barely
seems here for the meeting. He sits on the right of her in

Kahlan's office, Rayon on her left, and Makeddah's earth teacher, Preston, next to Rayon.

"The ball is tomorrow. I hope you are prepared," Kahlan says, looking only at Makeddah, then her gaze averts to Matt. "Matt, are you sure it's not too much?"

"Yes, I'm sure."

"Okay, then there is a slight change in plan." Kahlan slides a paper down the long table using magic.

"Masquerade?" Rayon recites from it. Rayon smiles up at Makeddah. "A really good change in plan."

"Yes. It's good. But remember, royalty, Guards, sorcerers—many people will be there. Mostly the rich people of Korzon who suck up to Haggard."

Makeddah sighs, "Why am I going?" She doesn't want to sound like a brat, but she still doesn't get it.

Kahlan nods, "Makeddah, I fear I have kept you up here for too long, and we have hidden you when we should have been showing that you are here. We need to show Haggard *and* the traitor that you are ready for the fight."

Rayon gasps, "She's revealing herself?"

Kahlan looks at Makeddah, "Yes, unless you are uncomfortable with that."

"Um," Makeddah feels a weight in her chest, "I don't know."

Kahlan smiles, "It's okay, you choose what you want to do. The main point of this trip is to find Haggard's weak points and see what we are up against. None of us has been near him in a long time."

"Intelligence gathering," Matt says. He nods off to the side and rubs his eyes. "We can do that."

"I hope you're all ready."

Makeddah looks at Matt's somber face. She hopes so, too.

Thirty-one

Makeddah wishes the beasts pulling her carriage would stop jolting it. Still, she's glad to be inside, feeling as if she's traveling the world—free from the Guard, from the Center, free to be herself.

She grasps two parts of freedom, but the last always eludes her. How is she supposed to truly be herself, surrounded by a kingdom of watchful strangers? The masquerade means no disguise forced by Kahlan, but she still doesn't recognize herself. Rayon can slip into roles and elegance under pressure—while Makeddah feels unsteady, uncertain which face she wears tonight.

Rayon drilled her in elegant manners that never sit right, each lesson grating against Makeddah's instincts. Every forced phrase or question leaves her resentful of the act. She worries about blending in, about being invisible. Yet, the most important people she's meant to find are total unknown—faces, clothes, even behaviors are a mystery to her.

Her dress looks incredible. That isn't the problem. Well, it may be. What if it's *too* beautiful? It's not as if she can just go out and change, can she?

Makeddah glances at Rayon, who is as beautiful as ever in a big, red skirt and the corset has a slight V-cut with puffy sleeves. Makeddah's own black lace dress fits modestly up to her collarbone, with long sleeves. She wears a thick shawl to hide her glowing birthmark.

Her hair is up in a bun, and brown paint is on her lips. She glances at Rayon, noting the deep red color on Rayon's lips that complement her blue eyes. Makeddah stares at the carriage wall. She reaches out, meaning to touch the wall for reassurance, but her hand moves toward her mouth instead. She stops herself, grimacing at the unpleasant taste of her polish.

"You'll be fine."

Makeddah looks up at Preston. His smile is as calm and effortless as could be. He and Matt look nice, in dark suits with white button-up shirts and sashes. They look like two completely different men, though. Preston has a dark complexion, dark green eyes, and wears glasses. He almost reminds Makeddah of the earth. His skin is the color of mud, his eyes the color of healthy grass. Scruffy, calm, and laid back, yet in control and sweet. He seems much more mature than nineteen, more like sixty.

Makeddah wrings her hands. "I'm going to get all clammy."

Preston slowly shakes his head. He's not a fast talker. It takes him a while to respond with, "Don't worry about anything. You will do just fine."

Makeddah looks over to Matt, who is sitting next to her. He doesn't say anything as he looks out the small window.

But minutes later, when Makeddah hears the carriage wheels hit stone, Matt finally looks up and says, "We're here."

Makeddah knows they've arrived as the carriage slows. She hears laughter and shouting outside. The carriage turns before stopping.

Matt and Preston step out, offering their hands to Makeddah and Rayon.

Rayon reaches for Preston's hand first as she steps carefully down from the carriage. Makeddah puts her gloved hand out to Matt, starts to stand, but then turns back to her seat. She almost forgot her mask. She quickly puts the white mask over her eyes and it sits just above her nose, then accepts Matt's hand. Stepping down from the carriage, she steadies herself, still a little intimidated by the small heel she's wearing.

She looks up at the big castle, and her breathing slows. This was supposed to be her home. This was supposed to be where she grew up. It is beautiful and ugly all at the same time. It could have been beautiful forever if not for the rule of an evil man.

She sees many people waiting outside. No one has opened the door yet, and the bridge is roped off.

Two pillars on the castle's far sides remind her of a picture from Rayon's book. The huge wooden door towers above. Beyond the castle's perimeter, stone ground gives way to forest outside the surrounding moat.

Carriages depart behind her. Vendors approach guests, hoping to make sales. Makeddah grimaces as some are dismissed by the wealthy, their clothes and attitudes making social lines clear.

She puts her hand up to her mouth, not to chew her fingers, but to stop from saying something. Would she have been just like these people? She really hopes not.

"You okay?" Makeddah looks up at Matt's question.

Is she?

The big wooden doors open, and trumpets sound to welcome the guests. "As I'll ever be?"

Matt shakes his head. "Sounds like a question."

"It is," Makeddah says. She sees Haggard has guards stationed in front of the castle, and she asks, "Haggard has guards?"

Matt shrugs, "We call them bodyguards because they are only big and brawny to keep the villagers out."

Rayon hears this and pipes in, voicing Makeddah's question. "What about his sorcerers?"

"He likes them close by his side, I'm guessing," Matt says.

He puts on his half mask and offers his arm. Makeddah places her hand in the crease of his elbow, nodding. "I think I'm ready," she breathes.

He nods. "Then let's invade your first home."

Makeddah hears trumpets, over and over. Names are being called as people enter. "The rich people who mainly live in the city, just a few miles from here. They don't come to the village just for fun; they come for this." Matt explains. "If they need anything on any other day, they'll send their servants. But they have enough in their city."

As they move through the courtyard in front of Rayon and Preston, Makeddah notices there are no plants or flowers. It looks dull and lifeless. There is a ripped flag above the door everyone is walking through. Makeddah can tell it is the Kingdom's emblem. But can only see parts of two swords, the tree and half of the wind symbol.

Haggard ruined everything her parents built.

"There used to be a fountain there," Rayon whispers back to Makeddah, pointing at the place where a rug is covering the ground. "It was broken when Haggard invaded. I guess he never refurbished it."

"Oh." Makeddah nods and waits for her turn to walk into the room; she doesn't really want a history lesson on the night Haggard became King.

When they arrive at the ballroom, in the back of the room, she sees a large chair and two smaller chairs on either side of it. The thrones for Haggard and his children.

Makeddah hopes his children will be here. Perhaps they could speak with one of them. Rayon says they don't live in the castle, but Haggard makes them go to big events. No one even knows their real names, something their mother wanted for them.

Rayon and Preston immediately separate as they enter, with Rayon heading for the snack table. Makeddah hesitates, gripping Matt's arm tightly instead of letting go. She squeezes so hard that Matt glares at her and mutters, "Ow."

She clears her throat and releases her hold.

Makeddah's nerves spike—she sees all the fluffy dresses and anxiety twists inside her. Did she miss something? Is her birthmark shining through? Should she approach others, or will that just make her stand out more?

Watching Rayon move easily through the crowd makes Makeddah feel like she's at the starting line, unsure what race she's running.

Matt raises his brow. "I'll go talk to her." He nods his head at a plump woman who's looking around the room reprovingly. "Maybe she'll have some gossip." He searches the room. "You start with him." He points to a man at the end of the snack table to the left. "Then I'll try to sneak out and find out where he keeps his documents. I'll try to find his weak spots and see how many sorcerers he may have. He's bound to have bragged to someone about it. You start spreading rumors about the Guard. We need people to start telling us stuff about this traitor.”

“Okay. I can do that.” Makeddah stands straighter and injects some poise into her steps. She spots her target at the snack table. He is standing there eating a cracker with fish and cream on top. She glides over to his spot and pours herself some of the red stuff in a bottle. She sips it, and all poise is lost when she coughs.

“That’s terrible.” She looks at the glass like it’s a rat she’s just caught.

“It is, isn’t it?” Makeddah looks up at the man, but she can’t tell how old he is because of his mask. It covers his hair and most of his face. It’s white, but has streams of black running through it, giving it a cracked appearance. He clears his throat. “It’s very expensive.” His voice is deep like a man’s, yet it seems he is hiding his true identity. “It has the worst side effects. More horrible than the taste.”

Makeddah remembers Rayon’s lesson on etiquette for these things. She twirls a piece of her hair, then leans against the table. “I can’t even imagine that.” But she stands from the table after realizing how this might look. *Too seductive!* She thinks to herself.

“Yes,” he nods. “It’s called being drunk.”

Makeddah puts a hand to her mouth. “Is that wine?” She whispers to him. “Oh. I hope my sister doesn’t drink any.”

Makeddah can’t tell if a smile is rising on his face, but he does chuckle. She offers her hand. “I’m, um, Lady Brooke.”

“Lady Brooke?” He nods but doesn’t give his name. “Lady Brooke, would you like to dance?”

“I don’t dance. I don’t like music,” she says, waving at the instrumental players as if they were playing something boring and unamusing. “But I do like to talk. Do you?”

He takes her hand before she can refuse, and she forces a nervous laugh, masking discomfort. Did she give permission for this? She scolds herself—she came for information, not to get distracted. She steels herself against the unfamiliar flutter in her chest, reminding herself of the real purpose that brought her here. There's no room for softness, not with Isaac still so close in her mind.

She puts her hand in his, and they sway to the sound of the music. "What would you like to talk about, Lady Brooke?"

"Just a scandalous thing." She tries her best gossipy-girl voice she can. "Have you heard of the place called the Guard?"

"I don't think I have," he dismisses it quickly. "Now, let me twirl you."

"I don't twirl like a Princess." She says plainly.

"But you are, aren't you?"

Makeddah stops, but he doesn't. She is forced to dance along. She says, "I don't under—"

"Did you know, even real Queens and Princesses don't feel like they are on a day-to-day basis. Every woman here tonight has the right to feel like a Princess." He dips down to her ear. "To feel beautiful."

"And you give them that right? Seems a bit demeaning if you ask me." This feels wrong, and she wants to get out of this guy's arms as soon as she can.

His mask makes her even more suspicious of him. He is hiding more than his identity.

"I don't give them that right; they give themselves the right. And I'm sure you haven't, yet." He says, "I'm going to twirl you now."

"No."

"Fine, I'll find another woman to twirl." He starts to walk away.

"No, wait." Makeddah grabs his arm. *Only because I need to talk to him about the Guard,* she tells herself. *Nothing more.*

Especially not to be spun. "But I guess you will have to spin me, huh?"

"I guess so."

She whirls under his arm twice, and he dips her. Not even a second later, he pulls her up, meeting her eye to eye. But she looks away before any real contact happens. "What is your name anyway?"

"Prince 1. Since I'm the first son. Prince 2," He nudges his head to a tall and broad man standing alone in a corner. "Is having the time of his life if you can't tell. You know, my father often forgets—"

"Wait, Prince?" Makeddah chokes.

"Yes, and I am betting you are not a richy rich city girl."

"I am…" Makeddah says. "Something like that."

"Really? My father wouldn't invite anyone less than a richy rich, but you're something like that? Are you a maid? And if not, then honestly, I could only think that maybe you're some kind of help. So, Lady Brooke, who are you, really?"

Makeddah pulls herself away from the dance and does something so unlike herself, she flips her hair and puts her hand on her hip. "Well, Prince 1, I believe I am a Princess by your standard." She turns on her heel, almost falling. At this point, she glides away, feeling the sway of her hips as she walks. But soon she believes that it must look utterly ridiculous, so she stops.

She will never tell Rayon what she did, but she liked it.

The Prince. She almost slandered the King in front of the Prince.

As a waiter walks by, she points to a glass. "Is that alcoholic?" The waiter shakes his head. "Sugar?" He shrugs. Makeddah takes the glass and gulps it down. Very sugary. Just the spike she needed. "Thanks."

She watches as the Prince starts to walk her way, but the plump woman Preston was talking to pulls him into a dance. Makeddah laughs as the woman moves him all around the dance floor. She grabs water from another tray as she walks by and sips, looking around the room for another person to interrogate.

She looks around for Matt, but he must be gathering the info from Haggard's files because she can't spot him.

She sighs and brings her finger to her mouth, but remembering the glove, she shakes her head, turning to walk away from the table. An arm grabs her before she can take her first step.

"Leaving already?" Makeddah turns and finds herself in front of the only unmasked man in the room.

Haggard.

Thirty-two

He looks exactly like the portrait Kahlan showed them but he aged. He has a few more lines on his face and greys run through his dirty blonde hair and beard.

The room goes silent when he speaks. Everyone must be thinking the crown on his head screams, "I ripped this crown from the rightful King's head." Or maybe that's just her.

He's wearing a long red and black robe. His outfit consists of several items that Makeddah doesn't know the names of, and she doesn't believe that a shirt, pants, or accessories would do the items justice.

A sudden confidence goes through her, one that she has never felt before. "King Haggard." She smiles, then shakes her head. "Why, what an awful name."

He only laughs.

Makeddah smells alcohol on his breath. She silently vows never to drink it; it will only remind her of him. Her smile is gone now.

"It is quite a name, though, is it not?" He's pudgier than Makeddah would have thought. But he *is* handsome, very handsome. The look of pride and accomplishment on his face makes her want to throw up. And now, she wants to take the thought back. He's not handsome. He's hideous.

She looks out at the crowd. They are no longer dancing. Everyone is staring at Haggard. Everyone is staring at her. Makeddah feels the weight of their stares like bricks being thrown onto her chest. But she notices that six people aren't staring.

One is Rayon, who is dancing with a man… no, *the other Prince*. She is dancing with Prince 2. Prince 1 is back at the snack table, but he *is* staring.

Makeddah feels Haggard's hand on the small of her back, and she tries hard not to throw it off her and walk away. Like father, like son. Both do things without permission.

"Let's dance."

"I've had my fair share of royalty tonight, thank you." She grimaces.

"Well, I've chosen you for my first dance of the night. I think you'd like to take it." She doesn't answer, so he sings, "Everyone is *staring*." Makeddah scoffs. As if she cares. They will stare anyway. "And I have no shame in taking your life if you don't." He gives her a small push on the back, and the crowd parts as they walk to the dance floor.

They land in the center, next to Rayon.

Rayon is oblivious until she notices Makeddah and makes a puking motion. Makeddah feels him hold her hand and swing around to the front of her. He lays his other hand on her waist.

She doesn't react.

She doesn't like the feel of this. She hates it. It is almost as if the motions are happening to her, not with her.

The music shifts from happy to slow and soulful in an instant. When Makeddah puts her hand on his shoulder, she realizes it isn't fat that makes him look pudgy, it's armor under the clothes he's wearing.

"Where's your wife, Haggard? Why should she not be your first dance?"

"That old news?" He laughs. "I've made sure I will never see her again."

"You don't want your children to have a mother?"

Haggard laughs, "Correction. I don't want to have a wife. She ties me down." He pauses, and a tension grows between the two. "I know who you are," Haggard says as he sways.

"You do?" Why is Makeddah not nervous? She should be nervous. Yet, speaking to him gives her confidence. Or is it because her sister is right next to her and she can feel *her* confidence, which makes Makeddah feel ten times better? "How wonderful for you."

"Mm, and to think of all these years of the Princess being silent." Haggard shakes his head. "I heard your whole Guard is afraid of a traitor." Haggard smiles big and broad.

"Yes, all but one, I suppose?"

"Or two." He steps back and twirls her twice.

Makeddah doesn't think about his last comment, but she stores it for later. "You want to kill me. Don't you?" Makeddah asks him as she comes back from the twirl. "You never wanted your sorcerers to do it. You want me to be killed at your hand. Just like my parents."

"No, no, no." He swats this away, "You see, you are very special. I would like to keep you for other things," he says in a devilish tone, but he doesn't look at her with lust. It seems he says it with envy and pride at the same time. And Makeddah knows his desire as soon as he says, "To show that not even the Lion Heart Princess can defeat me."

"I think," Makeddah says, "you're going to be sorry once you see I won't be your slave. Once you see I am stronger than you could ever be. I will not be your trophy."

"I hear your friend Grace died. How many tears have you cried?"

The smile on Makeddah's face rises just to taunt him. "Oh, Haggard, tears don't make you weak. I pity you for not knowing that. You know what a weakness is? Ego. Which, it seems, you have enough of." Makeddah rolls her eyes. "I don't know why you don't respect me more; you wouldn't even have a kingdom if it weren't for my family."

"Is that so?"

She nods. "Yes, you wouldn't be rich. You wouldn't have something to brag about." She raises a brow. "You'd still be dead inside, of course, but that's neither here nor there."

"As dead as your parents?"

Makeddah freezes, fire coursing through her body. She pushes him away from her and slaps him. "Something I should have done the instant I set my eyes on your ugly face." She spits at him, wipes her face, rips her mask off, and throws it at him.

He knows who she is, she should be able to tell the world.

Makeddah walks up to the stunned Rayon and grabs her arm. She walks out of the room calmly and without a trace of fear. She doesn't know why Haggard lets her, but she does not care what that vile man is thinking.

She stomps out to the village, only to see she is being followed by the whole party. Every eye is on her, which, for the first time, is what she wants.

"Hello everyone!" Makeddah shouts. People start turning to look at her, and the silence is palpable. You can hear the crickets chirping. "I am so sorry about the hurt this man puts you all through. Acting as if he is higher than you, killing your families, taking your money. But I promise you, soon we will take him down. Soon, no one will be afraid of him. But I need you all to start *now*."

Makeddah turns around to find Haggard standing there, his mouth in a tight line, and his sons behind him. "Because he is just a man. But you," Makeddah swings back to the villagers. People start coming from their carts, looking up from their work, and even a few gather from their homes. "You are not just people. You are *my* people."

She spots the confused faces, and fire runs through her veins. "I am Princess Makeddah Brooke." She finally says and gasps erupt. "I feel your strength. Show it. You've endured him this long; now it's time to fight back."

She turns back to Haggard. "Have fun, King." She smiles. "Because the Princess has spoken."

As if on cue, Rayon makes them both disappear.

Makeddah falls to the ground. She looks up and around. They're under the veil of the Guard. She stands and wipes her knees. She looks wide-eyed at Rayon. "I'm shaking." Makeddah holds her hand out. She's shaking so badly that Rayon has to stop it.

"But that was awesome," her sister giggles, looking at Makeddah as if she were some warrior hero. Rayon smirks. "And to think, you were just the magicless girl in a Witch Center. Now you are the girl who slapped Haggard, and spit in his face, and told everyone in the village to be brave enough to do the same." She stands back, folding her arms. A smile spreads across her lips, and she shakes her head at Makeddah. "How's that for special?"

Makeddah is still shaking, but now she feels like anything is possible.

Thirty-three

The whole world still seems out of place, but some-how, she feels better. Like it will mend in time. She actually slept like a baby after Preston and Matt got back safely. And she had no nightmares. None.

She's been battling these nightmares every single night for days, weeks even, but they disappeared last night. That weight on her chest was lifted, and she felt comfortable for the first time.

So when Makeddah and Rayon walk into the lobby to get breakfast, Makeddah moves lightly, her mood lifted. While Rayon is practically buzzing, still fueled by adrenaline.

"You should have seen my sister." Rayon sits down at the table next to Mira. "She danced with the Prince and—"

Rayon whispers, "from what she tells me, he was quite smitten with her. Prince 2 was smitten with me, of course."

"You guys got to talk to the Princes?" Mira's voice drips with awe. "Ugh, Matt said that nothing much happened, just that he found some promising files of Haggards, then he moped in his room. I really wanted to go." She moves the potatoes around on her plate.

"It's not really all that," Makeddah says, though she's still full of excitement, and she's not sure if it's from slapping Haggard or accepting who she is. "What are their real names anyway?" Makeddah asks as she picks up her mother's book. She's read the whole thing but still carries it around like she's holding a piece of her mother.

"It's a rule not to reveal a royal baby's name until the age of one in Korzon, but the mother didn't want them to give their names out at all. They were already two by that time." Makeddah knows that part. "And when Haggard did something to her, the sons decided to keep their mother's wish. They don't even leave the kingdom."

She didn't know that. Makeddah asks, "Did something to their mother? Like killed her?"

Haggard said he would never see her again, but Makeddah didn't read into what that meant. Now she wonders if he killed his own wife.

Mira shrugs, "When I was still living in the village, he said that he had a sorcerer send her to prison. He basically keeps his sons in prison, too, never leaving their place."

Rayon looks up, "I thought they didn't live in the kingdom?"

Mira shakes her head, "They do, they just never leave and only show their faces for big events like yesterday. I always wondered if they are like their father or if they hate him."

It must be so terrible to have a father like that. If they are like him, it must be because he raised them that way.

They have no choice like the sorcerers.

And if they aren't like him, they are living in their own personal hell. Even though the Prince didn't seem to be all that upset about it, Makeddah would hate to be in the Prince's shoes. He probably doesn't even care, which makes her feel sick.

People walking through the ghoster catch Makeddah's attention. She turns her head and spots Isaac and Aaron entering, accompanied by a small boy and a tall woman. She realizes they must have found some new recruits for the Guard. Now the high of last night is even better today.

Mira stands and walks directly to the boy and his mother, ushering them gently away from Isaac and Aaron. Meanwhile, Makeddah looks up to meet Isaac's gaze. Isaac looks directly into Makeddah's eyes and smiles warmly at her. Despite their earlier disagreement, he still finds a way to make her feel welcome. Aaron attempts to speak to Isaac, but Isaac instead walks over to join Makeddah's table.

"How was the ball?"

"It was fine," Makeddah says. "I thought you guys would be gone for two more days?"

Isaac shrugs, "Well, the village went a little crazy after last night, so we didn't want to stay out for too long. We decided to come back. I didn't see what happened, but we heard about it through some villagers. I want to hear it from you."

Makeddah sighs, "Kahlan told me to reveal myself if I felt comfortable, so I did. It's not a big deal."

"She's being modest. She was incredible." Rayon explains the whole thing, but Isaac watches Makeddah the whole time as if she is the one telling the story. Makeddah instantly feels she should have kept her hair down this morning. That she should have put some of that lipstick on. She should really do something with her awkward hands because them fumbling on the table makes her look nervous.

She looks down at them and swallows, then moves her hands below the table. Oh no, slouching. She's definitely slouching. Should she sit straighter? Makeddah follows her thoughts and sits straighter, but she feels so awkward that she has to slouch again.

"Wow, Sunshine," Isaac says. "Seems you will really make a difference?"

"No." Makeddah shakes her head. "But you have definitely made a difference for that boy and his mom."

"We hope." Isaac glances at Aaron. His blue eyes land back on her, and she sees something in them, something she can't describe, but it makes her feel uneasy. "But you, that's the whole village you are talking about, I'm serious."

Aaron huffs. "It's not really that much of a difference if Haggard is still on the throne, don't you think?" Makeddah looks up at Aaron and glares. "Just saying."

She knows he's right. "Well, we need to start working on that plan. The plan was to outsmart him. I think we can do it. He doesn't seem *that* intelligent."

And as she says it, Makeddah feels a chill down her spine.

She inhales and looks around the room, but no grey eyes. She can feel it's close because the ice rolls down her spine; it makes her shiver. Her breath shows up in the air, as if the room around her is turning cold.

Rayon stares at her. "What the heck?" Rayon blows out, but her breath doesn't condense.

"It's here." Makeddah says.

Makeddah quickly scans the room, then stands up and heads to the hallway. She senses footsteps following her, but keeps her focus ahead, not turning around. Behind her, she can hear Rayon, Isaac, and Aaron following closely.

"What's here, Makeddah?" It's Isaac asking.

Makeddah pushes into her room, and a sudden heat passes over her. Her sweat glands open, and she feels it start to pour down her body. "The thing with grey eyes. I know it's here. I feel it."

"Mak, gross, you're sweating like a pig."

Makeddah grimaces at Rayon. "I can't help it. Why are you guys not sweating? Do you not feel this heat?" She fans herself, and then it's gone. The heat and the cold. It's gone. It's like it stays only for a minute, then it leaves.

"What thing with grey eyes?" Isaac asks, the only one lost in the conversation.

"This isn't going to work," Makeddah says and rubs her head. "This traitor is not going to keep staying here. I'm done with them." Makeddah looks Aaron in the eye. "They're the reason that thing is here, I know it."

Aaron shakes his head. "But I don't have the answer, Makeddah."

"I know that," Makeddah says as Rayon hands her a cloth. Makeddah takes it without thinking. She rubs her face and arms and throws it to the side. "I need your guys' help. We've got to get this thing out of here before more people get hurt."

"Okay," Isaac says, "But *I* need to know what we're talking about."

"Hold on." Rayon puts her hand up. She says something, then an image of Belle appears. Makeddah runs over and stares at Belle over Rayon's shoulder. "Belle, what's going on?" Rayon and Makeddah glance at each other. Both are thinking the same thing.

Belle wipes her head where there are little beads of sweat. "Rayon, Makeddah, Mother Lianne is awake." Belle laughs. "You guys need to come. Hurry, she really wants to see you."

"Really?" Makeddah smiles at Rayon, then looks to the guys, "Um, Aaron, fill Isaac in. Do all you can to figure it out, please." Makeddah looks at Rayon. "We need to go."

"We have to tell Kahlan." Rayon runs a hand through her hair.

"We can!" Isaac says. "Just go."

Rayon grabs Makeddah's hand, and they rush to the ghoster together. Makeddah reaches for her key, locates it, and presses the button. They emerge above ground, then vanish again as the ghoster activates.

When they appear in the cottage, Belle runs into a tripping Makeddah, and they both straighten themselves up before Makeddah says, "How long has she been awake?"

"Well, she's been awake since…" Belle counts in the air. "Ten minutes. Ten minutes she's been awake." She wipes her hands on a towel to remove the dirt she had on them. "We need to get to the infirmary." She grabs a bag Makeddah hadn't seen from the table.

"Did you get some clothes?" Makeddah asks.

Belle bobs her head. "Yeah."

"Some water?" Rayon asks this time.

"Yes. I've got a toothbrush, clothes, shoes, a hairbrush, and her glasses." Belle adds proudly, "I've got it, guys. I've got everything down. I'm taking care of every single thing."

"That's a lot to take care of." Makeddah says, doubting.

"I realized that. And I told you both that I would take care of her." Belle smiles her sweet smile. "So, while I wasn't blowing up stuff in training, I was there. This is me taking care of her. I know what to do." Belle runs, and Rayon and Makeddah follow without hesitation.

They hurry through the infirmary, heading to the back room that Makeddah remembers from the previous week. As they approach the door, Makeddah comes to a halt. Rayon and Belle rush ahead inside, but Makeddah pauses, her eyes lifting to meet Alda's across the room.

She's crying in the corner. Makeddah furrows her brow and shakes her head as she walks to Mother Lianne's bedside. Mother Lianne smiles at the three of them and reaches out to hold Belle's arm.

"You girls are so beautiful," Mother Lianne says in a shaky voice.

Makeddah's frown goes away. "You're awake." She sits on her bed. "I'm so happy you're awake. Rayon and I have so much to tell you. Half of it, you probably already know, but I'm so happy you're awake."

"Shhhh." Mother Lianne's finger goes to her lips. "I need you girls to listen to me, okay. I won't be awake for long."

"What are you talking about?" Rayon asks, and Makeddah flashes back to when Grace died. The way she woke up and, a second later, fell asleep again.

Permanently.

"Why won't you be awake much longer?" Belle asks.

Makeddah can't believe this is happening. She's been hoping for her great-grandmother to wake up. She never thought of *staying* awake, just figured it would happen.

"I can't explain, just listen." She looks at Rayon. "You want so many things, my dear girl. You will find the things you truly want when you dig deeper. You will find the thing you truly *need* when you dig deeper. You will need to choose. The choice won't be easy. But it's one or the other." She smiles. "I have faith you will make the right decision."

Mother Lianne turns and takes Makeddah's hand. "You are the Princess, and you will be a great Queen. You have family in the North, your mother's family. Let them guide you, because to lead a kingdom at such a young age, you will need guidance. When you defeat Haggard—"

"If I—"

"No, I mean when." Mother Lianne nods. "When you defeat Haggard, stay close to your friends and family. Don't forget them. Don't forget your people, for then you will have all you need to defeat any enemy. Now," Mother Lianne turns to Belle. She runs her thumb over Belle's cheek. "Belle."

"No." Belle shakes her head as tears roll down her cheek. "This is not happening."

"Please, Belle…"

"No." Belle pulls away. "Nope."

"Let me talk, dear."

"Why?" Belle wipes her face violently.

"Let her talk!" Alda shouts, the first time she's said anything since Makeddah entered the room. Alda looks like a completely different woman, more emotional, more vulnerable, but Makeddah can't figure out why.

Belle looks up at her mother, sadness clouding every feature of her face. Belle sits slowly, letting Mother Lianne take her hand. "You are so special, my girl. You're different from the rest. I know you think you aren't, that you're a useless girl, barely even a witch, but you are *so* special. You have yet to see the great things you can do. I'm so sorry, you can't get to know that yet. But I knew it the day you were born." Belle stays silent as tears roll down her face.

"Okay, I've said my peace, and now I would like to go in peace." She closes her eyes, and no one says anything for a long while. Makeddah starts to open her mouth to speak, but Belle shushes her. They sit for three more minutes, and their grandmother's body falls back to sleep.

Makeddah is so confused. It's as if she's dead, but she's not.

Belle sucks in a breath then runs out of the room. Rayon stands motionless, Alda rubs her eyes, and Makeddah sniffles.

"I don't get it," Rayon says. "I really don't get it."

Alda's nose flares and her forehead creases. "High One takes out the witches who don't get well. Grandma asked to be one of them because of the pain she claims, but I said no. High One tried to say she was taking up space and to let her go, but I am *not* letting that woman touch my grandmother. I'm not." Alda shakes her head and walks from the room.

Now Makeddah knows why Alda seems different. She looks like a girl, not a woman. She's just a scared girl trying to cling to the last thing she has of her mother. Even though Mother Lianne isn't the *last* thing. Alda has several of her mother's things, but Mother Lianne is the last *living* thing.

And Makeddah realizes she knows how Alda feels. She wishes she could have something from her mother, too. Animate or not.

Rayon holds Mother Lianne's hand, and they all stand in silence. This can't happen again, no more death. Makeddah isn't sure she can take it anymore.

Thirty-four

It's so calming at the Witch Center. Now, whenever Makeddah thinks of the Guard, a headache follows. She was on such a high then plummeted to a low and now she is just at peace. She and Rayon haven't reached out to the Guard, not wanting any contact until returning becomes necessary. According to Rayon, that's tomorrow.

The spring breeze feels so good on Makeddah's skin, she wants to stay home longer. "You okay?" Belle asks, putting on her gardening gloves.

"I'm great." Makeddah closes her eyes, basking in the sun's warmth. She wants to savor it while she can. In the Guard, even the outdoors hide under thick trees that keep out the sun's heat. "You?"

Belle is already watering her flowers, picking off thorns and bad seeds with a strained determination. "I'm better than I thought I'd be. Knowing Mother Lianne doesn't think she's going to wake up is terrifying, but somehow I'm not terrified. Mom on the other hand…" She shrugs, her hand trembling briefly. "School ends next week, and these tests feel like a boulder pressing down on me. Do you guys have to do that?"

"No. Not me, at least." Makeddah shakes her head; she's glad for that. She never liked school. "How's training been going?" Makeddah asks and her sister frowns at her.

"Tell me something about the Guard to distract my thoughts from school."

Makeddah doesn't know what to say. She told her a lot when they first came down for the battle. But then she remembers one thing she never told her. "Every Friday, they have a fight night."

"A what?"

"It's like swordplay, but instead it's with elements, and they battle it out." Makeddah smiles, thinking of it. "I've only been once. I missed yesterdays, and one was cancelled because of the whole battle thing last week. But I'm pretty sure they'll do one this Monday. They want to start doing more since we're really preparing for a battle now."

Belle smiles. "That's cool. None of the other witches would think so. They frown at my swordplay."

"But you're different. You're like me."

Belle's smile falters, "Mother Lianne said I was different; I just don't believe her. I've blown three things up, I've made something disappear, but I was only supposed to make it orange." Belle throws off her gloves and sits on the bench next to Makeddah. "So exhausting." They sit in silence, then Belle laughs, "I see Rayon is still romance crazy. Has she found her way around the witch rules, yet?"

"Nope. She's asked Kahlan, and Kahlan says that she was only able to marry because she didn't have a Center, she didn't need a pendant." Makeddah picks a coin up from the ground and rubs the dirt from it. "So that left her disappointed."

"And I didn't know if I should ask this because I didn't want to upset you," Belle says, glancing at Makeddah. "That book in there about the Queen, the one you were reading yesterday. That's about your mother? Your real mother? How are you doing with that?" Belle only heard the news because of Mother Lianne. They haven't talked about it since then, and it's been a few days.

"I'm fine. I'm kind of wishing I knew what life with them would be like, but I'm so glad you're my family." Makeddah sets the coin down, her voice tightening. "But I'm not fine about something else. This whole thing about the traitor is eating at me. I have to go back to the Guard, and there's someone there who doesn't care if I live or die, someone who wants me enslaved by Haggard. It twists in my chest every time I think about it."

"Well, why haven't they just taken you already?"

"That's the first question I would ask." Alda says as she walks out and sits next to Makeddah on the bench, squeezing Makeddah in the middle. "And I bet you have asked that question a few times yourself."

Makeddah smiles at Alda. She's only come out of her room a few times, and that was for dinners, but now she looks like she's better. Like she's sad but hanging on.

"Yeah. They knew I was there; they didn't take me. They must know I'm here; still, nothing." Makeddah feels it's like a shadow always following, whispering threats but never striking. "What is the point of wanting to enslave me if they'll never really do it?" Makeddah shakes her head and nestles her forehead onto Alda's shoulder. "I miss being young, before any of this."

Alda chuckles, "You still are young."

"Doesn't feel like it."

All eyes go to Rayon as she steps outside the cottage, calling out and pointing at the sky. "I told you it'd be clear skies and sunny."

Belle rolls her eyes at Rayon and then exclaims suddenly, "Oh, are my cookies done?" She jumps out of her seat and runs into the cottage. Rayon runs in after her, saying something about the first bite.

"Belle is so different now," Makeddah pouts. "It feels as if I've been gone for years."

Alda puts her arm around Makeddah, gently squeezing her shoulder. "You're only feeling this way because you're torn apart inside. You want to come home, to be with family, but you love where you are at, don't you?"

Rayon comes out and lays down a blanket for everyone. Belle joins them with a plate of cookies and distributes them, making sure to grab one for herself as well.

Rayon takes a bite, "She loves Mira, Matt, Isaac, and Aaron—"

"Aaron is a bit too far," Makeddah laughs. When Rayon gives her a look, she frowns, "I'm kidding. How did you even hear us?"

Rayon replies, "Magic ears."

"How is Aaron?" Belle asks.

"Oh, please don't be like me little sister," Rayon says. "You'll never be able to marry him. Not in such a cruel system that is witchery. Especially, if you want to be a Head Witch." She sighs.

"I don't want to marry Aaron." Belle cringes. "I'm fine on my own." Belle bites into a cookie. "And I will never be a Head Witch; I don't ever want to be a Head Witch."

"You're a Parish," Rayon says. "Of course, you do. And when we get to that meeting today, you'd better tell High One so." Rayon twirls a piece of her hair. "Oh yeah, and she wants you there too, Makeddah."

"Me?"

Rayon takes the last bite of her cookie. "That *is* your name."

Later, outside High One's office, Makeddah stands with her sisters on either side. She's never been in High One's office. High One doesn't seem to really care for any of the Parish girls. Especially Alda. When it comes down to which Head Witch she likes the least, it would be Alda. Makeddah is positive.

But she doesn't know why.

Alda is the most powerful Head Witch. And from the story Alda told Makeddah about Haggard coming to reign, the reason Makeddah is even in the Parish family is because of High One. Yet, she treats Alda like she's still a kid and not valuable.

Rayon steps forth and knocks on the door three times. They wait patiently until the black door opens slowly on its own. A girl walks out laughing, and all three of them watch her giggle away.

"Come in," High One says.

Makeddah steps inside and is enveloped in a cherry blossom smell. She peers around the wall to see High One at her desk. Belle cowers next to her, Rayon seems as confident as ever, and considering this meeting is about the two of them, Makeddah isn't sure how to feel.

Rayon and Belle always have a meeting with High One towards the end of the school year. Makeddah and Rayon had already planned a trip down here so Rayon wouldn't miss it. This time, it's only different because Makeddah was asked to go with them.

"Take a seat," High One says, and with a flick of her wrist, the door closes.

Makeddah and Belle take a seat at the desk while Rayon remains standing.

"Rayon, you first, I suppose," High One says.

Rayon walks around and examines the books on the shelves. "Yes, High One." Rayon talks with dignity and moves like a woman, and it doesn't look ridiculous to Makeddah. If Makeddah tried to do that herself, she would feel out of place.

"You will be sixteen in…"

"Six months."

High One glances up. "Twenty-one in five years and six months. A special day for you, no?" High One doesn't try to get an answer but continues. "I see you have done well at the Guard with their witch. She has given you a hundred percent on every test but one."

"That one was rigged."

"Still a ninety-nine, Miss Parish." High One looks at a few papers. "You want to be considered for the Head Witch in five years? Then you want to take the test?" High One gazes up. "Don't step on that book."

Makeddah looks back. Rayon picks it up and tilts her head at it. "*The Stars*?" She gasps. "Is this a top-notch spellbook?" Rayon says it with wonder in her eyes.

"No, now give it here."

Rayon passes it to Makeddah, and Makeddah starts passing it up to High One, before noticing it looks like an old journal. High One snatches it from Makeddah and drops it in her desk drawer, slamming it closed.

Rayon stands behind Belle's chair. "Yes, I was wondering if I could be considered sooner," Rayon says as if the conversation wasn't interrupted. "Or take the test sooner. That is, if you see my potential earlier than I turn 21. I have aced every single test I have been given for nine years. I'm always at the top of my class and am extremely knowledgeable in the witch world. I believe I would benefit the Head Witches even at my young age."

High One slowly nods and doesn't answer for a while. "No. You will follow the same procedure as every other witch."

"Unless you see my potential earlier?"

High One hesitates. "Sure." She moves her papers. "You will be considered in five years and six months. After the consideration, you may be able to test for Head Witch amongst other girls."

Rayon smiles and bows. "Thank you so much for the guarantee of consideration."

High One tightens her mouth into a straight line.

Makeddah looks beyond her to the wall that has her many, many books. The desk is weathered, and the chairs are creaky, but they are well-maintained. She sees the picture of the sea on the wall.

"Have you been there?"

High One looks up at Makeddah, then at the painting. "Western Kingdom. The Horron Sea. Yes. It is a beautiful place to paint. Or buy a painting, I should say."

Makeddah laughs. "My friend Grace has—had a painting like that. She died that night the sorcerers came."

"Which time?" High One asks.

Makeddah scratches her cheek. "The second time. She was the wife of the man who was here to pick me up. The painting was hung in her office. She said it was the place where they got engaged." Makeddah smiles down at her hands. "I'd like to go there someday."

"You just might," High One says, and Makeddah swears she can see the corner of her mouth twitch into a smile. "Belle Parish. Did you want to be considered or test for Head Witch?"

"No, ma'am."

"Are you sure?" High One goes through the papers again. "I believe in seven years we will need someone like you to be considered."

"Someone who blows stuff up?" Belle whispers, amazed that High One is even saying such a thing. Makeddah smiles at her sweet and airy voice. "No, ma'am. I wouldn't like to be held to a standard. I'd rather be a gardener and make cookies while wearing slippers. I don't care much for magic." Rayon pinches Belle. "Ow."

"Don't say that," Rayon snaps. "Of course, you want to be a Head Witch, remember? Of course, you like magic."

"No, I don't." Belle turns to High One. "I truly don't, and if I will be looked down on or kicked out for thinking so, I don't care. I like myself with or without magic, and with or without the Center or the pedant."

Makeddah smiles. Belle is so much braver than her.

High One nods and writes something on the paper, says something about expectations for next year, then puts all the papers in a file. "Okay, then our meeting is over. You will not be considered nor take the test unless told to or you feel otherwise in the future."

"Thank you." Belle's dimpled smile shows up. Belle stands first, Makeddah second.

"And Makeddah, how are you?"

Makeddah freezes. She knows she was called for a reason, but it still shocks her when High One asks. "Fine. I think I'm fine. I haven't decided yet."

"Ah. I hear you have stirred up quite the rebellion in the village."

"Oh, yeah." Makeddah glances at Belle; they were just talking about that earlier. "I wish I could see it."

"You should; it's not a long trip. Your kingdom is making its voice heard. I'm sure one of the girls could ghost you." High One stands much shorter than Makeddah, barely a head taller than when she was sitting. But wisdom seems to ooze from the woman. "Your parents would be proud."

"I believe they would be. But not because of what I'm doing, because of who I am, and who I'm doing it with." She intertwines her arm in both Belle's and Rayon's.

High One grimaces at Rayon. "I suppose."

They start to walk away, but Makeddah stops. "And you would be dumb not to see Rayon's potential. But as she said, thank you for your guarantee of *early* consideration." And she turns and walks away.

Thirty-five

"Where?"

Belle points at the person standing at a cart. "I think that's him."

They're taking a risk walking to the village, but after High One encourages it, Makeddah feels she must. Now, both crouch behind a tree, watching the village as the sun rises high and people sell their trinkets.

Belle says, noting the description of the man Alda mentioned. "He's the one who said that he knew the princess was still alive."

Makeddah nods, about to say something, but the doors to the castle open and Haggard walks out, followed by sorcerers. "Where are his sons?" Makeddah asks. She is disappointed they aren't there. She is interested in seeing them again. Prince 1 had something to hide. She wants to know what it was.

"Oh, no. Haggard's collecting," Belle whispers, anxiety creeping into her voice. "I hoped he wouldn't be doing that today."

Makeddah can't hear from the tree what he's saying as he approaches the man that she and Belle were just talking about. The man shakes his head. His wife appears and trembles, pleading something to her husband. The man shakes his head, looks at Haggard, and says something to him.

Makeddah can't see Haggard's face, but his body movement tells everything. He stands stiff, his hands balling into fists at his sides. The man begins to walk away, but one of Haggard's sorcerers stuns him, and he crumples into Haggard's arms.

"This…" Haggard shouts so that all in the village will hear. "This is what happens when you decide to follow the Princess's orders and disobey mine." Haggard turns the man to face him. He grabs the man by the collar and yells to the sorcerers to take him away.

Makeddah clenches her teeth, trying not to rush into the village. Belle whimpers next to her and asks, "What do you think they're going to do to him?"

As if to answer her, Haggard says, "Death happens."

"We don't care," a man shouts. "If it ends with the village being happy, then we will die. For her."

A woman steps up and nods. "For the Princess."

Makeddah doesn't know whether to smile or to run out there and stop it. People will be dying because of her. They'll be torn apart because of Haggard's selfishness. Makeddah shivers at the thought of it. At the thought of the witch who was torn in two.

Haggard laughs and walks away, unbothered by their loyalty. He motions the sorcerers to take the two who spoke up, and they still chant for the princess as they are dragged away.

The wife trembles and watches her husband be dragged away to his death. But as Haggard disappears, people start chanting, "Bring back Korzon!" Haggard doesn't try to stop them. Even as his sorcerer looks ready to strike, Haggard juts his chin up and continues.

People continue to gather and shout as the castle doors close.

Makeddah takes Belle's hand, and together they hurry away from the village toward the Center.

When they're halfway back to the Witch Center, Makeddah slows to catch her breath. "He's evil. There is no reason he is doing all this," she says.

"Yes, there is, Makeddah," Belle replies, shaking her head. "For power. As terrible as it may be, people do things like this just because of selfishness."

Makeddah groans. She's right. That's exactly what he told Makeddah that night. He wanted her to be captured so that he could rule over her. To demonstrate his power to everyone. She grimaces at the thought and looks down at her sister.

"I'm proud of you, you know?"

"You are?" Belle asks, her big blue eyes filling with a sparkle Makeddah can't help but love.

"For telling High One you don't care about titles, because they're nothing. Being a Head Witch is just being a normal witch with a better title and *slightly* more training." Makeddah rolls her eyes. "Nothing special."

"Rayon seems to think so." Belle takes Makeddah's hand to examine it, stopping Makeddah. "Why are you still chewing your nails?"

"Ugh. You sound like Isaac," Makeddah mutters, biting her lip.

Giggling, Belle squints at Makeddah's hands and turns the palm toward her. "Whoa, when did this happen?" Belle looks up at Makeddah. "When did you get this scar?"

Makeddah pulls her hand away and rubs the scar. "The weirdest things have been happening to me." She rubs her nose and resumes walking. "Chills up my spine, randomly falling, scars, grey eyes. No one, except Matt, knows what I'm talking about, and he won't tell me."

"Maybe it has to do with the traitor."

Makeddah shakes her head. "At first I thought that, but I don't think so. If it did, Matt would definitely tell me or at least tell Kahlan, and the traitor would be gone by now. But there's something not adding up about the traitor," Makeddah says, pondering the events of the last few weeks. "Before Grace passed out after the battle, she said, 'It's them,' like the traitors were right there, looking at us. Then Haggard said that there were two. So, he or she must not be working alone."

Belle falls quiet. Their steps echo between them before she asks, "How were the dances with those Princes?"

Makeddah shrugs her left shoulder. "Just Prince 1—but it was weird, awkward, but a little intriguing. It was as real as it was fake. I wanted to puke, probably because Haggard is his father."

Belle nudges her with her shoulder, "There must be one man you don't hate."

She scratches her cheek. "Isaac and I are liking each other." Belles eyes go wide, "I have not told anyone, not even Rayon."

Belle giggles. "So you are boyfriend and girlfriend?"

Makeddah shakes her head. "No. At least, I don't think so. I don't know," she sighs. "But Belle, he is so handsome, charming, and kind, and he likes me. So I felt guilty dancing with the Prince. The Prince made me feel strange. He was familiar and he…" Makeddah remembers the dance: the way he talked, how he moved with her—the twirl, the dip, his eyes.

Makeddah stops. Her smile turns into a frown. Her heartbeat picks up. She tried so hard not to look into his eyes then, but now she remembers them. She remembers those eyes. She thinks of everything. The hair, the voice, the body shape… the hands. The eyes.

"No." The revelation shatters her heart in two. She chews on her already bleeding nailbeds, hoping some explanation comes to mind. "No." Makeddah wonders how she hadn't seen it sooner. Her gift of seeing out-of-place things had failed her when she needed it.

Belle takes Makeddah's hand from her mouth. "What?" Her brows furrow tightly together as Makeddah hesitates to give her an answer. If she says it out loud, it will be even more true. Feel and sound truer. How can she even deal with that?

She doesn't know, yet again, how she can deal with the truth.

But she looks in her sister's eyes, a stern expression on her face, and says it out loud. "I know who the traitor is."

"Who?"

Makeddah starts piecing it together. Mira mentioned that both princes were two when Haggard started ruling, which must mean they were either born super close together or they are twins. The ball turned into a masquerade at the last minute, probably because Isaac knew they'd be there and he wanted to conceal himself from the Guard. Grace and Haggard's words both pointed to two traitors.

"It's Isaac. Isaac and Aaron are the traitors."

"Are you sure?"

Makeddah can't talk anymore; she and Rayon have to go. She needs to tell Kahlan. And she already knows, this will break her heart too.

Thirty-six

Makeddah stands in front of the crowd. Kahlan is right by her side. She hated having to leave Belle and Alda a day early, but she had to. Rayon doesn't even know what's going on, but Makeddah rushed to Kahlan and told her everything.

Standing in front of the crowd, Makeddah feels exposed and overwhelmed by the noise and gazes directed at her. A mix of disgust and anger twists inside her, fueled by anxiety over what she has just revealed. She told Rayon not to listen, afraid of how upsetting it would be for her as well.

Rayon reluctantly stayed outside of the office as Makeddah talked to Kahlan. Now she sits front and center.

She sees everyone—sleepy, confused, and looking at her like she's stolen something essential from them. The guilt gnaws at her, knowing she has indeed taken more than their sleep. She searches the crowd for Isaac. Unlike the others, he seems alert; his calm presence somehow comforts her, even now, despite the swirling conflict inside. Her feelings confuse and betray her; anger, longing, and regret battle for control.

Makeddah forces herself to look away from him, desperate to regain control of her thoughts and emotions. If she lingers, she fears her composure will shatter under the emotional strain.

"Okay, settle down." Kahlan's voice brings Makeddah back. "Thank you for coming out of the comfort of your beds to be here tonight."

Makeddah looks down at Rayon and Mira, and they both shrug at her, asking what this is for. Makeddah swallows.

"For some time, we have been searching for the traitor. It has taken a toll on us all. But certain things have come to light for us. Some for the better and some for the worse." Kahlan frowns and looks over the crowd. "I am irked to know that any one of you could have done this. But I'm even more *displeased* to know that you are close." Kahlan's voice is quiet, but she clears it and looks up above the crowd. "Isaac and Aaron, please come forth."

Makeddah sees the deep shock in their faces as they turn to her.

"Quickly is preferable," Makeddah says, trying to get this over with.

Gasps erupt, Makeddah almost thinks it's fake. Staged. This is like a play, and she is a puppet playing along with the act. But it's not, and she will never be anyone's puppet.

She can't look at them, though she knows Isaac is staring. Isaac stands in front of Makeddah, and Aaron stands in front of Kahlan. Both are as still as rocks.

"I have figured out some things, some secrets. Secrets you have been keeping from us." Makeddah tries her best to keep her voice steady as she looks at them both, but it cracks. She clears her throat and goes on. "The secret that you are Haggard's sons." Everyone looks at each other, whispering starts, and it becomes loud, distracting Makeddah. "Quiet, please." She glances over at them all. "You will all have time to gossip later. Isaac and Aaron, we have reason to believe that, because Haggard is your father, you are the traitors." She turns to Isaac, him being the oldest. "Do you deny this?"

"We are…" Isaac takes a breath, his jaw twitching. "I am the son of Haggard, but—"

"Isaac, we do not give you any last words besides your confirmation." Makeddah shakes her head. "The pain you have caused… well, they say actions speak louder than words." And just like that, Makeddah is cold inside. Not like the weird chill up her spine, but a pit in her stomach, an emptiness.

She steps back and faces the crowd, trying to be cold and detached. She wants them to feel the pain she feels. The anger that boils inside of her.

"You can go," Kahlan says. "Makeddah will be the one to lead you to your room and out of the ghoster."

"Makeddah, please,"

"If you have any complaints, tell the trees. I'm sure they'll be happy to listen," Makeddah says. "Isaac and Aaron Weathers, you are now banned from the Guard. If you are to return, we will be forced to imprison you. If you agree, say, 'I agree.' If you do not, we will be forced and just—"

"I agree," Isaac says without a stutter.

"You are all dismissed," Kahlan says, and the crowd disperses. When they are all gone, Makeddah walks Isaac and Aaron to their room.

Makeddah stands by the frame, watching Isaac pack. So many words left unsaid to him, so many feelings she doesn't understand. It's so miserable. She wonders if they even feel anything at all. Any remorse, any pain. But she knows when they leave this Guard, they will run to their father and tell him everything. It disgusts her.

"You okay?" Isaac smiles sadly. "I've been calling your name for the last few seconds."

She looks up and sees Isaac standing there with his backpack on his shoulders. She glances at Aaron, but her gaze falls on Isaac again. "I don't want to talk to you, okay?"

"Makeddah, I know, I'm sorry." He looks so desperate, his eyes pleading with her, but she doesn't care. "I'm sorry that you think I'm the traitor. I'm sorry for lying to you."

He grabs her hands in his and pleads with the same blue eyes that got him here. "I would never, in my life, hurt you."

Makeddah jerks her hands away. "You already did. You told me your parents were dead. Killed by Haggard. You're just like them, like all of them." She scoffs, bitterness coating every word. "There isn't a single person I've met here who hasn't lied to me or kept a secret. It hurts, Isaac." Her voice cracks as she fights back tears. Knowing a breakdown is near if she looks at him any longer, she spins on her heel and heads to the lobby, heart pounding with hurt.

"I wanted to tell you…"

Makeddah stops but can't bring herself to face him. "That's what everyone says. I wanted to do this, I wanted to do that, I wanted to *tell* you." She brushes away a tear, emotion spilling over. "Why does everyone want and not do?" she demands, finally turning to him. Her voice is raw. "Please, I don't want to hear it. I'm done—done with trusting, done with getting hurt." She rubs her cheek, her words heavy with sadness. "You told me to trust you, and I did. That was my mistake."

Makeddah turns around and leads them to the ghoster. She stops and sees Mira there waiting to send Isaac and Aaron. Isaac walks inside the room, turns around, and faces Makeddah. He doesn't say anything this time. Aaron does.

"Makeddah…"

"Stop, please. Stop making excuses."

"I'm not making an excuse. You know I don't make excuses." Aaron waits for Makeddah to listen. When she crosses her arms, he goes on. "Isaac is stupid. He says stupid stuff. He told you to trust him, knowing he was lying. But, Makeddah, believe me when I say he didn't lie to you when he said our father died. Yes, Haggard is our father, but that man on the throne—he's never been a real father."

Makeddah licks her teeth. "Thanks for the insight." She holds her hand out. "I need your ghoster keys."

They look at her, hesitating. Aaron slams his key into her hand; Isaac places his gently. "I wish this weren't so hard. I wish you believed us."

"Why should I, Isaac?" She's really asking him. She wants him to give her a reason to believe him, to trust him.

"Talk with me. Please. I'd rather be your prisoner than walk out knowing this is what you think of me," Isaac says as he holds her hand with the key in it. "Sunshine, please."

She looks at him, desperate to give him a chance. Then she glances at Aaron. "Mira, can you take Aaron and give us a moment?" Mira takes Aaron a little way down the hall, and Makeddah turns to Isaac and says, "Talk."

He sighs. "My father was a good man, from what my mom said. He was a good man up until a certain point, when he changed. She said he flipped a switch, and he just became a bad man. He wanted revenge and wanted sorcerers. He wanted power, and he was determined to get it. We did not choose to be his sons, but we wanted to make sure we would still have a chance to see our mother if he ever let us. We told him we were leaving, but he said that we had to come to parties and show our faces if we wanted to keep her alive."

"Is she alive?"

Isaac shrugs, "I don't know, but we weren't risking it." He steps closer to her, and the space between them disappears. "Trust me when I say we are not the traitors. But I understand if you have to let us go now." He pulls her chin up so she is forced to look him in the eyes.

A tear falls from her eyes. "I don't know if I believe you."

He nods. "Okay." He wipes her tears with his thumb and kisses her cheek. She feels him linger there, his warm lips imprinting on her. He pulls away, but only goes to her ear. His lips brush her ear as he says, "I would never hurt you, Sunshine."

Her heart pounds. Keys clenched in her fist, she turns and walks away.

Aaron stands near the ghoster and Isaac joins him.

Mira is holding back tears, and Makeddah doesn't know if she has any last words. So when Makeddah rubs her back, Mira sniffles and nods.

She looks up at Aaron. "I knew something was wrong, I just didn't know I was dating the son of a man who killed my family. I hate you. I hate everything about you. I am so glad I found that out sooner rather than later." Mira wipes her tears.

"Send them." Makeddah walks away, dragging every last step.

She gets to her room. Her chest is empty, her lungs are void of air. She falls back into her wall, clenching her fists, feeling that if she lets go, something bad will happen. Something dark will stir in her like the day of the battle. So, she hangs on for dear life.

She sucks a breath in, tears fall down her face, but she doesn't move. Her body doesn't shake. She's completely still, as the tears fall from her eyes. She sees Rayon and Mira, then Matt comes into view. But all she does is stare at the wall. A whimper finally escapes, but another doesn't come. It's too much. One more and she'll break down completely.

How can this be so much? It's not like he's dead. But he's ripped her open like she didn't know anyone ever could. Now she longs for him again, for his touch and his lips and his voice. She doesn't know how to believe him, but one part of her does.

He wouldn't hurt her.

People are outside in the hall looking at her. Laughing, she thinks, or maybe they're gossiping. Or watching the Lion Heart slowly descend into madness. She can't tell. She tries to look over, but she can't. Her body is frozen in place. Then she finds the will to move, but all she does is bury her head in her hands.

"Do something," she hears.

She feels strong arms pick her up and lay her on the bed. Someone throws the comforter over her still body. She rolls over and cries into the pillows. The bed bounces, a wet rag is placed on her head. She feels someone hug her from behind and a hand stroking her hair. But now that she's here, crying into the pillows, she can't stop the tears. She lies here, vulnerable to the world and her emotions. Emotions she never thought she would have.

The feeling in her body is nothing like she's ever felt before. It's like a piece of her heart being ripped away, or her lungs collapsing on the spot. She can't breathe, she can't talk, she can't move.

All she can do is cry.

She believed, at the start, that being a Lion Heart meant she was special, that it offered her the life she'd always wanted. So, she broke down her walls, trusted, and did things she would only dream of doing before. But now, she wishes she hadn't.

Being special is doing her more harm than good.

Thirty-seven

Makeddah wakes up. Her mouth is dry, her lips and eyes crusty. She rubs her eyes and glances behind her to see Rayon, the one who hugged her from behind last night. Turning to her other side, she sees Mira still asleep. Makeddah carefully rises, gently slips out of bed, and tiptoes toward the washroom. In the bright lights, her reflection looks even worse than she feels, if that's possible. Her body appears colorless; her eyes are red and glossy, her lips are dry and white.

Makeddah's lips tremble, and she clings to the water basin as if it might anchor her. Weakness pulses inside, deeper than tears. She shakes, mind racing. How could they keep the lie alive for so long? Their care felt real. That's the cruelest lie: You trust people, invest everything, and realize they never did the same.

Except they did care, maybe just a little. At least Isaac did. Makeddah thought of him being her boyfriend one day, but now it feels like that could never happen. For all she knows he was only acting the whole time.

She quietly walks back out to the room, noticing Mira and Rayon are still asleep. Lost in her thoughts and confusion, she decides to leave the room altogether. As she passes through the lobby, she feels several people looking at her, but says nothing in response. She grabs a biscuit, biting into it with more force than she intends. She wipes her mouth, then consciously slows her actions.

"Hey."

Makeddah jumps and glances to her right. Matt. "If this is what it felt like to lose Grace, I wish you never had to go through it."

Matt narrows with a small smile. "Worse."

Makeddah feels foolish. Of course, it feels worse. He lost the love of his life and his child. She banished the guy she liked.

And here Matt is, being kind about her naivete. Why is Matt being so kind? "Do you need anything?" He asks

Makeddah feels dozens of eyes pricking at her. She crosses her arms defensively. "Maybe for people to stop staring," she snaps. Then her voice cracks, low and raw. "Yes, I need more. I want to know where this scar came from. I want to stop crying. I want to stop feeling so wrecked inside. I need… I need a hug." She kicks the floor, whispering, "A real one. I'll ask Rayon."

"I can hug you."

Makeddah gives a short laugh. "You don't hug."

"Well, neither do you."

Makeddah meets Matt's steady gaze and can't hold back. Tears threaten, blurred by confusion—his kindness, the world shattering around her. She collapses into his arms, not sobbing, but clinging, desperate for comfort. The warmth startles her. She hugs tighter, starved for relief, silently begging for the strength to hide her wounds.

She stays in Matt's arms as long as is granted, realizing he is a comforting hugger. "Thanks," she says when she finally lets go. He steps back.

"You're welcome." He looks down. "Is it bad…" He shakes his head and looks up at her, whispering, "Is it bad that I'm not grieving Grace like I thought I would? That I only ever really grieved my child? I want you to say that it's terrible."

"Well—"

"If you say it's bad, then I'll just hate myself," he goes on as if she hadn't started to speak, "like I need to. I'll know I'm wrong and that I should be wrong. I should feel guilty for it, and maybe I will. I shouldn't have said anything. I said I wouldn't admit that to anyone."

Makeddah shakes her head. "Did you love her?"

Matt gives no answer, only stares at her.

"I know you loved her, right?"

He seems to snap out of it and nods. "Of course I loved her. How could anyone doubt that? How could *you* doubt that?"

Makeddah puts her hand on his shoulder. "Then, no, you're not a terrible person. It's okay."

"But why?"

"Because your child never got to live. Grace did." Matt tries to dodge her eye contact, but Makeddah doesn't falter. "Why do you want to suffer? I don't get it."

He swallows. "Never mind. I'm just tired and shocked about Isaac and Aaron. I think I'll go rest." He starts walking away. "And about that scar… I'm trying my best."

"Thanks." She stops him before he leaves. "You knew I was a Princess this whole time?" She hasn't had the chance to ask him, and she's not sure why it comes to mind now, but it does. When he bows, she believes his answer is yes.

As he walks away, she feels a hint of anger, but she already knew the answer. He said he knew all of her secrets. All of the adults in her life have hidden things from her.

Makeddah grabs a plate of food to bring back for Mira and Rayon. When she returns to their room, both are awake. Rayon is straightening the bedcovers while Mira assists her.

"Hey." Makeddah shuts the door behind her. Mira rushes up and gives her a tight and quick hug. "Thanks."

Rayon walks up and caresses Makeddah's arm. "Are you okay?" Makeddah shrugs. "Please, just tell me you're fine."

"I am. I'm better than last night." Makeddah sets the food on the dresser. She scratches her back, it feels the same as when she got her birthmark.

Mira stands next to Makeddah but stops short and both Rayon and Mira look above Makeddah's head.

Makeddah looks up and she sees her birthmark floating above her and smoothly moving in front of her. She lifts her hand and her birthmark lands safely above it.

"Oh my nature, Makeddah. You're a full-bred." Mira breathes.

"What? How does that even happen? I didn't train for the last few days."

Mira smirks, "It just chooses when you are ready. You're ready."

Ready? This moment could not have come at a worse time. She doesn't feel the least bit ready.

Makeddah drops her hand and the birthmark disappears. She thought she might feel different, but she still feels empty.

"Congratulations. And now that whole show is over." Rayon steps back and folds her arms, "Let's cut to the chase. Why did you do all that last night without consulting me?" She frowns at Makeddah.

Makeddah is taken aback but attempts not to show it, leaning against the wall and narrowing her eyes at her sister. "What?" she asks. "He was the traitor, Rayon."

"Who?" Rayon asks. "Aaron… or Isaac."

"What is that supposed to mean?"

"You know exactly what I mean." Rayon shakes her head and points at the door. "You know for a fact that Isaac is not the traitor."

"Rayon, he lied," Makeddah says, hating the accusation Rayon is making. "*They* lied. They are the sons of Haggard. They just told everyone. Why don't you believe me?"

"I believe they are the sons of Haggard. But that's not their fault, and you know that." Isaac said that last night. Rayon shakes her head, her voice softening. "Mak, do you want the truth?"

"Of course, I want the truth. I always want the truth."

Rayon slaps the back of her hand to the palm of the other slowly as she speaks. "The truth is, everyone lies, Makeddah. Everyone keeps secrets."

Makeddah narrows. "That's not good."

"No, it's not, but it's true." *You* are the one trying to live outside of the truth—lying to yourself." Rayon points. "Now, the Guard has to move, and the traitor will still be with us, and it is your fault."

Mira gasps. "Rayon."

"The truth?" Rayon's voice quivers, not with warmth, but with anger barely masked. She chuckles—a hard, brittle sound. "You're getting impossible, Makeddah. You know that? Sending Isaac and Aaron away did no good and helped no one. And you'll carry that weight, alone."

She looks just like Alda.

"*You* want the truth, Rayon?" Makeddah steps back and glares at her sister. "I don't care what you say."

"Yes, you do, Makeddah." Rayon grabs Makeddah's hand, her voice softening again, and Makeddah hates that she listens. "Because you love me. And I love you. I am the only person who will tell you this." Rayon grabs a piece of bacon and sits on the trunk at the end of the bed. "The only reason you sent Isaac off is because you're afraid to admit that you care about him and when he lied, it was the first time you felt that kind of betrayal. You should have talked to him first, listened to what he had to say. You're selfish, Makeddah. Now you have to stop this higher than thou attitude."

Makeddah looks at the wall. "I'll stop when I want to." Even she cringes at the words that leave her mouth. She sounds like a prideful little kid. "You may think it's not Isaac, but I do. You say you love me, so you need to trust me."

"Love and trust have nothing to do with each other right now." Rayon says, biting into the bacon. "But I'll support you, until it goes wrong, then I will be there to tell you I told you so." Rayon takes the other few pieces of bacon from the plate, "And I *will* tell you." Then she walks out of the room.

Makeddah stares at the ground. "Do you think she's right?"

Mira looks up to Makeddah. "I'm in my second stage of my grief—depression. Depression clouds your head. My head is clouded; I'm not sure what to think."

Makeddah looks at the door through which Rayon left. She won't let Rayon say I told you so. Makeddah isn't selfish—Rayon is. Always trying to outdo everyone, make the best marks, and rise above others.

Yet, the truth aches inside Makeddah, a silent confession she hates but can't silence.

It claws at her, leaving her hollow, every breath a reminder.

Thirty-eight

Makeddah faces the crowd with the worst headache of her life. She knows Rayon will sit in judgment, glaring at her with nasty glances, while Mira mopes beside her and Matt lounges in the corner, paying no mind at all.

Each glance at the crowd intensifies Makeddah's headache, turning her stomach as well.

Makeddah walks up to Kahlan, who stands on the platform where they had been the night before banishing Isaac and Aaron. Makeddah stands beside her in silence until Kahlan greets her with a quiet hello.

Makeddah doesn't say hi back. She just leans toward Kahlan and whispers, "I think it's better only you talk today." She tries to smile. Her head stops her.

Kahlan nods, and they both face the crowd. The feeling claws at Makeddah, dragging up last night and her wish for all of this to just end. As she knew would happen, Rayon fixes her with judgment—sisterly and sharp, making Makeddah's stomach churn.

Makeddah can feel people staring at her, not because of where she stands, but because of last night—the same reason they stared at her this morning—but Makeddah isn't ready to break down again.

Ever again.

"Hello, everyone," Kahlan says. "We understand you all were deprived of sleep last night, and I know you will hate what I am going to tell you next." Kahlan's voice sounds unlike her own. It's small and weak. It doesn't command attention, nor does it lend authority. Maybe Kahlan is hurting just as much as Makeddah. "We have to relocate."

Sighs erupt around the room.

"I know it will be hard," Kahlan continues, "Especially trying not to be noticed, but our Lion Heart and all of the earth teachers will help us with it."

The whispers, rolling of eyes, and pouts make Makeddah mad. She doesn't know why. She feels they should be grateful not to have the traitors anymore. But they're just complaining because they have to protect themselves.

"Okay." Kahlan looks over the crowd and makes everyone quiet themselves. "Now, you must all pack your backpacks and pack any supplies you may need. You will all have rooms and have all that you need there, like I've provided before. It is not a far walk, it is an abandoned refuge close to Stonehaven hill." She says. "Lastly, there will be no fight night tonight." People sigh even harder this time. "We're sorry, but with all this change, we will need to recuperate. But to get some steam out, we will reschedule the fight night for tomorrow, and Friday is still on the books. So go on, we will see you back here soon." Everyone gets up and does as they are told.

Makeddah dreads the day ahead. Not only does she have to muster all her strength from her earth element, but she has to take people back and forth and back and forth. It will be easier for Rayon and Kahlan because their ghosting takes only a second, but it will still be a long day.

None of it eases Makeddah's headache. If anything, each task worsens the feeling.

After two hours, everyone in the Guard begins lining up, and people are organized into pairs. While Rayon and Kahlan quickly ghost in and out with their abilities, Makeddah and the other earth-breeds move at a slower pace.

This isn't her first time, but Makeddah is still amazed by the process. She holds the hand or arm of the people walking with her, and the ground vibrates. She feels her feet sink in first, and the rest of her body follows underground. When she opens her eyes, there is a pathway leading to the other Guard.

"I can't see!" someone behind Makeddah shouts.

Makeddah looks back at Preston. He smiles at her and looks at the girl he's holding. "I know." And they start moving. Makeddah can see perfectly fine, as if a lamp is guiding the way. But the one next to her can't.

Preston mentioned something about that. That earth-breeds are the only ones able to see underground without light. Which confuses Makeddah, but she hates to admit that she does not understand the process.

Makeddah leads the other earth-breeds down a windy and long path. She remembers exactly, as if she had gone several times before instead of only once. Curve left, turn right, curve right. But it's mostly straight ahead. Thirty minutes to and from.

The earth-breeds take much longer than the witches. They can only walk with two people at a time—one person for each hand. Makeddah makes this trip twice. As she is about to start her third trip, she's glad to see that not many are left. Rayon comes in twice while Makeddah stands there, looking over the remaining Guard members. Everyone is still lined up. Makeddah tries to count the ones left.

A blonde woman with one hand on her hip and a frown taps her foot impatiently and addresses Makeddah. "So, can we get going?" Makeddah looks up, grabs a child's hand first, and prepares to guide the next group. The woman mutters, "Little brat."

Makeddah glares up. "What did you call me?"

"I didn't call you anything. I just want to go." Makeddah looks at the woman, who smiles despite her attitude. "Can we?"

Makeddah clasps the woman's hand, feeling the ground vibrate below her feet. Once she senses everyone has joined the line, she guides the third group underground.

The day's trips take around six hours. Makeddah is exhausted by the time she returns to retrieve her belongings. The only ones left are Mira and Matt. The other earth teachers grab their own things, Rayon gets her stuff, and they all wait for Kahlan.

Kahlan glides out of her office with a backpack and a box. "Last trip," she says with a smile.

"I'm gonna miss this place," Mira says with a shake of her head, then her gaze falls to Makeddah. "Ready?"

Rayon takes Matt, Kahlan ghosts out, and the earth-breeds follow underground.

When they get to the new Guard, Makeddah and the others slowly rise above ground, and Mira almost falls over, as did everyone before her. She hasn't done this before either. Makeddah holds her up and sweeps her hand over the land. "Welcome home," she sighs.

"Wow." Mira watches people flood into the building.

It reminds Makeddah of the Witch Center. Four large brick walls surrounding it, but there is one gate three times as tall as Makeddah, similar to the one at the castle. They won't be living underground anymore.

Makeddah explains the dynamics, as it is quite different here. "There is no ghoster room for our rooms and the lobby but when they move the Units, we'll have a ghoster for that."

They walk in through the big gate and see plenty of little homes and cottages like they have back at the Center.

Kahlan explained that this was a commune years ago then became a refuge from Haggard. But Haggard discovered them because they had no shield protecting them. Now with the traitors gone and protection, they will be safe.

Mira says something to her, but Makeddah only nods absently, distracted as she scans the grounds for Rayon.

It takes Makeddah a while to find her, but ten minutes later, she sees her sister against the wall of a home watching the groups of people complain. The noise gets to her as she stands next to her sister. She almost forgot about the headache, but now it's worse than ever.

"Kahlan wants us to meet her over there," Rayon shouts over to Makeddah. "We should go now."

"Okay."

Rayon takes Makeddah's hand and weaves her through the people. When they get through the crowd, they walk towards a little shed and Rayon knocks on the door.

There is no answer.

Makeddah turns and looks at the crowd, rubbing her temple. Finally, Kahlan arrives and she looks like she had just as long a day as Makeddah.

"Thank you for meeting me, I wanted to show you to your new temporary home." She starts walking ahead and Rayon and Makeddah follow.

Something that is completely different from the Witch Center is the ground is all hard gravel. No beautiful roses, no grass, no gardens. It looks sad compared to the Center.

But as they walk Makeddah gets a look at Stonehaven Hill. It is abundant and green. Beautiful.

Kahlan leads them to a large home. It is probably three times the size of her cottage at the Center.

When they enter, Makeddah sees a big room. There's a small wooden coffee table and three sofas in the shape of the letter U.

Rayon's jaw drops, then grows into a grin. Makeddah follows her gaze. It's a snack cart and there is a cooler next to it.

Rayon asks, "We get our own food bar?"

Kahlan nods. "I'd like to work with you more on things Makeddah. Start growing your leadership skills. So, you both will be staying over there—" she points to a door on the right, "And I will be staying there." She points to a door on the left wall. She leads them to their room, "We will have meetings every morning and night making sure things are running smoothly here."

Kahlan opens the door with a flick of her wrist and Rayon enters first and gasps, "No way."

Makeddah pushes in. It is not a room like they had at the last place as Makeddah suspected. It is a small home. The living room is bigger than the one at their cottage in the Witch Center. The small kitchen has a circular wooden table with four chairs. There's a door on the right and two doors on the left.

"It's like we have our own house." Rayon runs to the first door on the left, opens it, and peeks in. "Washroom." She does the same with the other door. "Room. My room. I chose it, now it's mine."

Makeddah walks to the other door and cracks it open, inhaling the scent of earth. The bed is the same size as the last one, but all to herself. She looks at the window area and steps into some dirt, but she picks it up with her hands and makes it disappear.

"Makeddah," Kahlan says as she knocks softly, "meet me outside in twenty minutes."

Makeddah lies on her bed and mumbles "Okay." Then falls asleep.

Kahlan hadn't made home assignments yet, so that is Makeddah's duty. Makeddah's duty also includes creating schedules for training times, tests, and classes. Kahlan provides Makeddah with a layout of the refuge, including the number of members in each family and everyone's names.

So, Makeddah sits out in her little lobby and sets down all the paperwork. She stares at the piles, then bites her nail and starts working.

After two hours, five paper cuts, and three hand cramps later, Rayon emerges from their apartment. "Hey, want to help me?" Makeddah asks.

"Well, I'm not like you—saying no just for the sake of it—but no," Rayon says, glancing over the papers. "Mira needs me for something, so have fun." Rayon turns and starts to walk away.

"Rayon, are you still mad?"

She turns back to Makeddah and puts her hand on her hip. "No. I'm not mad. I never was. You were... I just thought you were stupid."

"Okay thanks, I think. Bye."

"Hey, when the bad guys are found, make sure to tell them that *you* were the stupid one, k?" Rayon puckers her lips into a small smile.

Makeddah rolls her eyes. "Yeah, sure." She watches Rayon leave the room. By the time she posts the room assignments and training schedules, it is dark outside. She's ready to sleep. But when she goes to get dinner, Mira begs Makeddah to let her see her apartment.

So, Makeddah gives her a quick tour after she has eaten a plate of food. "Wow," Mira says. "It's so nice. Matt and I have an apartment too, but it looks like everyone else's." Mira stops, "Oh, my nature. When is your graduation? You're so much farther along in a month then I ever was."

"It's the day after tomorrow." Makeddah says.

Mira gasps, "I need to figure out what you are wearing."

Makeddah really doesn't care but offers, "I loved your graduation dress."

"Okay, perfect. She takes a blank sheet of parchment and a pencil and makes herself at home on the sofa. "Maybe I should make Rayon a dress as well. Mine is all finished, it's…"

Makeddah looks around as Mira mutters on. "Hey, Mira." The muttering goes on and she grabs Mira's shoulder. "Mira." Mira finally looks up, "Where's Rayon? She said she was going to be with you."

"I haven't seen her all day."

Makeddah looks at the door that swings open and sees Rayon rush in. Without looking back, Rayon goes to her room. Makeddah calls after her, and Rayon turns, giving a fake smile. "What were you doing?" Makeddah asks.

"Hm?" A false look of innocence. "Oh, just… eating. Goodnight." She shuts the door to the room and doesn't come out again.

Thirty-nine

Rayon

It's a nice new place, but it's all wrong, Rayon contemplates as she stares at the ceiling. They should be here with Isaac and Aaron, not without them.

She hears Makeddah's clock go off in the room next door and quickly puts her back to the door. A few minutes later, when she hears Makeddah open the door to her room, she snores or pretends to. Makeddah closes her door. Rayon hears the click of the latch as it goes into its socket, and the front door opens and closes.

She pops out of bed and rushes to the closet. She brought only a few clothes: some pants, two T-shirts, and three dresses. She picks out a dress and flats. Seeing Makeddah isn't there, she heads to the washroom.

"Slob already," Rayon says under her breath, irritation flaring as she sees the toothbrush lying out with the bottle of paste open. She throws Makeddah's nightclothes and training suit under the counter, huffing softly, and gets ready herself, jaw set.

She writes a note for Makeddah and sets it on the counter, hesitating as doubt flickers in her eyes. "Just in case I'm late," she mutters, voice barely above a whisper. Before she tries to ghost out, she looks at the coffee table and grabs the book lying there, clutching it tightly to her chest. She hugs the book and nods with a shaky breath, then ghosts from the Guard, pulse racing.

Rayon lands in the center of her living room—the living room in the Witch Center. She opens her eyes to emptiness. She looks at the table, spots a paper, picks it up, and reads it. "Good going, Belle," she whispers.

Setting the book and paper down, she creeps over to her room and knocks quietly on the door. "Belle!" she whispers. "Belle, I'm here. Belle, open up."

The door swings open. "You could just open the door."

"I wasn't sure if I'd walk in on you changing or something." Rayon throws her hands up in defense. "I know how you get with your privacy."

Belle pushes Rayon out of the way and softly shuts the door. Rayon sees her sapphire blue eyes, bagged with dark circles, and senses the exhaustion radiating from her. Belle's finger goes up to her mouth, "Shhhh. I don't want Mom to hear us." She glances anxiously over her shoulder.

"I know, I got your note." Rayon says, "Well, you first."

Belle walks out. Rayon follows. Belle shuts the door quietly. Exiting the cottage, they walk four minutes in silence.

290

Rayon glances at her. "Are you sure High One doesn't know?"

"Yes, I'm sure." Belle waves to someone walking by. She rounds a corner and stops. "Are *you* sure this is the right thing to do?" Belle glances at the door where her hand rests on the knob. "Because if it isn't—"

"It is. I'm sure."

"Okay." Belle bites her lip and nods. "They're in here. But we have to leave as soon as we get in." She looks back at some of the witches walking around. "I don't want to risk getting caught."

"Okay," Rayon says, following her gaze. "Have you ever ghosted before?"

"Yeah. I've only done it once successfully, but… yeah."

Rayon smiles. "Okay. Don't kill him."

Belle swallows and opens the door. Before Rayon's eyes are two guys with blonde hair and blue eyes. One with a sad smile and one with no smile at all. The two guys she knows as Isaac and Aaron, but everyone else in the Guard knows them as the traitors.

"I won't," Belle answers. She shuts the door behind her, takes a big breath, then grabs Aaron's hand. "This may hurt." Then they're gone.

Isaac stares at the place Belle and Aaron were two seconds ago. "Is it seriously going to hurt?" he asks Rayon.

"Oh, please, I'm experienced." Rayon grabs Isaac's arm. "It won't hurt a bit, but you'll probably feel a little tickle."

Isaac smiles bigger. "Rayon, thank you."

"Don't thank me until we've found the real traitor. Maybe then I'll feel better about doing this behind Makeddah's back."

"How is she?"

"It's not been two days. She's pretty horrible, but soon she'll be fine." Rayon raises her brows. "Ready?"

He nods. And Rayon and Isaac disappear.

"Put this on." Isaac pushes a blonde wig to Rayon's chest.

"Excuse me," she says, brushing the wig away. "I happen to like my hair."

"Our father will notice you both," Aaron says. "He has seen your mom. And he… just put them on." He gives Belle a brown wig.

Isaac pulls out a picture. "You need to look like them. Do you have any makeup or eye color changers?"

Rayon laughs with a glance at Isaac. "Eye color changers?" She studies the picture of the blonde and the brunette. "Who are they, anyway?"

"Princess Jasmine of the Eastern Kingdom," he says as he points to the blonde, "and her sister Francesca." He points to the brunette.

"What color are their eyes?" Rayon asks. When Isaac says brown, she smiles. "I learned a little elite trick from Kahlan last week. No eye color changers needed." Rayon closes her eyes and slowly brings her hand to her face, and she feels it morph. Changing the shape to a square instead of a heart, and the eyes brown instead of blue, with a tanned skin tone, and smaller lips. She sees the image in her head and tries to get everything down to the last detail. Then she claps. "Looks good?"

Isaac nods as Aaron tilts his head.

Next, Rayon does Belle. When Belle is completely changed, they both look like two entirely different girls.

The boys take out one dress each from their backpacks. "This is better kingdom attire."

Belle walks out into the woods to change, and Rayon just snaps hers on her body. When Belle comes back, Rayon says, "You realized you could have just magicked it on?"

"Do you know me?" Belle's eyes go wide. "I'd kill my-self."

Rayon rolls her eyes. "Don't you think your father will know that you've been kicked out of the Guard since the traitor is feeding information back to him?" Rayon stuffs her clothes into Isaac's bag. "And don't they know that you two are in the Guard, trying to take away his title?"

"The title he loves more than his sons?" Isaac nods. "Yes, he does. We haven't figured out why he hasn't just thrown us in the dungeon yet. I try to talk to him as little as possible. And we'll avoid him. He shouldn't be in the castle right now, so we should be fine."

Rayon looks at the village looming ahead. "I'm about to go into the castle with a Prince. Wow, my life is much more interesting than I thought it would be a month ago. Thank you for that." Rayon pats her wig. "How do I look?"

"Perfect," Isaac smiles.

They walk into the village. Belle on Aaron's arm and Rayon on Isaac's. Rayon hears the people say things like, "The princes" and "Who are they?"

She smiles at the attention. Maybe she shouldn't enjoy it so much, but it makes her thrive. She sashays onto the bridge. "I really hope we don't see your father," Rayon whispers to Isaac.

He scowls, "You and me both."

Once inside the castle, they get bowed to by some bodyguards and servants, then go straight back for the opening across the courtyard. They walk to the apartments, going to Isaac's first. They get inside, and Belle lets out a long breath as though she has been holding it the whole time, and knowing her, she probably was.

"Okay," Isaac says, "We just need to grab a few things from our apartments, then to the library."

"Will the library have what we need?" Rayon asks, taking in every detail of his room. It's big—bigger than the new apartment she and Makeddah just got. There's a king-sized bed with a gold frame and sheets, a fireplace with two chairs and a coffee table, and, in the corner, a mahogany wardrobe and an antique-looking desk.

The place is bare despite the few luxurious items. Even the nightstands look like they'd cost more than the village houses.

"No, but there is a passageway from it and that is how we will get to my father's office and break in. Find whatever we need there." Isaac stuffs clothing into a duffel. "Can you transport this back to the Witch Center? I can't walk around with it."

Rayon puts her hand on it, and in the blink of an eye, it's gone. "The proper term is ghost when you're talking about moving one place magically to the other, by the way, not transport."

Isaac looks up at her from the pile of clothes he's pushing under the bed. "Noted."

Aaron leaves the room through the back door with everyone following. They go through a thin hallway outside and another door, stepping into a different room that Rayon likes much more. It has the same layout with the bed, the fireplace, and the wardrobe in the same place, but this one features a red rug that spans from one side wall to the other, as well as bookshelves filled with books on every wall.

"Mind if I pop in here every once in a while, you know, to grab a book?" Rayon asks, still in awe over the size of the bookshelves. She knows they have different tastes in books but she can't get over these bookshelves.

"All yours," Aaron says, rushing through a door in the side wall. He hands her his bag and she ghosts it to the Center.

They walk out the front door and down the stairs; they're further from the exit than before. "How many apartments do you have here?" Rayon asks.

"The King's suite, which is in the center, then six around that," Aaron answers. "Hopefully, it will be the Queen's suite soon."

Rayon looks back at him and grins. She hopes so, too.

They walk to the library without any interruptions, except for the few bows from maids. They walk to a staircase; Aaron goes up first, Rayon and Belle following, with Isaac in the back looking out for them. When they get to the library, Rayon sees a man standing at a table.

"Prince 1," he bows. "Prince 2," he bows again. "How may I help you?"

Isaac flashes a smile. "I came in to tell you to take the day off. If my father has a problem with it, tell him to take it up with me." Isaac pats the man on the shoulder whose face shows no emotion. "Good day."

"Good day, Your Highness." The man leaves without a question.

Isaac runs to the books on the back wall.

"They seriously don't know your names?" Belle asks.

Isaac searches through the books. "No one does. Our mom wanted us to be able to leave the castle and not be known as Haggard's sons."

Belle picks up a dusty book. "How'd you keep your identity concealed all this time?" She dusts off the book and blows on it, coughing a second later.

"We walk to the woods, change there, and go wherever we please," Aaron answers. "The sorcerers are the only ones who know our names. The bodyguards, maids, and servants aren't allowed out of the castle anyway."

"Interesting," Rayon turns to look up and down the library walls, "Why this library is so small?" Rayon gazes back at Aaron. "And yet I still want it."

"You're a very envious girl," Aaron says.

"Yeah," Belle laughs. "Always has been. Always will be. When Rayon wants the stuff…" Belle rolls her eyes as if she's heard this line a million times before.

"Rayon gets the stuff," Rayon finishes with a smile, moving her finger over more dusty books. "Everyone should know I get what I want."

"Got it," Isaac says. "Prepare to be amazed." He pulls down a blue book, and nothing happens, not for a few seconds. Then, to Rayon's left, a door opens to reveal a larger silver one. "To the tunnels." He walks to the silver door and pushes it open.

"After you," Aaron says.

Rayon follows Isaac to a dark room. When Rayon slips down a step, she realizes it's a staircase. A dark staircase that is only lighted by the light from the library, which fades when the secret hideaway door closes. "Prepare to be amazed," she says, just as Isaac did. Summoning an orb of light, she throws it to the ceiling and points her fingers down the length of the staircase. The light follows her finger down and glows over the whole staircase, and they all start moving.

"Show off," Belle says, but her voice is so light and sweet that Rayon almost laughs.

"Down here," Isaac says as he turns right into a thin hallway. Orange lights from the ceiling come on as they move past them. Isaac makes another right, and they walk for a few minutes until he stops. "Okay, the door's up there, but it opens to the fire pit in my father's office."

"Fire pit?" Belle asks.

"Yeah, the fireplace," Isaac says. "I don't know if it's on."

Rayon steps up the stairs and presses her face to the door. "No. No heat." She takes a breath and opens the door slowly, and beams when she sees inside. "See, no heat," she whispers, then peeks in farther. "And no evil King. Take my hand."

Aaron takes it, and they ghost into the office so they don't have to walk through the fireplace and dirty their clothes. Rayon hears a door shut, then sees her sister and Isaac a second later. "Okay, where do we look?"

Aaron squints, "Everywhere."

Rayon rummages through the desk while the others looks through bookshelves.

They are making too much noise, which is not good. And with every second they search, Rayon's fear of not finding the traitor increases. It gives her anxiety. Something that she hates. Whenever she's scared, she's really scared. No one knows but her, not even Makeddah. Something bubbles up in her stomach and rises to her chest, and her lip starts twitching.

She shakes out the feeling, but now she's thinking of the bad things that could go wrong. She looks up and sees the damage done to Haggard's office. "Guys, cover your tracks when you finish an area. Come on, we can't get caught," she says in an even tone, not matching her feelings inside. *Confidence.* She thinks to herself. *Confidence.*

"Nothing in the desk," she says.

"Nothing in his bookshelf," Isaac says, straightening it up.

"Hey, I've got something." Belle whispers.

Rayon's eyes turn to Belle. A worn leather black book opened to the last quarter of pages is held in Belle's hands. Belle looks Rayon in the eyes. This is it. This is the key to the traitor. Rayon runs to it and sees scribbles and scrawls that are barely legible.

Somehow, she feels it in her gut. "This is it. This is what we need." But before Rayon can get the whispered words from her mouth, the doorknob turns, and she straightens.

Isaac looks up, a bead of sweat rolling down his head when he whispers, "It's Father."

Forty

Rayon

Yes, I suppose." Haggard is now at the open door speaking to someone.

When Rayon hears Haggard, her first instinct is to ghost out of there, but she knows that's not what Belle is thinking. When the door finally opens—it seems like it takes forever—Rayon inhales a big breath. *Confidence.*

Haggard steps in but stops when he sees his sons and the two girls in front of him. His face is unreadable when he says, "Son?"

Rayon smiles and stands up straighter. *Confidence.*

Isaac bows. "Father."

"What are—"

"We wanted to talk with you, so Cephas told us instead of standing outside like commoners to seat ourselves in here." Isaac smiles but it's not his normal smile. It has no warmth behind it, which sends a chill up Rayon's spine. "Right, Cephas?"

Haggard turns and the bodyguard nods, hiding any trace of the confusion he might have had before the heads turned to him. "Yes, Your Highness."

Rayon glances behind Belle's back. *Haggard's book is gone. Haggard's book is gone.* Rayon repeats to herself over and over. Belle must have ghosted it out. She hopes her sister is smart enough to do that. That's when she notices the man in all black standing in Haggard's shadow. Black hair and brown eyes, freshly shaved face and one earring on his left ear.

She notices it is the man her mother spit at when they were invaded. *What was his name?*

"But aren't you standing?" The man asks.

"Yes, Eliab." Aaron says.

A lightbulb goes on in rayon's mind. *Eliab.*

Aaron continues, "We heard Father coming and we stood," He scans Haggard. "Just like you've always taught us."

Rayon's impressed with how quickly they come up with the lies. She's good at lying herself. That truth would make Makeddah shiver. But looking at them, they are experts.

"And who are these lovely ladies?" Haggard takes Belle and Rayon in completely, making her feel that if he studied them long enough, he could figure out who they are himself.

"Princesses Jasmine and Francesca, Father," Isaac says as Belle and Rayon curtsy.

"Here to wed?" Haggard asks, holding Rayon's gaze.

"We hope soon enough," Rayon smirks telling her sick stomach to quit churning. "Your boys are very stubborn, wanting to stay bachelors forever. I guess that's why I like them," Rayon giggles.

Haggard smiles. "Well, good. Pour them drinks."

"Not necessary, Father," Aaron says. "We are going to take a tour around the city, but first we wanted to come and apologize for our actions."

Isaac nods in a sorrowful way. "We will no longer go to that Guard place. They have kicked us out, something about us being traitors." Isaac waves it away showing its insignificance to him. "That's when we realized our fault in being traitors to you, Father. We hope you can forgive us. We're just glad to be home."

"Well," Haggard nods. "Good." He summons Aaron with his finger and drops his voice, but Rayon can still hear. "But I need you at the Guard. We need the Parish girls on our side." Haggard pulls away and smiles.

Aaron clears his throat. "Why?"

Haggard's smile fades, and his mouth turns into a straight line. "Because."

"Because...?"

"Because they are very important." Eliab says. "*That* is why." Rayon wants to punch the guy, but she stands there as if she's oblivious to the conversation. "Can you get back in good graces with your little Lion Heart?"

"We'll try our best." Aaron nods. "See you at supper."

"Yes." Everyone turns to walk out but then Haggard calls out, "Sons." Aaron and Isaac turn around, and when Rayon circles to see him, she notices the smile on Haggard's face has returned. "It's good to have you back."

Everyone wants to dive into Haggard's diary, but all four decide to wait until tomorrow. Rayon can't completely disappear from the Guard all day or someone might notice her absence.

So, she ghosts back to her room at the Guard, rips off her wig, and morphs her face back into her own. She looks into her wall mirror and flips her hair. "Good to be me. No offence Princess, but I'm way prettier." She shimmies out of her dress and puts on the garments she bought, then walks out of her room.

She doesn't get far before she stops. Two sets of eyes are turned to her. One just staring—Mira—and the other judging—Makeddah. "Oh, hey." She waves and walks to the kitchen.

Makeddah stands. "Where have you been? I didn't see you at breakfast or lunch. You totally missed your magic practice." Makeddah looks at Rayon's feet. "And why are you wearing no shoes? You could get a splinter on these floors."

"You sound like me." Rayon laughs and grabs a slice of bread. "Calm down, I wasn't feeling well. I told Kahlan that I wouldn't meet her today."

"You weren't feeling well in your room?" Makeddah asks. "Mira and I checked it an hour ago. You weren't there. I have been here almost all day, and I didn't see you go in or out."

"You have your ways, I have mine." Rayon twirls one of Makeddah's curls, "See you later."

"No shoes," Makeddah says.

"People can deal with it." Rayon waves it away.

"Hey, will you be there for my fight tonight?"

Rayon pauses, it's not like she has anything better to do. "Yes, I'll be there."

Makeddah smiles, "Thanks."

"I'm feeling better and want to grab some food, you coming?" Rayon waits for the answer, but she is hoping it is a no.

"No," Makeddah answers and Rayon hopes the relief is not written on her face. "Fasting before the fight."

"All right." Rayon walks out of the door into the lobby without another word. Makeddah is going to be suspicious. Rayon wanted to avoid this, but the fact that her sister is nosy doesn't help. She needs to be more careful.

She can't tell Makeddah about Aaron and Isaac, or she will be upset. Rayon will be the bad guy, and Makeddah will give her the silent treatment. And the fact that Belle is in on it too will be worse for Makeddah to hear. Not only one, but both sisters keeping a secret from her.

"Wish she could take a lie every once in a while," Rayon mutters to the ground.

She steps out of the lobby and onto the hard gravel. "Oh, that hurts." She walks on her tippy toes on her tippy toes and hops to the food bar, but the gravel does not soften.

"Need help?" A deep voice says. Rayon glances over and sees Preston. He looks down at her feet. "Oh, here." He slides over his slippers.

"No, it's okay." Rayon smiles. But her mind goes back to the night of the ball, which makes her think of Isaac and Aaron, which then makes her think of the diary. So, her smile is gone. She looks at the slippers, then slips them on. "Thanks."

"I saw the way you were reading that book a couple days ago." Preston says grabbing his own food. "Must be really good."

Two days ago? "Nope. Not at all actually." She shudders remembering all the plot holes in the book and the bad dialogue. No action and no romance. "I've read many bad books, but that has to be in the top ten worst books I've ever read."

It takes him a minute to respond, but he finally says. "Wow, you still looked absorbed."

"I guess. I have to concentrate to read bad books, or they never get finished."

Preston smiles. She pops a grape into her mouth and smiles back. Kahlan emerges from the dinner crowd, and Rayon straightens. She forgot to cancel their training today. "Shoot," she says under her breath. "I've got to go." *Before Kahlan spots me,* she doesn't say out loud.

Preston looks back and starts to say something, but Rayon turns the corner faster than he can get his words out. She finds the nearest home and leans against the wall, closing her eyes. How could she forget? She never forgets to inform her teachers of absence. That's Makeddah and Belle's thing, not Rayon's.

She waits for a full two minutes with her eyes closed, then she peeks one eye open. As soon as she sees Preston standing there, she nearly drops her plate of food.

"What the heck?"

"What are you doing?" Preston asks, his smile still there.

"I forgot to tell Kahlan I wasn't able to make it today, so now I'm here." She lifts her plate of food. "Is she gone yet?" Preston checks around the corner for her and nods. "Good."

She wants to sit but the gravel will be too uncomfortable. So, she stands and eats. Preston looks amused, then creates a small wooden table with two chairs. He pulls on chair out for her and she smirks. She sets her plate down and sits.

Preston joins her, and it's the first time she's surprised by him. He doesn't hang out with her. He barely does with Makeddah, usually only for lessons and sometimes outside of that, but not much. Rayon stares at him as he eats a piece of chicken.

"You can go," she says. "You don't have to stay with me. I'm good alone. I appreciate the gesture though."

He laughs. "I'm just making sure you don't steal my slippers." When Rayon tilts her head, he points to her feet.

"Oh." Rayon slips them off, but he pushes them away, his face saying it was a joke. So, she puts them back on and her gaze lingers on the perfectly crafted wood table.

Her mind goes to the fact that she could have ghosted herself shoes, but she was too clouded to think of it. Now, she is too intrigued by the man sitting across from her.

Silence hangs around them, which she doesn't mind. She likes noise, but she's no hater of silence. It seems like Preston doesn't mind, either.

After seconds of silence, he looks up and his gaze comes to her. He stares at her, and she stares back, unsure if it's turned into a staring contest. He finally says, "You don't think it was them." It's not a question. "Is it because they're your friends?"

"Why do you say I don't think it was them?"

"The way you looked at Makeddah while she was announcing them as traitors." He shrugs. "You looked like you didn't believe her. Like you knew she was wrong."

Rayon chuckles. Her face must tell more than she believes at times. "It's not because they're my friends, it's because they aren't traitors. I know it," she says, without adding the fact that they are in her Witch Center and things haven't burned down yet.

"I don't think it's them, either." He scratches his head. "If you ever need some help finding the real one, I'm here."

Rayon lifts a brow. "Thanks." She peeks up at him, a grin playing her lips "You were looking at me when she was banishing them?"

"Yes," he replies.

"Why?"

A smile rises on his lips, "Guess."

Instead of guessing, she bites her lip and continues to eat. She is living in a book right now and if she plays this right, she will get a fairytale ending.

They finish their plates of food in silence, then he takes her plate. Standing, she slips off his oversized slippers and slides them to him. With a nod, he's gone.

She ghosts to the lobby and stares at the door leading to their apartment. She does not want to face her sister but she can't avoid her now.

She opens the cracked door and sits on the couch next to Makeddah, who is concentrating on a schedule or something. Rayon isn't one to get into her thoughts when she's around people. But right now, it almost seems overwhelming. Makeddah always says it depends solely on her, but it doesn't. Not really. It depends on anyone who cares and wants to catch this person.

Now, Makeddah isn't even looking for them, and Rayon is here trying to pick up pieces that are glued to the floor. It's fun, it's an adventure, and it's exhausting.

"Rayon, I'm putting you in a white dress."

"Huh. What?" Rayon looks down at Mira, who is lying on her stomach on the floor. Rayon didn't notice she was there.

"For Makeddah's graduation."

"I thought those were casual." Rayon looks at the dress Mira is drawing.

"No." Mira looks up and bites her pencil, "Well, the first time you guys went to one, yes. But this is our Lion Heart Princess we are talking about."

Rayon smiles. "I like dressing up." She looks at Mira's sketch pad and back up to her. "I thought you were in the depression stage?"

"No, I'm in the 'you only live once' stage." Mira smiles. "Because you do."

"The circle of grief," Rayon says, "who would've thought it'd be so complex?"

Forty-one

Makeddah looks everywhere for Rayon. She is about to fight for the first time on fight night. She is determined to win. She will be picturing Isaac's face and how much she wants to pummel him for lying to her.

He said his mother and father died—killed by Haggard. That was untrue. They don't even know what happened to their mother. Why would he lie about something like that? And his literal father is Haggard who is perfectly healthy on the throne that is supposed to be her family's throne.

His face seems like a fun thing to punch right now.

Kahlan and Matt are coordinating the Units to be moved right now and Makeddah hadn't seen Rayon all morning, and when she saw her earlier she sensed Rayon was lying. She can't prove it though, if she felt sick, she felt sick. But where was she?

Rayon is supposed to support her, be there for her. But maybe Rayon hates Makeddah because of her sending Isaac and Aaron out of the Guard.

She's wrong, they have to be the traitors. And once she realizes her mistake, she will come crawling back to Makeddah and say "I'm sorry for yelling at you, I was wrong. Let's be the best of sisters again."

But tonight she does not need an apology, tonight she needs her sister to show up.

She finds herself sitting alone in the dingy washroom preparing for her fight at nine. She has fifteen minutes before it starts. The other fights were mediocre. No one seems ready to battle Haggard.

Maybe their excuse is that they just spent all day yesterday moving and today getting settled but it doesn't seem like a great excuse.

Makeddah basically orchestrated everything and she is ready now more than ever to fight.

They should be angry, they should be pumped.

Makeddah watches the clock tick, maybe Rayon just didn't want to see the first fights but will show up any minute for hers.

"Hey, you ready?" Mira walks in and sits next to Makeddah.

"Yeah, is Rayon here?"

Mira shrugs, "I didn't see her. But it's pretty packed for your fight because the Lion Heart Princess is about to be on the stage."

"And about to win." She smiles. "Matt is the ref?"

Mira nods, "I'll be judging so go kick some fire butt."

"I'm using fire too."

Mira stands, "I know." Then she walks out like she doesn't have a care in the world.

Makeddah takes a breath and stands.

She's ready.

As she walks to the Units, she notices Mira was right, this place is packed. This must be the fight of the night.

They are in the Water Unit, which Makeddah chose because she wanted to smell the way Isaac smells while she won a fight.

And she is fighting an opponent of his, Mikko. Which makes it even better. Once she beats Mikko, she will prove that she is better than Isaac and she can let off some steam. Two birds with one stone.

Makeddah spots Rayon in the front seat talking to Preston. She waves before they get ushered in but she's not sure if Rayon saw her.

The Water Unit smells salty and feels humid. Her feet sink in the sand as she follows Matt and Mikko to their starting spots.

She hopes she can predict Mikko's moves. He's trained with her a few times after Grace's death, and she's seen him do one of these before. She should have the upper hand.

Matt takes a red flag from his pocket and waves it high then tilts it to Mikko and next toward Makeddah.

Matt clears his throat, "Shake hands."

They do as he says.

He raises the flag high and cuts it between them then steps back.

Makeddah knows Mikko does not go straight for the kill, so she will have to initiate.

She steps up, and throws a fireball, trying to psyche him out but instead he smiles and tilts his head. "Come on Makeddah, that will not work. Let's try again."

"This isn't a lesson Mikko, don't treat me like your student."

Mikko stops smiling and snaps back as if someone just slapped him. "Fighting while angry? You shouldn't do that, Mak."

Makeddah voice is low as she asks, "Yeah, why not?"

"Because you either lose brutally or you win and regret the things you done and said. Are you sure you want to continue?"

She stares and tightens her stance. She must be ready at every moment. "Yep."

Mikko glances at Matt, who shrugs, then back to Makeddah. "Okay."

Makeddah is done with the talking. She throws five fire balls from her palms and kicks two from her feet.

Mikko blocks them with a fire shield and when the shield goes down, Makeddah can see the confusion in his eyes.

She doesn't know why he's acting like this. She barely knows him, he barely knows her. Yet, he seems genuinely hurt.

He makes swords of fire in both hands and starts to chop away at her. She mimics the motion and starts to duel.

There's no clinking of swords and the fire mainly collapses on each other. She has a feeling he is trying to tire her out.

She looks into his eyes and pictures Isaac and all the lies. She pictures Alda's lies. Haggard's evil acts, Grace's death. She pictures everything that has ever worked against her and she fights.

She fights until she feels numb. The fire is leaving her body as if she has been doing this her whole life. As if it's in tune with her anger.

She punches, she kicks, she blocks. And he does the same. A fiery wall burning in her eyes, she forgets everything.

When her chest starts heating up, the wall comes down. Everything slows and she finds a ball of fire on her chest as she flies through the air. She's about to lose and the world is slowing down so that she can feel the loss.

She hits the ground with a vicious thump and rolls backward towards the wall.

Tears escape her eyes and she watches through them. Matt is holding up a red flag in Mikko's direction, but Mikko doesn't look happy. He just nods and walks over to help Makeddah up.

Makeddah stands on her own and wipes the sand off.

"Are you okay?" he asks.

Makeddah scowls at the pain shooting through her arm. "Fine." And she walks away.

The crowd is loud and even in the midst of that she hears Rayon call out her name but she does not turn.

She stomps out of there as quickly as possible with balled fists.

She was supposed to win. She was supposed to prove something.

The only thing she ended up proving is that she is a loser.

She feels like she can't breathe. She walks to the ghoster and clicks her key to ghost outside. Her breathing gets faster, and her anger is flaring.

She throws fire at the tree and the grass around it catches fire. She watches the crackling flames laugh at her. She drags her feet to them and drops to her knees.

"Why?" She tells herself that she doesn't know who she is asking, but she does. She half expects an answer to come from the Creator but he's silent amid her crises. "Why are my parents dead? Why are my friends' liars? Why am I a failure? Why did you make me this way?"

She wants Alda. She wants Alda to explain what this all means but she feels like she has no one.

Not even the Creator is on her side.

Forty-two

Rayon

Makeddah peeks into Rayon's room for the fifteenth time and an hour later, when she finally stops, Rayon gets out of bed and puts on a dress. She puts her pillows in place, adds a magic red wig, and makes her alarm clock sound like a snore—which is harder than she thought it'd be—and smiles at her work. "Genius. I am a genius."

She walks to the center of her room, closes her eyes, and she's gone.

When she appears in the room Isaac and Aaron are staying at in the Witch Center, the first thing she sees is Belle sitting on the back of a chair looking over Aaron's shoulder, reading the diary.

"Hey, I thought you would wait for me."

"Well, finally, you're here. What took you so long?" Belle asks.

"*Hello*," Rayon rolls her eyes and walks over to their chair. "We have a nosy sister on the other side."

"Are you talking about you or Makeddah?" Belle quips.

"Oooohh, cat fight," Isaac says, coming from the back room. "What?" He shrugs, looking at the stares he's getting. "How is Sunshine?"

Rayon shrugs a shoulder, "she lost in fight night."

Isaac asks, "Fight night on a Tuesday?" Rayon nods and Isaac bites his lip, "To who?"

"Mikko. She was pretty torn up about it. But when we find the real traitor, you guys can come back with me, expose them and watch her graduate today." The boys are silent, "You'll come back after we find the real traitor, right?"

"Just like my father will be disappointed to know, no, we're not. Ever." Isaac laughs at Rayon's horror-struck face. "I'm kidding, but Aaron and I agreed. We aren't needed here right now. Other places need teachers. Korzon isn't the only kingdom or village."

He pauses finding the words, "And I need to give Makeddah time to forgive us for lying. I don't want her to feel like she is being smothered by us," Isaac glances at Belle and Aaron who seem preoccupied by the journal. "Please." He takes out a letter. "Give this to Makeddah." He takes a breath and closes his eyes. "Tell her to reach out when she is ready."

"Well, where are you guys going?"

"We're going to try to help some people. It's always been our dream to help the less fortunate by lending a hand in teaching them their elements." He smirks, "Oh, and try not to find out how to get married until we come back, okay?"

Rayon shakes her head. "What? Why?"

"Because I want to be a part of the big enlightenment. And if the guy is there when we find out, I want to walk you down the aisle." Isaac smiles his big broad smile and winks.

"You're pretty cocky to think I'd ask you."

He shrugs, a smug look on his face. "I call it confidence."

Rayon smirks, no wonder she kept screaming it in her head yesterday.

Rayon throws her arms around him. "I'll wait."

They let go of the embrace.

She looks at Aaron at the clearing of his throat. He is standing and handing the book to Belle. Isaac moves to Belle as Aaron makes his way to Rayon.

It takes him a moment to say, "Okay, I wrote a letter too." He waits for her to say something, and when she doesn't, he takes it out of his back pocket and hands it to her. "Give it to Mira." Rayon takes it, and the instant she starts to move he stops her. "Don't open it!"

"I'm not going to open it, dummy. I already know what it says, duh."

"No, you don't," Aaron says, folding his arms.

"Yes, I do. I've been doing this a long time." Aaron furrows his brows at her. She smirks. "I'm a romance consultant."

"To whom?"

"To the fictional people, duh."

He frowns, "Stop saying duh."

"Sorry. I'm overwhelmed." She stands on her tippy toes and hugs Aaron. It's only after a few seconds that she feels him relax and hug her back. "She was really broken up about you too. Are you sure you want to bear your heart to her in a letter and not face to face?" she says, letting go.

"I'm sure." His scowl tells her to not continue any further.

"Okay, okay. Sorry." She puts the letters in her pocket. "Okay, but I don't want any love letters coming through me so eventually you guys will have to talk to the girls yourselves."

Aaron turns to Belle and Isaac. "You're ridiculous."

"You're just now noticing?"

Isaac claps. "Enough about us, have you guys found anything?" he asks Belle and Aaron. It seems his two minutes of reading over Belle's shoulder was not profitable.

Aaron shakes his head, but Belle is flipping through the pages herself, skimming every page. Rayon scoots Isaac over and peers over Belle's shoulder and attempts to take the book, but Belle pulls back.

"I'm better at reading," Rayon says.

"Don't mess with me, Ray. I have been taking care of our crying mother all night and morning." Belle's eyes widen, "And she got really mad and yelled at High One. A lot. I'm scared of her. I think High One is, too." She turns to the book and skims again. "I may not look tough, but fighting off the prissy little witches has given me some skin, so back off."

Rayon throws up her hands, "Fine."

"I found something. Something weird." Belle screws up her face. "Guys, I don't think this is Haggard's diary. Unless Haggard talks in third person and his first person refers to someone else."

Rayon squints at the words on the page. Belle reads out, "'My son has finally obtained the Lion Heart. We can do the work for her. We can finally work for her and throw Haggard to the side.'" Belle looks up with a breath, then reads again. "Down here it says, 'The plan is in place; the girl will die. She knows too much. My son feels no remorse.' This was written the day you guys fought the sorcerers."

"Grace," Isaac says. "Someone planned to kill Grace."

Son? No remorse? Rayon is wracking her head as to who would be close enough to Grace but also feel no remorse. And though she knows it seems impossible she keeps coming up with one answer.

Belle looks up. "Who is Matthais?"

"Matt?" Rayon rubs her lips as Belle glances up with a nod. "I mean, of course, it's Matt. Of course. He had it written all over him."

"Not really." Isaac crosses his arms. "I never suspected him. And it doesn't make sense; he killed his wife?" The question lingers in the air between them. "Grace said 'them' when she was dying. Them who? Not *just* Matt. And it's too easy. We couldn't have found it already. Keep looking."

"'Matt and Jo have taken care of the witch; the battle is on.'" Belle flips through the pages. "And there is plenty more of that. He mostly says Matthias but it is clearly Matt in other paragraphs. And I checked the front page of the diary. It belongs to a man named Eliab."

Aaron's face darkens. "Haggard's right-hand man, the lead sorcerer of the Korzon sorcery clan."

Rayon won't ever be able to forget him. He invaded their home. He is always by Haggard's side. Him and his stupid earring.

But Rayon's brain looks over the resemblances between the two. Dark hair, dark eyes. But their faces don't look the same when Rayon thinks back to it. Eliab is ugly and has rough edges. Matt is softer with a more likable face. "Why was this in Haggard's office?"

Belle narrows at the book, "It also says something about the Parish girls, too. He's talking about us again." Belle gapes, her brows creased with worry. Isaac takes the book and looks down at its page.

"Listen, Rayon," Aaron snatches the book from Isaac and pushes it at her. "You need to warn Makeddah, make her read this."

Rayon nods, "Belle, are you coming?"

"No, I'm going with mom to the graduation. Go tell Makeddah."

Rayon does not waste any time ghosting to the Guard. She lands outside of their apartment and looks inside. "Mak!" she shouts out. No answer. She sees her room door open and peeks inside. Not there.

She runs out to the courtyard. She looks around and finds Mira giving people instructions for the graduation.

"Mira," she says out of breath. "Where is Makeddah?"

"Stonehaven. She told Kahlan last minute that she wanted the graduation there."

Rayon sighs, looking over at the hill.

"She's with Matt and Kahlan so she's good."

Rayon's eyes go wide, "Matt is with her?" Rayon gives Mira no explanation for her sudden reaction she just ghosts out.

Forty-three

The dress is beautiful, the day is bright, but Makeddah is still not satisfied. She looks down at the nice black leather that flows out at her waist. Mira spent all her time on changing her graduation dress to make it a full skirt and overlaid it with beautiful black lace. She covered up the open patch where Mira's birthmark is and instead cut out a back piece that perfectly encircles her birthmark.

But her favorite part about this dress is that the sheath her father used to wear fits perfectly with it.

She wanted to carry her parents with her on this day.

As she takes her breaths, she practices holding her birthmark just as Mira did at her graduation. She must be perfect. No one is graduating with her so she will be the only focus.

She goes over her steps, knowing she only had little time to practice.

She looks up as Kahlan and Matt set up the chairs and stage. Kahlan has already protected the area so she will have to invite people in soon.

She catches Matt's gaze and he saunters over. "How are you feeling?" he asks.

She shrugs. When she looks over at him, she notices the sweat that has accumulated on his brow. He was just helping Kahlan rearrange the chairs, so she doesn't look too deeply into it.

"Thank you, Matt, for being there for me. I know it's hard for you since you used to hate my guts but now, I'd like to think of you as an old and wise friend."

Matt grimaces. "Old, really?"

She chuckles and Kahlan begins ushering people through so she tries to hide behind the crowd so that she can make her big entrance soon.

"I'm nervous about remembering all of my steps," she admits.

Matt clears his throat. "You'll be fine. I'm going to help Kahlan organize the people." Then he is gone.

Makeddah rolls her eyes and mutters, "So much for being there for me."

Finally, the last of the people make their way through and Makeddah sees Kahlan signal to her that they will start in five minutes.

With an inhale, she practices holding her birthmark in her hand again. But instead she jumps and it drops as she hears Rayon call out her name.

"Mak, I need to talk to you."

She looks out of breath like she ran here. Makeddah brushes her off. She has barely been there for Makeddah and she can't take another chewing out right now.

"Go sit down, Rayon."

"Mak, it's serious."

"I can't handle anything serious right now. I am graduating. Now, please, go away."

Rayon opens her mouth to speak again but Mira is coming up behind her and pulling her away so that Makeddah can make her entrance. She sees Rayon join Alda and Belle and they are all whispering, if not bickering with each other. But Makeddah focuses on herself.

Everyone sits, she thumbs her sheath, and she stands tall.

Kahlan announces, "Hello, everyone, and thank you for coming. Makeddah came into the Guard with no knowledge of her gifts. No understanding of how it worked or who she was. But today we will see our Lion Heart Princess present herself to us. Graduation has only been a small step in her journey and we celebrate with her. I am so very proud of this young woman."

Kahlan moves from the stage and Makeddah starts to walk down the aisle, holding her birthmark in her hand. She stands up tall and stares ahead at her destination on the stage.

When she enters the stage she lets her birthmark fall and looks up at the drummer in the back, that again, appeared from nowhere.

She glances back to Matt, who is fidgeting, and to Rayon who is glaring at him.

Makeddah tells herself not to get too distracted. She takes her sword out and holds it high, feeling like an imposter after her loss from the night before.

She takes a warrior stance and moves swiftly across the stage then sheaths her sword.

As her hands lift to the sky, the elements fly up one by one. First earth, next water, then fire, then air. She swirls them above her head and wishes for them to stay put while she takes hold of her sword again.

She again raises the sword to the sky, in between the elements moving swiftly in a circle above her.

She looks down to the crowd and they erupt with applause.

Again, feeling like a fraud, no smile is brought to her face. She covered a two minute routine and she doesn't even think she deserves to be a Lion Heart. She doesn't deserve to be their Princess.

Though the crowd is still clapping and cheering. One person stands out to Makeddah in the back. He wasn't there a minute ago and now he is clear as day, a smirk on his face.

Makeddah would never forget his dangly earring.

She points her sword towards him. "How did you get in here?" She says it too quietly for the people to hear but Eliab grins as if he heard her every word.

Eliab throws a beam of black magic at Makeddah but it is slow and weak. He is just wanting attention now. And he gets it. People start screaming and scramming and he makes his way to the stage.

Rayon, Matt, Alda and Belle are quickly behind him.

"Makeddah—" Rayon starts but she is interrupted by a glare from Eliab.

When she cowers, he smirks and looks at Makeddah.

"Take me." She says, "I don't want anyone else hurt."

"Well, sorry, I am here for more than just you." He looks at Matt who stands straighter and walks to him with a straight face.

"No. You don't get to have him. You take me and me alone."

Rayon speaks out before Eliab can answer, "Matt's his son." She lifts up a black book and Eliab glares at her. She glares back, "Yeah, I was with the Princes and we found out about all your secrets."

Makeddah is still computing what Rayon said. "Son?" There's a crack in Makeddah's voice, but she shakes it away. She turns back to Matt. "You're his son?"

Rayon frowns. "Yes, Makeddah, he is."

Eliab's mouth twitches, "I told Haggard those boys could never love him." He chuckles.

Rayon doesn't take to his comment. Instead she asks, "And who's Jo, Matt? The real woman you love, or is there such a thing?"

Matt tries to jump at Rayon, but Eliab holds him back. "Don't worry, son. She's not our goal here."

Makeddah clenches her fist. When she stretches out her hand, Eliab sends sparks at her with a flick of his wrist. Makeddah falls backward onto the stage. Eliab pushes Matt to her, and Matt walks up and grabs her arm. She sees Alda, Belle and Rayon try to reach for her but magic flies from elsewhere and they are stopped.

Eliab grins. "Jo!" he shouts. A silhouette comes and goes, and Eliab, Matt, and Makeddah go along with it and the last thing Makeddah remembers is the look of horror on her mother's face.

Makeddah wakes up on the grass. She feels different. Like she's been hit and consumed with darkness. It's in the pit of her stomach, the back of her brain, covering her heart. And when she opens her eyes, all she sees is black. Yet, it's bright outside. The sun is shining.

But she isn't.

Someone roughly pulls her up to her feet. "Calm down!" Makeddah says. "Or I'll pass out on you again." She glares at Matt. He doesn't say anything, he just keeps moving. "Where's your father, huh?"

She doesn't remember the chain being put on her. She doesn't remember Eliab leaving. She just remembers landing next to a waterfall and passing out. She's not even sure what time it is. But when they come out of the woods and

Makeddah sees a bunch of small and wrecked houses, she knows they're in the village.

She looks up at the sky. The clouds are covering the sun, making her feel worse inside. "Can you at least tell me why you did it?" This time Matt glances over. "Why did you act like my friend? Like I could trust you?"

"It was my order," he says as if that will be enough for her but knowing it won't. They turn right then left and they're out in the open village.

"Why did you follow it? You could have just been there, not let me bother you. You could have sat in the background instead of making an effort with me. But you didn't." She tries to tug her arm from his hold, but he tightens his grip. "You made a friend in everyone."

"I didn't want to." He stops walking. "I followed my order; I brought you to the Guard. Then you… you had to be Miss Braveheart. You had to like me. You had to be around me and make me—" He shakes his head, stopping his sentence short. "It wasn't my fault."

"So, it was mine? So, everything was my fault?" Makeddah scoffs. "I'm a kid. I needed someone. You're not a kid. You could have sent me away, Matt."

He tugs her along. "No, I couldn't, Makeddah. I really couldn't."

As they walk in silence, Makeddah reflects on the way everything happened this morning. Rayon tried to warn her, and she didn't listen.

She could spend her time blaming herself or Rayon for not trying hard enough but instead she is just worried. Every thing that has happened is because of her, and her family is constantly in danger because of it.

Makeddah sees the castle come into view. He's taking her to be Haggard's slave.

And when she tries to use her elements, it doesn't work. Something must be restricting her right now. Then she remembers her first lesson in the Guard. They are magic binding chains.

She walks alongside him and tries to think of all the things she wants to say to her family and her friends. The first being, "I'm sorry."

She swallows back a lump in her throat. "Was Rayon, right?" Makeddah realizes she has to specify because Rayon has been right about a lot of things lately. "Did you not love Grace?" He doesn't move other than the slow walk they're taking. "When I asked you if you did, did you lie?"

He clears his throat.

Makeddah feels tears coming, but she doesn't let them fall. She looks around the village to try and stop them. They pass a vendor's booth, and she sees a big brown spot on the ground next to it. It takes her a second to realize that it is dried blood.

"That's from your rebellion," Matt says, nodding to the dried blood. His brows are furrowed when he says, "To answer your question from earlier…" he pauses, going up the bridge leading to the castle. The bodyguard's nod, and the doors swing open. "Yes," he says. "Everything is your fault."

Then he pushes her in.

She does not remember the castle from the night they came to the ball. There were too many people. Too much noise and she was distracted.

But she sees it perfectly in the light of day. They walk into the courtyard and she looks up at the cloudy sky, then she takes in her surroundings. The ground is a dirty grey stone. The pillars and wall are the same dirty stone color.

There is a broken fountain in the center of the courtyard, it seems like they put a mallet to it and just beat it down until it could barely stand. No water flows from it and is covered in mud which Makeddah finds odd. She remembers it being covered by a rug during the ball.

She sees straight ahead that there is an opening to another part of the castle but Matt pulls her away before she can look deeper. Matt pushes her along, and she steps into the room the masquerade ball was held in. Now it looks completely different. There are no people, no food tables, and only four bodyguards.

Matt leads her to a door. Two bodyguards stand in front, one takes a ring from his pocket that has probably twenty keys on it. He searches for two different ones and unlocks the door for them.

They step into the smaller room, and again there are two bodyguards. These ones are standing in front of a large gate. They wait for the door to be closed and locked before they open the gate that has its own sets of locks.

Matt drags Makeddah down the stairs and to the left. Makeddah then notices that she is in a prison. All the cells are lined up on her left and right sides.

Matt shoves her into a cell and the bars shut on Makeddah, and she looks up at Matt. He removes the chains and begins to shut the gate. She has a slim chance, so she throws fire at him, but it bounces back and hits her on the shoulder.

He sighs, "Can't use that stuff in here."

Makeddah hisses and snaps her head back to him. "I've got that, thanks." He rolls his eyes and starts to walk away, but Makeddah steps up to the bars. She tries to reach her hand through, but a shield blocks her. "Matt!" she shouts before he walks out of her sight. He looks back at her. "I'm hungry."

"Makeddah, please."

"Matt, I'm serious," she calls, and as if on cue, her stomach growls. He rolls his eyes again. She wants to do the same just for looking at him.

"I'll get you some food."

Makeddah hears his footsteps receding, then it's silent. She peers into the cell across from her, but it's too dark to see inside. She looks up and sees a small yellow light hanging from her ceiling, identical to the ones in the hallway.

She sits back on her cot. It's hard and uncomfortable. It's not going to help her to relax before she's enslaved. She holds her shoulder; it is a little sore where she hit herself. She hopes it's not there in the morning.

She hopes she can escape.

Matt comes back with a plate of mush. It looks like they boiled a bunch of things together until it got really soft then slapped it onto the plate.

She holds back the bile rising in her throat. "You live in a castle. You can't give me something better?"

"Prison food, Makeddah."

"Oh, is it your order to give this stuff out, too?" He frowns at her and walks away.

Maybe it's because of the shock of everything or the fact that her brain is barely working, but she isn't sad anymore. She's just hungry and tired.

She eats the gross slop—which tastes as bad as it looks—then throws the plate to the side. The bodyguard in front of her cell switches positions with another and stands there like a rock.

When she thinks of today, it only brings her questions and a headache. She is sure she's had a thousand headaches since being at the Guard.

What did Matt mean by his order? Why is she so tired? Why hasn't Haggard made her his slave yet?

What about Matt and Eliab being so different from other sorcerers? The sorcerer Isaac killed was kind of the same. They don't have a rotten smell and decaying skin like the other ones. What makes them so different?

She lies back on her cot and looks up at the brown ceiling, down to the water stains near the water basin, and at the dirty grey sheets. It's gross here. But it's as if her body isn't aware of that. She falls asleep right there on the cot, the exhaustion taking over.

Makeddah pops up at the sound of her bars creaking open. Matt pulls her up and puts chains on her wrists, behind her back. "Come on. Haggard wants to see you."

This is it. Makeddah thinks. *He's going to cut off my hair and make me bow to him.* She walks in front of Matt, and they turn right, walking up the stairs to where a bodyguard opens the big gate, and they step into the other room. Just like yesterday, the two bodyguards wait for the gate to be closed and locked before they open the door to the ballroom.

Makeddah notices there is now one throne up on the stage. She didn't notice that yesterday, but she remembers the three at the masquerade ball. But today the throne looks different, bigger. Maybe it's because the two smaller thrones that were there before aren't anymore.

Haggard is sitting on that big throne with a smug look on his face, and he's not alone despite the other thrones missing. Eliab is standing on his right side, and when Matt stops Makeddah in the center of the room and bows, he walks up and stands on Haggard's left.

"There's no point in asking you to bow to me, now is there?" Haggard pouts.

"Not really," Makeddah says.

He makes a *tsk, tsk, tsk* sound. "Fine then, let's get this meeting over with." He grabs a paper and looks over it. It takes him forever to put it down. And when he does, he grabs another paper and looks over that one. Then he gives it to Matt and looks at Makeddah. "Well, you've been very busy in the past month, haven't you?"

Makeddah shakes her head. Month? That doesn't sound right. It must have been longer than a month. Feels like it's been eight months, not one. She looks up at Haggard and sighs. "I guess so."

"Yes." He nods. "It's been manifested to you that men are real—though they weren't the first ones you've seen. But *you* didn't know that." He giggles like a little girl. "You've found out you're a Lion Heart. You started using that, practicing day and night. You've met Princes, killed a man—"

"I didn't kill a man. Your son killed him." Makeddah wishes she could cross her arms.

"Well, good for him." He continues, "You've seen a friend die, danced with a King, and started a rebellion. Graduated." He shakes his head and folds his hands in front of his chest. "Very busy, indeed." His eyes trail from the ground and up to Makeddah. He has a devilish grin on his face, "Did you find the other traitor?"

"What?" Makeddah remembers when she danced with him at the ball, he said two. She believed him. That's why Isaac and Aaron made so much sense. But now? Nothing makes sense. "What do you mean?" She looks at Matt, "What does he mean?"

There can't be another. The closest people to Matt are Kahlan and Mira. It can't be them. But it could be. Could it be?

But Matt does not answer, he looks away. Haggard chuckles, "There are two traitors, but I guess you hadn't figured that out yet."

Another person in the Guard working among them. Then she thinks to the grey eyes and the voice that is so distant in her memories, but it was a woman. A familiar voice. She just doesn't know which familiar voice.

Makeddah looks around, waiting for his point. Was he just trying to rile her up now for his satisfaction?

It doesn't take long before he gets tired of the silence. "I think the most important thing of all is that you've discovered you are the Princess." He shakes his head, a smile showing excitement. "How did that make you feel? To know you have a kingdom, but you'll never rule it. To know you'll never see your parents? To know you're the one who put the witches in danger and everyone else in the village who serves you? To know the only reason your witches were in danger was because I wanted you to be my slave."

His pure joy makes Makeddah sick.

"So, are you going to do it?" She asks. "Are you going to put shackles on my feet and force me to bow to you?" Her gaze falls on Eliab, Matt, and then back on Haggard. "I only have one favor. I want you to tell my family and my friends and my people that I love them and that I'm sorry. That's it. Then I'll submit to you."

He stares at Makeddah, the joy completely removed. She knows she's not ready, she knows her life ahead of her will be everything she hates. She's going to have to think about all the things she's failed at. All the things she's progressed in. All the things she wanted to do, while mopping floors and bowing to him.

"No."

Makeddah snaps her head up when he says it. "No?"

"No."

"What? I thought that was why you took me. I thought that I was here because you wanted me to submit to you."

Haggard nods slowly, "I did."

When he gives no further explanation she says, "And you don't, now? Why not?" He doesn't answer, just stares at her. Even though she doesn't know him too well, she knows this isn't his typical behavior. "Are you just going to sit there and look at me? At least say something smart back."

He sighs. "I want to challenge you. You have discovered that Korzon is your kingdom, and I know you want it back. So, I want to give you a fair shot."

Makeddah looks at Matt, but even he looks confused. She turns back to Haggard. "Are you joking? Are you playing some sort of game?" she asks. "Something tells me you don't give fair shots."

"I don't. And this is why it is your lucky day." He smiles. "I'm feeling merciful. I will give you food tonight and tomorrow and let you have a good night's rest. I'm done with you now." He waves for her to go away. "Bye."

Makeddah squints at him, but Matt descends the stage and grabs her so her eyes fall to the ground. They walk through the door and through the gate, down the stairs, and to her cell. When the chains are off her and she's inside of the cell again, she puts her hands on the bars.

"Matt, what is he doing?" she asks.

"I don't know, Makeddah." he says, "Eat and get some sleep. I'll see you in the morning." And then he's gone.

Forty-four

hallenge? Makeddah can't stop thinking about it. What kind of challenge is Haggard talking about? Why was he acting so weird?

She eats the food she's been given. It's a better meal than the last one, but she still can't enjoy it. Not only is she in prison, but she's in a prison that's supposed to be owned by her. The weird part is that she's being locked up so she can try to take her castle back.

She can't fathom the reason Haggard decided not to enslave or even kill her. It must be a good one because he's no fool.

She notices for the first time that the prison is almost completely silent, and she wonders if she is the only one there. Did Haggard keep her isolated to trip her up?

Makeddah lies down, and the light in her cell shuts off. One of the bodyguards yell, "Lights out!" And small yellow lights in the hallway are the only things allowing her to see.

She wants to be ready for this challenge, meaning she will have to sleep, but sleep escapes her.

Her mind races. What are Rayon, Belle, and Alda doing right now? She hopes they don't come to rescue her. If she fails, then she fails, but she doesn't want them to be involved. Maybe if she stays away from the witches, none of them will die brutal deaths anymore.

Her thoughts wander back and forth, but it always comes back to Matt and Grace, Isaac and Aaron. All the mistakes she's made and the thoughts she's had about them. She's most upset about pinning the traitor problem on Isaac and Aaron. Rayon's going to be able to say I told you so. She didn't think she should believe Isaac when he told the story, but he was telling the truth. She knew there were no lies in his eyes.

Eventually, she falls asleep. Maybe because her head hurts so much and she tries not to think anymore, or maybe because her body knows what's about to happen tomorrow. Her mind and her body agree to keep her as rested as possible to give her the best possible chance.

A man pulls Makeddah up, and she opens her eyes, but sleep wears on them and they shut again. She coughs and feels the cold chains wrap her wrists together. "It's time already?" Her voice sounds sleepy.

"No." She knows it's Matt talking, even though she hasn't seen his face. "He's giving you breakfast outside of the cell."

Makeddah wishes she could rub her eyes, she wishes she could bite her nails or do something more than be pushed and pulled down the prison hallways. Instead of making a right, they make a left. There's still a gate and door, but this time they arrive above ground, the sun beaming through the windows and into Makeddah's face.

"Why is it so bright today?" She turns her face away, making the hot sun hit her cheek.

Matt drags her down a hall and through a door into a small room with a round table and one chair. He sits her down and takes away her chains. "Don't even think of doing anything stupid. It's only for you to eat breakfast."

Makeddah wrings her wrists and rubs her eyes. "Thanks, you're such a gentleman." She crosses her arms and sits back in the chair, staring at the table. A weird tension grows in the room as she waits for the food. Just as the silence becomes too much, the servants come, and she exhales, not realizing she was holding her breath. She doesn't like being in the room with Matt. The one who truly betrayed everyone.

The way her stomach feels now tells her she won't want to eat. And she's right. She only picks at the food. It looks delicious. Potatoes, eggs, ham. It probably tastes better than it looks, but she can't eat.

When Matt demands her to eat at least half of the potatoes, she does. Not because she is listening to him, but because these poor servants made food for her and she doesn't want to disrespect them by picking at it.

They sit there for a half-hour more and then the chains go back on. Matt leads her to the ballroom they were in the night before, but Haggard isn't there on his throne.

"Where is he?" She asks, getting her chains taken off for the second time. Matt doesn't answer, which seems to be his thing now. Eliab isn't up at the throne either but standing in the corner of the room. She examines the room. It's just them, and ahead, right behind the throne, are two swords crisscrossed to make an X.

The silence in the big room makes Makeddah uneasy. There is not even a sound of breath. She can hear her heart beating in her eardrums. It's loud and heavy. That is, until

Makeddah sees the bodyguards pull open the doors and she sees Haggard waltz through. He walks up to the throne, the bodyguards and Eliab and Matt bow, then he sits.

"I was starting to think you were backing out of the deal," Makeddah says. "Not that we've actually made one yet."

"Well, hello there, little Princess?" He smiles down at her. "Do *you* want to back out?"

"I want to end this," Makeddah says. Despite her nerves, it's the truth. "And I want to end this now. It is my kingdom. It is my right." She looks around. "You stole it from my parents, and that means you stole it from me."

He scratches his brow. "Do you really think I care?"

"No. I don't." She says it because *she* cares, and she has to give herself some confidence before she challenges this horrible man.

"Okay, stop talking now. I will tell you the challenge." He taps his fingers on the arm of his throne. "You battle against my sorcerer, Eliab." He smirks like he has come up with a way to defeat Makeddah. "You give me what I've asked for and win? You get your castle back. He beats you? I get to keep it, with no complaint from you. And whoever loses goes to prison, meaning you, when Eliab wins."

Makeddah rolls her eyes. "*If.*" Haggard shrugs at her. "So that's your challenge? Why'd you change your mind about me, Haggard?" She crosses her arms. "Why are you letting me do this?"

He ignores the question. "You do this, and the last man standing wins."

"No death, just dominion?" Makeddah asks.

Haggard purses his lips in thought. "I think I like the sound of that. No death," he grins, "just dominion."

"Fine. Challenge accepted." She walks up the steps to the throne and sticks her hand out to Haggard. "We start the moment it's set." Haggard's face lights up. "And I'm sorry to be cruel, Haggard, but you killed my parents. The *least* you deserve is prison." Makeddah scoffs. "You deserve death row, so either way you're getting off easy—"

"Actually," he sings then laughs. "I didn't."

Her hand drops, "You didn't what?"

"Kill them." He laughs again and stands. "I didn't kill your parents. I only imprisoned them. But in the special prison. The one no one knows about." He puts his hand out, but she doesn't offer it. "Our challenge, Makeddah."

"My parents are alive?"

Haggard grabs her hand and shakes once. "Set."

As soon as he releases her hand, she's blown back from the stage with a sting to her stomach, rolling three times before the wall helps her come to a painful stop. She throws her wood shield up, wiping herself off and coughing a few times. She closes her eyes for a split second.

Help me, she says in her heart. And though there is no answer, she feels the strength muster in her bones. She feels the weakness fade.

She looks up at Eliab, now more confident than ever. "Is that the best you can do? Make my hair a little messy?"

Eliab laughs, but she's not intimidated. "I don't get it." Eliab walks up. "You've been training for a month, and I've been training for years. You really believe you can beat me at this?"

She lets go of her shield. "I do."

"Why is that?" he shrugs.

Makeddah shakes her arms out. "Because I'm better than you. Not physically maybe, but in every other way. I've got something on my side that I'm sure you've never had." She throws her fire at him. The sound of the blaze makes her feel peaceful. The blasts of black magic come for her, but it's like they can't touch her.

As soon as she stops shooting out her fire, she ducks. The black blaze leaves him and flies right over her.

"Stop!" Haggard shouts with a smile. "No, no, no, no, *no*." He shakes his head and strokes his chin, a thing Makeddah has seen Aaron do multiple times. "This is all wrong. You shouldn't be fighting *that* Eliab. You should be fighting Eliab Matthias."

Makeddah shakes her head. "What? Who's Eliab Matthias?"

Haggard points at Matt. "Matt. You should be fighting him."

Forty-five

Makeddah's heart drops. No. She shouldn't. She shouldn't be fighting Matt… Matthias. Matthias is his real name. He said Eliab, not Matt, not Eliab Matthias.

How was she supposed to know?

He tricked her.

Makeddah looks at Matt, that name sounds so strange in her head. That's not who she knows, but she's never really *known* him anyway.

"The deal I worked out wasn't with him," Makeddah frowns.

"And the deal I worked out wasn't with *him*." Haggard points to Eliab. "So, what's the compromise?"

Makeddah wipes her forehead with the back of her hand. "There is none. You won't let there be one. So, I'll be the bigger man." *Which is ironic because I'm not the man, and I'm definitely not bigger. But it'll have to do,* Makeddah thinks. "Matt's down and I win?"

Haggard smiles. "I am a man of my word."

"Fine." She waves Matt forward. He hesitates but takes the place of his father. "I really wish it wasn't this way."

He says nothing, but his eyes say he agrees.

"Start," Haggard says.

Makeddah throws the first ball of air, but he throws black magic to her at the same time. She dodges it and sees, as it passes her, that it has a silver glow to it. That his magic is beautiful. He moves more swiftly than Eliab, maybe because he has archery training behind him. Moving swiftly and quietly is needed for that.

Makeddah turns back to him, and he's starting again, throwing balls right in her area, but not *at* her. It's odd to see him using magic. She's so used to the bow and arrows that the real him is foreign to her. She summons her air. Water comes next, sweeping him off his feet. He falls backward to the ground, but without skipping a beat, he gets up and runs straight at her.

Makeddah freezes, but at the last minute, throws her arm up to form a wall, any wall. She isn't even thinking, and when she looks at it, she sees it's a dirt wall. A dirt wall that crumbles the moment Matt hits it. He steps back, taken aback at the sight. "I thought you were no good in earth." He wipes his brow.

"I'm efficient enough to graduate." Makeddah chuckles nervously. She crosses her arms into an X and pumps them forward at him. The air knocks him off his feet and into the wall. "And I see you're good. But not good enough, Matt."

"Hey," he gets up, coughing and wiping himself off. "What happened to that thing about helping the world's self-esteem?"

She doesn't know what he's talking about until a faint memory passes of her training with him and talking about that very thing. It makes her smile. It's just like she is fighting a comrade, but she knows she's not. Still, despite herself, she smiles at the memory.

Makeddah walks up to him, panting, and wipes the dirt off his shoulder. "I'm sure you have enough self-esteem." She punches him square in the jaw. "I just hope it's dwindling." She kicks him in the gut and throws down a fireball. But he blocks it, leaping up to her, and pushing her with his magic with great force.

She slides back a foot and hits the ground on her back. Her breath leaves her. She's not sure how to bring it back. She knows she's learned how, but the lesson escapes her. Her eyes start to water as she heaves.

Matt comes over and steps above her with a smile. "Your move."

She doesn't know why he doesn't just end her there.

She breathes in and decides to do something he won't expect—she sinks into the ground. He can't come down here, and she only needs a minute. She gets her breathing controlled and puts on her game face.

Knowing exactly what her plan is.

"Makeddah, what are you doing?" She hears his muffled voice.

"You're talking a lot right now, *Matthias.*" She wipes her face and puts her hand to the roof of the ground, feeling the vibration of his steps. "Funny, because I didn't know you could do that since you went full sorcerer on me." She swallows.

Cracking her neck, and with one more breath, she's above ground.

Makeddah kicks and water flows from her foot and pushes him back into the wall. He tries to run at her, but she uses the force of air to push him back, then surrounds him with a circle of fire, pinning him to the wall.

"Your son is a good teacher, Haggard. Both of them are." She throws up an air ball and lets it fall to the ground, disappearing.

Matt tries to throw his magic at the fire, but it bounces back and hits him in the shoulder. "Can't use that stuff in there," Makeddah says, reciting the words he said last night. "Your wife was a great teacher too, Matt." She makes the fire go away with a sweep of her arm and Matt trips forward. "I believe it's your move now."

He wheezes on the ground. "Give me some space."

"I thought you'd be better than this," she laughs.

He glares up at her. "I didn't practice. I *don't* practice. The only time I did was for about a month before I joined the Guard. I had only been a sorcerer that long when my father ordered me to go. And stop mentioning Grace."

Makeddah shouts, "It's your fault she's dead!"

"I know that!" he yells, then blows out a breath. "Don't you think I know that? I never cared about her, *that* was just a ruse. But I lost my child, that… that was not a ruse. *That* was never planned." He inches toward Makeddah, shooting magic at her. She tries to block them, but it gets harder as he throws one after the other. "It was never planned that I would be this way. *Weak*. I'm weak."

He keeps going until she backs up into the wall. She puts up a shield, but it will only hold for so long. "I hate this," he says. He stops throwing, and Makeddah lets down her shield. She pants, he's too close to her now. His hands shake by his side. "I hate knowing that I would have had something that I never thought I could have." He grits his teeth. "Instead, I become weak. I get shown up by a Princess. I lost the only thing that could have brought me joy." His eyes never waver from Makeddah's. His gaze is completely focused on her, and it makes her skin crawl.

"That's your own fault." Makeddah feels her heart cramp at the words, but it's the truth. "Because not everything is my fault, Matt. Maybe I am the reason you were there, but you are the one who befriended us, welcomed us into your home, and made me stronger than I ever have been. Everyone believed it. Mira, Kahlan, Grace believed it. But what they didn't see was that you were hiding a monster underneath it all. A sick monster."

He slams the wall behind her. "I wish I hadn't." He turns away and runs a hand through his hair. "I wish I could have said no."

Makeddah pushes him away from her and stands up from the wall. The words come from her mouth, but she's not sure she's the one talking. "Said no to what?"

"To her. To *him*." He points at his father. "But you're right. I made my bed. Maybe I should lie in it."

"That's where we agree." She throws the air at him, making him fall to the ground. She builds a box of fire around him like before, this time keeping him on the ground. She turns around to look at the throne. Eliab and Haggard are both gaping.

"What? Are you mad I won? Surprised that your sons despise their fathers?" She's fuming, but she's happy. Angry, but ready to rule the world.

Thank you. She tells the Creator.

They both look speechless. Not able to say a word. And Makeddah loves it.

"Makeddah…" Matt pauses, "Your birthmark."

She throws her hands up without turning to him. "What about it?"

"It's glowing," he says with a tone of awe and fear.

Makeddah whips around to look at him. "It's supposed to."

Haggard shakes his head. "No." He swallows. "It's glowing gold."

This makes Makeddah mad. He's just trying to throw her off. So, she throws her fire at Eliab. He moves his shoulder for it to fly past him, but Makeddah's quick to make a whip out of vines. The whip takes hold of Eliab's ankle, and she pulls him to her. He's shocked, he wasn't expecting this from her. With a lasso, she tugs the sword from the wall behind Haggard, holds it tight in her left hand, and pierces it into Eliab's leg.

Eliab screams out and Makeddah stands tall.

"Last one standing," she says, her breathing labored, but that doesn't stop her from being confident in her victory.

Haggard still looks dumbfounded. "You didn't compromise."

"No," she tells Haggard. "I won both my deal and your deal. It's my kingdom." She sucks up the fire from around Matt and sets vine chains around his wrists. "Now, step down so that I can take what is rightfully mine."

"I don't think so," Haggard growls.

"Are you serious?" Makeddah wipes her temples with her wrists and stares at him. "I won fair and square. I *want* my kingdom. And now, I *won* my kingdom. So, step down Haggard."

"No." He stands. "Sorry, but that's not happening." He pulls down the second sword from the back wall. "Because now it's time you fight me."

"That wasn't the deal, Haggard," she yells.

"Well," he shrugs. "It is now."

Forty-six

Haggard comes down on Makeddah with his sword. She manages to dodge him. "No, Haggard. You cannot change the rules." She glances at where Eliab lay. She needs the sword.

It's still there… but Eliab isn't. Haggard comes for her. Fire surges in her palms as she pivots, stopping Haggard from stepping closer. "Where'd he go?"

"Who?" Haggard asks, his sword still up and ready to strike.

"Eliab." She points and grits her teeth. "Where did he go?"

Haggard looks around. His face first is shocked then turns to disbelief. He was there, Makeddah can swear he was there. But now he's not. He hesitates. She runs.

She swings around and dashes for the sword. Haggard goes after her, but she holds it up and blocks him. The swords clink with rage.

"I should have known you'd change the rules," she says, pushing against him with all her might.

"I should have known you'd be stronger than I anticipated." He pushes at her, and she stumbles back but regains her balance and comes around to slash at his side.

Right when he decides to go for her heart she ducks and rolls. He falls forward, and Makeddah backs up. "Haggard, please stop."

"No," he says, and Makeddah hears his voice crack. He runs at her full force, and she readies her sword but instead kicks him in the knee when he gets close enough. "Ah!" He falls backward.

Makeddah glances around at the sorcerers and bodyguards staring at the two. They seemed to be stunned in place, but she is not taking a risk.

She pushes the bodyguards against the wall with air and chains them back with vines, then she runs through the door out into the courtyard. She searches, her eyes not landing on one thing. "Where is Eliab?"

She hears Haggard grunt and pant as he stumbles after her. She whirls around with a smile on her face. "Out of practice?" He bends on his knee and looks up at her, and his eyes go rigid.

He wants to kill her.

He brings his sword right at her forehead. She grabs it and cries out as it cuts her hand deep. He laughs and she lets go, ducking. Then he grabs her neck and lifts her off her feet. Her eyes bulge. She grabs his hands then tries to swing her legs. Her momentum isn't great, but she gets him in the sternum, and his grip loosens with the blow. His hands are burning from touching her. He coughs as he drops her.

"Haggard, stop," she pleads with him. She can't keep this up. It's either him or her in the end. He starts lifting himself to his feet. "Haggard, I don't want to hurt you."

He laughs then charges at her, but she is quick to throw fire at him. He nearly dodges it, but she hits his ear. He screams out but continues to run towards her.

When he reaches her, she throws one more kick and two punches all with the heat of the fire. "I'm sorry," Makeddah says as she grabs her fallen sword, opens the earth slightly for him to sink into the ground, and stabs his hand with the sword, piercing it through the open earth. He yelps and tries to reach for the other sword, but she stabs his other hand with that one. "I really am," she says when he gives another cry of pain.

"No," he whines. "You're not."

"You won't stop!" She shouts. "You'd never stop if I didn't hurt you enough to."

Haggard whimpers and Makeddah feels a tear rush down her cheek. Blood spills from his hands and she has to rip her eyes away.

"Haggard…" Makeddah kneels and looks him in the eyes. "Why did you change your mind about enslaving me?"

He shakes his head and mutters the word "no" over and over.

"Tell me," she pleads. "Just tell me."

"I don't know!" he cries out. His eyes flash with realization. "I don't know." His lip trembles. "And that scares me."

Makeddah stands, speechless.

He looks lost. Her heart almost breaks for him knowing that he feels just as lost as she did not long ago.

Of all the answers she thought Haggard would give, that wasn't one of them.

When there is movement by the ballroom doors, she looks up. Sorcerers. Many stand there, staring as the others did. More appear by the entrance to the castle, as if they'd been summoned.

"Tell them to leave," Makeddah says to Haggard. "This is between you and me."

"I didn't do that," Haggard breathes. She can see that he wants to escape but his hands are pinned to the earth, bringing tears to his eyes. And though he acts tough, he's in pain, and it's bad.

Makeddah steps over Haggard and marches back into the ballroom. Matt is standing. He's ready for battle. He heaves and wrings out his wrists; his chains are broken off.

Makeddah feels herself droop. She does not need this.

As he runs to her, something stirs in her belly. Strength, she recognizes. But from what? Matt goes for her neck, but she learned something from almost being strangled by Haggard.

She burns his hands before he can wrap them around her. "What is it with you men trying to take me by the neck?" But the fire is so hot it turns his hand into burned and raw flesh. He looks like he doesn't know what to do with them.

She kicks Matt, but her air element makes the kick strong enough that he flies over Haggard and into the broken fountain. He lands with a thud.

Makeddah flips her hands and out come fire swords.

Matt clings so hard to the broken fountain that Makeddah feels like he wants to become one with it, hoping to escape her wrath. But her swords will teach him. Teach him that he can't hide from her.

"Want to be like him?" she motions back to Haggard with a fiery sword.

"Please. No."

She turns her left sword into wood. It changes from the handle down to the sharp tip. "This is my kingdom." The sorcerers step up but she holds her fire sword at them, not looking their way. Matt trembles like a little kid hoping his mom won't yell at him in front of his friends. He nods at the sorcerers, and they back up. She lifts his chin with the wooden sword. "I am Princess Makeddah, and I will take my kingdom back."

She presses the wooden sword hard into his thigh. "Ask me." The words hang between them.

"What?"

"I could kill you right now. Ask me not to," she says with determination behind her tongue.

"This isn't you." A tear falls from his eye.

"Rules change, people change," she says. "I know my place now. Do you?"

All the hurt he has caused her and those she loves has built up and now she wants justice.

He flicks his eyes to the sorcerers and Makeddah feels the weight of them start to creep up once more. But she swiftly moves her fire sword over the castle ground, surrounding her and Matt with fire. "I would rather watch this castle burn and you people be brought to justice than to let my kingdom slip into the wrong hands again. I will burn with you. I am not afraid." As she says the words, she knows they are true. She wants fairness brought back to Korzon, and if comes at the cost of her life, she is okay with it. She is not afraid.

Matt's eyes tell a different story. She realizes that she is sad. Sad for him. Sad that he will never get to know what real love is. That he will continue to live in rot.

She asks him, "But you are, aren't you?"

He swallows. "Princess Makeddah, please don't kill me."

Makeddah lifts her chin. Her wooden sword crumbles to the ground and turns into a pile of dirt. He lets out a whimper.

She releases the fire sword and stands tall.

"What was this all for?" She feels her lip quiver. She does not want to cry, not right now. "Why did you bring me to the Guard? Why not kill me on-site? The first time you and I left the Center. Why not take me out kill me then go on your merry way?"

Matt scoffs, "You were worth more alive."

Makeddah narrows. "Matt, you aren't telling me something, what is it?" She feels a sense of déjà vu from when she cornered him to ask about the traitor. "Tell me."

He drops his head.

Makeddah throws wood cuffs around Matts hands. "Fine." She gives up on him. He will not tell her, so she'll have to find out for herself. Somehow, some way.

She parts the circle of fire and grabs Matt by the collar, using air to help drag him out. When they reach the stone leading away from the castle, she drops him on the ground. The castle is in flames, yet she is relieved.

Three bodyguards standing at the castle entrance look mortified. She narrows her eyes at them. "Whose side are you on?" she asks, knowing she'll be able to see through any lie that they tell, but they tremble and bow before her. She looks down at Matt, but he is only staring at the ground. She makes eye contact with one of the bodyguards. "What do I do now?"

They look at each other. "Contact the League of Kingdoms, your Highness."

"Thank you," Makeddah says. "Take him."

They rush up to take Matt, and she stands back from the castle.

She draws water up from the dirty moat and releases it down on the flames inside the castle. They all dissipate in an instant.

She sees the sorcerers run to the entrance, ready to fight, "Matthias," she says with spite behind her tongue, "tell your sorcerers to go throw themselves in jail."

"Do what she says." He tries to sound tough but says it in a higher pitch, and his voice catches.

As all the sorcerers run, bumping into each other as they go. Makeddah motions to two of the bodyguards. "You two go lock them in, and you…" she points to the last one standing, "find a way to contact the League so that I can tell them that Haggard has been dethroned and Princess Makeddah is the one who has him in custody."

Makeddah hears a whimper behind her and looks down at Matt again, but it is not him. She looks behind her and the person who stands there is Alda. Makeddah breathes a sigh of relief.

Now she feels the weight of it all, and she cries.

She runs into Alda's arms and when she pulls away, she sees more witches and Full-Breeds, it almost seems like it is the whole Center and Guard showed up just for her.

Makeddah looks at one of the Head Witches standing behind Alda and points to Matt, "Please ghost these guys into the prison. Haggard is still in the courtyard, with swords in his hands," she says, hoping no backlash comes on her for that. But they don't say anything, just walk to Matt and inside to Haggard.

"Are you okay, Makeddah?" Alda asks.

"I'm amazing," she says in a tired voice.

Alda rubs her cheek, "You got him."

She nods, but she has gained more than her kingdom.

"I believe now." Is all she says and Alda smiles, hugging her tight.

Then Rayon and Belle come into sight and Makeddah pulls them close to her.

Makeddah looks at Rayon first and smiles, tears welling up in her eyes. Belle nudges Makeddah's shoulder and Makeddah smiles harder. Her family and everyone she knows were ready to go into battle for her. And she couldn't be more grateful for them.

She finally looks up to Alda, a little pang in her chest and her smile falters. "I got my kingdom back." Her gaze drops, "But Haggard said something back there." She doesn't know if she has fully processed it. The words feel heavy as she says them. "He said my parents are alive."

Forty-seven

*T*oday is the day. Coronation.

Makeddah studies her reflection. The golden dress looks marvelous against her brown skin, full and weightless in a way she's never felt before. Her hair is in a braided updo, and her neck is layered in gold jewelry. She looks more royal than she feels.

It's been two weeks since Haggard's defeat.

The sorcerers were imprisoned immediately. People cheered so loudly Makeddah's ears began to ring. After telling the whole story to the Guard, she almost got trampled by the people's excitement.

The League of Kingdoms contacted her, congratulating her and saying they wish they could have courage like her.

They promised to transform the castle into what it once was.

Everyone is safe. That is what matters.

But questions still swirl in Makeddah's head. Haggard said her parents are alive, being held in a prison. When she told others, they didn't believe that. They said it was a cruel lie. It was a stab to make her fumble. It was his last way to make her feel pain.

But what if it wasn't?

If they are alive, the crown does not belong to her. She should be searching for them; they are the rightful rulers.

And the grey eyes—they linger in her mind. What was it? Did it have something to do with Matt and Eliab or is this just another thing that she will have to face soon?

And another thing—

"Are you ready?" Kahlan stands behind her, smiling. Bringing her back to earth. "You look beautiful," Kahlan tells her.

"Thank you." Makeddah clasps her hands together. "Alda chose the dress. She said gold and purple were our kingdom's colors before."

"She has great taste." Kahlan adjusts the train. "She raised an amazing young woman."

"Maybe you will too, someday."

Kahlan shakes her head, "I don't think it's in my cards." She straightens out the train on Makeddah's dress then Makeddah swirls around to face her. "Perfect."

Makeddah turns to her, "Kahlan, thank you for everything. And—I'm sorry for being such a brat."

"You were questioning everything. I understand."

Kahlan leads Makeddah to the big wooden doors. Voices spill through—excited chirps, chatter, laughter.

Makeddah pauses.

She is about to step into the same room where Haggard held his masquerade ball not long ago, the same room where she defeated him and his sorcerers.

But this time there will be a crown on her head.

The noise on the other side turns into music.

"That's for you." Kahlan says.

Makeddah inhales, staring straight at what lies ahead, and nods.

Two men swing the wooden doors open. She looks ahead at the great crowd. But she must focus.

What lies ahead? she asks herself.

Alda is standing on the stage near the officiator. Makeddah's grandfather beside her. She still can't believe she has another family out there.

Rayon and Belle stand at the front, hands clasped. And Mira is beside them.

Makeddah's breath catches. She takes a deep breath, calming her nerves.

Finally, the music lulls and it is time for her to walk.

Kick step, kick step—that was Rayon's advice, and it seems to be working.

The golden rug beneath feels like a cloud. She is floating. Floating towards her destiny. Striding forth, she stops in front of the officiator.

The officiator talks, his words blur in her ears. The crown is what speaks to her.

It is tall. Arched like rainbows. It has four points, one dips toward her forehead, two frame her ears, and one at the back. Raindrops lay at each rainbows point. At the top, beautiful branches stretch upward.

She takes the small golden cup. The emblem is engraved in it. Makeddah watches her reflection.

She drinks—five sips, as ordered. Water, air, earth, fire. Magic.

Makeddah bows her head, the crown making itself a home there.

As she rises, something moves inside her. Warmth, fullness, overwhelm.

Makeddah faces the crowd.

Belle gives her a thumbs up. Mira claps quietly. Rayon mouths, *posture*. Makeddah straightens and smiles.

A man's voice rings out. "I present to you—your Lion Heart Queen."

Cheers erupt around her. The earth shakes and she waves.

Haggard's reign is over. But somehow, she knows, that was only the beginning.

The celebration is louder than Makeddah anticipated. People cheer and play music. Kids run and parents dance. Makeddah stands at the edge of it, watching rather than joining.

Flags ripple through the air, carrying Korzon's emblem. Her first order of business is to change the bodyguards' official name back to Sentinel as her parents had it. They will also be bearing Korzon's emblem.

Everyone is celebrating; she isn't.

There are too many things she does not understand.

The League of Kingdoms hasn't arrived yet. They will be teaching her how to rule her kingdom, but they said they weren't prepared. Of course they weren't, they probably expected Haggard to be reigning forever. It's not as if they stopped him.

But she hopes she can put those thoughts aside. She's ready to dive in and learn more about this world.

She watches Rayon spin across the floor in a white dress Mira made.

Belle sits nearby with Mira at a table, deep in conversation.

Makeddah contemplates escaping up to her room. She has too many things to do.

"Makeddah,"

Alda.

"I need to speak with you."

Something in Alda's voice catches her. Something is out of place.

They step away from the crowd and into the quiet night just outside of the doors. "What is it?" Makeddah asks.

"I didn't want to say anything until I was sure." Alda answers, "Now, I am."

Makeddah's heart races. *What lies ahead?*

Alda hesitates, glancing at Kahlan. "Kahlan… is meant to be our High One."

Makeddah blinks, "What?"

"We haven't had one born in years," Alda continues, "But Kahlan wasn't raised in our Center." She meets Makeddah's eyes. "Trust me. I can feel it."

Makeddah glances through the open doors to the crowd. Kahlan and Preston stand together, smiling, unaware.

Makeddah starts connecting the dots in her head. Her white hair, her icy blue eyes. Her power.

Makeddah brings her finger to her mouth and chews on her nail.

"But… why are you telling *me?*"

"Because you're Queen." Alda lowers her voice. "And something isn't right here. I've never wanted to burden you girls with it, but I know High One is hiding something. I've suspected it for months."

Months. Makeddah's thoughts spiral and it comes back to one thing.

The traitor. Haggard said there were two. Makeddah started to think it was Eliab and Matthias. But no, that can't be because Eliab was never in the Guard. So, who is the second traitor and are they still among them?

Makeddah's superpower starts to activate, and she feels something is out of place. She does not feel like they are safe.

Maybe she should disregard everything Haggard said. Pretend it was all lies. But she has a gut feeling she shouldn't. She knows something is off and her gift never fails her.

Makeddah watches over the celebration. Her people. Her kingdom. More uncertainty. More questions.

And one remains.

What lies ahead?

Acknowledgements

I first want to thank God for giving me the gift of imagination, and for blessing every part of this journey. Though it took me years to find the courage to do this, I am deeply grateful to my Lord and Savior for leading me in this direction.

To my mom—thank you for fostering my creativity from such a young age. You have always been a constant supporter of anything your daughters set their hearts on. Even when we failed, even when we changed our minds, you never let us give up. You were always on our sidelines. I know you were scared for me to put this out into the world because you wanted to protect me from criticism—but I also know that comes from seeing me as your baby girl. Thank you for loving me through it all and for being such a shining light in my life.

To my husband—my amazing husband—thank you for standing beside me through the endless days and nights of overthinking, plotting, questioning, and dreaming. You've supported me through every challenge, from writing to navigating social media and everything in between. I've already begun books two, three, and four, and book three is inspired by you—so there is more thanks to come. But for now, thank you for your patience, your encouragement when I'm down, and for always being my number one.

To my sisters—you have both been such incredible supporters from the very beginning. Your love, your humor, and yes, even the chaos of our childhood helped shape this story more than you know. I could not have written a book about sisters without you. Thank you for always having my back.

To my editor, Kelly Murray—thank you for being the first to read my novel in full and for offering such thoughtful advice, guidance, and support. Your help with editing and formatting gave me the confidence to take this step toward publishing. I am so grateful for you.

And lastly, to my ARC team, to those who bought my book, and to everyone who found me—whether through Amazon or social media—thank you. I would not be here without you. I am truly overwhelmed by the love and support surrounding this release.

Thank you, thank you, thank you.